Praise for

Home on the Range

"I've been so eagerly awaiting this book by Ruth Logan Herne—and it's even better than I'd hoped. An overprotective cowboy daddy and the therapist masquerading as a woodland fairy princess called on to help his daughters . . . What could possibly go wrong? Just everything. The whole delightful story is full of fun twists and poignant turns. *Home on the Range* is a great new installment in the Double S Ranch series."
— MARY CONNEALY, author of *No Way Up*

"*Home on the Range* showcases Ruth Logan Herne's ability to write wounded, damaged characters grasping for grace with both hands. My heart ached for Nick's loss, Elsa's guilt, and little Cheyenne's desperate need. As always, Herne's story is sprinkled with hope and gives the reader glimpses of the One who came to save. A satisfyingly happy ending left me sighing with contentment."
— MARY JANE HATHAWAY, author of *The Pepper in the Gumbo*

"In *Home on the Range,* the finely crafted second story in the Double S Ranch trilogy, Nick is caught in a downward spiral of repeating his father's mistakes and no amount of cowboy gumption is going to fix things. But Elsa, a family therapist who sought refuge in Gray's Glen to escape her own tragic past, defies her fears and conventional wisdom to connect with Nick and his daughters, bringing a soothing balm to this hurting cowboy's wounds. Ruth Logan Herne explores the darkest recesses of her characters' souls and bring light into the shadows, giving hope to the lost and healing to the broken. This latest story is no exception and one of her finest!"
— JAN DREXLER, award-winning author of *Hannah's Choice* and *Mattie's Pledge*

"A child in crisis, a hunky but clueless single father, and a reclusive therapist with a big secret . . . Intrigued? I sure was. *Home on the Range* is a fabulous story of hope, faith, and real-life family drama. Filled with heart-tugging emotion, delightfully sassy bantering, and a cowboy to die for—what's not to love? I loved it so much I quickly ordered the first book in the series. Well done, Ruth Logan Herne!"

—VICKIE MCDONOUGH, best-selling, award-winning author of *Sarah's Surrender,* book 3 in the Land Rush Dreams series

SS DOUBLE S RANCH, BOOK 2

HOME
on the
RANGE

A Novel

RUTH LOGAN HERNE

MULTNOMAH

Home on the Range

Scripture quotations are taken from the King James Version and the Holy Bible, New International Version®, NIV®. Copyright © 1973, 1978, 1984 by Biblica Inc.® Used by permission. All rights reserved worldwide.

The characters and events in this book are fictional, and any resemblance to actual persons or events is coincidental.

Trade Paperback ISBN 978-1-60142-778-6
eBook ISBN 978-1-60142-779-3

Copyright © 2016 by Ruth Logan Herne

Cover design and photography by Kelly L. Howard

Published in the United States by Multnomah, an imprint of the Crown Publishing Group, a division of Penguin Random House LLC, New York.

MULTNOMAH® and its mountain colophon are registered trademarks of Penguin Random House LLC.

The Cataloging-in-Publication Data is on file with the Library of Congress.

Printed in the United States of America
2016—First Edition

10 9 8 7 6 5 4 3 2 1

To Seth, my second son:
This one's for you, my guy who stayed close
to "home on the range." You've grown to be
a wonderful man in so many ways. I'm
proud of you, son. And I really love the
sweet wife and adorable grandkids!

ONE

*N*ick Stafford stared at the half-buried, round-roofed dwelling and realized he couldn't go through with the elementary school principal's edict. Not if it meant meeting with a hermit who lived in a toadstool shack tucked so deep in the forest that woodland mice couldn't find it.

A hobbit house. No way on God's green earth was Nick Stafford about to risk his daughters' mental health by having them counseled by a recluse who lived halfway to a mole hole. No matter what the girls' principal said.

What was next? A hollow tree?

He did an about-face, ready to stride away, and came face to face with a dryad.

Cool gray-green eyes appraised him from beneath a hooded cloak, Celtic friendly, except they weren't in the lush green hills of Ireland. They were in the forestland of central Washington, and the thin spring leaves did little to protect him from today's chill drizzle. Which made her hooded wrap more sensible than his bare head.

A dark dog moved their way, darting furtively through the shadowed edges of the small, rounded property.

"Achilles. Stay."

The dog paused, peering at them through the dense undergrowth edging the rain-soaked clearing.

"Dr. Andreas?"

The rain and shadows shifted. An oblique ray of sun made

quivering raindrops sparkle along the mostly bare branches framing her. The quick change to filtered light forced his pupils to adjust.

He thought she winced when he said her name, but maybe it was the dance of light. With the shadows bobbing and weaving, he couldn't be sure, and when the sun broke through, brighter and stronger, nothing but a mild, placid expression stared back at him. "Elsa, please. And you are Nicholas Stafford?"

"Yes. Mrs. Willingham recommended you, and just so we start on the same page, I'm not here by choice."

"Then leave."

She didn't blink, didn't move, and for a moment he was caught up, staring into Monet-like watercolor eyes, absolutely gorgeous if you liked whimsical characters in a fairy-tale setting.

He'd tried for a fairy-tale ending once. But he'd crashed and burned because no matter what he did to make his princess wife happy, Whitney Stafford hadn't been ready to take the role of queen seriously. She ended their marriage after abdicating the throne to run off with the court jester, a.k.a. one of the ranch's rodeo-riding hired hands. She'd abandoned her husband, her vows, and, worst of all, two beautiful daughters to become a rodeo cowboy–chasing buckle bunny.

But he couldn't possibly have heard correctly. Did the wood nymph just tell him to go? What kind of therapist did that?

She moved toward the door, reached out, and twisted the handle. The door opened easily, no key needed. Of course if you were this far off the grid, maybe no key was ever needed. He started to follow her, but she turned, effectively blocking the entrance. "You're still here."

"We had an appointment." He stretched out the last word, miffed by her mandate, his life, his lack of choices, and pretty much everything known to man, and despite what his older brother, Colt, said, he was not one bit depressed. He was simply mad about everything, and that was his God-given right.

"Mr. Stafford—"

"Nick is fine."

"Mr. Stafford," she continued in a cool, clear voice. "I don't want to be here either. Which means our sessions are doomed, so why waste time? You have a life, dysfunctional, of course"—an easy shrug and her matter-of-fact expression said that was a given—"but you haven't done irreparable harm, so you're free as a bird. I have a life as well, and I appreciate my privacy more than most these days, so let me save us both from a dead-end path we needn't take. Go home. And if things continue to spiral downward and out of control, take my sister's advice and find a therapist you do want to see. I'm closed."

She took one step back and shut the door in his face.

She couldn't do that, could she? They had an appointment. He'd even set up a reminder on his phone! He'd scheduled time to see her, against his will, and he'd followed through.

You followed through because Angelina and your brother hounded you until you walked out the door. Left on your own, you'd have conveniently forgotten the whole thing. Do you want to make the same mistakes your father made thirty years ago? Or try to fix things for the girls by expending some kind of sincere effort? Cheyenne nearly got killed earlier this spring because you refused to compromise. But of course—the voice of reason paused as if resigned to being brushed off—*the choice is yours. Again.*

Well, he *was* here. He'd shown up as promised, and finding her little hut in the woods hadn't exactly been a cakewalk.

He glared at the door and lifted his hand to knock.

A long, low growl from behind him said the dog wasn't all that enamored by his presence either.

Nick was pretty sure this couldn't get worse, but then a brightly colored bird winged its way to the tree alongside the house, squawked, flapped its wings, and screeched, "You're a jerk! You're a jerk! You're a jerk!"

The dog sank back on his haunches and barked twice in agreement.

Nick conceded defeat. The bird was right. He dropped his hand and started to back away from the door, hoping to escape before the dog attacked while the bird pecked his face off. Where was his trusty Remington long barrel when he needed it? Sixty feet away, in the rack behind the seat of his extended-cab ranch pickup truck.

The dog barked again, but this bark didn't sound threatening. It sounded sad, if such a thing was possible, and the croon in the bark said the mutt was either looking forward to hand-to-paw combat or he wanted someone to pet him.

Nick crouched and tapped the path beneath him. The dog ambled over. He sank onto the stones and flipped to his back, waiting for a good scratch.

"You're no watch dog, that's for sure," Nick said as he rubbed the dog's belly. "As far as protection goes, you're on the low end of the scale, my friend."

"Dumb dog! Dumb dog! Dumb dog!"

Nick glared up at the raucous bird. "Listen you rude, loud pile of feathers. No one needs your guff, okay? And you're so stinking ugly, no one more than twenty miles north or south of the equator would even use your feathers to decorate their hats. So there."

"You're arguing with a macaw." He hadn't heard the door open but was kind of glad it had.

"Just having my say," he returned, not looking up. "The bird's obnoxious and it poops when it roosts." He shrugged a shoulder toward the offending pile to the dog's left. "Reason enough to make pie out of it right there."

He'd figured to tick her off, because she had animal-loving, tree-hugging, far-left liberal written all over her eccentric outfit, but she surprised him by laughing. Only her laugh sounded rusty, like his.

"I can't deny I've been tempted."

"Is there more to your menagerie?" He angled his gaze up while still petting the dog. "Stray monkeys and elephants, perhaps? A dinosaur or two? *Jumanji* inspired?"

Her smile deepened at the mention of the fantasy movie. "No, just these two. Why are you still here?"

He studied the dog, then her, assessing. "I'm not sure. Now that I know the dog's not going to maul me, I could have simply walked to my truck, backed around, and left."

"But you didn't."

"No." He stared around and shrugged again. "I'm in a bind. I've got to do something to jump-start my oldest daughter, and the principal . . . your sister, right?"—he met her gaze and she nodded slightly—"gave me your card and threatened further action if I don't get help for both my girls. So here I am, in the last place I ever expected to be."

"In the woods, petting a dog?"

He frowned at her deliberate misinterpretation. "Hunting down a therapist to fix things that never should have been broken."

"Ah." She sank onto one of two garden benches, still damp from the quick rain shower. "Life has a way of doing that, doesn't it?"

"You got that right." He kept petting the dog, and when he paused, the hound pulled his head around and pushed it against Nick's flank, a silent plea for more. "I've got two daughters. Cheyenne and Dakota."

"Western girls."

"Except they're not," he answered instantly, as if denying the girls' ranch identity was important. And it was, to him, but that was part of the problem. "Well, they weren't western girls, that is. Washington girls, sure, but not *western,* as in riding and roping. Is there something wrong with a father wanting what's best for his children? And who has the right to question that?"

"Is it the questioning that's hard or the fact that your definition of *best* is being criticized?"

"What do you know about it?" He sounded petulant, but he didn't care because he was sick to death of people second-guessing his choices, his ideas, his deeds when it came to the girls and just about anything else these days. He shifted to face her. "Do you have kids?"

"No."

"Do you work with kids?"

"Not currently."

"So what makes you an expert on them or me?"

She accepted his question with a nod, and between the hood and the curved chair made out of bent forest limbs, he felt like Luke Skywalker chatting with Yoda, only he actually *liked* the Star Wars character. "You search for understanding."

Yup. Yoda, all right. He sighed.

"And yet, when others want to help, it has to be on your terms, your way."

"Not always," he shot back, indignant, and when she didn't meet his gaze, he realized he was angry . . . again . . . because she'd hit the truth and he didn't like it when people hit the truth. He sighed and stood with one last pat to the dog. "Listen, this probably won't work."

She nodded, quiet.

"And it's silly to waste our time."

She accepted that as well, still quiet.

"I—" He shrugged. A quick breeze shook the baby leaves above him, sprinkling him with fresh raindrops, chilling him despite the warming spring temperatures. "I'll get on my way, and one way or another, we'll muddle through. Families have been doing this a long time. I don't expect we're any different than most."

"And that's all right with you?"

Her voice didn't change but her question hit home. "I—"

"To settle on chance rather than taking firm steps to set your children on the right path?"

Put that way, he sounded pretty stupid and self-centered, as if he knew what was best for the girls. If he'd known that, for real, they wouldn't be in this hot mess of crazy right now. Cheyenne was about to fail her grade, and Dakota pretended acquiescence while she did what she pleased, a dangerous combination for a first grader.

"Sometimes people just need someone to talk to. Someone they're not trying to protect. Someone who'll listen to their complete thought without building instant brick walls of rebuttal."

"You think I should bring them to see you."

She lifted her eyes to his, and when she did, he recognized something he hadn't seen when their gazes locked before.

Pain. And that realization inspired added caution. "I don't know anything about you."

"A valid point. The kind of thing a responsible parent would say. What would you like to know?"

"Why are you buried in the woods?"

She made a face at the stone drive leading up to her small home, then raised a brow to him. "You found me, which means I'm not buried."

"You're avoiding the question."

She shook her head. "I said that I'm a private person."

Nick had been raised between two brothers. His older brother, Colt, jumped headfirst into every situation, confident of his success, always needing to prove himself, while Trey, his adopted younger brother, found his paths made smoother by faith in God and humanity, but Nick knew both men. Their outward natures hid a lot of internal junk. Being stuck in the middle made him privy to a wide family spectrum. "And that answer says you're either not capable or not comfortable living a normal life surrounded by everyday occurrences. So why should I trust my children with someone who has clearly shrugged off everyday existence?"

"Privacy equates to inability." She mused the words with a measured look at him. "Interesting assessment."

"Hey, fixing you isn't on my agenda, and while I appreciate the way you've put together the setting"— he flicked his attention to the house, the dog, and the talking bird—"this is all a little too surreal for me. Thanks for the time, Doc. Send me a bill and I'll put a check in the mail. I'm going to guess you don't do a whole lot of online banking out here."

"No charge," she answered smoothly as she rose from the bench. "I wish you well, Mr. Stafford. No offense taken."

"None meant, ma'am." He reached out to shake her hand and felt like a fool when she didn't extend hers. "Well, then. Have a good day." He did an about-face, strode back to his truck, climbed in, and backed it around before aiming the big V8 up the slope. He turned onto the main logger's path, carved out over a decade before and kept clear by an avid group of hunters, and followed that to the county road.

He was right back where he started. The principal wouldn't be happy, his family wouldn't be happy, and hey, news flash! He wasn't happy.

He stopped for gas, picked up a package of his favorite popcorn treat, Halfpops, then went for broke and bought two more and ate all three bags on the way back to the Double S. He stuffed the empty bags into one of the storage bins behind the seat so the girls wouldn't see them. He was careful with their snacks when they were at home, more so because he knew Angelina would feed them anything she pleased at the ranch. Since he respected and possibly feared the former Seattle detective who had agreed to marry his know-it-all big brother, he held his tongue about it and the girls weren't worse off.

Whitney would have a fit if she was here, and you know it.

He knew it and he didn't want to care. But something about a woman leaving her husband and two beautiful little girls meant he must have done something drastically wrong. Otherwise, why would a woman turn her back and walk away from her children?

You tossed aside a chance to help two little kids? What are you thinking?

Elsa shoved the mental scolding aside and moved toward the house. She knew exactly what she was thinking. She didn't dare let herself get drawn in by another anxious parent, even if the guy was a twelve on a "smokin' hot cowboy" one-to-ten rating system. Sure, he needed help. She saw it in his eyes and heard it in his tone, even as his words refuted her sister's directive.

You want to help him. No. Strike that. You're intrigued about helping the girls, especially the older one. You've worked with kids like her before, and you're good at what you do. Isn't it time to move on? Especially if it can help this child? And if you help the big sister, the younger one benefits as well. Are you willing to let Will Belvedere's depraved choices steal more of your life?

"You're a jerk! You're a jerk! You're a jerk!"

Elsa didn't need the bird's ill-timed reminder. It was there in the mirror's reflection, in the set of a stubborn man's shoulders, the understandable question in his eyes. Who in their right mind *would* bring their precious children to a therapist with her mental health record? No one. Not if they knew her history.

He was right to run hard and fast, and she was just as right to let him.

The phone rang as she finished laying out food for Hoyl in the parrot cage. She raised the phone, read her sister's number, and clicked

End, but Rachel wasn't fooled by that. She called right back, knowing Elsa couldn't resist two tries in a row, just in case something serious had happened. She answered the phone as she opened the front door for the bird to return to his cage for the night. "Hey, Rach. What's up?"

"Stop ignoring my calls; how did the appointment with Nick Stafford go?"

"Patient/client privilege, HIPAA rules, leave me alone."

"Stick to basics, then," her older sister insisted. "Did he show?"

She could answer this honestly and keep the guy temporarily out of trouble. "Yes."

"Good."

"You sound genuinely pleased," noted Elsa as she wired the bird's cage shut. "Why?"

"His daughters are delightful, even if Nick is oblivious," Rachel replied. "They're smart, funny, and have a lot going for them. But it's real tough when you're old enough to understand that your mother's new boyfriend is more important than her children."

"You think they know?" Nicholas Stafford had seemed more protective than the average angry single dad she'd met while in active practice in a Seattle suburb. She wouldn't have labeled him as a rash talker in front of his kids, but then she'd been wrong before. A tight sigh wound its way up from gut level. She forced it back, determined to stride forward.

"It's Gray's Glen, small town USA. Of course they know," said Rachel. "Wives running out on rich husbands, chasing rodeo cowboys, ditching kids. Please, that's a reality TV show with no cable bill involved. Dakota might be a little less informed, but Cheyenne was older when Whitney took off. Trust me. She knows."

Mother abandonment, the toughest scenario for any child to surmount. Bad enough when inadvertent, like death, but the raw, ragged-edged emotions left by a mother's deliberate abandonment could leave lifelong scars and present challenging behaviors.

"When are the girls coming to see you?"

Rachel wanted definitive answers. Elsa could throw the guy under the bus and tell her sister he wasn't going to follow through, or she could give him some time to figure out what he wanted to do. Life and emotions weren't as cut and dried as her big sister seemed to think. "Once again I'll cite patient/client privilege and leave it at that."

"Elsa."

"Rachel." Elsa blew out a breath as she studied the deepening shadows surrounding her forest home. "I understand the district's concern, and I'll keep you in the loop. For the moment, you're about to end the spring semester, all the kids will be on summer break soon, and then they have the entire summer to try and make headway. This isn't a quick fix, ever. You know that."

"I do, but Nick Stafford has already shrugged off my concerns for seven long months. We'll have to hold Cheyenne back a year, and while that's not the end of the world, I don't think being labeled as stupid by her peers is going to help anything. Her self-image is already soured."

"You can't just pass her?"

"Not and live with myself," Rachel retorted. "But I don't want to add to her passive/aggressive plate by pushing her over some unseen edge." She paused, sucked a quick breath, and backtracked. "Sorry, I didn't mean that the way—"

"You're fine, Rachel. And you're correct, the stubborn, quiet ones can brew a head of steam no one notices."

"I won't ask any more questions, but I want you to know that if you need information from me, I'll share," Rachel continued, and Elsa knew not all school administrators were that accommodating. If they were—

No, she wouldn't look back and wouldn't cast blame. There was plenty of it to go around. From a clinical point of view, she understood not everyone could or would be saved. But every now and again, when shadows loomed and she remembered the sound of little Christiana Belvedere's voice, she wondered what would have happened if she'd called the school with her concerns that day. Would they have taken steps to hold the children there?

Probably not, but she'd never have the chance to know because she never made the phone call.

And then it was too late.

Her sister's words bothered her all night. Or was it the look of defeat in Nicholas Stafford's troubled brown eyes that messed up her sleep? In any case, she questioned her snarky attitude and her judgment well into the next morning. Finally, she stormed into the house, picked up the phone, and hit Nick Stafford's number. He answered on the second ring, which meant he wasn't crazily avoiding her. "Double S Ranch, Nick speaking."

"Mr. Stafford, this is Elsa Andreas." Was he hauling in a breath? Looking around him, uncomfortable? Peeved and considering hanging up the phone without another word?

Stop creating the scenario and let it occur naturally. Why is it so easy to use your training on everyone except yourself?

"Yes?"

"I've been reconsidering our conversation yesterday."

"The one where you held all the cards and treated me like some kind of low-level species beneath your dignity?"

"That would be the one." To her relief, he laughed, so she waded in. "I've had time to think about the girls and their current situation and how I might be able to help."

"Doctor, I—"

"Here's the thing," she went on, ignoring his objection. "You and I don't have to be best buddies for me to be effective with your children. And yes, I decided I wanted a more solitary setting last year, but a love of solitude doesn't negate years of education and practical experience in family therapy. My sister has legal means at her disposal to ask a court to order your children into therapy, but is that what you want?"

"Absolutely not." His voice went hard.

"My thoughts exactly. Here's my suggestion. You come over here again—"

"Or you could come here, save me the drive to Middle-earth."

"Funny. Like I haven't heard that before." Rachel tweaked her about it all the time, but she had to hand it to Nick Stafford. It sounded funnier coming from him.

"Your steady barrage of company makes Tolkien jokes, Doc? Why do I suspect that's not the case?"

"Reiterating," she drawled, disregarding his comment, "you could come over here and our first session could be a family session. You get to know me, I get to know all of you, and the noisy bird is a great conversation starter for kids. It's neutral ground, Mr. Stafford. Kids do better on neutral ground. And yes, at some time I'd like to come there. With your permission, of course. Rachel and I were raised on a ranch up north, so animals, hay, dogs, and farm equipment are a comfortable setting for all concerned."

"You're a ranch kid?" Doubt speared his voice.

"Not everyone finds their home on the range, do they?" She left the question rhetorical and moved on. "My familiarity with their setting might make sessions at your place beneficial."

"My father's home, you mean."

His father's home? She'd been tapping a pencil against the tabletop. She stopped. "You and the girls don't live on the ranch? I assumed—"

"We live in town, but I work here, so the girls are at the ranch fairly often."

"I see." And here might be conflict number one, because with a huge spread like Sam Stafford's Double S Ranch, why wouldn't his son be living on the gorgeous rolling acreage spreading across the rich plain of the fertile Kittitas Valley? Too much family proximity? An aversion to the ranch? Separation of job versus daily life? Her mind jumped to possible scenarios, any of which might have an effect on the girls' behaviors.

He sighed, and he didn't try to cover it. In fact, he might have exhaled extra loud for her benefit, and when he did, she almost smiled. "Unless you prefer the long drive to Ellensburg," she continued. "They have many good therapists there, and I won't be offended."

Seconds mounted, and when he did speak, she knew she'd made her point. No one had extra time these days, and single parents suffered from lack of time more than most. "When should we come?"

She wasn't about to let scheduling mess up progress. "My schedule is flexible," she replied smoothly. "Yours isn't. What works for you? Do the girls have after-school activities we need to work around?"

"They do, but they're free on Thursday and Friday this week."

"Does that work with your schedule?"

Again the pause, but he didn't make her wait too long before he conceded. "I'll make it work."

"Perfect. Thank you. I'll see you and the girls on Thursday at five." She hung up the phone before he could answer. She was pretty sure he'd prefer being a no-show if she gave him the chance. He'd put Rachel off for most of the school year, which meant he was adept at shelving problems. Reticence in his tone indicated he was cornered, and Elsa had been a western girl for a long time. Born-to-the-saddle cowboys never liked being cornered. Now it was up to him.

She moved toward the door, set down the phone, and walked outside.

Clean spring air had swept away the smell of winter mold from leaf clutter and needle droppings. Birdsong surrounded her, bright and vibrant, assorted visitors singing welcomes as they cared for northern nesting grounds.

She used to love springtime. The dance of new life, resurrection, rebirth. She'd reveled in the fresh angle of the sun, its sharper rays, a more defined warmth. On her parents' ranch, they'd be birthing puppies, piglets, and calves—a true season of renewal. Her brother, Ian, and his family would come to help, even her littlest nephew. Ian had bought an old-timer's house up the road and fixed it up for his growing family so they could all be part of the ranching process. When Nick said he lived in town, her internal radar had spiked, but she'd been in Gray's Glen long enough to hear a little history. And current history in Gray's Glen revolved around Sam Stafford and the Double S.

She drew on her cape and stepped outside. The bark-like voice of a heron paused her. It was joined by another great blue, then another, and as she turned toward the honking voices of pterosaur-looking birds, a sweeter, more melodic tune made her stop. Moving slowly, she peeked around the corner to find the songster. On the southeast side of the shed, in the lee of a faded, peeling shutter, a purple finch knit bits of grass and weed in quick, decisive motions. His bright plumage danced in the warming sun, and when his mate flew in with more nesting material, he bobbed a quick look of true love her way and kept right on working as she flew off in search of more goods.

A young pair, most likely. Hurried, with no last year's nest to guide them, but the fury of first love and babies pushed them to commit. Did they stay together out of need or desire?

An age-old question that niggled present-day anthropologists.

She stared around her small holding, suddenly dissatisfied, and with a swoosh of her cape, she strode back inside and gathered her art supplies. She piled them into the car and followed the logger's road to a higher elevation where dense foliage welcomed her. She pulled her cloak close, set up the easel, arranged her colors in nonspectral order, and let the shadows draw her in.

Up here, she was safe amid somber grays, blues, and browns.

Brightly colored birds singing songs of love didn't find cozy nesting corners in the gloomy chill, and when she'd applied paint thickly to the eighteen-by-twelve canvas, she took a razor blade from the side pocket of her bag and began carving muted images of shadowed trees and lifeless branches, light along the edges and growing darker inside.

Like her.

TWO

I 'm going because I have to, not because I want to," Nick reminded his family Thursday afternoon. "My kids are not crazy, I am not depressed, and we don't need any backwoods therapist to tell us otherwise." Nick Stafford put an exclamation point at the end of his statement by tearing the memo of his appointment into confetti-sized pieces, then letting them sift softly into the nearby kitchen garbage can as he faced off with his future sister-in-law, Angelina Morales.

"Fat lot of good that'll do you," muttered his brother Colt as he passed by on his way outside. He paused, kissed Angelina good-bye, then shot a sympathetic look his brother's way. "Go easy on him, honey. He's the sensitive type."

"Sensitive?" Angelina encroached on Nick's space with a spatula, and he had to draw up all his manly reserves not to cringe. He'd known Angelina for a while now, and she wasn't afraid to use whatever weapon happened to be at hand. "This is not sensitive. It is stupid—so stupid a blind man could see. You tell me"—she pointed outside where Nick's two daughters romped with her son—"what it is that you fear and I will fix it for you."

"I fear nothing." He met her gaze and grabbed his hat as if dismissing her, but Angelina had been a decorated Seattle police detective for years. She didn't do "dismissed" easily. She rounded the counter and scowled up at him.

"There was plenty of fear on your face when we prayed for Cheyenne to live a few weeks ago."

Well, okay, he'd been downright scared to death then, when Cheyenne tried riding a ranch mount with no one around. She'd taken a nasty blow to the head when she fell off. Seeing her unconscious in the hospital bed about took his breath away. But Cheyenne was all right now, she'd promised to do her schoolwork, and there was ranching to be done.

"Do not put anything ahead of the health of these children, Nick Stafford." She folded her arms and braced her feet, ready to stand her ground or do battle, and Nick was pretty sure she'd be fine either way. "You heard the principal. For Cheyenne to remain in school, even if she's held back, she needs counseling."

"She needs academics," he growled. "The rest will take care of itself."

"How's that been working out so far?" she wondered, facing him. "Oh, that's right. It hasn't. If you let your stubborn, overinflated Stafford pride get in the way of this child's success, I'll—"

"Stubborn, yes, but not overinflated, surely." Sam Stafford came into the room and winced. "Nick, it's really okay if you don't repeat all the same downright foolish mistakes I've got on my record. Take the girls to go see this woman. What have you got to lose?"

His father was offering parenting advice?

Sam Stafford, a man who put the ranch above everything else, including his three sons, had the nerve to advise him?

Anger didn't just crawl up Nick's spine; it vaulted. And at that moment he wanted to go toe-to-toe with the man who'd made everything more important than raising children. But then he noted how Sam gripped the back of the chair for support. How his pallor had grayed with the simple effort of walking into the kitchen. Sam Stafford was ill, and Nick bit back the words he wanted to say. Now wasn't the time or the place, and if Sam didn't recover, that time might never come.

He glared from one to the other, put his hat firmly in place, and strode out the door. What he wanted to do was to ride high into the hills of central Washington under the guise of shifting cattle and sorting calves, but he stopped himself halfway to the barn.

I don't want to talk to anyone.

I don't need anyone.

He had his girls, this beautiful ranch, a nice home in the fairly new subdivision overlooking Gray's Glen, and he wanted for nothing except . . .

He sighed and really longed to punch something—anything— and if his brother Colt strolled by right then, he'd be the most likely target. He didn't, which left Nick downright frustrated and unnerved but not one bit depressed, no matter what the rest of his family thought.

"Daddy, look!" Six-year-old Dakota did a death-defying leap from a tree limb, tossed in an aerial spin, then rolled like a tumbleweed when she hit the ground. "I almost stuck the landing," she yelled across the wide expanse of fresh green grass. "Wanna see me do it again?"

His heart hadn't *climbed* into his throat when she twirled off that tree branch.

It leaped.

"Uncle Colt's going to saddle up True Moon for me tomorrow," added Cheyenne from the porch, with just the right touch of in-your-face attitude. "He said I'm doing great with the pony and I'm ready to graduate to the bigger horse."

All the more reason to pummel his brother, for sticking his nose in where it didn't belong, although True Moon was a gentle mare, perfect for learning, which meant Colt was probably right. That made Nick madder yet.

He stared at the girls, so marvelous and beautiful, both of them longing to be true ranch kids. The fact that their mother hadn't wanted ranch life for her girls didn't bother them. It bothered him. For just a moment he wondered what the cloaked therapist would say about that. He pushed that aside and addressed Cheyenne. "We are not discussing this now. Gotta go."

Dakota scrambled his way, not caring where they were going or why.

Cheyenne shuffled along, eyes down. The stubborn set of her jaw took him back a couple of decades to the reflection he saw in the daily mirror. She climbed into the back seat, fastened her belt, and stared out the window, chin in palm, disenchanted with everything.

Dakota hopped in, pulled the shoulder strap at least five feet farther than necessary, seated the buckle with a firm *snap,* and sat back. "Why are we going home so early?"

"We're not going home," Nick told them as he steered the truck down the curving drive.

"Is it a surprise?" she asked, wriggling. "I love surprises. Good ones, that is. Can we stop at our house so I can feed Stripey? She's probably hungry by now."

"Her name's not Stripey; it's Snickers," Cheyenne scolded from her side of the back seat. "She doesn't even *want* to come when you call her that. Stripey's about as dumb a name as you can find for a cat without stripes."

"That makes it more special," Dakota declared in a smug voice. "And cats don't come to anybody, usually, so you're just showing how much you don't know."

"Dad, she's such a brat!"

Nick glanced up in time to see Dakota mime Cheyenne's face and gestures in an absolutely perfect caricature of her older sister. "Dakota Mary, cut it out."

"I didn't say anything." Dakota pointed to her left. "She just likes bossing everybody around, and if they don't do things her way, she acts like a big baby."

"I'm not the six-year-old," Cheyenne shot back smoothly. "But I suppose when you're in first grade, you think you're big stuff. For a little kid."

"I'm almost seven, and I'll be in second grade soon, and you'll be staying in third grade, so there won't be too much difference, will there, Miss Smarty Pants?"

Nick had just turned down the first gravel-covered, winding road when Dakota fired that shot.

Cheyenne's head jerked up, and for the first time in months he saw real emotion on her face. "You don't know anything. Shut up."

Dakota pressed her mouth into a thin line, then smiled and stayed quiet, knowing Cheyenne wouldn't be able to resist glancing her way, and when she did, Dakota swung her back toward her sister and looked out the window, humming as if nothing Cheyenne did bothered her.

Which only made Cheyenne angrier.

He made the next turn, deeper into the forest, pretty sure the girls needed a boxing ring instead of therapy. But maybe that's why they needed therapy. Weren't little girls supposed to be more easygoing?

"Are you about to dump us in the woods?" Cheyenne wondered as he aimed the car through a long copse of trees. "Like Hansel and Gretel? Dad, do you have any idea where you're going?"

"I do." And when the small hillside bungalow popped into sight at the last minute, Cheyenne made a light whistling noise through her teeth and Dakota screeched, amazed. "It's like half gingerbread, half wicked witch," she said. "Dad, who lives here? Why are we coming to their house? *Is* that a house?" she added, as she scrambled out of her seat belt. "Like for real?"

"Hi, girls." Elsa didn't wait for them to come to the door, and Nick was grateful for that. She moved through the doorway with an easy smile, not too big, not too small, and he had to hand it to her. She looked way more comfortable talking to them than she had when she had spoken to him. "I'm Elsa."

The girls stared up at her like she'd grown two heads or perhaps suspecting the smoke from the chimney came from a simmering cauldron inside.

"No jokes?" she asked, glancing from one to the other. "Like where's my braid? Why aren't I wearing gloves? Can I freeze whole cities with a wave of my hand?"

"It's not nice to make fun of people's names, is it?" Dakota asked, puzzled. "I think Elsa's the prettiest princess of all, except maybe Cinderella, but they both have long blond hair, like you. So that's nice, I think."

"Thank you, Dakota. And this is Cheyenne?" She shifted her attention to his oldest daughter. "Cheyenne, it's a pleasure to meet you."

Eyes down, Cheyenne dug her toe into the forest floor.

"Shall we go in?"

"Why?" Dakota asked.

"It's warmer," said Elsa as she held the wooden screen door open. "I haven't had a fire in three days, and it was great, but the rain and the wind from this new storm pushed me to break down and make another one."

"But the sun's out now."

"When half of your house is underground, the dirt keeps it cool in the summer and protected in the winter," she explained lightly. "But this time of year, when temps go up and down quickly, sometimes I need a little fire to take the chill off."

"Your house is weird," Dakota announced as she stepped through the outside door. "Not inside. This is kind of normal, but outside it's really weird."

"Dakota." Nick frowned down at her. "That's impolite."

"Yet apt." Elsa swung the door shut as they all filed into the broad front room. "It's an odd house because it started as an octagon built into the side of the hill. So three sides of the octagon are buried and five sides are open to the outside with windows. But the last person added that room to the side, so it messed up the configuration. Now it looks like a crooked mushroom."

"Why would someone bury a house?" Dakota's expression said that made no sense, and Nick couldn't disagree. "I think that means I'm right, Dad. It's definitely weird."

"Maybe not everyone likes the same things, DakoDUH." Cheyenne shot her a sharp look from across the room. "Maybe some people like things done a different way. Just because you don't like it doesn't make it weird."

Dakota plopped onto the edge of a big chair, clearly more at ease than her older sister. "I didn't say I didn't like it," Dakota answered reasonably, with just enough edge to try to set her sister off. "I just said it was really weird. That's all."

"And you were right," Elsa told her easily. "Mr. Stafford, would you like to sit here?" She pointed to the couch facing the fire. She didn't give Cheyenne any direction, which was probably for the best, because if she did, Cheyenne would most likely pick the exact opposite to do. He took a seat, set his cowboy hat down on the table, and breathed deep.

"You paint?"

Elsa turned to look where Cheyenne was pointing and nodded. "Not well, but yes."

"All of those are yours?" Cheyenne wondered and moved toward the clutch of canvases leaning against the far wall, taking her own sweet time doing it.

"They are."

Nick sat stiff and straight, kind of like the collar around his neck. Was this woman going to beat around the bush all day? Pretend this was a social visit? Put things off? Because one of them had things to do, a lot of things. They were in the thick of spring planting, a new crop of designer seed calves was due to start dropping out of handpicked heifers, and his father had a Friday afternoon appointment for a follow-up to his health problems. On top of that, he'd promised to help rebuild town buildings lost in the wind-fed spring fire a few weeks back, and they were almost ready to start erecting the walls of their new log cabin church. Inactivity didn't exactly work for him. He was just about to nudge things along when Cheyenne made a face of disinterest at the paintings and came back their way. "We've got *pretty* pictures at our house."

Nick stared at her. Not only was that inconsiderate, but they really didn't have all that many pictures in the house, except of the girls. Whitney had taken a few of the things she'd liked from the walls, and he'd never thought or cared about replacing them.

Elsa accepted Cheyenne's statement easily. "I've been in a blue-gray funk for a while. It's probably time to change it up a little."

"Well, they're ugly."

"Cheyenne." Nick stared, aghast. "Apologize."

She rolled her eyes. "Sorry!" She said it in a smart aleck singsong voice as she fell into a seat, and there was nothing in her attitude that seemed one bit sorry about anything. "I just don't see the point in painting stuff that comes out dull and grungy."

"What colors would you use, Dakota?" Elsa seemed unaffected by Cheyenne's insolence as she directed her attention toward his younger daughter.

"Purple!" Dakota's smile said purple was exceptional. "And maybe pink, but not the baby pink stuff."

"Oh, of course not," Elsa agreed. "Far too common."

"Right!" Dakota bobbed her head, grinning. "I like dark pink with silver sparkles the best," Dakota continued, while Cheyenne seemed quite content to say as little as possible. "Dad got me a shirt like that for Christmas and I love it so much!"

"Bright and sparkly works for me," Elsa told her. "Sometimes I like quieter colors. And sometimes I like things bright and festive."

"Me too!"

Nick was just about to move things along by bringing attention back to Cheyenne, when a mad flutter of wings brushed the front door.

Cheyenne's head snapped up, startled.

Dakota's mouth dropped open, and then she screeched in excitement.

"You're a jerk, you're a jerk, you're a jerk!"

Cheyenne's brows shot up. So did Dakota's.

"Let me in, let me in, let me in!"

"That would be Hoyl." Elsa moved easily as if she hadn't planned for the bird to return just about then.

"That's *your* bird?" Dakota breathed the question, eyes wide.

"You're letting it in here?" Cheyenne's voice squeaked, and she pulled back into the corner of her chair while Dakota stood up, fascinated.

Elsa opened the door. The bird fluttered in and went straight to his perch near the cage. "*Bawk!* Don't stare, don't stare, don't stare! Let me in, let me in, let me in!"

"He's talking." Dakota made a full-fledged, wide-eyed look of surprise and did a dramatic tumble onto the couch cushion. "I didn't know you could really teach a bird to talk, Elsa! I thought it was stuff on TV!"

"Does he know what he's saying?" Nick asked as Elsa swung the cage door wide for the macaw. "I mean, is he just saying words or did he really want to come in?"

Elsa shook her head as the bird settled into his cage with a last flap of bright red wings. "I don't know. Sometimes it seems as if he knows what the outcome will be, but then he can be totally random."

"You let him out of the house on purpose?" Cheyenne had stayed tucked in her seat, but now she stood up and crossed the room, staring at the noisy bird. "You let him *out* of the house and he *comes back*?" she asked again, as if the concept was unbelievable.

"He does. He likes to fly free, but he loves to come home."

Her words struck Nick hard. He'd thought that about Whitney a few years before. That she'd have her fling and realize there was nothing better than home sweet home.

He'd been mistaken.

"I can't believe he comes back." Cheyenne breathed the words softly. Moving closer, she extended her hand toward the cage, then re-thought the idea quickly. "Does he bite?"

"Hasn't yet," Elsa joked. "But birds don't come with guarantees."

"He's beautiful." Cheyenne stared up at the bird, eyes wide. "How did he get so many pretty colors? Birds around here aren't colored like that."

"If he was living in the rainforest, he'd blend," Elsa explained. "Bright blossoms, green leaves, yellow flowers. The colors there are bold, like Hoyl. If he lived outside in the Pacific Northwest, he'd stand out and become food for some wild creature."

"Then why let him out?" Cheyenne turned completely and aimed a full frontal look at Elsa. "Why risk his life? Isn't it better to keep him safe in here?"

"Ah, the age-old debate of safety versus freedom." Elsa studied the bright-toned bird and made a face of regret. "It's a difficult choice every day because you're right, Cheyenne. One day he might not come back, but if I never give him the chance to be himself, what kind of person am I?"

"Sane?" Nick meant it as a joke, but when she winced, he got the same vibe he'd noted the other day.

"I've been called worse." She said the words, but the tight set of her jaw gave her away. Poking fun at mental health was unacceptable, and maybe everyone in her profession felt the same way. "So, Cheyenne."

Nick held his breath because they'd been there for twenty minutes and this must be the moment of truth.

"Yeah?" Cheyenne looked back over her shoulder, and he had to give it to Elsa. The bird had been a total icebreaker, just like she predicted.

"Mrs. Willingham is my sister."

Cheyenne's face drooped. "Oh." She turned her back on the bird and returned to her chair, looking utterly alone. "I should have known." She directed a hard look at her father. "I told you I didn't want to do this, but did you listen? No. You never do." She sat, eyes narrowed, piercing Nick with the intensity of her gaze. Looking from father to child, Elsa saw the resemblance. Not a physical pairing, but a personality pair, for sure. Their stature and expression mimicked each other. Sometimes that meant if she could help one, it helped the other. Other times it just meant they were both rock-solid stubborn.

Elsa sat back in her chair, hands folded. "Do you like Dr. Seuss's *The Cat in the Hat*?"

Cheyenne made a face. "Um, for babies. Yayuh."

"Remember how the cat got into trouble?"

"By getting out every toy there was!" Dakota bounced on her couch cushion, excited. "And he bounced up and down with them! And then he fell down, and so did everything!"

"Yup." Elsa didn't say anything else. She just sat back and let Cheyenne take a moment. "The cat got himself into big trouble, and then he tried to solve it by doing more dangerous stuff. He also had an amazing magical machine that came along and cleaned everything up. Real life isn't like that."

Cheyenne gulped visibly but didn't hesitate to blow Elsa off. "And now comes the lecture about making good choices." She groaned, dramatic. "They sent me to the school counselor this year. Boring!" She sang the word, still confrontational. "What's wrong with hating school? What's wrong with wanting to just stay home? What's wrong with being different?"

Nick shifted his attention to Elsa, waiting for the answer too, but she shrugged and stood. "Good questions. We'll address them the next time we get together. Girls, can you each take one of these dog bones out to Achilles? He's in the yard, waiting patiently. I want to talk to your dad for a minute."

"I'm not coming here again. Ever." Cheyenne snatched up her hoodie, didn't grab a dog treat, and stomped out the door, letting it slam behind her.

"I'll feed the dog!" Dakota took two biscuits from the bin Elsa held out and skipped out the door. "Sorry my sister's a brat!" she sang out as she opened the screen door, just loud enough for Cheyenne and the grownups to hear her. "See you soon, Elsa!"

"Thanks, Dakota."

Nick had stood up when Cheyenne flounced out the door. He picked up his hat as Elsa turned his way, and he cringed slightly. "Those are my girls."

She said nothing, and that wasn't exactly the answer he was looking for. "So what do you think?"

She glanced out the door before drawing her eyes back to him. "They're girls."

"Like, normal?"

She winced as if wondering how he could be so far off, then raised one questioning brow. He interpreted the silent message and sighed. "Can we help them?"

She stared out the door where the girls had climbed into the extended cab of his truck. Dakota perched in her seat, animated as ever, and Cheyenne sat as far away from her outgoing sister as she could get, quiet and withdrawn, gazing out the window at nothing. "We'll need time. She's not exactly happy."

"She used to be."

Elsa's look of interest invited him to continue.

"A long time ago. She and my wife were very close."

"And your wife is no longer in the picture."

"No." Talking about this pinched his collar tighter, but maybe that was because he never talked about this. He glanced down, wondering what she thought. Did she lay the blame squarely at his door? Because he was pretty good at doing that all by himself.

"Hoyl, huh?" He changed the subject with a glance toward the bird. "The mythological bird blessed with immortality for refusing the forbidden fruit when Adam offered it in the Garden of Eden."

She smiled at him, and when she did it was like the way the sun broke through the other day, making things brighter, more vibrant. "You paid attention in school."

"Jewish Studies 101, at a time when I thought it was important to expand my consciousness."

"You no longer feel that way, I take it?" she asked as they walked outside and approached the truck.

"I'm storing the wealth of somewhat useless knowledge for another time," he answered. He put his hat back in place and dipped his chin toward the pickup. "Between them and the ranch, I've got my hands full. And helping the town get things back in order. I never thought . . ." He stopped the comment before finishing it and frowned, wishing he hadn't started it at all.

"You never thought?" She led him gently, and when he brought his eyes to hers, it was there again, depths of empathy in a calm sea of pale green and blue.

"About being a single parent. It wasn't something I'd ever consid-ered or thought about or planned." He shrugged. "It was the last thing on earth that I wanted to happen. And then it did. So here I am."

She kept her eyes on his.

She didn't smile or nod or smooth it over with empty words. She simply let her gaze meet his, and then she took a small step back, break-ing the connection. "I'll see you tomorrow. Same time?"

Like he had a choice? And even if he did, this time frame allowed him a full day of work, and that was critical right now. "Sure."

She nodded, waved to the girls, and walked back to the house while he climbed into the truck. Cheyenne nailed him instantly.

"I'm not coming here again, Dad. Not *ever*. Never!"

He started the engine, praying for words, longing for wisdom, and then he remembered what Elsa had done in the house.

She'd moved the conversation on to something else, so he tried that. "'Kota, do you really love the shirt you got for Christmas that much?"

"The most!" She beamed at him with such openness and love that he had to sometimes remind himself not to play favorites. "Carly Jansen has one just like it, so some days we pretend we're twins!"

"Maybe their family will take you in," Cheyenne muttered.

Normally he'd scold her. Make her apologize.

He didn't. He aimed a smile at Dakota and said, "I'd miss you too much, kid. I like my girls at home. With me."

His words made Dakota smile and squirm, happy. Cheyenne did neither, but she stopped arguing as he crested the hill. A light-bulb mo-ment made him reexamine his parenting skills. Cheyenne engaged him with confrontation constantly. What if he didn't engage? What if he moved on, like Elsa did today? Would it lessen the arguing and call a halt to the regular standoffs? It couldn't hurt to try.

He turned the truck onto their street a few minutes later and pulled into their classic colonial on the indistinctive suburban street, not far from the girls' elementary school. He parked the truck in the drive, grabbed his hat, and started for the house, then paused, letting the girls pass him.

"Nick, hey!" Ray Morris waved from next door as he mowed his lawn with freshly sharpened precision blades. "Listen, if you're pressed for time and need me to do some bush trimming for you, just say the word. I've got vacation coming next week and you know I don't mind helping out."

"I appreciate the offer, Ray." Nick grabbed the mail, opened the house, followed the girls inside, and was immediately surrounded by neutrality.

Was it walking into Elsa's odd cottage, seeing the bird's vibrant plumage, or driving into forest he hadn't explored in nearly two decades that made his home seem bland? Pale walls, white cabinets, light wood accents, plain lighting. He stood still, gazing around. If he wanted to, he could pick this house up, move it into any suburban subdivision in the United States, and it would fit, and for some reason that bothered him today. Why should a sit-in-the-saddle western man bide his time in a faded existence?

He set his hat down on the counter like he always did and realized the reason the hat always looked out of place was because the hat *was* out of place in his house. He stared around, but then Cheyenne screeched at Dakota from upstairs.

Reality broadsided his musings, but for a moment he saw a decade of choices flash before him, most of them wrong.

Could he fix them?

The girls' shouts shoved the question aside, but as he climbed the stairs, it wasn't the dark hat against the white background that he saw. It was a glimmer for the future, a possibility he'd shoved aside long ago. Why did he live in the land of manicured lawns when the wide-open range owned his heart? Why couldn't he begin anew? Both girls longed for what he'd been denying them until the past few weeks, a chance to be true ranch daughters.

He hurried upstairs to tackle the current confrontation, but with a lighter step than he'd known for a while. Once the girls were tucked into bed, he pulled up pages of possibilities on his laptop.

Staying stagnant had lost its appeal, and as he bookmarked house plans to share with a local builder, he wondered why he hadn't done this sooner.

Probably because your father kept telling you to.

He drummed a finger against the tabletop because the mental reminder was spot on. Sam had been urging him to build a house on the ranch from the beginning. He hadn't done it for two reasons: one, because his father urged him to; and two, because Whitney wanted a normal life, as she called it, away from unglamorous farm work.

He'd done as she asked because he wanted to show his father that sacrificial love bound a marriage.

And how did that all work out for you?

The stabbing thought cut, but not as deep as it used to. The wife who claimed to want a normal, all-American suburban lifestyle had left him for a rodeo cowboy, and the irony wasn't lost on Nick. He called local contractor Josh Washington and set up an appointment to meet.

As he passed the mirror at the top of the stairs, he paused. A hint of Sam Stafford gazed back at him: like father like son, and now like daughter, boots-in-the-mud stubborn. If he changed up his paths, maybe he could unmire himself from chronic mistakes and keep Cheyenne from following a similar pattern.

Trying to mold her according to Whitney's plan had been foolish. He didn't see that soon enough, and now those choices were the only scrap Cheyenne had left of her mother, compounding the error. A part of her longed to be the ranch kid she wanted to be, and another part yearned to make her absentee mother proud. Cheyenne was her own conundrum.

But *he* was here. He was the parent. It was up to him to smooth the way, and as he moved toward his room he realized that parenting wasn't easy, and it didn't even feel all that natural some days. He'd noticed that more lately. But it was the most crucial job he had, and one way or another he aimed to do it right.

Sam Stafford had messed up three boys because domination of the beef market outweighed everything else.

Nick had every intention of showing him how wrong he had been.

THREE

*L*ast year's *Washington Cowboy* review of eligible bachelors had gotten it right, Elsa decided as she settled fresh food and water into the bird's cage a few minutes after Nick and the warring factions known as his daughters left.

Nick Stafford most definitely had the best eyes, just like the reporter declared. Which meant she might need to weigh other possible circumstances contributing to Cheyenne's anger. New relationships could add fuel to a smoldering fire, and if Nick was seeing someone, that might be a causative factor. So now she had to come up with a nonintrusive way of asking the wealthy rancher about his love life.

Awkward, but she'd keep it smooth and simple, a trait she'd learned from several years of practice. The number of single parents had grown, and that put new questions on the table. How would he react?

Well, that would be strictly up to him.

Hoyl squawked, flapped his wings, and dipped his beak, scolding her for some perceived action.

She ignored him as she scrounged through a wooden filing cabinet and pulled out a worn file folder. She put Cheyenne's name on the tab, jotted a few handwritten notes on a legal pad, and tucked the pad inside before she filed it away.

Memories came, swift and deep, thoughts of old files, former clients, polished desks, comfortable seating, and a five-gallon water dispenser. She glanced around, tugged her sweater tighter, and tried not to measure the difference. She'd gone from part of an upscale professional practice in Sammamish to a forest cabin. Instead of designer fish in a ten-thousand-dollar aquarium, she had a rescue parrot and a trusty dog, the only outside relationships she'd allowed into her life in thirty months.

So who needed fixing more? Her or the kid?

Physician, heal thyself.

Easy to say, tough to do. She shoved the warning aside. It was too cold and damp to paint outside, so she set up an easel in the living area, grabbed her paints, organized her palette, and paused.

She didn't want to paint.

She didn't want to draw.

She—

A tear found its way down her right cheek. Another one snaked a path down her left side, and pretty soon wet tracks found their way down to her chin.

Get a tissue and calm yourself. Move on. Without the paints. Break free. What are you waiting for?

She couldn't, not today. Facing Nick Stafford, seeing his two beautiful children, sensing his dismay, she'd felt trapped.

So what else is new? You've been trapped for a long time; you're only just admitting it. Look ahead, gaze forward, make a move. God gave you so much, so very much. Why waste it?

Finch song broke the moment, an inviting array of notes, twittering just beyond the bedroom window.

Another finch returned the favor from the opposite side of the house, each tweet and chirp welcoming the sun, the growing warmth, the newborn leaves of shade.

May the God of hope fill you with all joy and peace. Paul's salutation to the Romans gave a tender thrust, a green tendril defying stony ground. *In him shall the Gentiles hope.*

She wanted hope again. Rachel might have been her typically pushy big sister self, but she'd been right to urge the Stafford family

toward Elsa. The urge to help Cheyenne was strong. As long as she
didn't blow it. Again.

"She loves you! She loves you! She loves you!" Hoyl screeched the
declaration, then danced along his perch. "She loves you!"

"It's a good thing your old owner wasn't a rapper," she told the bird
while she swiped more tissues to her eyes and nose. "My dad loves the
Beatles too. But don't start singing 'Eleanor Rigby' or I might banish
you to the shed. Let's keep things upbeat, you and me."

"You're a jerk! You're a jerk!"

So much for upbeat where the bird was concerned. She blanketed
the cage and surveyed her surroundings. Normally now she'd pretend
to eat, grab a book, or watch an old movie.

None of that held any appeal tonight.

The finch called again, letting others know he'd found his one true
love and this spot was taken.

She'd wanted that before she'd left the coast. She'd longed for a
happily-ever-after, a couple of cute kids, and a minivan. Who in their
right mind thinks a minivan is cool?

She did, then. Before the earth tipped sideways and she slipped into
the abyss.

She glanced outside.

The evening sun shimmered along still-damp leaves. She grabbed
her cloak and the keys to the car, then pushed out the door before she
could second-guess herself. She started the car, backed around, and
drove up the drive, then turned right at the top of the rise. She drove
into town and focused on the bright angled sun, not the lengthening
shadows.

She parked at the general store, walked up the steps, went inside,
and breathed.

She loved the fun mix of goods in Hammerstein's store. She picked
up a basket, ordered some fresh cold cuts and a half pound of cheese

from the deli, then browsed the country aisles while she waited for the meat to be sliced.

A cowboy hat caught her eye. Made of tan straw, the women's version sported two jeweled turquoise wings on the side, and between the wings lay a tiny cross.

Roots and wings. She'd preached that often in the city.

She lifted the hat, set it on her head, and checked the mirror. *Awesome.*

She loved it. Totally and fabulously, she loved the hat, the look, the whole deal. Funny how she'd hurried to leave her parents' ranch, yearning to achieve her goal of attaining a high-class education, and here she was, tucked in the hills, wanting a cowgirl hat.

"Your order's ready, miss. And the hat looks great, by the way."

She acknowledged the deli clerk, lifted the hat carefully, and set it back on display. She had no need for the hat, no matter how good it looked. Her budget didn't possess a column called discretionary spending, and the cool price tag said the hat was a pipe dream, nothing more.

She gathered the cold cuts, splurged on a pint of her favorite ice cream, and bought a six-pack of fresh yeasty rolls. When she got outside, she hauled in a deep breath, ignored the evening darkness, and drove her car back home.

Her phone buzzed a call from Rachel as she parked outside her wooded bungalow. "Hey. What's up?"

"Just saying good night. I was thinking you might want to come over on Saturday. Hang out for a little."

Rachel offered the same invitation each week, and every week Elsa said no.

Not this time. This time, as she grabbed her sack of groceries, opened her front door, and let herself in, she accepted. "How's noon for you? I just bought some ham and roasted turkey at Hammerstein's. We could make subs."

"I'd love that." Rachel kept it simple, like Elsa would if the roles had been reversed. "Noon's perfect. See you then."

"Will do." She hung up the phone, made a quick sandwich, and put away the food before she sat down to eat. Achilles poked his nose up under her arm, as if asking what she'd been doing, leaving him at that hour.

She fed him a bite of sandwich, then sat back, petting the dog with one hand and eating with the other.

She'd been stuck a long time. It was time to come unstuck, and it didn't matter if it was Cheyenne's insolence, Dakota's perky nature, or the pain in Nick's eyes.

Right now she felt like living, and that hadn't happened in a long time.

~⟶€☺

Seeing Elsa Andreas was better than a cowboy's draw to a new truck, Nick realized as he pulled into her drive on Friday afternoon with Cheyenne. Why the magnetism?

He wasn't sure, but he squelched the emotion as he put the truck into park.

She walked toward them and smiled, and although Nick had been out of the game a long time, that smile made him feel better than he had in years. He climbed out his side and prayed Cheyenne wasn't going to make a big deal out of meeting with Elsa. Her hissy fit at the ranch had been quite enough.

To his relief, she climbed out quietly, turned, and slammed the door, but she didn't yell, screech, or pout, and he was grateful for that. She walked forward, chin down again, but he noticed she glanced around, as if looking for something. The bird, maybe?

Elsa set down the flowerpot she'd been holding and eased off gardening gloves. "Let me just set these here." She spoke mildly, as if she kept her expectations at bay on purpose, and set the gloves down. "You brought something."

Cheyenne exhaled loudly. "My report cards. My dad thought you might want to see them."

"Are they awful?"

"What?" Cheyenne darted a surprised glance up.

"Your report cards. Are they wretched, horrible, terrible things you wish you never had to see again?"

"Yes." Cheyenne slipped a quick glance up to Nick, as if admitting how bad the reports were put a sizable nail into her coffin. "Did you want to see them?"

"Nope. I want to burn them."

Cheyenne's brows shot up, and then a spark brightened her gaze. "For real?"

Elsa bent low. "Does looking at them make you happy?"

Her instant head shake underscored the emotion. "No." She whispered the word as if vocalizing the admission at full volume made things worse. "No, it doesn't."

"How can we face the new if we're stuck in the old?" Elsa looked up at Nick, matter-of-fact, and he had to hand it to her. She'd made her point in less than a minute, a point he'd been trying to make for over a year.

"It was too warm for a fire inside today, and I'm glad of that," Elsa shot over her shoulder as she lifted a handful of wood shavings and tossed them into the round fire pit centered in the yard. "If you both grab some of these, we can have a little fire going in no time."

Nick had returned to Elsa's version of the Shire, unsure of his role in hobbit-land. As he watched how deftly Elsa handled Cheyenne, he decided he'd follow her lead. If she wanted him there, he'd stay. If not, he'd leave, and with a lot less trepidation than he'd felt the day before. Despite her odd house, cranky bird, old-world cloak, and sorrowed eyes, Elsa Andreas knew her way around kids and was exactly what he needed. He indicated the dry chips with a quick wave. "Got a lighter?"

"In the house," she told him. "It's in the first cupboard to the left of the sink."

What kind of therapist allowed strangers to roam through her house and belongings while creating a hermitage in the woods? It made no sense, did it?

He went inside, found the lighter, and came back out. He crossed to the fire pit, bent low, and hit the trigger. A tiny flame teased, smoldered, then grew. He was just about to lean back, satisfied, when Hoyl offered his opinion from the tree above them. "You're a jerk! You're a jerk! You're a jerk!"

Surprised, he lost his balance and sat down hard.

The flame went out, but the thin shavings smoldered, edged in red, while curling smoke rose upward.

"Ultimate fail," he grumbled as he shot a scorching look to the bird. "Chicken stew, pal. That's all I'm saying to you. Chicken stew."

Cheyenne laughed and Elsa grinned. As he leaned forward to re-apply the lighter, Elsa laid soft, cool fingers against his hand. "Let's try this instead." She motioned for them both to lean forward and blow, coaxing the smoldering wood flakes into flame. And when the three of them puffed air from opposing directions, a bright golden flame erupted from the center, licking and curling the dried bits of wood, sending defined smoke skyward. "Let my prayer rise up like incense before you," she said softly, and then she smiled at Cheyenne. "We made fire."

"We did!" Cheyenne seemed genuinely pleased to be part of this little ceremony.

"We should let it take hold a little more, and then the three of us are going to turn the past into the ashes it so richly deserves. God gives us the grace and talent to keep the good memories tucked inside ourselves, but I think he'd scoff at the idea of dwelling on the bad stuff. So we won't."

Cheyenne looked a little skeptical. "We just do it? Is that allowed?" She kind of squeaked, as if she couldn't believe it was all that easy, and Nick agreed. He didn't think it was all that easy either, but then Elsa didn't live with his daughters.

"That's where everything starts, isn't it?" Elsa sat back on one of the old benches alongside the fire pit and held Cheyenne's gaze. "With making a decision. And then we go from there."

"It can't be that easy," whispered Cheyenne, and the strangled note in her voice broke Nick's heart. Why hadn't Whitney seen what her desertion would do to their children, their family? Why hadn't she weighed that into her decision?

She saw. She knew. She didn't care. Get with the program, won't you? The internal voice sounded miffed with him, for good reason. Cheyenne wasn't the only one who'd spent too much time mired in old thoughts and what ifs.

Elsa waved a nonchalant hand. "The beginning is always easy, Cheyenne. We see what we have to do and recognize it. It's the *doing* of it, day by day, building a base of goodness and joy, that takes the effort."

"The good choices thing." Cheyenne looked over at Elsa and frowned. "I hear that a lot."

Elsa burst out laughing.

Surprised, Cheyenne laughed too, and then Nick couldn't help but join in, only nothing was funny. And yet, it was.

"Oh, kid." Elsa swiped a hand to her eyes, still laughing but dabbing moisture away at the same time. "There's generally a reason we hear the Good Choices lecture repeatedly. It's because we're caught in the cycle of making bad ones."

Cheyenne's wince said she'd been called out.

"But here's where we start anew. Right here. Right now. Mr. Stafford, can you grab us some of those bigger kindling sticks behind you, please?"

"Nick."

She looked up at him and hesitated. Was she thinking getting too familiar was a bad thing? Because right now he was thinking he'd like to be a lot more familiar with the blond-haired therapist who wasn't afraid to set fire to a bad past. She blinked, then smiled, and the smile didn't need words. "Nick, then. Can you grab us some of that?" She pointed behind him and he stood, then paused, smiling down at her until a hint of color rose to her cheeks.

He turned, walked across the pavers, and picked up a pile of thin, dry sticks, then applied them to the little fire. Within a minute the fire had grown to broader proportions, spreading to the edges of the fire pit wall.

"Now let's have those report cards."

Cheyenne carefully opened the big envelope. One by one she withdrew the folded sheets of paper and handed them over to Elsa. She sat back down, timid again, waiting, but then Elsa surprised her again.

She handed her back one paper. "Last quarter, last year. Crumple it up and let it fly."

Cheyenne frowned. "You're not going to read it?"

"Didn't you already tell me it was terrible?"

"Yes." Cheyenne made a face of disbelief. "Except adults always want to say stuff a thousand times as if you don't get it."

"So you got it. You just didn't care."

Cheyenne cringed and shot a look up to Nick. "Basically."

"Exactly why we're doing this." Elsa pointed to the paper. "We're refusing to let this kind of thing bother us forever. It's a ridiculous way to live, really, and who wants to be caught on that kind of treadmill?" She tipped her look to Nick, and he shook his head, hands splayed.

"Not me. Anymore," he added because he'd been caught in a similar cycle, so maybe Elsa had him stay for a reason.

"'Today's a new day, with no mistakes in it yet,'" Elsa said lightly. "That's from a book I read as a child, *Anne of Green Gables,* a marvelous story about an orphan girl who has to deal with a crazy number of changes and messes up repeatedly. Charming, actually."

"Messing up is charming?" Cheyenne hiked her brows in overdone surprise again and glanced at her father. "Not in our house."

"There's an old saying that says laughter is the best medicine," Elsa told her. "It means that embracing the joys in life is healthier than letting the sorrows drag us down. If we can learn to shrug off our frailties and foibles, the world becomes a much better place."

"What's a foible?" Cheyenne asked.

"A mistake. And our frailties are our weaknesses, the things that hurt us most. So if we take charge of the moment and begin anew, we've stepped forward. And that's always the best way to go." She directed her gaze toward the crumpled report card in Cheyenne's hand and sat quietly, one brow lifted, allowing Cheyenne to make the decision, and when his oldest daughter tossed the negative report into the fire, Nick's heart softened.

Positive steps. Forward progress. Embracing the future.

This was all stuff he knew. How had he let himself and his daughter get stuck in a hurtful past? He knew better.

As Elsa handed Cheyenne one report after another, her smile deepened until he glimpsed the happy, carefree girl she'd been before Whitney took off.

"So." Elsa handed the empty envelope back to Cheyenne and stirred the flames with a fire stick once all the reports had met their fate. "We have the envelope."

Cheyenne nodded.

"We can burn that too, if you'd like, but if you look inside, there's nothing in it, so no real reason to waste it, right?"

Cheyenne shrugged, looking at the plain manila envelope. "Right."

"So instead of burning it, we can refill it over time. Use it as a place to put good thoughts and feelings. Good reports, wherever they come from. If your grandfather compliments you, have him write it down, and if he's too busy, then you write it down. If your dad tells you he's proud of you, write it down and tuck it into the envelope, and pretty soon that envelope will be filled with the new you. The you that you want to be."

"Filled with reminders." Cheyenne smiled at the thought, as if she'd just had an epiphany.

"Exactly." Elsa nodded. "We all need reminders, especially when we let old memories or bad memories take over. We allow them too much power and they become dangerous. We want the good, the bright, and the beautiful to have the power. Not the uglies."

"No uglies." Cheyenne whispered the words, chin down, and Nick's heart went out to her. His eight-year-old daughter was far too young and innocent to carry the weight of the world on her shoulders, but hadn't he done the same thing when his mother took off and left him behind? He had, and to hear his brother yap about it, Nick was still trying to fix that old wrong to this day. But then, Colt was flat-out stupid.

"That's the goal." Elsa reached out and touched a gentle hand to Cheyenne's soft cheek. "We banish the uglies and embrace God's beautiful. Together."

Cheyenne took a deep breath, and when she nodded, Nick felt like he could breathe for the first time in years. "Okay."

Elsa stood. He did too. Cheyenne followed suit, clutching the envelope. She darted a quick glance to the fire and breathed deep.

"When should we come back?" Nick asked, hoping Cheyenne wouldn't buck the idea. She looked more at ease right now, but he knew his daughter. If she started obsessing about something, her anxiety grew.

"How does a Tuesday/Thursday rotation work for you guys?"

He shook his head. "Thursdays are good, but Tuesdays aren't. The girls have gymnastics lessons then. And dance on Mondays and Saturday mornings."

"Busy schedules." She looked up at him, but he noticed she kept Cheyenne's reaction in her side vision, and when Cheyenne's face darkened, Nick was pretty sure he'd just been accused, tried, and convicted in record time. "Can dance be switched from Mondays?"

He shook his head. "Recital time is coming, but then they have the summer off."

"So Mondays and Tuesdays are out. Unless you come either before or after your lessons, Cheyenne."

Cheyenne looked surprised to be included, and Nick saw the obvious once again. He avoided including her on decisions because it fell into argument, so he made decisions without her. He was the grownup; that's what he was supposed to do, wasn't it?

But seeing the growing interest on her face when Elsa included her, he recognized another mistake.

"After dancing is good. I'm usually pretty tired after gymnastics class."

"Gymnastics puts a lot of stress on the body, so you should be tired," Elsa told her. "Great workouts, but lots of pressure."

"Did you do gymnastics?"

"Not me. We didn't have the time or means to be that devoted to one kid and one sport, but I had a friend who went through two broken wrists, one dislocated shoulder, and three sprained ankles. She made it to Junior Nationals, so she was very good."

"Junior Nationals?" Cheyenne whistled softly, like she did for the ranch dogs. "What'd she do then?"

"She quit."

Cheyenne stopped moving. "After making it that far?"

"Yes."

"But why?" Disbelief marked her gaze. "Why would anyone get that far and stop?"

"She realized she was living her mother's dream, not her own," Elsa answered. "Her mother had worked with Karolyi, a very famous coach in Texas, and she was a true lover of the sport, but Ashley realized it was time to start living her own dreams."

"So she just stopped?"

Elsa nodded. "Later she said that decision opened a whole new world for her. Now she's married, she's got two kids and another on the way, and you know what she does?"

Cheyenne shook her head, still looking stunned by the thought of making decisions on her own, and that was Nick's fault, all the way.

"She runs an online gymnast outfitting company out of her house. She took her knowledge and applied it to a business she loves because it leaves her time to be home with her kids."

Cheyenne turned as another revelation brightened her eyes. "Like you, Dad."

"Right." He smiled down at Cheyenne, but it wasn't exactly the same. He'd magnified the problem by staying the course. He'd kept the girls in Whitney-inspired activities, even after they'd made their wishes known. "We'll come by Monday after dance class, then. Around five thirty. Does that mess up your dinner time?"

"An advantage of being alone is flexibility." She aimed a smile at Cheyenne. "Five thirty is fine."

"See you then." He put his hat back on his head and started for the truck, but instead of getting in his side, he rounded the hood, opened

Cheyenne's door, then gave her a hand up. She smiled up at him, almost shy, as if not expecting him to do the sweet, tender things he used to do automatically.

The brightly plumed bird flew into a nearby tree just then. He flapped his wings twice as he settled on a limb, cocked his rainbow-colored head, and stared at Nick without calling him names. This time he didn't have to. Nick had been kind of a jerk for a while now, and it was well past time to change. He waved a hand toward Elsa as he came back around the truck. "Thanks, Doc. We'll see you Monday."

She nodded, quiet, but when their eyes met, he paused, wishing he had a private moment to say how good it felt to see Cheyenne's real smile once more. "Well."

"Well." She smiled slightly, and when she did he reached up and tipped the brim of his hat ever so slightly, total cowboy, as he smiled back.

Her color rose as he climbed into the truck. As he backed around, the image he took with him was Elsa in her woodland garden, gazing at him as if he'd done something right at long last.

It felt good.

He went back to the ranch to pick up Dakota, and while the girls played with Noah in the late-day sun, he searched out his father in the downstairs office. "Can we talk?"

Sam pointed to the chair. "Sit. I'm too tired to stand long, and if you're going to yell at me, it's better if you don't loom."

As if his father allowed anyone to yell at him, ever. Nick ignored that and took a seat. "I'm thinking about building a house here, on the ranch, like you've suggested. Am I still okay to go ahead with that?"

"Nothing would make me happier, Nick."

He'd made his father happy.

Nick had expected at least a half-dozen "I told you so's" because Sam thought living away from the ranch was dumb, and he hadn't hesitated to tell him so. Facing the man who'd led the way in running one of the best ranch operations west of the Mississippi, he realized Sam had been right. Had he let Whitney color all his decisions?

In a way, yes, because a husband was supposed to take care of his wife. That wasn't just preacher talk; it made sense for a man to look after his own. Maybe if Sam had cared for Nick's mother the way a real man should, she might have stayed.

Or perhaps you married the wrong person for the wrong reasons and things played out the way they were going to anyway. Sound familiar?

And then Sam kind of ruined the niceness of his calm reaction by saying, "I'm going to restrain my excitement because if I offer hearty approval, you're liable to change your mind, but yes, it's an excellent idea. What were your thoughts and which building lot would you like?"

His father had subdivided several good sites edging the long, sloping drive nearly fifteen years before. To date, each one of the sites remained empty because no one in their right mind would choose to live under Sam Stafford's critical eye. A combination of illness, sensitivity, and Angelina's rolling-pin logic had cultivated Sam's awakening faith. On top of that, Nick loved this ranch. He belonged on this ranch, and building a home here for his girls might reglue the bonds they'd let fray. Living here could give Cheyenne and Dakota some of the stability they'd been missing. "I thought I'd use the west-facing lot overlooking the southeast corner. I'll give the house a deep setback to give us the best view."

"You talk to anybody about building yet?"

Nick shook his head. "I wanted to get square with you first."

"Consider us square." Sam smiled, then coughed, long and hard.

"Are you all right?" Nick moved to his father's side quickly. "I thought you were getting better."

"I'm fine." Sam growled the words, always annoyed at any sign of weakness in himself or others. "It just takes longer to get over things when the liver's not happy."

"What did the doctor say today?"

"Same thing they always say," Sam grumbled. "You're sick, give your body time, you're getting older, be patient, blah, blah, blah. That's their way of saying they're not sure what's wrong or what to do, but they're mighty quick to send a bill for services rendered. How'd the appointment with the shrink go?"

Shrink? Elsa wasn't a shrink. She was a degreed professional, deserving of respect even though she wasn't exactly playing by the book. "She's not a shrink, Dad. She's a psychologist."

"Same difference."

"Do you want me to answer the question or not?"

Sam huffed, then got quiet.

"It went all right. Elsa—" He paused, then corrected himself. "Dr. Andreas seems nice. Quirky . . ." He thought of the bird and the dark paintings and the furtive movements of the dog. "Cheyenne seemed all right with her and that's what matters."

"That's not how it sounded before you left today," Sam remarked. "Cheyenne threw a fit, and you almost had to hogtie her to get her into the car."

"I thought you were sleeping."

"You'd have to be dead to sleep through that racket," Sam declared. "And I'm not there yet. So if this woman got Cheyenne to calm down and want to come back, I'm chalking it up to a miracle."

Nick stood and nailed his father a withering look. "I'd say the miracle is seeing you drag yourself into church these days."

"Angelina says it's God's grace," Sam retorted, but they both knew the truth. Nick's father had spent decades shrugging off faith and family until earlier this year. Then he got sick and Angelina reminded him that time might be running out. Maybe it was the illness, maybe it was prayer, but for some reason, he listened. At last. "By the grace of God, if he sees fit to give me enough time, I want to see my sons happy, and I want to make a difference in the town."

Nick snorted. "Better late than never, I guess."

"We've all made mistakes." Sam's expression soured enough to remind Nick that he wasn't exactly error free. "I'm just hoping for time to fix them. The good Lord willing."

Nick wanted to make a smart retort.

He didn't. He bit his tongue because he suddenly remembered something about late harvesters coming to work and getting paid the same wage as those who'd toiled all day. The parable stuck in his craw.

God's grace, flowing free. The choir sang a song about that now and again.

Free for whom?

His father had run roughshod over anyone in his path for decades, so how a simple change of heart rendered him salvation was anyone's guess. Nick sure didn't get it.

You might if you truly listened. And possibly humbled yourself.

He strode outside, disgruntled.

When he drew up alongside Colt and Angelina standing by the foremost paddock watching Noah, Dakota, and Cheyenne play, he pulled a picture of a log home out of his back pocket and handed it to them.

Angelina looked at the picture and smiled, and when Colt realized what it was, he turned and clapped his hand on Nick's shoulder with way more force than necessary. "You went to the clue store? At last?"

"Hush," Angelina scolded, exasperated. "Be nice. What is the matter with the men in this family?" She glowered at her future husband, then grabbed Nick in a big hug. "I'm so proud of you. When and where?"

"I'd guess late summer or fall by the time the excavation is done. I'll know more when I've talked to Josh. I want to put it on the east side of the drive, just beyond the second curve."

"Wonderful view from there," Colt agreed while he aimed a look of doubt Nick's way. "So, what finally inspired this?" He put his hands up and let Nick off the hook. "Never mind. Doesn't matter. I'm just glad you're doing it."

"Dakota will love it." Angelina glanced at the three kids, then Nick. "Cheyenne might take a little more time."

"The kid who's insisting on learning the ins and outs of ranching will give me a hard time?" He shook his head, confident. "I doubt it."

Colt and Angelina exchanged looks, then Colt shrugged as he watched the trio try to fence in one of the pregnant cattle dogs by using a pile of winter-fall sticks near the barbecue. The Aussie was having none of it and finally leaped over their latest attempt, scurried under the lowest fence rail, and ducked into the barn. "I want to be *on* the ranch, in a house that suits the ranch."

He watched as Dakota scolded Cheyenne for something, then flounced over to Noah, effectively cutting her older sister off. He started to move forward, but Angelina stalled him with a hand to his arm. "You don't have to fix everything," she reminded him softly, then raised the brochure with her free hand. "Focus on the big stuff. Pick your battles. The rest will work out."

"If I'd listened to you a year ago, Cheyenne wouldn't have gotten hurt last month." He folded his hands and sighed. "How'd you get so smart and then fall for a loser like my brother?"

"No one's perfect," she told him, smiling, and when Colt said, "Hey!" she laughed and tugged him close for a quick kiss.

"Noah! It's time to come in!" Angelina's mother waved from the far door.

"Not yet!" protested the three-and-a-half-year-old. He immediately turned and appealed to Angelina for respite. "Mom, do I have to? We're having fun!'

"You have to do what *Abuela* tells you this time and every time," she called back to him and pointed toward the house. "Tomorrow is another day."

He grumbled, yanked off his miniature cowboy hat, and stomped his way across the yard and up every single step, glowering.

Nick gave a light, quick whistle. "Girls? Gotta go."

"Dad, there's no school tomorrow," Dakota called back. "We get to stay up late on Fridays."

"Family meeting at home."

Dakota groaned and fell dramatically to the ground.

Cheyenne rolled her eyes and started their way, but not before reminding her younger sister that she was a big baby.

Dakota screeched that she wasn't, and instead of overreacting, Cheyenne continued their way. "Can we have ice cream after the meeting?"

"If your sister behaves herself, we can walk down to Hammerstein's ice cream window," Nick told her, loud enough for Dakota to hear. "But first, the meeting."

"Dakota, come on. I'll give you first pick of seats."

Dakota scrambled up, amazed. "For real?"

"Yes."

Dakota raced across the yard, waved to Colt and Angelina, then tried to pull herself into the big truck. Nick reached down, scooped her up, and deposited her into the extended cab seat with ease, then offered a hand to Cheyenne. She climbed in and tipped a smile his way, sweet and open, the kind of smile he used to see all the time.

He wanted that smile back. He'd messed up, wasted time, and acted stupid, but if he could reclaim Cheyenne's good nature, he'd be the happiest man in Gray's Glen. "Pretty smile, little lady."

"Dad." She squirmed, embarrassed, but pleased too, and when he reached in and put a hand on her cheek, he thought they might just be able to fix things pretty easily.

lsa heard Nick's truck pull into her driveway Monday afternoon. From the look on Cheyenne's face, they'd had a rough bout. Maybe more than one.

Cheyenne jumped down from the truck cab, stomped up the path in the chill, steady drizzle, arms folded and jaw set as Elsa swung open the door.

Trouble at the O.K. Corral.

She let Cheyenne in, then let the door swing shut behind her as she stepped out to meet Nick on the covered stoop. "Bad day?"

"Bad few days," he admitted. "The afterglow of your Friday session lasted about three hours, until we had a family meeting about selling our house and building a house on the ranch."

"Ah."

"That's it?" He stared at her, then at the door and motioned inside with his hand, clearly upset. "I thought it would make her happy. She's constantly on me about learning to ride, to help with chores, to feed stock, to be a ranch hand, and the minute I took a step in that direction, she freaked. How am I ever supposed to make her happy?"

"Are you free later? To talk?"

He frowned and looked around, impatient, then grunted. "Yes."

"I don't want to keep her waiting, but maybe you and I could discuss how that all went down. Is there someone who can watch the girls?"

"My brother's fiancée or her mom would do it, I'm sure. I just—"
He banged his hand against the post. "I take one step forward and two

steps back. Every time I think there's progress, there isn't. I don't know what I'm doing wrong."

"Are the other Staffords the calm, quiet, patient ones?"

His scowl deepened before it softened. "Exactly one of us fits that description. My younger brother, Trey. Maybe the bird's got my number, because the rest of us are jerks."

"So, then . . ." She led him with an expectant expression.

"Take a breath and be patient."

"Bingo." She stepped back and waved him off. "Come back for her in an hour, then meet me at the Coffee Shack. I could use a cup of something delicious and strong tonight, and some good conversation wouldn't hurt either. Maybe we can figure out together what sent her right back into the spiral."

"You don't mind taking the extra time?"

For a kid? No. She didn't mind at all. "I'd rather figure out her triggers now than later. It evens my playing field."

"All right." He'd removed his hat while talking to her, a gallant gesture, like days of old, and when he put it back on his head, she had to wrestle her heart into submission. Cheyenne was her primary responsibility. She'd work with the agitated girl and then deal with the grumbling father.

She walked back inside, sat down, and waited.

"I'm not talking." Eyes down, Cheyenne glared at her feet. "Not now, not ever. I don't like my life, I don't like adults, and I don't want to be anywhere. Ever."

Elsa sat back, silent.

"I mean it." Cheyenne darted a glance her way. "I might as well stop coming here because I don't want to talk to anybody. Ever."

"All right." Elsa picked up the local weekly paper and opened it. The kitchen clock ticked off seconds in light, staccato rhythm. Achilles was sound asleep, and Hoyl had his head tucked beneath his wing, napping. Other than the clock, utter silence filled the small space, and Elsa let it do just that, ignoring the time and the girl.

"This is a waste."

Elsa set the paper aside, glanced at the clock, and nodded. "Six minutes and eight seconds. Excellent for your age."

"What's excellent for my age?" Cheyenne drew her knees up, locked her arms around them, and glared. "I don't do anything excellent, or hadn't you heard?"

"When the pity party is over, let me know, okay? And remember, I get paid whether or not you get helped, so it might be smart to accept some help, figure out who and what you're mad at, and who or what you're afraid of, and move on. But that is, of course, entirely up to you."

"I'm not afraid of anybody," Cheyenne retorted, and the chin went down again. "Not anyone," she mumbled into her knees.

"Oh, good. This should be easy, then. If it's an anger issue, I can just give you a couple of pills to take every day and you'll be fine. Excellent."

"They have pills that make everything better?" Cheyenne asked, and interest brightened her face. "Really?"

Elsa made a "get real" face at her. "Of course not, I'm messing with you. There's no such thing as a cure-all pill. Which is why your dad brought you here."

"I suppose you're the next best thing." Cheyenne rolled her eyes. "Just my luck."

"Did you put anything in your envelope this weekend?"

"No."

"Did you try?"

"No."

"Ah."

"Why should I put anything in a dumb old envelope when my dad is talking about building a new house over on the ranch?" She leaped to her feet, facing Elsa. "He knows my mom hates the ranch, he knows she wouldn't like living there, so why does he have to go and try to ruin everything?"

"Your mom's feelings are important to you?"

"Yes! And they should be important to him too, but he thinks it's a great idea. Well, it's not! It's a stupid idea because Mom will think everything is just the way it was, and then she'll come back and look for us on West Chelan Pass and we won't be there!"

Elsa tread cautiously now. "You don't think she'll figure it out?"

Cheyenne glared at her.

"Like maybe she could look up your dad's name on the computer or ask a neighbor? Or is our town too big for people to know where you're living?"

Cheyenne stared at her, then dropped her gaze. "Telling her where we are isn't the same as her finding us all by herself."

A child's prayer and wish, rolled into one, longing for a mother's love. Elsa softened her voice even more. "Having her stroll in and say hi to everyone. Hug her daughters. Rejoin the family."

Cheyenne's eyes watered. Her chin quivered. "She can't do any of that if she can't find us, and she won't want to come looking at Grandpa's."

"So that's a problem."

"Yes."

"How can we solve it? How can we let her know where you are so there's no confusion?"

"I don't know." Cheyenne frowned. "How could we do that?"

"How would most people do it, honey?" Elsa made a phone from the fingers of one hand and held it up to her ear.

"We don't have her number."

"I hear the mail service is still delivering letters."

"We don't have her address. I guess she moves around a lot," she added, quick to make excuses.

"Well." Elsa leaned forward, casually, putting her chin in one hand. "If this was a game, the move would be all on Mom's side, wouldn't it? You have no way of reaching her, but she can reach you anytime she wants, can't she? Because you're in the same town and the same school as you've always been, and Dad's got the same phone number he had when she left."

Cheyenne frowned. "I suppose." She said the words but didn't look any too happy about it.

"But sometimes we want to make it as easy as possible for someone to come back," Elsa said gently. "So they don't get upset and change their mind."

"I keep everything picked up nice." Cheyenne whispered the words like a quiet confession. "All my books and toys and my stuff so there's no clutter around."

"Because you like it that way?" Elsa asked, and she wasn't a bit surprised when the nearly nine-year-old girl shook her head.

"Because I want her to love our house again. She liked things cleaned up and put away all the time, so maybe if she walks in and sees it that way, she'd like to be there."

The gravity of the child's extended efforts when the mother had made none spoke to the emotional tangle left behind when a mother abandons her children. "You're very thoughtful to remove any kind of barrier that might discourage her. That shows a good heart, Cheyenne."

Cheyenne's wince said more than words. "I just want her to be happy."

"And here."

Cheyenne frowned. "Huh?"

"You want her to be happy and here," Elsa repeated. "Because she's your mother and you love her."

"I can do more things now," Cheyenne replied. "Way more than when she was here before."

The thought that a child should have to work so hard to earn a love they richly deserved broke Elsa's heart, but she kept her voice calm. "Such as?"

"Helping with things. Taking care of Dakota. Putting away dishes. I tried to help when I was little, but I'd mess up and she'd get mad."

"Thank you for trying," Elsa told her.

Cheyenne shrugged and dipped her chin back against her folded legs. "It didn't work then, but it might the next time."

Hopeful waiting . . .

Enduring . . .

Praying . . .

Elsa wanted to grab Whitney Stafford and shake her. A responsible adult would take one look at this child and see the suffering and pangs of loss in her eyes.

A mentor's words came to mind. *There's a reason selfish people cause misery. Because they're selfish.*

Looking into Cheyenne's sweet face, seeing the pain and concern dogging her, Elsa wasn't in the forgive-and-forget mode. She wanted to have her own personal face-to-face with Cheyenne and Dakota's mother and tell her how beautiful, special, and wonderful her children were, but self-absorbed people never saw the whole picture. They saw themselves, dead center, even if the real image lay twenty feet to the left. "How does Dakota feel about moving?"

"Fine, I guess." Morose, Cheyenne stared at the tops of her knees, unmoving.

"And is Dad excited?"

"Very." Cheyenne looked surprised when she said it. "It's a really nice house he wants to build."

"And you like being at the ranch," Elsa supposed.

"I *love* it," Cheyenne corrected her. "I never want to go home while I'm there."

"We moved when I was little," Elsa mused, sitting back. "My sister is four years older than me, and she cried every night in that new house. She loved it later, but it took a while. And making new friends was hard for her because she left hers behind in her old school and the old neighborhood. It's kind of nice that you don't have to worry about that though. You'll be in the same town, same school, same friends." Cheyenne's affect flattened, a mental health red flag, so Elsa shifted topics. "I received a note from the school today saying that you've been offered a place in the summer school program."

A tear slid down Cheyenne's cheek. Then another. "I know. I hate school, I hate going, I hate people looking at me, and now I have to go more." More quiet tears followed with increasing speed.

"What if I told you the school offered a different option?"

The girl's forehead furrowed. "I don't know what that means."

Elsa put her elbows on her knees and leaned forward. "My sister has given us a choice. We either agree to keep you back in third grade—"

Cheyenne gulped hard, as if realizing how badly she'd messed up.

"Or you make up your grades over the summer, pass the requirements, and then you can move on with your class. She also said that if you'd prefer to be tutored at home, that would be fine."

Cheyenne's eyes went wide as she recognized the possibility of reprieve. "Could you do it?" She half-whispered the words, strangling on hope. "Teach me, I mean? I would like that, Elsa."

Cheyenne's optimism tempted her. Elsa had been in such a hurry to get off the ranch, to move on, to achieve her goals. As she matured, she realized how much she missed the normal give-and-take of ranch life, and then it was too late. Her father retired, they sold the ranch, and her parents moved to an island in Puget Sound, so when she wanted to go back, she couldn't. Because it was gone.

Right now she'd love to get out of her stuck-in-the-mud existence, rejoin the world, and hang with two cute kids on one of the biggest spreads in the Pacific Northwest. Tempting, but impossible, but she couldn't slap Cheyenne down first thing. "We'll have to look into the arrangements, okay? But honestly, kid, if they're willing to offer this second chance, I think you'd be downright silly not to take it."

The sound of truck wheels ended their discussion. Elsa stood. So did Cheyenne, but slowly. "You'll think about it though?" She came close and peered up at Elsa. "About teaching me?"

Something softened inside Elsa, the child's words and pleading expression pushing her toward a new normal of caring. Joining. "I'll absolutely think about it. Wouldn't you prefer a regular teacher though?"

Cheyenne made a face. "No." She folded her arms around her middle, still glum but not as angry, and led the way out the door. She didn't say a word to her father. She walked past him, climbed into the truck using the small step on the side, sat down, and fastened her seat belt silently.

Nick looked her way, then back toward Elsa. "Half an hour?"

She nodded. "I'll be there."

"Okay." Concern deepened his features. Regret shadowed his gaze, and for a brief moment Elsa was tunneled back to another rainy day, another child, another father.

This is nothing like that, her brain scolded instantly. *Stop drawing parallels. Run inside and put something else on. You're meeting Nick Stafford for coffee in twenty-eight minutes. Do something with yourself.*

Like this was a date?

It wasn't. It was a consult with a distraught father about his obsti-
nate daughter. She did take time to clip her hair back and apply mas-
cara to darken her fair lashes.

It might not be a date . . . but there was no rule that said she needed
to look pale and washed out.

The bird woke up long enough to stare at her, disapproving, but he
kept his opinions to himself, a rarity. Achilles slept on, curled on his rug
in complete comfort, a serene moment, well deserved. She let herself
out the door, climbed into her car, and headed for town for the second
time in a week and felt almost normal doing it.

Nick drove back into town, frustrated with himself, with Cheyenne,
and with the whole situation.

Elsa had reminded him to be patient.

Patience had never been his strong suit, and he grimaced, remembering, as he walked through the Coffee Shack's front door. The scent
of fresh-roasted beans and rich vanilla welcomed him, and when he
spotted Elsa scribbling notes in a booth, his universe seemed to right
itself slightly. "Hey." He slid into the worn oak booth and refused to
examine why it felt good to be there. "Am I late?"

She shook her head, finished whatever she was writing, and
looked up.

Beautiful.

Soulful eyes, shining tonight. She'd clipped her hair back, away
from her face, but the long blond mass had spilled over her left shoulder
as she wrote, like an old-world painting, all blond and rose and pale.

"You're building a house, I hear."

"Hoping to," he replied. "Hey, Mavis. Just coffee for me. Elsa, what
about you? Coffee, tea? Dessert?"

"An iced mocha would be perfect," she told the waitress. "And if Mr. Stafford is buying, then a piece of lemon cake would make me happy. Somehow spring and lemon cake make a nice pairing."

"That does sound good." He turned toward Mavis again. "Make it two lemon cakes, and can you pack one to go for Angelina?"

"And not your brother?" Mavis frowned. "Troublemaker."

"Make it two," he conceded, smiling. "I'll call it a wedding present and be done with it."

"Your brother's getting married." Elsa sat back as she made the observation.

"As soon as we have that church built." He indicated the construction area down the road. "We pledged to help put this town back together after the fire, and the church is the current focus."

"Noble."

"Long overdue," he argued, as they waited for their order. "My father kept us separate from the town for a long time. Except for basketball with Coach Irvine. That was our one major connection with the town growing up. School and shooting hoops."

"Rancher elitism." She made a face. "Who knew that was a thing?"

"Yeah, well, it was kind of the feudal lord and the peasantry and preposterous," Nick replied. "Colt and I don't agree on a lot of things, but we agree on this. We want to change people's perceptions of the Double S, and surprisingly my father has arrived at a similar conclusion. I'm not sure if it's guilt, illness, or a blast of faith-based common sense from my future sister-in-law, but I'll take any improvement I can get. For the first time in a long time, we're almost on the same page. Some of the time."

"Families are a tricky business," she agreed as Mavis brought their cake and coffee. "What made you decide about this new house now?"

Would it sound weird to confess that he'd never been at home in his own home? That he'd been out of place for a long time? He decided it would and stuck to basics. "Availability of labor. It's construction season and the girls have been pushing to learn more about the ranch. To do that effectively, we'd be smarter to live on the Double S. I've been in trouble with Cheyenne for over a year because all the area ranch kids can ride and work in the barn. Most of them have been sitting saddle for years, and my father brought us up that way too. So in trying to do right by building us a home there so they can learn the things they want to learn, I'm clearly doing wrong, but let me just say"—he leaned forward, dismayed—*"there is nothing clear about raising girls.* Not one thing. Girls and women are the most confusing creatures known to man. And that's all I've got to say about that."

She laughed, sipped her iced coffee, and shrugged one very pretty shoulder. "You have a valid point, and of course it's not the new house that put Cheyenne into a tailspin. It's leaving the old house, the one she shared with her mother."

"But Whitney's been gone for three years." He frowned, not understanding. "She doesn't want to leave the memories? Because that last year wasn't all that memorable from what I recall, and how much can Cheyenne remember from back then? She was little."

"Have you noticed that Cheyenne keeps things nice and neat and clean?"

He nodded.

"And that she's trying to be helpful with chores?"

"I figured that's what kids do as they mature. They take on responsibility."

"They do," she agreed. "Especially when they're hoping to impress their mother when she does come back."

"No." Did he look as surprised as he felt? Dumbstruck? He hoped not.

She hauled in a deep breath. "Yes."

"She thinks Whitney's coming back? She hasn't breathed a thing like that to me since the first year."

"She wants to be ready when that happens. Her mental scenario is that Mom walks into the house, sees how helpful Cheyenne has become, and stays forever."

Nick's heart sank.

He'd felt exactly like that when she first left. Angry but hopeful. Sad and yearning. Bitter but longing. He'd spent months filled with unanswered questions from an untraceable wife, except when she sent him the divorce papers. And even for a short while after that, he wondered when she would come to her senses.

She didn't.

He did.

But not sensible enough, because how could Cheyenne be harboring these thoughts and never share them? "Why hasn't she said any of this to me?" he asked Elsa. "Is it that she doesn't trust me?" He braced his forearms on the table, leaned forward, and spoke more softly. "Or am I the bad guy in all this? Why would she be waiting and hoping and never say anything?"

The common sense of Elsa's answer tweaked another nerve. "Because if we say unbelievable things out loud, other people's expressions can chase the dream away. So we keep it safely tucked inside until we're ready to give it up."

He'd done the same thing with his father years ago, hoping his mother would return. Did he hide it as well? Was this a case of like father, like daughter?

"I can't believe this." He studied his coffee cup, then sighed. "How do I fix it?"

"You can start by talking to her openly."

"Ha." He sent her a bemused look. "You've seen how far that's gotten me."

"I know." She made a face of sincere sympathy, but Elsa had no kids. Could she really understand that he felt pretty much like a failure as a dad? "It's really the best way. Usually kids have two parents to play against each other after a marriage breaks up. That way they can dole out the guilt, grief, and blame. But in this case you're it, Nick. You're all she's got, and she doesn't know how to resolve the mental and emotional issues hitting her. And of course by messing up the school year, she's under greater pressure now. The school has offered her a chance to do summer school and stay in her grade."

"Or be tutored." Nick nodded. "Mrs. Willingham e-mailed me today, and this is really decent of her. Getting Cheyenne to summer school wouldn't be easy, and finding someone with the patience to tutor her won't be a piece of cake either. Speaking of which, this cake is pretty darn good."

"It is." She hesitated, ate a forkful of cake, then set the fork down. "Actually, she's hoping I'll do it."

"You?" Nick stopped the fork and stared at her. "You're a psychologist. Why would you spend your summer tutoring a kid, even a really cute one like my daughter? I'm pretty sure most therapists don't grab tutoring side jobs."

"Because she needs it?" She pressed the back of her fork to the last crumbs of cake, forcing moist crumbs to fill the tines. "I'm not exactly practicing my chosen profession at the moment. Hence the *gratis* work with Cheyenne."

"I'd noticed. Do you want to tell me why?"

She hesitated slightly, then shook her head. "Nope."

"I see." He didn't see. He didn't see at all. To have someone come waltzing into the ranch, being part of the daily routine, and know little about her?

You knew nothing about Angelina, and that's worked out to everyone's benefit. You knew a lot about Whitney and got blindsided. What's wrong with giving this idea a chance? She's the principal's sister and Cheyenne likes her. So do you, actually.

"There is a problem with this idea."

Nick shoved the mental nudge aside. "I'm listening."

She set her fork down. "I have to be careful not to get involved with my patients and their families. I have to maintain a professional distance, and I'm concerned that I won't be able to do that effectively if I'm working with Cheyenne on her feelings *and* her schoolwork."

"Hard to maintain a sense of personal detachment," he said slowly.

"Exactly. And while I'd love to help Cheyenne and she's already beginning to trust me, I don't want to mess up our counseling relationship."

"Become attached."

"Yes."

"Is that so bad?" She started to reply, and he held up a hand. "Elsa, we don't know each other."

She conceded that by dipping her chin slightly.

"You were a ranch kid. When you see the Double S, you'll notice I don't do anything without a plan of action. But right now my plan of action with the most precious thing in my world is failing. I don't fail." He lifted his shoulders. "It's not in my genes. And yet my wife left me and our kids, my oldest daughter is mentally spinning in circles, and I don't know how to fix any of it. So yes, I'd like to take a chance on you. I'd like for you to come and work with Cheyenne, if you wouldn't mind and if you have the time. This is the first time Cheyenne's asked anyone for help. For her to ask you is a big deal. Huge. And I'm going to be honest here. I think we're supposed to form attachments as we go through life. I'm pretty sure half of my father's problems were from lack of attachment to people, so if we can break that cycle too?" He raised his coffee mug in salute. "I'm all in."

She stared beyond him for long, slow ticks of the café clock, then stuck out her hand. He shook it lightly, and when he did, a warm feeling stole over him, as if her hand in his was right somehow.

She pulled her hand back and stood, then waited while he paid the check. When he'd squared up with Mavis, Elsa moved forward, ahead of him, and a spiced scent drifted back his way. *Delicious.* "So. We have an agreement?"

She turned on the café steps and looked up at him with a gaze that mixed hope and something else. Something winsome and indefinable, the same feeling he got at her eccentric woodland home.

"You think spending my days with a bunch of hard-driving, cattle-herding, church-building roughnecks sounds like a good idea?"

It did, and he couldn't resist saying so. "From where I'm standing?" He aimed an appreciative smile in her direction, and when the blush rose to her cheeks, he knew he'd made his point. "Absolutely. And if you've got time on Saturday, why not start right away? No sense wasting time, is there?"

She hesitated, then nodded. He walked her to her car, and when he swung the door wide, she looked up at him and smiled, surprised. "Thank you."

"You're welcome, Elsa."

She started the engine and drove off. He watched her go, more hopeful than he'd been for a while. She'd gotten Cheyenne to open up. That had to mean something. And she seemed comfortable with both girls, as if their well-being was important.

He'd spent a long time wondering why their mother hadn't felt that way, but hearing Elsa talk about Cheyenne held up another reflection. His.

He'd been guilty of the same things. Trying to steer the girls in the direction Whitney had laid before them. He'd tried to maintain a sense of normalcy in an abnormal situation. If he stopped living in the past, perhaps Cheyenne's emotional attachment to it wouldn't be such a stumbling block.

Elsa's taillights blinked out of sight over the rise.

Something stirred inside him. A sense of hope, rekindled.

He drove back to the ranch, picked up the girls, and hustled them home to bed. As he passed the curve where he planned to put the new house, peace flowed through him.

Cheyenne might not like the idea of a new home, but Nick knew it was the right thing to do. And the thought of having Elsa help out over the summer might make the whole thing less confrontational.

As he came downstairs from tucking them in, his phone signaled a text. He pulled it up and smiled instantly when a picture of Achilles popped up. Underneath the shaggy dog's photo was a caption. "He is, of course, part of the summertime deal. Have dog, will travel."

His grin deepened as he texted back, "We've got two pregnant Aussies, a proud father Aussie, cats, and chickens. As long as he doesn't mind sharing the barnyard, it's an open invite."

"Deal."

Just that. Nothing more, no wasted words.

He liked that. It was unusual to have a quiet woman around, wasn't it?

Unusual in his experience. But nice.

FIVE

June first. Elsa walked by the wall calendar and refused to turn the page. She couldn't stop June from coming, but she could pretend it hadn't arrived in the privacy of her little home. Would she ever be so busy and vital again that she wouldn't notice? She hoped so.

Her phone buzzed and Nick's number flashed in the display. "Nick. Good morning."

"We've got a problem here."

A single dad, a lot of work, two kids, and a wide assortment of angst sprinkled liberally. Problems were going to be a given. "Explain."

"Dakota wants to come to Cheyenne's session tonight. I told her no, and I explained the situation before they got on the bus this morning, but she looked sad and Cheyenne looked triumphant."

Besting her little sister sounded pretty normal in Elsa's book. "Bring Dakota with you when you drop Cheyenne off this afternoon. I'll tell Dakota that I'll be there on Saturday and that we'll work together then. That will prep Cheyenne for sharing me with her sister."

"You're okay with starting Saturday?"

She was, and that surprised her as well. Being around Nick Stafford and those girls made her feel alive again. "How's nine thirty in the morning? We'll give it a couple of hours this first time and see how that goes."

"And then lunch, here at the ranch."

"I don't want to be a bother, and we might want to keep my roles separate," she argued, while a part of her thought lunch at the ranch sounded lovely. "We don't want to create a dependency."

"Well, now, I think you create some kind of dependency any time folks develop a relationship or feelings, don't you? I'm not sure how you can get around that."

"Nick, I—"

"Cheyenne trusts you," he continued. "Dakota thinks your bird is cool, and I can't remember the last time I could carry on a comfortable conversation with a woman who didn't have her own agenda in mind the whole time. Can't we just leave it at that? Friendship with professional benefits? And we never settled on a pay rate for the tutoring. Is twenty-five dollars an hour acceptable?"

"I don't need money."

Silence greeted her words, and she could almost see him weighing her old car, the odd house, the dated clothes, but he didn't need to know that she existed on a government subsidy to offset her loss of income when she left the well-heeled practice. That wasn't exactly the kind of thing that inspired confidence in parents of needy children.

"I have to pay you. It would be wrong not to," he argued. "I appreciate that you're not practicing therapy now and that you're not taking pay for seeing Cheyenne, but this is different. If you don't do it, I have to hire someone who will, and I don't want to do that because Cheyenne talks to you. That in itself is a step forward. We'll compromise."

Learning to compromise was a big part of a healthy emotional base. "I'm listening."

"I pay for the tutoring, with food thrown in."

"Nick, I—"

"Every decent job comes with a benefit package attached, and when you taste Isabo's cooking, you'll realize that the benefits outweigh the paycheck. Can we do three hours a day on the clock?"

Three hours was a reasonable amount of time to spend on missed schoolwork. "Three should be plenty. And I like benefits as well as the next person," she told him. His answering laugh chased more shadows away.

A new day. A new season. A new time.

"Good morning! Good morning! Good morning! *Bawk!*" Hoyl hopped along his perch, wings flapping, feathers out, as if dancing.

"That is a crazy bird, Elsa."

"He thinks he's Mandisa." She hummed a few bars of the singer's popular hit tune. "I haven't got the heart to tell him he doesn't sound anything like her."

"I'll see you this afternoon. With two kids."

"I'll be here."

She shouldn't be excited about seeing him.

She was.

The thought energized her. She pulled the living room apart and gave it a thorough cleaning, windows and all, and by the time she got the room put back together with the windows thrown open, fresh air invigorated the surroundings.

She pulled a half-dozen planters out of the small shed behind the house and lugged them to the front yard. She'd known they were there last summer, but she'd left them in the dark shed purposely. Now she hosed them off, set them around, and added potting soil to her shopping list.

A few weeks ago the idea of a shopping list would have meant hours of mental preparation. Now it seemed almost normal.

Because you've taken steps forward, on your own. Welcome back. And let me just say . . . it's about time.

It was, and she couldn't even hate her conscience for the slightly mocking tone because it felt good to be teased. She showered and changed before the girls' arrival, and when Nick hopped out of the truck, he smiled at her.

And she smiled back.

"Elsa!" Dakota raced her way and hugged her legs. "I've been wanting to see you!"

"And here I am." She squatted to bring herself down to Dakota's level. "How are things, Toots?"

"So good." Dakota held up her fingers and ticked them off individually. "First, I got two stickers on my paper because I got done first and had everything right."

"Bonus!"

Dakota grinned. "Yes! And then my kitten threw up on the couch and Daddy didn't get mad. He just said babies do that sometimes and we cleaned it up."

"Wise words," Elsa noted, and she slanted a quick smile up at Nick.

He shrugged, humble, but his expression said he'd aced the moment.

"And then we're here!" She spun around, nearly smacking Elsa in the face, and when Nick took Elsa's arm to help her stand back up, something clicked again, as if it was right to have his help. "Can I stay?"

"*May* I stay," Elsa corrected her mildly. "And the answer tonight is no, but . . ." She angled a frown down when Dakota started to whine. "I'm coming over to the ranch on Saturday to do some schoolwork. Would you like to do some schoolwork with us?"

"I love schoolwork so much!"

Cheyenne snorted. Elsa ignored her rude reaction and palmed Dakota's head. "It's a date. I'll be there for a while, and maybe one of these times you guys can show me the ranch. When the weather's nice."

"We can do that Saturday!" Dakota aimed excited eyes up at Nick and grabbed his legs. "Right, Dad? If it's nice out?"

"Not this Saturday, sweet pea." Regret deepened his voice. "I'm working on the ranch because Colt and Murt are on the church work crew from one until dark," he added. "How about if we all meet at church on Sunday and then go back to the ranch and we can show you around. Would that work, Elsa?"

It would if she accepted the invitation. She'd stayed away from church for a long time. The insensibility of a loving God versus evil men left her angry. If man was created in God's image, why did humans have such a hard time choosing good over evil?

"I can show you the kitties and our dogs!" Dakota let go of Nick's legs and did a little dance. "BeeBee and Kita are going to have puppies soon!"

Puppies.

She bent low again, excited by the prospect of puppies, of new life. "My mom used to breed dogs when I was little. She let me help take care of the dogs and help with the birthing, Dakota. I absolutely, positively love puppies. Like this much." She spread her arms wide. Dakota grinned and a slight smile softened Cheyenne's features momentarily.

Nick lifted one brow as he waited for her decision. He didn't push, didn't encourage. He simply waited, and that made all the difference.

"Let's see how Saturday goes, okay?" She couldn't pretend she was too busy for Sunday, because the fact that she did little was obvious.

"Sure. And bring Achilles along."

She had planned to bring him, but would he behave in new surroundings? "He's not cattle savvy."

Nick shrugged. "Does he come when you call him?"

"Most of the time." She stretched out the word *most,* and he laughed.

"There'll be plenty of us on hand to keep an eye on him. And he might like a chance to run in the sun."

He probably would, Elsa decided. She'd kept him shadowed, just like she'd kept herself in obscurity. Nick didn't press. He didn't sound disappointed. He sounded strong and hopeful.

She liked that. "Cheyenne, I'm going to have you help me clear out that shed. You left your good clothes at home, right?"

"Yes. Aren't there laws about this? Against child labor?" the bright girl asked. "I think there are."

"Not when it falls under the heading of therapeutic endeavors," Elsa assured her. "Grab some gardening gloves from that box. You and I are going to put the finishing touches on an in-depth research study I call 'work therapy.'"

"Are there spiders?"

"Quite possibly."

"Great." Cheyenne pulled on the gloves as she turned back to Nick and Dakota. "I'll see you guys in an hour. If I survive."

Nick watched Cheyenne tug the grungy gloves into place. He looked surprised but backed toward the truck, smiling. "You've got this?"

"I do."

"Okay, then." He waved, helped Dakota up, then waited while she fastened her seat belt before he backed around and pulled away.

Elsa watched them go. Dakota leaned way up in her seat and waved good-bye.

Cheyenne ignored her.

Elsa waved back.

As they crested the slope leading onto the logging path, Nick turned. When he saw her watching, he paused the truck and smiled. Just that, as if seeing her with his daughter was something to smile about.

"I'm ready."

"Me too," Elsa replied, but was she?

Maybe. Maybe not. But she wanted to be ready, and that was half the battle.

Nick pulled into Josh Washington's driveway, grabbed his house plans, and waited while Dakota undid her latches. Once done, she hopped out behind him. "Well done." He high-fived her before she raced to the backyard to see what Josh's kids were shrieking about as Josh moved his way.

"Hey, Dakota."

"Hey!" She dashed by him and disappeared through the wooden gate.

"Do we dare trust them out there?"

"Sammy Jo's back there. She knows we're going over plans so she got her homework done early."

"I owe her."

"I promised her a chance to help build this summer."

"For real?"

Josh nodded, firm. "She looks like her mother, but she's got a builder's blood and she loves jumping in on jobs. So she'll crew with me on the housing project at the lower end of town. And that child has a way with fine carpentry. Pretty amazing, and patient, besides."

"I think it's great," Nick replied as he thought of all the stumbling blocks he'd put in Cheyenne's path the past three years. Why hadn't he recognized that God and nature had created her to be unique, and everything else built from there? He laid out the plans on Josh's extrawide worktable, and as they talked, Josh jotted notes in the margins and at specific spots on the house plans.

"How soon can the logs be delivered?"

"Late July."

Josh shook his head. "Can't do it then, Nick. I never turn down work, but with the repairs and rebuilds to the houses in town and over-seeing the church project, I can slip in small jobs here and there, but there's no time to get to a new build like this until October. That spring fire caused a lot of damage and spurred two things. A whole bunch of insurance claims and more work than my crew and I have seen in years."

October?

In his head, he and the girls would have been moved in by October.

"I don't want to hold you up," Josh went on. "If you need to pull in someone else to do this job, I understand, Nick. No offense taken."

Josh had worked in this town since he was a kid at his father's side, doing odd jobs. He'd stayed through thick and thin. He'd married a great gal, had a wonderful family, then lost his wife to cancer two years before. And when Nick was a gangly high school freshman, it was Josh who schooled him under Coach Irvine's direction on how to pump fake, pivot, and deliver a perfect shot to the hoop, nothing but air.

Nick shook his head. "We'll hold back until you can fit us in, Josh. I've waited this long; a few months won't matter. I want the best, and that's you."

Appreciation softened Josh's dark-toned features. "Sounds good. Can I make a couple of suggestions?"

Nick nodded.

Josh pointed to the plans. "You nearly double your living space if you make this a walk-out basement by moving the house to the crest of the slope." Josh pointed to the lowest level of the plans.

Nick whistled lightly. "I hadn't thought of that, and a finished basement like my father's would be great. I've never liked that our house in town is on a slab."

"Newer builds have done a lot of that," Josh remarked. "Especially as you head east and the state gets drier."

"I didn't realize how handy a basement was until I didn't have one."
Nick began unpinning the set of plans.

"Do you have more than one copy?" Josh paused him and tapped
the house plans.

"I do."

"Leave this one here. I can wrap my head around how I want things
done with a visual. That's been one of the toughest things about jumping in so fast with the church project. Hurrying isn't my style, but I've
never seen so many folks work together to get a job done. It's like an
old-fashioned barn raising, and your brother's been on hand real regular. Of course, he's waiting on the church for a wedding, and a wedding
can push a man to speed, sure enough."

"I figured the church was keeping you crazy busy. I'd be here
more often, but Colt and I decided I'd take lead at the ranch and he'd
put in more time down here." Josh lived a scant two blocks from the
big fire that had raged through town that spring, a fire that con-
sumed multiple buildings, including the original Grace of God
Community Church. "I know my father has you putting in a lot
of hours over there."

"I am," Josh agreed. "With your father's funding, we'll have the
exterior done soon, and we're subcontracting a lot of the interior work.
That fire destroyed a great deal, but these unexpected jobs will keep
food on my table for the next year. With money tight and so many folks
not liking change and mad about most everything, life was looking
mighty grim a few months ago." He lifted his chin and stared out the
front window overlooking the small western town. "I don't mind admitting I cried the night of that fire," he added honestly. "Susan and I
got married in that church. We've been raising our children there, going
to services, being involved. Watching it burn was like a knife in the
back."

"It shook my father the same way," Nick told him.

"I wouldn't have thought I'd have much in common with Sam Stafford, but when you lose someone you love and watch the memories burn away, well . . ." Josh shrugged. "It's a rough go. The fire wiped out part of my family's history. But now?" He nodded to Nick's plans and pointed to a jam-packed bulletin board hanging on the far wall next to the landline phone. "I'm hip deep in work, I'm scheduling into fall and winter, and I'm hiring crews, which means a big boost for our local economy. Out of bad came good."

Nick had spent the last years being a churchgoing man to set a good example for his girls. He wanted to believe in something bigger, grander, and kinder than mortal man. Faith in God wasn't easy to swallow, and faith in people was tougher yet, and that went right back to his mother and his wife, walking out the door and never once looking back.

Was it people who turned the bad around for good? Was it God? Or was it the combination of faith-filled people working for God?

He had no answer, but working side by side as the town came together to rebuild, he'd gotten to know more folks than he had in all his growing-up years, and he liked it. For the first time in years he felt like he might be where he was supposed to be. "Let me know when the excavation crew is coming in, and I'll make sure nothing's in the way."

"I'll order the survey done and the utilities to be flagged," Josh replied. "And I'll note which trees you want left untouched. Digging might damage roots to some, and they might not all survive, but we'll trim out as needed once the structure's complete." Josh stuck out his hand. "Good doing business with you, Nick."

"Same here."

Dakota fussed at having to leave, but Nick stood his ground. "We've got to pick your sister up at Elsa's place. Let's go."

"And then Elsa's coming to our house on Saturday!" She caroled the words as if singing in a musical.

"Well, the ranch," he corrected her. He realized he didn't want Elsa to see them at the house on West Chelan Pass. He wanted her to see them where they belonged, at the Double S.

He pulled into her yard, hoping Cheyenne wasn't quite ready to leave, but she was. She'd tugged a sweatshirt over her lightweight top, and as she went to remove it, Elsa waved her off. "Wear it home. I'll get it on Saturday."

Cheyenne grinned in delight, an expression Nick hadn't seen much of lately. He missed her bright, crinkled eyes and her cute, winning smile. "Thank you, Elsa! I had fun!"

She enjoyed cleaning out a shed?

Normally Nick would have a hard time believing that, but Cheyenne's expression confirmed her words. She climbed into the truck, humming, fastened her belt, and didn't say one mean thing to Dakota. That was worth some therapy right there. He leaned out his window before he backed the truck around. "Nine thirty Saturday, right?"

"I'll be there." She met his gaze straight on.

"Much obliged." He lifted his cowboy hat in a little salute. "See you then."

Elsa steered her car past a small back-to-basics-style Christmas tree farm, hooked a right turn, then stopped on the long, winding gravel driveway.

She'd grown up on a northwestern ranch, surrounded by hills and fields of hay and corn, but nothing like this.

The Double S fanned out above and beyond her, stretching to either side, dwarfing other local farms she'd seen along the way. Massive barns extended along the stone drive to her left, while acres of pastureland rolled east. Green hills rose successively above the sprawling two-story cedar-sided house facing the daily sunrise.

Gorgeous.

Patterns emerged in her artistic mind, fields below giving way to pastureland in a patchwork landscape, utterly beautiful.

Above the main-level barns were higher elevation pastures, dotted with trees, merging forest and farm into a blended existence teeming with cattle.

Rachel had said the Stafford holdings were impressive. She'd alluded to money, but nothing the elementary school principal had said prepared Elsa for the stunning natural beauty that lay before her. She breathed deep, put the car back into gear, and parked it in the shaded area at the far side of the ranch house. Before she was able to exit the car, Cheyenne, Dakota, and an adorable little boy raced her way down the broad concrete walk.

"I'm so glad you're here!" Cheyenne grabbed one hand.

Dakota clutched the other. "Me too!"

The little guy kind of stared at each of them, then her, then shrugged and stuffed little hands into tiny blue jean pockets, total boy. "Hi."

Irresistible seemed to be a Stafford trend. "Hi. I'm Elsa."

He peeked up at her as a dark-haired woman stepped outside the door and crossed the wide porch. "Elsa?"

She nodded and moved forward, a kid on each side and one in front. "Yes."

"I'm Angelina, the house manager and Noah's mother." She swept the boy a fond look. "And I get to ride herd on these two regularly."

"And she's going to marry Uncle Colt as soon as the church is built," bragged Cheyenne. "Uncle Colt works on the church every chance he can because he says the waiting is just about killing him."

"Is it now?" Elsa exchanged a look with Angelina and decided she liked this woman instantly when Angelina rolled her eyes.

"You will soon find that handling men around here is not unlike handling children or cattle. Of course, that might be more Stafford than gender," Angelina mused with a skeptical smile. "I'm still deciding that issue."

"A wicked combination either way, darlin'." The screen door opened and a broad-shouldered, square-jawed cowboy stepped out, grinning. "Dr. Andreas, I'm Colt Stafford. Pleased to meet you."

"Elsa, please."

"Mighty pretty name for a mighty pretty gal, but I don't expect my brother's figured that out yet, has he?" He aimed a direct look over her head, and when Elsa turned, she wasn't surprised to see Nick approaching. "He's a little slow on the uptake."

"I thought you were meeting Murt and Ty?" Angelina asked, shooing Colt toward the stone drive. A cool breeze rolled down from the western hills. She crossed her arms over her chest and shivered. "Kiss me good-bye and head out so we can get our work done here. Men are a bother."

He didn't look at all bothered by her words, and actually, neither did she, and when Nick's brother kissed his fiancée good-bye, he left no doubt he was a man in love. "See you tonight. Love you."

"Me too." She smiled as he crossed the graveled lot and climbed into an SUV with the Double S logo emblazoned on the front doors.

"Come on in." Nick moved forward and swung the door wide. "That breeze is chilly this morning, but tomorrow's supposed to be warmer, so if we decide to take a look around, it should be nice to do it then." He removed his hat, set it on the counter, picked it right back up when Angelina *tsk*'d him, and hung it on a hooked rack inside the door. "Where's Achilles?"

"I decided that today's a workday so not a good day to bring him along," she explained.

"Tomorrow, then. Give him a little sun."

She'd considered telling him no to the tour on the drive over. She'd weighed it and knew what her answer should be, but the minute she spotted the gracious, terraced land and the sprawling house, she felt like Elizabeth Bennet first seeing Pemberley.

"That would be really nice. We'll both enjoy it."

Angelina set out a tray of fresh baked goods and pointed out the single-cup coffee brewer on the counter. "The doctors want to run some tests on Sam, so I'm driving him down to the hospital this morning. Nick promised to grill sausages and dogs on the wood-burner grill outside for lunch later, and my mother will laugh in the face of her Latino roots by making one of the best Irish potato casseroles you've ever had. We've found it best not to question these things," she advised Elsa with a look that only a woman would understand, and Elsa did. "We just roll with them."

A man approached the kitchen from a side wing of the house. At first glance she thought he was elderly, but as he drew closer, she realized her mistake. Older, yes, but not aged. Ill health seemed to be taking its toll on him. Ashen skin and hollow cheeks gave him a gaunt appearance, but when he spotted her, a hint of steel sharpened his expression.

"Dad, this is Elsa Andreas," Nick told him. "She's here to work with the girls."

He started to extend his hand, then gripped the counter instead and looked downright aggravated at the necessity of it. "Welcome to the Double S, Miss Andreas."

"Doctor Andreas," Cheyenne corrected at the same time Elsa waved that off.

"Elsa is fine. It's a pleasure to meet you, Mr. Stafford."

"Where is your walker?" Angelina crossed her arms over her chest again, but this time Elsa was pretty sure that temperature had nothing to do with the gesture. "You're being stubborn and uncooperative, and if you fall on your way into the professional building, it will serve you right."

"I won't fall because you'll give me your arm," he retorted. "Dang fool walker is for dang fool old folks, and when I need one of those to get around my own blasted house, it's time to call the undertaker."

"Perhaps our infirmities are meant to offer a dose of humility." Angelina tipped her head slightly. "Have you considered that, Sam?"

"I expect I'll be humbled on a regular basis before this thing is done," he grumbled as he made his way to the door. Angelina moved alongside and offered her arm, and the big man grasped it gently. "Thank you, my friend."

She smiled at him, their height difference minimized by his stooped stature, as if standing straight proved too painful. "You're welcome, as always. We'll be back later, although maybe not in time to have lunch with all of you."

"*Vaya con Dios y bendiciones!*" A busy-looking woman entered the kitchen from the opposite direction. "I'll have lunch waiting unless Sam needs to eat as he waits."

"If you're making those special potatoes, Isabo"—he turned and sent her an expectant look from the doorway—"I'll enjoy them when I get home."

"They'll be ready," she promised, and when Elsa shifted her attention to Angelina, she read the gravity of the situation in the other woman's face.

Sam's illness added another layer to the broken family dynamics, which meant she needed to find out more about his prognosis. Children dealt better with the elements of life and death when they were prepared for them.

Sam and Angelina went through the door, and Elsa wondered why Nick didn't move forward to offer his assistance. Was it to salve the older man's pride or because grievance lay between them?

And that added a different layer of mortar to the already hard walls of being born Stafford.

A part of Nick longed to assist his father to the door, but Sam would only shrug him off. Nick had spent a lifetime being shrugged off. He should be used to it by now, but he wasn't, so he let Angelina help his father. Angelina wasn't mired in old hurts where Sam was concerned. In Gray's Glen that put her in a miniscule minority status because at least two-thirds of the town hated Sam Stafford, and at least half of them did so with good reason. The others just went along for the ride.

Colt and Nick were determined to turn that around. Sam's change of heart would help make that possible, if he lived long enough to see it through, and right now that appeared to be a big if.

"Girls, come on over here to the table, and let's get organized, shall we?" Elsa set a bag down on the broad braided rug, and a smaller one on the table. "Who can get me crayons, scissors, pencils, and erasers?"

"I can!"

"Me too!"

The girls dashed off to the corner of the great room to gather supplies, and when they hurried back to Elsa's side, their looks of anticipation blessed Nick. He'd put off meeting with a therapist for long months because of stupid, Stafford pride. He was a moron, plain and simple, and right now he wanted nothing more than to stay inside and hang with Elsa and his daughters.

Isabo would take a rolling pin to him if he tried, but it might be worth it to coax Elsa's smiles. He started to pull out a chair when one of the ranch hands yelled his name.

"Nick!"

The ranch hand's bellow from outside came at the same time Nick's phone buzzed a 911 incoming text. He raced out the door, looked up, and saw the catastrophe unfolding from a distance but could do absolutely nothing to help. He ran for the ranch Jeep. One of the ranch hands jumped in alongside, and they torqued up the hill as the huge tractor careened over the small embankment and into the slow-running creek below.

The first thing he hoped was that Hobbs was all right.

The next thing he figured was that he'd have to kill the old-timer for taking that upper corner too sharp with a monster-sized rig.

He paused the SUV as a summer hand ran his way. He let the kid jump in behind Brock and raced toward the creek's edge. Fear tied his gut into a massive knot. They hadn't had a serious ranch accident in over a decade because Sam ran a tough, tight ship. Accidents cost lives, time, and money, and for all his father's faults, Sam Stafford took safety seriously. As he spotted Hobbs making his way up and out of the creek bed, Nick knew the old man's days of running tractor were over, but he had no idea how to break that kind of news to one of the hardest working cowboys he'd ever had the pleasure to team with.

Nick jumped out of the Jeep as soon as it drew to a stop. "Hobbs, get in." He helped the old man into the backseat. He motioned for the younger ranch hand to take the wheel. "Get him to the emergency care clinic. If they can't handle this, run him right to the hospital."

Nick turned his attention back to his devoted old friend. "Are you okay to ride in this?"

Hobbs brushed the question off with old-timer ease. "I've rode in worse, and I'm just banged up. Maybe busted." Hobbs glanced down, and it was then that Nick noticed his arm hanging at an impossible angle. "Yup. Busted." He scowled. "Don't much care to run into your daddy at the hospital when I just wrecked a major piece of equipment," he muttered. "I thought I had it, Nick. I took that corner same's I always do, and then the next thing I knew, I was heading for the edge. Mebbe I ain't cut out to drive them bigger rigs."

"Let's get you fixed, then I'll ream you out, okay?"

Hobbs smiled thinly through the pain. "Your daddy will take care of that, more'n likely. I can stay, you know." He scowled at the creek bank where the monstrous wheel spun sideways, cutting the air smoother than a Dutch windmill. "We can fix this later." He nodded to his arm as if working with broken bones was okay, and from the stories Sam, Hobbs, and Murt spun around the supper table, it might have been, back in the day.

But this was a new time, and Nick sent Hobbs and the kid off to get medical care while he and Brock surveyed the situation. He called Colt and told him to gather Murt, the local sheriff, and anyone else he could grab hold of and get back to the ranch a.s.a.p. They'd all been working on the new church, but everything stopped when the call for help was sounded. In farming there was a time for every purpose, just like the Good Book said. If you missed that window of opportunity, you could mess up an entire year or more.

It took all afternoon and lots of good-natured ribbing as they positioned massive equipment every which way to haul the tipped tractor back to navigable farmland, and when they'd finally gotten the big rig back on level soil, Nick drew a sigh of relief. "Don't know how to thank you all," he told the group of men as the double winch lines eased the rig over a shallower embankment. "Tank, you got enough daylight to give it a look?"

"Plenty," the ranch mechanic told him. "Me and the kid can team up, then come up for supper in a few hours." He'd driven an old farm rig out to the accident site, loaded with tools. "I put a sack of sandwiches and cookies there too, Tim," he added when the rangy nineteen-year-old sent a longing look back to the ranch. "And Miss Izzie will hold stew for us. She promised."

"Thanks, Tank."

Colt smacked Nick on the back, a move that could have gone either way. Today it was a friendly gesture. "You handled this like a pro."

"I am a pro," Nick told him, irritated. It wasn't as if he needed

Colt's approval on anything. Ever. "I've spent twenty years doing what needs to be done, half of which you spent in big cities."

"What's the burr in your boots?" Colt asked. "This is a job that would have taken days on your own. We got it done in a few hours. You'd think we interrupted some hot date or—" He stopped and stared at the house, then his brother as they followed Murt and a couple of area ranchers into the newer SUV. "I forgot. The doctor was in." He made quote marks with the fingers of two hands. "That's a mighty pretty reason to want to get back to the house, little brother. I thought you'd sworn off women completely."

"Shut up."

"Hey." Colt lowered his voice so the other guys wouldn't hear as he paused Nick with one hand. "I'm not messing with your head. I think Cheyenne's got a better outlook these past few weeks, and while I'm no expert on women or raising kids, I can spot a happy face when I see it. For the first time since I've been home, my niece looks happy. And that's something I'm thanking God for."

Nick wasn't sure how to handle this. Colt had spent his life messing with Nick's head. To have him shoot straight and sincere was new and might take some getting used to. "Well, I was supposed to be back at the house to grill lunch for all of them. That didn't happen."

"Isabo and Elsa took care of things from what I saw, and when I stopped into the house to grab the waters, Elsa was cutting vegetables for the stew pot and the girls were helping."

"She was ticked, I bet."

Colt shrugged as they reached the SUV. "Didn't look ticked at all, and you might want to stop assessing every woman by Whitney's standards. A lot of women are willing to jump in and help out. Maybe Elsa's not the exception. Maybe she's the rule."

He hated that Colt was right and that he hadn't understood the measure of a good helpmate a dozen years before. Was he that blind? Or just stupid? Or was he so busy trying to create the perfect family to show up his father that he failed to look beyond appearances?

More likely.

They climbed into the car. Colt swung it around in an easy arc and headed downslope. "We're two men down now, what with Dad and Hobbs, and with the work on the church in full swing, there's not a lot of help around."

"Dad doesn't worry much, but he worries when we're short on help. For good reason."

"When's Trey due in?" Murt asked from the backseat. "He knows his way around." The youngest Stafford had followed his dream to Nashville years before. He'd stuck it out through hard times, made it big, and was setting everything aside to come north as they faced Sam's prognosis together. He was a solid singer and musician, and an even better ranch hand, and Murt didn't offer praise like that—or any, he realized—lightly.

"His last concert is Tuesday," Colt answered. "He said he'll close down the tour as quick as he can and get back here, but I don't know what that means."

"Then we slide by for a bit," Murt said. "Won't be the first time we've pulled double duty. Won't be the last." He climbed out of the SUV once it rolled to a stop. Angelina came out the side entrance to meet them.

"It's upright." She pointed to the distant hill and the tractor. "That's a good sign."

"It is, darlin'," Colt told her. He hauled her in for a kiss, then tapped the brim of his hat. "I'm on barn duty for those F1 cross babies due now. To everything there is a season, and this appears to be the season for calves, ready to drop for the next few weeks."

"Supper?" she asked and he sniffed the air, looking hopeful.

"Bring me some?"

"I will once the kids are in bed."

"My girls rope you into letting them stay here overnight?" Nick asked as he moved toward the kitchen door.

"They didn't have to rope hard." She slanted the noisy front room a fond look as she led the way back into the kitchen. "And don't even think of wearing that mud-spattered nonsense in here. Ditch it by the laundry room entrance and we'll take care of it."

Isabo came into the kitchen with a basket of fresh sweet peas. "I thought these would be stringy, but they're not. They're perfection. We'll do some fresh and some steamed tomorrow." She spotted Nick and turned her attention his way. "Your friend—the girls' doctor friend?"

"Elsa?"

"Yes!" Her face split into a wide smile when he said the name, as if just hearing it made her happy, and Isabo wasn't what Nick would call the effusive type.

"What about her?"

"Magnificent!" she declared. "With the girls, with Noah, with the kitchen." She stressed the last because Isabo had great respect for any-one who could hold their own in her kitchen. "She made the best bis-cuits we've ever had, warm and cheesy and good, and she was not afraid to take the girls to the barn when I was too busy."

"Translation: you wanted to see if she was tough enough to handle kids and half-ton animals without caving, and she passed the test," Nick offered reasonably.

"That is one way of putting it, yes." Isabo looked quite agreeable as she rinsed the peas beneath a stream of cold, clear water. "I like her."

Nick wasn't sure when winning Isabo's approval became important but figured it was about the time she walked through the door a couple of months before, after being holed up in a cabin with Angelina's little boy for two years. "I do too."

"Well, good." She waggled her head from side to side as if a momentous decision had just been made. "We are in agreement. Angelina, can you put the bread out with fresh butter?"

"Absolutely." Angelina withdrew two soft, fragrant loaves from the warming oven. She handed them off to Murt as the other guys trooped in, looking tired and hungry. "I'll finish serving supper, *Mami*. You take care of your produce."

Their combined voices brought the kids running into the kitchen. "You got it out!" Cheyenne clapped her hands together as if proud of Nick, and Nick couldn't remember the last time his oldest daughter seemed proud of him. "We were watching from down here, Daddy, and we weren't sure what would happen, but when Isabo said we should pray for your success, we did! And it worked!"

"I heard you guys took care of everything down here while I was stuck up there." He pulled her in for a hug and realized Colt was right. She seemed happier. Lighter. More relaxed since he'd brought Elsa into her life, which only made him feel bad for not following up on the principal's idea sooner. "How'd the schoolwork go?"

"So fun!" Dakota twirled around, grabbed a toy gun from a holster she must have borrowed from Noah, and took pretend aim at a bear head on the great room wall, tomboy to the max. "We practiced sounding things out, and I didn't know where to put my teeth with the letter *v,* but Elsa showed me and then it seemed like so easy! And she showed me how to figure out big math things right in my head. I just think of the bigger number, watch, Daddy." She pulled on his hand and then tapped a finger to her temple. "I'm adding twelve and seven, so I keep twelve up here and then"—she held up seven fingers—"I add the seven!" She counted up and waved her hands, triumphant. "It's nine-teen! And it was so easy. I don't know why I used to think it was hard to learn my numbers, because when Elsa showed me, it was so fun!"

Angelina cleared her throat.

When Angelina cleared her throat, it meant either you should lis-ten up because something momentous was going on beneath your nose or she was about to explode and take a rolling pin to your head. And since she was a former cop, he figured a rolling pin was better than a small, lightweight Glock, her pocket weapon of choice.

He looked her way. "Say it."

She tipped a look down at the girls and lifted one shoulder. "I don't need to say a thing. It's there, in front of your eyes."

He smiled because it was suddenly easy to smile, despite the tractor mishap. Hobbs was going to be all right, the tractor didn't appear to have suffered dire damage, and his precious girls were acting happy on a more regular basis for two reasons: he was encouraging them to be the rancher's daughters they deserved to be, and he'd finally taken outside advice and given the girls someone to talk to, to listen to, to hang out with.

The quirky therapist who preached laughter with sad eyes made him interested in getting to know her more, in hanging out with her. She brought out the protector in him, but why? He was pretty sure Elsa could take care of herself.

And yet . . .

Her choice of shadows and privacy didn't mesh with big city, big bucks therapy, and Sammamish was an upscale town snugged up to Seattle. So why was she here, living a hermit's life in the forest?

Does it matter enough to mess up the forward progress you see in your daughters?

It didn't, he decided. He wasn't some wet-behind-the-ears kid, crushing on someone. He was an accomplished man, a rancher who ran a big business. He used instinct to make decisions every day. Sure, he'd almost walked away that first night, tempted to let pride get in the way.

He gazed into his daughters' shining eyes and was mighty glad he didn't, because Elsa's quiet honesty seemed to have turned the tide in his favor at long last.

———◦◦———

Elsa pulled into Rachel's driveway on the upper outskirts of town. She climbed out of the car as Rachel's boys headed out back with their father on thick-wheeled Gators. Rachel was walking toward the house with a tray of dishes in hand when she saw her.

She paused, then smiled. "Got time for coffee?"

"Tea, yes. Or water. I've hit my coffee limit for the day." She followed Rachel into the house. Rachel set the tray on the counter, filled the kettle, then set it on to boil.

"You could just heat water in the microwave," Elsa reminded her. "I do it all the time."

"The kettle takes longer, allowing me to probe deeper."

"No probing required." Elsa made a face at her. "I was out and thought I'd stop by."

Rachel could have reminded her that she hadn't done anything impetuous since moving to Gray's Glen. She didn't. "I'm glad. What were you up to today that's got you wandering the roads at suppertime?"

"The Stafford girls."

Rachel's sigh of relief wasn't overdone. "Thank you."

Elsa shrugged. "Don't thank me yet, I'm just stepping in to help Cheyenne catch up on schoolwork over the summer. And maybe give her some tools to deal with the tough mix of emotions left to brew when mothers walk out on children."

"Nobody does it better, Elsa."

Elsa used to believe that. She'd always felt gifted when mixing children and therapy. And then she lost two beautiful children at the hands
of an angry, possibly brain-traumatized parent, and she'd done what so
many of her young clients yearned to do. She'd curled up into a ball
and hidden herself, mentally and emotionally. "Well."

"Mom called today."

Elsa winced.

"And your expression says she called you and you let your mother
go to voice mail."

"I wasn't exactly free to take calls in the Double S kitchen. I was
doing reading skill builders with Cheyenne, who is, by the way, quite
smart."

"I've got the test results to prove it," Rachel agreed.

"But she likes everything on her terms and her timeline, so we'll
work on that over the summer too."

The kettle began to whistle. Rachel got up, made the tea, and
brought it back to the table. "You think she can catch up?"

"Can? Yes." Elsa stirred the tea just for something to do with her
hands. "It's up to her. The stubbornness might get in the way, but we
have one very important trump card on our side."

Rachel arched a brow in question.

"Her grandfather." When Rachel looked surprised, Elsa nodded.
"It's clear that he loves those girls, and she wants to please him. So I'm
going to use that for leverage in the nicest way possible, but there's a big
question mark that goes along with that plan."

"Which is?"

"His illness."

"Ah."

"I'm not sure about the prognosis, but he doesn't look good, and
coaxing kids along new paths is tricky enough with no major potholes

along the way. If he doesn't make it, all this time and effort could be for nothing."

"Or it could strengthen Cheyenne to the point of being able to handle the unexpected twists and turns in life."

"That's what the books say." Elsa sipped her tea. "With kids, it's not nearly so predictable because stages of development vary. But it can't hurt," she added, and she wasn't sure if she was trying to convince Rachel or herself.

"Teaching her how to build a platform of strength will only help her."

"And help me in the meantime?"

Rachel smiled and tapped the mug of tea. "It did get you out of the cave and into the light, so yeah. I'd be okay with a fringe benefit like that. Because it's time."

"Maybe past time." She drank some more of the tea, then stood. "I've got to get home and take care of my mini-menagerie. They're not accustomed to my being gone."

"Which means they're about to enjoy a learning curve as well." Rachel walked her outside, then hugged her. "I'm glad you stopped by. When do I see you again?"

"I was thinking about going to church tomorrow morning."

Rachel stayed quiet, waiting.

"Nick invited me."

"I see."

"I'm still considering it, of course. There was an accident on the ranch today, so we couldn't talk it over, and I'm weighing it up."

"It's church, Elsa." Rachel's expression called her out.

"It's church, in a small town, with a single parent. I'm assessing possible implications."

"Not possible, probable. And, yes, folks would actually see you in church with a single guy. But at least you'd be back in church, so I'm voting for yes. Get over yourself and shove the concerns aside. Like you used to, Elsa Jean."

"Things were different then." She'd been braver. More self-assured.

"And can be again," Rachel insisted. "But only if you give them the chance."

She wanted to.

She'd seen that today, working with the girls, helping when a farm crisis changed up plans, jumping in like she used to years ago.

So the question wasn't should she step out.

The question was, could she?

lsa reached for her brush, then hesitated. Was she really getting ready for church, knowing Nick would be there with the girls? And was she a complete phony or only a partial phony, because would she have gotten up and ready if Nick wasn't going to be there?

No.

But she'd have felt guilty about it, so maybe God had been working on her for a while and she hadn't noticed. Or she'd ignored him because she was downright angry with him for letting Christiana and Braden down in their hour of need.

Like you did.

She set the brush down and stared at her reflection in the dresser mirror.

She'd run the gamut of self-help. She knew the rules of therapy, she understood the timeline, the grieving and guilt process, she could recite the textbook platitudes by heart, and she'd gone for professional help because she understood the value of it.

And still she heard their cries in the night.

Was there a God? Did he care? Did he shelter and embrace? And if he did exist, were Braden and Christiana safe in his arms, or was that a simplistic portrait the gullible painted to glamorize the reality of death?

Her gaze darkened, but then her phone buzzed an incoming text from Nick Stafford. "Heading to church in ten. Can I pick you up?"

No, he most certainly could not. Having a man pick a woman up for church in a small town like Gray's Glen spoke louder than a ring on the finger. Worse than that, if things didn't work out, everyone knew.

Then it became item number one on the small-town gossip circuit, so no, she'd get to church on her own, thank you very much. She texted that she'd meet him there and then laughed at herself.

She'd talked herself into staying home, holding back, keeping her distance, and the minute he made contact, she'd caved. And if she was truthful with herself?

It felt good.

———⁓———

"Elsa."

Her heart tripped faster when Nick called her name. As she turned, the two girls raced across the stretch of sidewalk to throw themselves at her. "Good morning, ladies."

"I'm so glad you came!"

Cheyenne grabbed one hand and Dakota latched on to the other. "Me too!"

"Will you sit with us?" Cheyenne wondered, but it wasn't in her demanding, petulant voice that had been getting her into trouble on a regular basis at home and at school. This was a gentler, kinder version and Elsa appreciated the difference right away.

"Yes, because you're precious and polite and not a demanding little twit."

Cheyenne blushed, then smiled. "I'm trying."

"Good." She shifted her attention up to their father, mentally scolded her heart to keep it from jumping into overdrive, and kept her face placid. "Good morning."

"Good morning." He looked at her, right at her, and even though he couldn't take her hand because the girls had grabbed tight on either side, his eyes said he wanted to, and that was enough for now. "You look beautiful, Elsa."

"You look mighty fine yourself, cowboy."

A tiny smile that couldn't be called a grin quirked his left cheek, and then he tipped one finger to the brim of his hat, cowboy style.

Her heart stutter-stepped all over again.

He led the way inside. If folks noticed them, they pretended not to, which was probably because some of them knew her story even though she'd kept out of the way. Still, in quaint places like Gray's Glen, people had a way of finding things out. Anyone with access to a computer could find her history in a one-point-five-second Google search.

Let it go . . .

The words from the popular song touched her. She'd come to church because it felt like she should, and now that she was here, she didn't want to fret. She wanted . . .

She glanced around the quaint Catholic church they were using while theirs was rebuilt. She didn't know what she wanted, but she'd like to start with peace. Peace of mind, peace of heart, to toss the scarlet cloak of guilt away. That would be a wonderful way to begin.

Nick handed her a songbook. The bright Sunday morning bathed the simple windows in light, and a bank of flickering candles winked and bobbed with each breath of soft late-spring air.

And when a lone voice from behind them began the a cappella opening notes of an old-time hymn, her soul grabbed on to the words like a sponge seeking water.

She knew the rules of wellness better than most. She could either reach for the elusive healing with all its aches and pains or wallow in solitude.

Dakota took her hand on one side.

Cheyenne took the other.

The hymn's words pitched up and rolled down, and for the first time in long years, Elsa joined in the song.

Within two minutes of the final hymn, Nick was sandwiched on the church steps by the town drunk and the elementary school principal he'd ignored the past year, who also happened to be Elsa's older sister.

Nowhere to run, nowhere to hide.

"I'm comin' here to get a little religion," the drunk explained, and when he hiccupped and swayed, Nick took him by the arm.

"Can I help you home, Johnny?"

"You're a good-for-nothin' Stafford so I don't think so," the older man argued, but he didn't look any too sure. Several people passed by. Two women sniffed and scowled. One old-timer rolled his eyes as if seeing Johnny Baxter drunk was nothing new. Johnny had lost his wife, his home, his kids, and his self-respect when his drinking caused problems at the Double S. A part of Nick knew he could have mimicked Johnny's outcome, except he was blessed to be born a Stafford with money and connections at his disposal when his marriage fell apart.

"Elsa, can you get the girls to the car?"

"I'll walk with you, sis," offered Rachel. Her glance sized up the situation as Elsa herded the girls north. "Cheyenne, that dress is lovely. The color is perfect on you. And Dakota, I love your pigtails. The matching bows totally rock the outfit."

Dakota was easily distracted.

Not Cheyenne. She turned as they started to walk away. "Daddy, aren't you coming?"

He was and he wasn't because someone had to see Johnny home before he made trouble and turned a nice Sunday morning into a hometown fracas. "I'll be right along."

"I don't need no help. I believe I said that." Johnny shook him loose and took a wobbly step forward. "I got nothin' but time, and I plan to spend it in church. It's Sunday, ain't it?"

Nick nodded about the same time his brother Colt caught wind of what was going on. Colt and Johnny weren't exactly buddies. "Church just finished," Nick explained, easy like, but he wasn't feeling quite as magnanimous inside. A tractor rollover had burned his family time the previous day. He wasn't about to let the town curmudgeon ruin Sunday, but he couldn't exactly leave him stumbling. That fact that most everyone else had done just that wasn't lost on Nick. He saw the reverend approaching from the side steps and breathed a sigh of relief.

"Service just ended, Mr. Baxter, but if you want time inside, we don't need to lock up yet," Reverend Stillman noted as he drew closer. "Father Mitchell said Mass early, and then we stepped in to do our service because he's been kind enough to give us church time while ours gets rebuilt."

"I don't much care for all the hoopla." Johnny squinted at the minister.

"I'm a simple man myself," the reverend admitted. "Come on up. I'll sit with you awhile."

Johnny blinked, then stared around town as if realizing where he was. He scowled at Nick and doubled up his fists. "If it weren't for dagblasted Staffords, I'd be in the money now. Sittin' pretty. I don't need to set in no church to know I was done wrong."

Nick stepped back when Johnny offered a weak side swing, and when Colt barreled their way, Nick grabbed his brother's arm and kept him at bay. "He's drunk and poor and pitiful and doesn't know where he is half the time," he whispered to his older brother. "Leave him be."

"He's spoiling for a fight, that's what he's doing," Colt shot back, not nearly as quiet.

"A fight we're not going to give him," Nick continued softly. "Didn't you just walk your sorry behind out of church?"

The reverend cleared his throat in a show of support for Nick's reasoning.

"Do unto others? Forgive us our trespasses as we forgive those who've trespassed against us? Any of it ring a bell, Colt?"

His brother sighed, long and overdone, as if contrite, but Nick knew better. If he let go of Colt's arm, Colt was liable to give Johnny a wake-up-call thrashing for trashing their name around town for two decades. "Let's head home. The reverend's got this."

Sheriff Bennett rolled down the street in his black-and-gray police cruiser. He stopped, idled the engine, and leaned out the window. "Beautiful day, gentlemen."

Nick followed his lead. "Best one yet. We're throwing smoked brisket on the slow grill, Rye. Do you and the kids want to come by later?"

Rye Bennett looked like he was weighing his answer as the reverend led the drunken ex-cowboy up the church steps, and when they moved through the church door at long last, he leveled Colt a stern look. "Get over it. No one listens to what he says anymore. It's time to move on."

"That's easier said than done when he turns up all over the place, telling everyone we ruined him, his life, his marriage, and his farm."

"He's not the only one holding a grudge against Staffords," Rye reminded them. "Helping with this church and coming into town might balm some wounds, but it doesn't happen overnight, Colt. You've only been home a couple of months. Give it time, man."

"He was in New York for a lot of years," Nick reminded the sheriff as he released his brother's arm. "If it's not going a hundred miles an hour, Colt needs to know why. Patience isn't his long suit."

"I'm patient when I need to be." Colt stared up the church steps, clearly unhappy. "I don't care what the old coot says about me, and I care less what he says about the old man because a good share of that's deserved and we need to fix things. But there are kids involved now."

He looked to where Elsa and Rachel were talking in the far parking lot. "And that changes things."

"It sure does," Rye told him. "It means you have to mind your manners and set the better example. And I can't deny, brisket sounds real good for later. What time should we come by?"

"Any time after three's good," Nick told him. He pointed up the sloped road and gave his brother a shot in the arm. "Ange is looking for you, and Noah's eying that playground. Let's give the kids some time to play before we head back to the ranch."

Noah ran their way just then, and Nick watched his brawny, in-your-face brother cave totally as the little guy launched himself into Colt's arms. "Why not?"

"And if Johnny Baxter comes wandering out of that church before you head home, leave him alone. Better yet?" Rye hiked a brow when the two Stafford men turned back his way. "Offer up a prayer or two. Spring's a tough time for him."

Nick and Colt knew that. Johnny had messed up his life as a younger man. Sam Stafford cut him no slack when he started hitting the bottle. They'd lost two pricey calves in one night because a drunken cowboy failed to tend the birth mothers properly. He'd been thrown off the ranch and fell behind on his home payments. He lost his home and his wife twenty years ago now. Since then he scraped along by getting sober once in a while, working here and there, receiving benefits now and again. It was a day-to-day existence that always seemed worse in late spring.

"Girls?" Nick called across the parking lot. "You want twenty minutes on the playground?"

"Yes!" Cheyenne looked delighted by the prospect.

"Yes!" Dakota echoed her big sister. Then they tore across the grass, looked both ways, and crossed the quiet street to join Noah, Angelina, and Isabo on the far side of the road. "We *never* get to stay and play on the playground! Thanks, Dad!"

Nick mulled her words as Elsa came up to his side. "They're right," he told her. "I'm always too busy to let them stay and play. There's always ranch work or house stuff or fixing . . ." He let his voice wander on purpose. "Why do I forget to just let them play?"

"You take responsibilities seriously." Her tone said that wasn't a bad quality. "A good work ethic is a wonderful thing, but worker bees need to examine their lives with greater care than most others. Are they pushing forward so much that they forget to relax and enjoy the sun?"

"Time is money on a ranch."

She didn't appear impressed. "Time is money anywhere. The skill is in learning to appreciate what you have and tether the constant desire for more. What is it you need that you don't have?"

"Nothing." That was true in a material sense, but not in other ways, because all he'd ever wanted was a normal family. He'd missed out as a kid, and when he married, that was his one true goal. A delightful, normal family. Healthy kids, loving wife. He'd been so determined to show his father how it was done. He'd met every demand Whitney threw his way, and it still didn't keep her happy. "Well, nothing money can buy."

She acknowledged that with a wise look. "Exactly. I didn't realize how fortunate I was, growing up on a ranch. Other than caring for the puppies, I resented having to help. I wanted to be a town kid in the worst way. They had the coolest clothes and the best cars. Our Walmart jeans and pickup trucks couldn't compete. So I plotted my course to be a well-educated city professional, and in the end?"

He waited for her to continue.

"I missed the ranch."

Nick understood the night-and-day rigors of living off the land. He loved the Double S, but he wasn't one to paint rosy pictures about it. "I hear you, but a ranch isn't just a postcard prospect. It's work, every day. It's living, breathing creatures, us against Mother Nature. It's reaching goals—daily, monthly, yearly. And if you fall short, you have to try harder next time."

"All well and good as long as we don't lose the beauty of the hills. The forest. The birds. The children," she chided gently. She swept the town a soft smile. "The little town trying to rebuild itself."

"Well, missy, while you're busy jawin' on all that utopia stuff, here's the reality." He tipped a knowing look down to her. "To everything there is a season."

"Ecclesiastes."

"Yup. And there's a reason the Bible understands simple people. We make up most of the world, and we have to plant when we're supposed to and reap when it's ready. We can't just glance at a clock and decide it's time to swing by the coffee shop, because if we miss that window of time before the rain, we've ruined thousands of dollars' worth of cattle food."

"But is that the exception or the rule?" she wondered. "Is every day that structured and important, or does it become a habit because it's in your nature to overachieve and possibly best your father and brother?"

"Both." He grumbled the word because she was right. Some things needed immediate attention, while others could be let go for a little here and there. "The problem is, I get worried if I let too many things go. It piles up in my head, and then I feel like the work's controlling me instead of the other way around."

"Will it be easier with Colt here?"

"Already is, but I'm not about to tell him that." Nick watched his brother dash from swing to swing, pushing kids from behind. "He's got a big enough head already. With my father and Hobbs down and out right now, we'll be working double time for a while. So that's a consideration too."

"Kids! Time to go!" Angelina tapped her watch. "We've got chores and berry picking back home."

Elsa's eyes lit up. "Berry picking?"

Nick nodded. "It's that time of year for the late season ones."

"I want to pick berries. I haven't done that since I went off to school. I used to make jam with my mother, and we'd freeze gallons of berries to use over the winter."

He scanned her church dress with no small measure of skepticism. "You're going to pick berries wearing that?"

"Of course not. I brought along some proper ranch clothes. Preparation is often the key to success."

"Perfect." It felt nearly perfect, like the kind of early summer day a body waited on all winter.

He looked down. Met her gaze. And when the color of her cheeks went deeper, the only thing he could think of was leaning down. Kissing her. Seeing if kissing Elsa Andreas would be as perfect and nice and delightful as he thought it would be, but the laughing voices of racing children made him put that thought on hold.

"Dad, let's go! Elsa, can you come? Dad said you might. Please?" Cheyenne skidded to a stop by her side, scattering pebbles and scuffing her church shoes. "Oops."

"I am coming," Elsa told her. "And clothes and shoes don't grow on trees. Someone works hard to make money to buy them. Don't take them for granted."

"Yes, ma'am." Cheyenne grabbed her hand as naturally as if she'd been doing it forever. "I'm glad you're coming over. Isabo is making strawberry shortcake and pie, and Daddy said he'd cook on the grill, and Uncle Colt said we could have a bonfire tonight to celebrate the end of the school year."

"And Mommy said we can make s'mores." Noah whispered the

words with a little boy grin as Colt drew closer. "She said they will be so dewicious!"

"Chocolate and marshmallows?" Cheyenne smiled down at Noah. "Noah, you're going to love them so much!"

"They're marvelous," Elsa promised him. Dakota came up, side by side with Angelina and Isabo.

"This is going to be the best summer ever," Dakota announced. She spun around, carefree, arms out. "Elsa, I'm so glad you're coming to the ranch with us! We're going to have so much fun!" She spun again as the group turned.

A small, roughed-up car wove its way up Center Street. It rolled through the stop sign as if there was no need to obey something as mundane as traffic rules, cruised to edge of the community park, and came to a halt. Nick was ready to scold the driver for disregarding the stop sign, but then a cloud shadowed the glare of late-morning sun, letting him see the driver.

Disbelief and raw emotion gripped him. His hands went damp. His breath caught. And if Colt hadn't had the presence of mind to put a firm "I've got your back" hand on his shoulder, Nick wasn't sure what he might do.

The door swung open. Mere seconds dragged like minutes as the driver pushed the door open farther and stepped out. "Cheyenne? Baby? I'm back!"

Dead silence reigned until the woman stepped forward, bent, and put her arms out.

"Mommy?" Cheyenne's voice broke, uncertain.

Dakota stared at Whitney as if she'd never seen her before, and Nick understood her reaction. Short, dyed blond curls had replaced Whitney's nut-brown hair. She'd done something with her eyebrows, giving them an unnatural arch, and the dress she wore like a second skin wasn't generally seen on Gray's Glen streets on Sunday mornings. Long legs ended in pointed-toe heels, and the only thing missing from the overdone look was fishnet stockings.

"It's me, baby! I've come home!"

Elsa slipped back, allowing Nick room.

Colt did just the opposite. He stepped forward as if shielding his brother, the women, and kids, and folded his arms across his chest in a formidable pose.

Cheyenne dashed toward her mother. Nick went to stop her, but she slipped away from his grasp and raced across the narrow road.

The force of Cheyenne's embrace knocked Whitney off her feet. Nick was pretty sure he was okay with that and didn't hurry to help her.

What was she doing here, with no warning?

What was she thinking?

And why was she dressed like that?

"There's much we need to learn." Angelina's voice came from behind him, and it wasn't her gentle, helpful tone. This was her cop voice, tough and succinct. "Don't believe anything without proof and make no assumptions."

Wise words.

He moved forward.

Dakota hung back, untrusting, and when he glanced back over his shoulder, she'd moved to Angelina's side. She tucked herself into the curve of Ange's arm, staring at the unfolding drama in total disbelief.

He stared in disbelief too.

He reached out a hand to Cheyenne as Whitney quickly brushed off the seat of her dress, and the way she turned to do it, so that everyone saw, made him cringe. She'd always loved attention, but this—

This was different, and his mind went to several unappealing scenarios. He wanted to send Cheyenne back to the group, but she clung tight to Whitney's hand as if never letting go. The look on her young face mirrored his confusion. He took Angelina's caution to heart and faced Whitney, arms crossed, legs braced. She'd broken a trio of hearts once. He had no intention of allowing her to do that again. "What are you doing here?"

She aimed a smile at Cheyenne. "I believe I live here." She arched her sculpted eyebrows as if she spoke the obvious, and when Cheyenne's smile grew, Whitney laid a confident arm around the girl's shoulders. "I realized nothing was more important than my children and my family, and so . . ." She lifted her shoulders. "Here I am."

"I'm so glad, Mommy! So glad!" Cheyenne embraced her mother once again, as if all her hopes and dreams had just come true. "I've been praying about this for so long! Thank you!"

"Oh, baby, I couldn't stay away forever," Whitney crooned, but Nick would have to be blind not to miss the cool stare she swept the gathered family. "Not from my girls."

Anger boiled up inside Nick.

She hadn't cared a fig about these girls when she ran off with a rodeo cowboy. She hadn't given a second thought to breaking up a family, abandoning her daughters, leaving her husband, and sticking him with over three thousand dollars in credit card bills that financed her getaway. And then the significant sum her lawyer demanded for the divorce.

Separate her from the girls.

Think first. Then act.

The bit of wisdom said he'd done some growing up himself, because three years ago he'd have acted first and regretted at leisure later. What had Elsa told him? *"In all things, put the girls first. What is good for them? What will work for them?"*

Dakota didn't look excited or welcoming. She looked terrified.

Little Noah stared, eyes wide, but then Colt handed him to his grand-mother, said something Nick couldn't hear, and moved their way as Isabo turned and walked toward the ranch SUV.

"Colt's here." She flashed an insincere smile his way but kept her arm snug around Cheyenne as if using the girl like a shield. "How nice."

Colt ignored her completely. He squatted down, faced Cheyenne, then indicated the group with a nod. "Ange is going to see you guys home so you can get changed, okay? Can you help her get the berry baskets organized? Can you help make sure there are plenty for every-one who's going to pick?"

She stared at him, then her mother, then her father. "But what about Mom?"

"Not sure," Colt replied smoothly. "But I expect there's some adult talking that needs to go on."

"There is, Colt." Nick smiled down at Cheyenne, but he saw the change already. She'd spent the last few weeks looking happier. Easier. More settled.

Not now.

Shadows darkened her eyes. She stared up at her mother, then her father, then took a step back toward Whitney. "I want to stay with Mom. She just got here, Dad, and she came a long way. Can't I spend some time with her? Can't she come to the ranch for supper with us? To the bonfire?"

The last thing Nick wanted was to have Whitney at the ranch. Ever.

She hated the ranch, she hated his job, she hated his father and the entire life the Double S stood for. The mockery that she ran off with a cowboy wasn't lost on him. He knew then it wasn't his life that didn't satisfy her.

It was him.

"Not today, Cheyenne. You've got to—"

"Why?" She took a step back and faced Nick square. "Why don't you want her around?" she shouted. "She's my mother and she came back to see me!" She stared up at him, trembling with anger. "Why can't you just let her come back? We need her! Elsa, tell him!"

Silence hung still and deep until a soft, sensible voice said, "Nick, Cheyenne's made a very good point. There's plenty of food and it's a perfectly gorgeous day."

"Elsa, really?" Cheyenne's gaze flew to the woman behind him, and while he appreciated what Elsa was trying to do, she didn't understand how deeply Whitney had hurt so many.

"Well, of course it's up to Dad, right?" Elsa stepped forward, smelling of springtime and sunshine and sweet moonlit nights. Her soft, flowy dress was a direct contrast to Whitney's honky-tonk-friendly outfit. She looked up at Nick, and he read the warning in her eyes, a message that had nothing to do with him or her and everything to do with Cheyenne.

"There is plenty of food and it should be a good time." He faced Whitney, and it took a supreme effort to hold back all he wanted to say. "We're heading back home now."

"To the house?" she asked, and Cheyenne shook her head.

"Dad's going to build us a new house on the ranch, Mom! It's beautiful, and he's teaching us how to ride and how to take care of animals. But if you don't like it," Cheyenne added quickly, "we can just stay in our old house. Like, forever! That would be just fine!"

Nick's heart melted while his backbone hardened to forged steel. How could anyone turn away from the longing in Cheyenne's voice and face? And yet Whitney had done that before. He had no doubt she'd do it again, but right now, Elsa was right. He needed to look out for Cheyenne first and figure out Whitney's motives second. If nothing else good came of this, maybe Cheyenne would see her mother's true colors before she caused more pain.

His beloved daughter had built up a fantasy, trying to rationalize and excuse her mother's actions, exactly like Nick had done as a boy. Maybe Whitney's surprise reappearance would give the girl the closure he never had. He took Cheyenne's hand and stepped back. "We'll see you at the ranch."

"I know the way." The smug look she sent him refueled his anger, but he walked back to the group as if he hadn't seen a thing.

"Elsa, can you ride with us?" Dakota clung to Elsa's hand like a lifeline. Nick firmly expected Elsa to smile politely and deftly remove herself from the specter of family dysfunction spiraling around them, but to his surprise she bent and kissed Dakota's cheek and said, "No, I'm bringing my car. That way when I need to head home later, I don't have to disturb anyone."

"Wise move," Angelina muttered as the girls moved ahead with Colt.

"I'm assessing variables and coming up with so many potential scenarios that I'm losing count. This is not going to be the day they expected." She indicated the girls with a quick glance. "I could duck out and go home, but that would create another action/reaction sequence, so I'll come and lay low while preparing myself to expect the unexpected."

"That's the only kind of attitude a woman can have around here." Angelina kept her voice soft as they walked back to the cars. "Just remember I'm trained in all kinds of defensive maneuvers."

"None of which will be needed," Elsa told her. When Angelina looked doubtful, Elsa added, "But it's good to know you've got my back. Just in case."

Nick climbed into the SUV, his thoughts churning.

Cheyenne hurried into her seat. Dakota moved more slowly, methodically, as if delaying her buckles might put off facing this stranger.

One too willing. The other untrusting. How was he supposed to make sense of this? And if he couldn't make sense of it, how could he expect the girls to? Whitney had deliberately broken their vows with her secretive life and her quick getaway.

He'd trusted his mother when he was a child.

She left without a backward glance.

He'd trusted his wife.

She ditched him and their daughters the same way.

He never wanted to be in those throes again, caught in deceit and lack of faith. He'd been there, done that, and the last thing on earth he wanted was to be involved with another dissatisfied woman. A part of him had been happy that Whitney stayed gone once time marched on.

But now she was back.

They made an odd convoy, following the turns and twists up to the ranch house, and as they pulled into various parking areas east of the first barn, a new thought hit.

How would his father handle Whitney's surprise return?

He didn't have long to wait because Sam appeared at the door as soon as Nick pulled in, which meant Colt had forewarned him. The old Sam Stafford would have needed no warning. He'd have simply tossed her off the ranch, and if she refused to leave, he'd have wasted no time in having her arrested.

But this new, gentler Sam—the one facing grim illness—Nick wouldn't stake a claim on how he'd react. He stood just outside the door, hanging on to the railing, but not as if he needed it for support. No, it looked more like he was tempted to wrangle someone and was holding himself back by sheer force.

Nick didn't pray often enough, but he prayed right now that this meeting of opposing forces wouldn't put his father into some kind of cardiac arrest or scar his daughters for life.

Was there such a thing as liver arrest?

He didn't think so, but he knew Sam was in rough shape, no

matter what kind of face he put on for show. And right now, Sam's stern countenance said he'd drawn on his reserves, full force.

"Grandpa!" Cheyenne raced to the porch, delight painting her face. "You'll never guess what's happened. Mommy came home!"

"Did she now?" He pulled her in for a hug looking like a sweet, old story-time bear, but the look he raised and pinned on Whitney said he'd protect what was his, regardless.

Whitney climbed out of her car, spotted Sam's hard gaze, and faltered. While everyone else moved forward, Whitney stayed silent and still, eyes locked on Sam, until Elsa moved in her direction. "Does coffee sound as good to you as it does to me?"

Whitney broke the standoff with Sam and looked at Elsa, really looked. Her eyes narrowed. She swept the group a look, but then drew her attention straight back to Elsa, and the expression on her face wasn't one bit pretty. "You must be Nick's newest little friend."

"Flavor of the month," Elsa agreed cheerfully, and Nick stared at her, wondering what she was doing. Saying. "Which reminds me, Angelina has chocolate truffle coffee in the kitchen. It's to die for, and I'm not even really exaggerating. Are you a coffee drinker?"

Nick thought Whitney would explode over the nonchalant dismissal, but she accepted Elsa's overture after a few long, drawn-out seconds of silence. "I could go for a cup, no lie."

"Then let's do it."

"Girls, head upstairs and get changed." Angelina pointed to the door. "Noah, you too. Cheyenne, can you make sure he gets play clothes on?"

"Sure." She hesitated before going inside, staring at her mother as if Whitney might disappear again. "You'll be here when I come down, won't you, Mom? Or you can come upstairs with me."

Nick wasn't about to let Whitney have the run of the house. She knew too much about their cash flow on the ranch, and she'd had the old combination to the safe. Wisely, he'd had the lock changed when he realized she'd taken him to the cleaners a few years before. "She'll be down here, honey. I promise."

"Okay."

Dakota followed, still quiet, an unusual circumstance for the gutsy child, but the look she shot her sister questioned Cheyenne's intelligence, and when she narrowed her eyes and sent the same look toward Whitney, his ex-wife had the decency to look uncomfortable, and that spurred Nick's memory.

She'd never been able to con Dakota the way she manipulated Cheyenne. Even as a tiny girl, Dakota had migrated more toward Nick, as if she sensed the insincerity in her mother. Was that possible in such a small child?

Nick didn't know, but Dakota's reaction made one thing clear: she had no vested interest in building a relationship with this stranger, and from the look on Whitney's face, she recognized the girl's reticence and was focusing her attention on Cheyenne. The fact that her actions could hurt Dakota didn't seem to matter.

She'd shown up out of the blue purposely. A responsible adult who loved her children would have tiptoed back into their lives, allowing the girls some time to adjust and react. And that responsible adult would have worn something less scandalous.

Whitney hadn't put her children first when she left. She wasn't prioritizing their well-being now, and that meant she'd come back for one purpose only: money. He saw it in her eyes as she glanced around, sizing up the ranch, and in her gaze as she clutched the too-large purse to her side.

"Lock up the silver," Colt muttered as he swung open the door. "And move petty cash upstairs."

Nick sighed but couldn't disagree. They moved inside where the smell of fresh coffee indicated Isabo hadn't waited for the unfolding drama. She'd set out plates of cinnamon rolls and danish, a new Sunday morning tradition, and as Nick and Colt went upstairs to change into ranch clothes, the last thing Nick heard was his father's voice. Deep. Hard. Guttural. "Sit here and tell me what you want."

"Well, to be here, of course." Whitney's voice sounded as fake as her eyelashes. "With my family, Sam."

Nick left her alone to face Sam's inquisition for two reasons. First, she absolutely deserved to be uncomfortable, and Sam Stafford knew how to make people squirm. Second, his father's newfound faith would be tested by Whitney's return, and that was something Sam had to deal with on his own. He'd grabbed the reins of redemption with both hands over the long winter, wanting to make amends.

Facing the woman who'd hurt so many might push that fledgling grace beyond its limits, or it might strengthen Sam's resolve. Either way, Nick was locking up the valuables.

SEVEN

I'm chalking this up to Murphy's Law." Angelina waved a long-speared fork around as she seared a flat of beef on the long griddle. Cheyenne had insisted on taking her mother to the barn. Nick and Colt went with them. Dakota too, but only because Nick snugged his beautiful little girl into strong, caring arms while Noah trotted alongside Colt, mimicking the big guy's swagger. "Anything that can go wrong will, and at the worst possible time."

A strong family unit could survive negative onslaughts, but it wasn't easy. A family riddled with thin cracks in its veneer might fare much worse. "Did you know her?" Elsa asked as she sliced potatoes for German-style potato salad. "Before she left?"

Angelina shook her head. "She left before I came on board. I managed the phone calls from creditors once she bled bank accounts dry and ran up a host of charge bills before Nick canceled them. She left on his dime, and it looks like she's trying to come back the same way."

"Does she think that's possible?" Elsa wondered, and Angelina's reply said more than the simple words.

"I think Nick tried to do everything he could to make her happy when they were married. The Whitneys of the world don't see that as kindness; they see it as weakness. I expect she's banking on a similar reaction now."

Ange's words made sense to Elsa.

Nick longed for happiness. She saw it in his face, in his gaze as they'd talked since meeting each other. But anger and distrust took its place when Whitney stepped out of that car. Elsa hadn't just witnessed the varied reactions; she'd felt them. Cheyenne, so desperate and needy, longing for her parent to love her as any parent should. Dakota, bush-whacked and mistrustful, holding back and staying outside the drama zone. She'd gone immediately to Angelina's side in full-blown safety mode. And Nick. His face and shoulders took on hard, definitive lines in his ready-for-battle stance.

Their reactions weren't the problem. They were normal mental, emotional, and physical reactions to unpleasant stimuli.

It was Whitney's false emotional state that sent chills of unease up Elsa's spine. Self-absorbed, self-protective, angry, and desperate made a dangerous combination on the human psyche—a combination Elsa had witnessed firsthand a few years before.

The healer within wanted to help Nick and the girls. The woman who lost two beautiful clients to the hands of an angry, unhappy parent three years before needed to run.

I lift up my eyes to the hills—where does my help come from? My help comes from the Lord, the Maker of heaven and earth. She shifted her gaze to the west-facing kitchen windows, recalling the sweet psalm. The bank of hills rolled to the majesty of mountains beyond. If she closed her eyes, she could see them rising in the distance.

I lift up my eyes to the hills . . .

Dark images swept her. If God was truly present, then how could such things happen? And if man had so much free will, then why bother with prayer? What good was it?

Raw emotion surged from somewhere deep within, from a place she'd tried so hard to bury, and yet it lingered still. If only she'd made that call—

Firm hands gripped hers.

Elsa moved, startled.

Isabo's strong Latina features came into focus. Deep brown eyes with hints of honey bore into hers with warm sincerity. "Do not fear, for I am with you. I will strengthen you and help you; I will uphold you with my righteous right hand." She clenched Elsa's hands, the touch and the voice reminding her of the here and now. "God sees and he knows, my precious child. And he will protect."

"Not always," she whispered. "Not always, Isabo."

Isabo's clasp remained firm, while her gaze stayed gentle and knowing. "We cannot blame God for the evils of people." Her voice was warm and soft like a pixie fire on a cool spring night. "We are inclined to sin. But if each of us makes her corner of the world as sweet and good as she can, she blesses many, unseen."

Angelina plunked down a fresh cup of coffee in front of her. "Drink this. You'll need it. My prescription's a little more hard-core than my mother's. We watch. We soothe. And we move before she can, just in case. And under no circumstances does she get those children alone."

They'd read her fear and didn't seem to think she was crazy. Funny, she'd felt crazy when she'd first come to Gray's Glen, but not anymore. Now she felt . . . stronger. More capable. More like her old self.

Was that because she'd stepped forward? Or was it because of the trust Nick Stafford put in her and her growing affection for those girls? Or maybe she was finally letting the shining light of God ease her heart, soothe her soul.

She took a deep breath, kissed Isabo's tan cheek, and lifted her coffee mug. "To peace and watchfulness."

Angelina raised her own mug in agreement. Their shared concerns indicated her instincts were on target.

Could they help Whitney?

Her experience said they couldn't if Whitney was a true narcissist, but that might be bitter experience talking. If Nick's former wife had come back to reclaim her place as the girls' mother, that wasn't necessarily a bad thing. Unless Whitney made it one, and Elsa had treated both sides of that scenario many times in her old practice.

She understood the lasting damage of parental abandonment. She understood the value of reconciliation, but she was glad to have Angelina and Isabo standing watch. She could use a dose of their toughness, and she wouldn't mind a cup of their strong, shared faith to go alongside the fresh, hot coffee. She'd spent a long time unconcerned with matters of faith except from a therapeutic, self-help angle. The constant of her parents' faith had been diminished by years of hard work and human accomplishment. She'd misplaced that youthful hope and trust. More than anything else, she longed to find that elusive peace and joy again.

"This day didn't go according to plan, did it?" Nick locked his hands on the top fence rail and tipped his gaze down to Elsa's while Rye Bennett's sister and brother led the girls around the riding ring on easygoing mounts. Rye, Jenna, and Brendan had lost their mother to cancer less than a year before. Rye had left his job on the Chicago police force to become the local sheriff and take care of his teenaged siblings.

"What was your plan?"

He shrugged one shoulder, musing. "A day on the ranch, showing you around, hanging with the girls, breathing. And maybe . . ." He slanted his attention to her mouth and raised his left brow slightly. "When no one was looking, of course."

"The best-laid plans . . ." She leaned on the rail beside him and kept her voice low. "How did the send-off go?"

He grimaced. "Not well. Cheyenne didn't understand why Whitney can't stay at our house. She thought I was being mean and selfish."

"Ouch."

"There's only so much you can explain to an eight-year-old," he went on. "Whitney wasn't exactly helpful, so I took it on the chin, big time."

"Where is she staying?"

"The Glen Hollow Inn on Center Street. Marcie said they've got a room she can have, and she gave us a good price."

"You're paying."

He stared forward, clicked his tongue against the roof of his mouth, then made a face. "That makes me a pushover, right?"

"For being nice?" Elsa turned her back on the young riders in the paddock and faced him. "Why does kindness make you a pushover?"

"She's got a long list of priors," he reminded her. "But I couldn't leave it that she'd be out on the street, and that might be what brought her back. I'm pretty sure she's broke, desperate, and—

"An alcoholic."

The lines between his eyes angled deeper. "You smelled it too?"

She turned back toward the horses and clasped the rail. "Anxiety, unnatural thinness, shaking hands . . ." She nodded. "And the smell, which means possible dangerous situations for the girls."

"I'm being nice to buy time," he confessed in a tone that matched hers. "I don't know what my legal options are, but things were a whole lot easier eight hours ago. When I was planning my perfect day." He bumped shoulders with her and then sighed. "I hate drama. I was raised in the midst of it, and the only thing I wanted as a grownup was a nice, normal life. A home, a family, kids, and a dog."

"Do you have a dog?"

He made a face that said yes and no. "Working dogs. The Aussies. But not over at the house. Whitney didn't like animals. Their smell, their needs, their hair. And I'm sorry you didn't have time to bring Achilles over."

"I figured there was enough going on."

"And yet you came." He faced forward, but there was a question in the statement.

"I thought of going home. Leaving you guys to it. But then I saw the desperation on Cheyenne's face and the distrust in Dakota, and I realized they were about to be thrust into the middle of a situation in which they bore no responsibility but would bear the full brunt as it played out. And so I came."

"For them."

She slanted a wry look his way. "How often does one get to see an entire theoretical schematic played out before her eyes?" He grimaced and she nudged him with her elbow. "I wanted to offer support and gain insight. Mission accomplished. And you were just explaining how you wanted a house dog but never got one," she noted.

"Marriage is a compromise, isn't it?" He gazed off, maybe watching the girls. Maybe not. "Once Whitney was gone, there wasn't time to throw a puppy into the mix."

He was right—and wrong. "Dogs are good company," she told him. "They're always happy to see you. They bring you presents from the woods. Some of those gifts are still breathing, by the way."

He grinned understanding.

"I don't know what I would have done without Achilles," she went on. "He's my sidekick. I'd have to say on a therapy-rating scale, a good dog nets a ten. Totally."

"They roll in decaying matter." His tone underscored his dog knowledge.

"There is that," she conceded, smiling. "But *Old Yeller* is my most favorite movie of all time for good reason. It's heartfelt family drama."

"And powerfully depressing."

"Sacrificial love, rights of passage, growing up, protecting the family," she corrected him. "But yes, a total tearjerker. I loved helping my mom with the dogs and the puppies, all of which I didn't appreciate properly as a child. When you build your ranch house, those girls should have a dog of their own. A big ol' sit-on-the-porch kind of dog, gentle and goofy. Speaking of which, I should get home and take care of my shaggy hound. And the crazy bird."

"One s'more at the bonfire." He laid one hand over hers, one big, strong, weathered, rugged hand and didn't just touch her hand . . . he touched her heart. "Everything else got messed up, but if I can roast you one perfect marshmallow, I'll end the day happy. How do you like them?"

"I can't."

He paused.

She gave his hand a light squeeze and stepped back. "I'm glad I came over. I'm sorry about the upheaval. I'm happy to keep helping Cheyenne catch up on her schoolwork, but today's bend in the road came with possible serious repercussions for those two. And right now, I want to be a nonjudgmental friend if they need to talk. Everyone else on this ranch has a history with their mother."

"Except you."

"And that gives me an advantage because my vision isn't clouded by past hurts."

"You make perfect sense."

He didn't sound all that happy about it, or content either. She waited.

He huffed a breath, thrust his hands into his pockets, and called the girls over. "Ladies, say good-bye to Elsa."

Dakota had just dismounted with Jenna's help. She dashed their way, slipped between the fence rails, and hugged Elsa tight. "But we're having a bonfire! Do you have to go? Really?"

"I do. But I'll be back once the term is over, and we can do school-work each day. All right?"

"Yes!"

Cheyenne looked less enthralled by the idea of Elsa and school-work on her daily calendar. Elsa ignored the expression as she faced her. "And I'll see you tomorrow afternoon, okay?"

"Do I have to come?" Cheyenne looked surprised, as if Whitney's arrival had solved all her problems. Elsa was pretty sure that wasn't going to be the case. "I mean, I like coming to see you . . ."

Her voice trailed off as Nick nodded. "We're still on. Let's not mess up the progress we've been making, okay?" He sent her a direct look, and Cheyenne stopped arguing.

"Can I come see you too?"

Dakota's soft voice said more than Cheyenne's. Today's events had unnerved the younger girl. Elsa was pretty sure Dakota didn't remember much about her mother, and the caricature that arrived today was more Cruella de Vil than Mary Poppins. Dakota was an intuitive kid. Quick, questioning, and not easily swayed. The suspicion in her voice and expression said she didn't want anything to do with Whitney, no matter who she was. "You can both come tomorrow."

"More shed-cleaning therapy?" Cheyenne's tone held an almost cocky note of belligerence, a step backward.

"Cheyenne." Nick frowned at her. "Don't be rude. I'm sure shed cleaning ranks right up there with inkblot pictures."

"Huh?"

"Never mind." He turned and walked with Elsa toward her car. "You don't mind them both coming?"

"Under the circumstances, I'd say it's a good move on Dakota's part. You know that old analogy about how a small ripple in the water causes a chain reaction felt round the world?"

"Yeah."

"Well, this is more like a tsunami, and the reactions will vary from person to person. Including you," she reminded him. "I'm glad Dakota wants to come. Better than hiding everything inside, hoping it goes away someday."

"Like me and Cheyenne."

"We're all different, Nick. And no one's perfect."

He frowned and scuffed the gravel lightly. "I wanted it perfect, you know?"

She'd recognized that from the beginning. "I know."

"Stupid, right?"

"No. What's stupid about wanting a warm, healthy, loving relationship? Nothing. But our first choices aren't always the best grounded."

"Like the parable of the seeds being sown."

It was a good analogy. "Rocky ground, fallow ground, and good ground. Yes. The reasons behind our decisions at one age might not be the most fertile choices for longevity. But we don't see it then."

He scuffed the drive again, then met her gaze. "Thank you. For being here. For taking the time. For caring."

She did care. Maybe too much, because being with Nick and talking with him wasn't just helping him. It was helping her. And it seemed to be growing in significance as time went on. "I'll see you guys tomorrow."

He watched her go.

She glanced into her rearview mirror just before she took the first curve of the drive, and there he was, rock solid, one hip cocked, watching her leave as if her leaving mattered, and as she drove away, she was glad it did.

He watched her go and wished she wouldn't, but he understood the logistics. Whoever said timing was everything had nailed the phrase, because he hadn't let himself think about dating or relationships or much of anything other than the ranch and the girls until recently.

Until meeting Elsa.

Yes, he admitted to himself.

Today the game board had been rearranged. Not by their fault, but that didn't matter, because once things were messed up for kids, they had to come first. He'd spent too much of his life wishing he'd come first to make the same mistake with his daughters.

He wanted to get to know Elsa better. He'd wanted the day to be a perfect blend of family, faith, and fun. To show her around the ranch, see her eyes light up.

It hadn't come close, but facing Whitney and dealing with Cheyenne's instant overreaction and Dakota's obvious fear seemed easier with Elsa around. Not because she was a therapist. He was pretty sure being psychoanalyzed could grow old after a while.

It was because she had the best interests of him and the girls at heart, and that made all the difference.

Hobbs came his way just then, one arm in a sling, the other holding a book. "Gonna turn in. They're supposed to cast this tomorrow." He glanced down at his broken arm. "And those pills they handed out sure make you tired." He started to move by, then paused. "You okay, Nick?"

He was and he wasn't, but he appreciated Hobbs's concern, especially in light of the older cowboy's accident the day before. "I'll be fine. I'm glad you're going to be all right, old-timer."

Hobbs snorted. "Sam out for the count, now me down, and Colt committed to helpin' in town. Trey can't get home soon enough to suit me, especially with today's little surprise appearance. I expect that's goin' to pull your attention away now and again, tryin' to set things right, one way or the other."

"Just another bend in the road, Hobbs." He looked down at the

old-timer's injured arm sympathetically. "You've got firsthand knowledge of that, don't you?"

"Well, yeah, but them bends could use a marker now and again. A
street sign. Somethin' to warn us what's comin'. That's all I'm sayin'."
Hobbs started moving off to the bunkhouse at the front of the near
barn. "G'night."

"Good night."

They were down two full hands at a terrible time. The town needed
help rebuilding, and he and Colt had pledged work, money, and
supplies.

And now, this.

He'd have to figure out how best to handle this new wrinkle at a
time when there wasn't time enough for the existing problems. Hire
more help?

Not so easy.

Work longer hours?

That could prove dicey or dangerous with Whitney back in town,
because the one thing he did know was that his ex-wife couldn't be
trusted, and that meant they had to keep a fairly close tether on the girls
while a long summer stretched ahead of them.

Angelina laughed at something just then.

Isabo replied softly and laughed with her, and Nick realized God
had sent him reinforcements. They might not be riding herd, although
Angelina was getting pretty good in the saddle, but with the Casti-
glione women on the ranch, minding the girls as needed, it would be a
lot harder for Whitney to mess with them. No one in their right mind,
or even slightly out of their mind, would intentionally mess with Angelina and Isabo, and recognizing that would make it easier to fall asleep
that night.

Cheyenne stomped out of the car the next night, arms crossed and her hair undone. "I don't see why I have to come here." She said it loud enough for Elsa and every forest-dwelling creature within a thousand-foot radius to hear. "I just wanted to go see my mother!"

Nick's pained expression said he'd been hearing her objections for a while. "Come on, Miss 'Kota. I'll help you down." She jumped into his arms from the back of the tall SUV and hung on tight, and Elsa couldn't blame her. Cheyenne didn't just look angry. She looked chin-in-the-air combative, and staying out of her way was in Dakota's best interests.

"Hey, girls."

Dakota peeked at her from Nick's arms, then looked at her sister. "Cheyenne told Daddy she hates him."

"Shut up, you little tattletale!" Cheyenne stomped in their direction. "Why do you have to open your mouth and spoil everything? You're such a brat."

"If I were holding a mirror in my hands right now and held it up just so"—Elsa pretended to hold a mirror up, facing them—"whose reflection looks bratty and angry, and who looks scared?" She playacted as if looking into the mirror herself, then faced it toward them. "Dakota, are you scared when Cheyenne gets angry?"

"Yes." Dakota wasn't generally meek and mild. "Usually I ignore her like Daddy says, but she was throwing things and saying bad words, and Daddy said she wasn't going anywhere, ever, until she learned to calm down and behave."

"Sounds like a fun evening already." Elsa motioned for Nick to set Dakota down. He did, but he kept a sharp eye on Cheyenne, which was probably a good idea. "I wanted to talk to you about the tutoring sched-ule too, once vacation starts later this week."

"I don't need tutoring, I don't need extra help, I don't need anything!" Cheyenne snapped the words in quick succession. "I know all the stuff; I just didn't want to do the stupid assignments. I'm fine on my own."

"You made a deal," Elsa reminded her in a matter-of-fact voice. "A commitment. We agreed together that you could miss summer school if you were tutored and passed the examinations to get into fourth grade. The choice has been made. Now it's up to you to either handle it graciously or mess it up, but there are no other choices. Once you strike a deal and give your word, it's given."

"Then I hate you too!" She stared at Elsa and then her father. "What is the matter with you two? Don't you get it? All I ever wanted was for my mother to come home, and now she did so I'm fine!"

"And on that note . . ." Nick blew Cheyenne a kiss, bent and kissed Dakota, and climbed back into the SUV. "I'll see you in an hour or so, okay?"

"All right."

Dakota scurried over to Elsa's side. If her father was leaving, she must figure Elsa would provide some sort of protection from her sister's ire. Elsa grabbed a can of mosquito repellent, put some on herself, then applied it to Dakota.

Cheyenne stayed off to the side, arms crossed, her left foot tapping the ground.

Elsa raised the bottle of repellent. "We're going into the woods and it's shady, which means mosquitoes this time of day." She waggled the bottle and figured she'd give it ten seconds. "Your choice. Bug spray . . . or mosquito bites. Either way, we're going."

Cheyenne glared at her, then Dakota, then Elsa again before stomping over and holding out her arms.

Frustration, anger, and impatience darkened the girl's naturally attractive features. So much to deal with at a young age, and yet some of it was self-imposed because Cheyenne rejected help on a regular basis. She misted the girl's skin lightly, then tucked the bottle up on a ledge. "Let's go."

"Where?" Eyes narrowed, Cheyenne looked around as if the forest had nothing to teach her. Elsa knew better.

"This way." She led them into the woods up an old trail, and as the woods grew thicker and greener, sounds greeted them. Birds, nesting or still building, chattered greetings and warnings. Frogs croaked here and there, and as they approached the small bog not far from the creek, the sound of spring peepers increased. "Hear that?" she asked as they broke through the forest's edge to a small wetland area.

"Crickets? Yeah. Big deal."

"Not crickets. Frogs. Tree frogs. Spring peepers."

"Jeepers, creepers, where did you get them peepers!" Dakota laughed. "Murt says that to me all the time! Where are they? I don't see them. And now they're quiet."

"You scared them with your big mouth," Cheyenne scolded. "That seems to be all you do lately, Dakota. Open your big mouth and mess up everything."

"If we're quiet, they might sing again." Elsa took a spot on a moss-covered log, then patted the natural bench. "Come. Sit. Listen."

Dakota took a seat alongside her, so close it was nearly in her lap. Cheyenne stood scowling, staring into the distance, her arms folded tight around her middle again.

For a moment nothing happened. Bird calls sounded back and forth, intermittent, the quick singing notes of finches and friends, followed by the soft, plaintive songs of mourning doves.

And then the peepers recommenced. All around them, from the trees above and the shallow pond stretching before them, the *ca-reeek! ca-reeek!* of tree frogs chorused a happy, lilting tune.

"This is creepy." Cheyenne stared around, looking up, looking down, then slipped over to the log and took a seat. "And this stupid log is scratchy."

Elsa ignored her. She sat, holding Dakota's hand, letting the amphibian chorus fill the evening air. And once they started, the tiny frogs sang out in full voice, blending and balancing their song of love.

They sat silent for long, peaceful minutes, then Dakota climbed onto her lap. She stuck a thumb in her mouth, curled her head against Elsa's chest, and sighed, peaceful. "I think I love this, Elsa."

The whispered words went straight to Elsa's heart. "Me too."

"I don't know what's so great about a bunch of slimy frogs croaking," Cheyenne offered, but she kept her voice quiet. The more respectful tone said the therapy wasn't totally lost on the older girl. "But I think I see one, right there." She pointed over and down and then frowned. "And one there. Only that one's kind of beige-y brown, and that one's green like my new shirt."

"Color-changing frogs."

"No way. Why do grownups always have to make things up? I hate that," Cheyenne scoffed.

Her words told Elsa that buildups, empty promises, and letdowns had left their mark, but with Cheyenne's personality, some of that could be self-imposed. "You're seeing them, aren't you?" She sent Cheyenne a sidelong glance. "That makes them real enough."

"Then they're different kinds."

"Nope."

Cheyenne arched her brows in disbelief. "They can really do that?"

"Camouflage. Their skin takes on the background color. As close as it can, anyway. I grew up in a yellow house, and if the frogs climbed the house, they turned almost white. Like dingy ivory white. And they have tiny suction pads on their feet so they can climb and not fall off. Radically cool."

"I don't believe you."

Elsa rolled her eyes and Cheyenne backed down. "Well, it doesn't seem real."

"Much better, because one thing I don't do is lie, my friend. We'll study them for our science lesson this week. These guys are our state amphibian."

"What is that?" Dakota joined the whispered conversation now that it seemed her life wasn't in imminent danger from her sister's wrath. "What is a Anne fibbian?"

"Something that lives on land and in water," Cheyenne told her, which meant she'd listened to at least some of her third grade lessons. "We really have a frog for our state? For real?"

"We do."

"Cool."

Elsa allowed herself a small smile. "I agree." They sat in silence for long minutes, and when she stood to go, both girls hung back.

"Do we have to leave?" Dakota asked in a tired voice. "I like it here."

"Can't we stay a few more minutes?" Cheyenne's voice implored her, and Elsa was tempted to say yes. It wasn't like they had anywhere to go. But part of Cheyenne's problem was the constant resistance and passive-aggressive choices, so she jutted her chin toward the path and said, "We'll come back another time, but we might not hear the peepers much then."

"Why?"

"Will they die? If they die, then this whole thing sucks," Cheyenne declared.

"Use appropriate language, please. You sound ill-mannered and spoiled when you talk like that. Do you hear how many of them there are?" She swept the broad, shallow pond and the surrounding trees a quick look.

"A lot," Cheyenne admitted.

"Exactly. The reason you might not hear them is because they croak less when the mating season is over. You hear some, but not nearly as many. This is their sound of courtship."

Cheyenne made a gagging motion with her hand, but she paused, quiet, before she left the open area. The frogs had gone silent when they moved, but now, with the humans edging into the forest, they started up again. First one, then another, then dozens peeping their way through the lengthening shadows. "It is kind of cool," Cheyenne admitted as they walked back through the woods. "The noise and the color-changing thing."

"I think so too."

"I'm tired, Elsa." Dakota's yawn punctuated her words.

She shouldn't break the rules of personal boundary, but Dakota looked as tired as she sounded, so Elsa bent and picked her up. "That better?"

"Yes."

The little girl tucked her head against Elsa's shoulder. The feel of soft curls and the smell of strawberry-scented soap and mac and cheese teased her senses. She'd longed for the same normal that eluded their father. Maybe it didn't really exist anymore. Maybe the Christmas card family was an illusion in these modern times. Or maybe people just didn't try hard enough.

Cheyenne walked ahead, less antagonistic than she'd been an hour before. Dakota snuggled against her like a baby chimpanzee, arms and legs locked on, and that's how Nick saw them when they moved into the clearing surrounding her odd little house.

"Someone's tired." He spoke low as he reached out to take Dakota from her.

It felt special, having him take the sleepy child, as if passing Dakota to her father was a natural thing between them.

He'd sent a knowing glance toward Cheyenne but didn't try to engage her, and when Dakota yawned widely, he tucked her closer to his chest.

"We saw frogs, Daddy." Dakota's subdued voice said she was close to sleeping. "So many frogs."

"I love frogs." He kept his voice quiet too. "We used to chase them when I was little, but there aren't too many on the ranch now. We mow all the fields, and frogs like to live where there are great hiding places."

"Plenty of those around here," said Cheyenne, but she didn't sound angry. She looked and sounded intrigued, like she'd never realized how many things could live and breathe in the woods. "So we're going to study frogs when you come over?"

Did she sound hopeful? Elsa thought so. "And adding and subtracting, number charts, clocks, money, writing, spelling, and reading."

She didn't balk or throw a hissy fit, a major improvement. "Can we learn more about the woods too?"

"We don't need books for that," Elsa promised. "We can take field trips and explore the woods all summer. Best way of studying."

"Okay." Cheyenne started toward the car, then stopped. She took a deep breath as if about to say something, then didn't. She climbed into the car, put her seat belt on, and waited.

"Baby steps," Elsa muttered under her breath. "The way we all learn to walk is by using baby steps."

"She's almost nine." Nick didn't sound quite so patient.

"Chronologically, yes. But emotionally, a fraction of her is stuck at age five, when her mother walked out. She was old enough to know something was wrong, and then to be abandoned . . ." Elsa grimaced slightly. "It leaves a kid wondering why it happened, what they did wrong. And then as they mature, they want to know how they can fix it."

"She did nothing wrong. She was a cute little kid, perfectly normal."

"And there we have the difference between the adult point of view and childlike perception. She'll come to realize that in time. But it's her journey, and she keeps going around in circles. Maybe Whitney's surprise appearance will shake things up, just enough to get Cheyenne off her treadmill."

"She should still be polite."

"Possibly the least of our worries right now."

"If she won't say it, I will." Nick faced her, and when he did, Dakota peeked through half-shut eyes and smiled, just for her. "Thank you. You're wonderful with them."

"I'll see you on Wednesday." She didn't ask about Whitney. It wasn't her business, and the situation was too raw. Time might soothe or stir, but there was no sense in pushing the issue now, because she was pretty sure Cheyenne would give them plenty of reason to discuss Whitney's return over the coming weeks. Which meant she had to maintain a professional distance and attitude with Nick.

She didn't gaze up into his eyes, although she wanted to. She didn't glance at his mouth, wondering, because these two precious children needed her to be on her A game. Their mother could turn out to be a normal, if somewhat selfish, lost soul, but if she was more than that—if she was dangerous or impaired—Elsa needed to be able to make a clear assessment. For years she'd been a strong, hard-working professional. Engaging with Nick's daughters made her feel that way again, and that was worth whatever sacrifice it took. Even if that sacrifice meant ignoring the growing attraction to their cowboy father.

~⁓⊂℮⌐

"So how did your little meeting with Whitney go?" Colt spun a chair backward and straddled it after they tucked the girls and Noah into bed, just like he did when they were kids. "Did you do what Ange suggested and keep it in a public place?"

"The park, yes. I bought her coffee and explained she'd be welcome to see the girls here twice a week after their lessons, she went ballistic, and a great time was had by all."

"Ouch. Sorry." Angelina's regret sounded real. "What about clothing?"

Nick frowned. "If you mean was she dressed in normal, appropriate, mother-friendly clothes, then no. Same kind of getup we saw yesterday, only the shirt was tighter. If that's even possible."

"So she needs a shopping trip." Ange made a note on a small pad. "And what about food?"

Nick stared at her. "What about it?"

"Well, we can't starve her, and she can't be underfoot here every day or Elsa will never make progress with the girls. So you either move in here and let her use the house for a short-term contract, or you pay out of pocket for food and the inn. And she might be more likely to accept changes or make changes if she's in a familiar environment."

"But then she'll want the girls to visit her there." Nick shook his head. "That can't happen, Ange. Not when we know she's been drinking, and who knows what else?"

"Did you bring up the drinking?"

"Yes."

"How'd she take it?

"Angry, bitter, antagonistic. The new normal, it seems." Nick folded his hands and for the first time in a long time, he asked his brother for help. "What do you suggest?"

Colt stared, surprised. "You're asking me?"

"As much as it pains me to admit it, yes. I'm too close to the whole thing. I can't see straight to know which way to go. You've got a better perspective."

Colt worked his jaw, then met Nick's eyes. "Surprise her."

"Huh?" Nick frowned. "With what? Flowers? Never mind, I'm

sorry I asked." He started to turn toward Angelina but paused when Colt smacked his arm. "Hey!"

"You asked, I'm answering, so pay attention," Colt ordered. "Treat her kindly. Be caring. Provide for her. Do what Ange said—let her use the house for the time being. Tell her she needs to go to AA and regain her self-control if she wants to see the girls, and then offer to pray for her. Invite her to church."

"Whitney was never a churchgoer," Nick reminded him. As much as it pained him to admit it, he glimpsed a hint of truth in Colt's advice. "You want me to go all 'let bygones be bygones' on her when what I want to do is run her out of town and pretend she did it of her own volition?"

"Kindness breaks down anger and oppression." Angelina drew his attention with her words. "Your brother's right, and I'm proud of him."

Colt grinned and winked her way. "That's my goal, schnookums."

She pierced him with a fierce look, then smiled. "You're such a boy." She shifted her attention back to him. "Nick, Jesus ate with unbelievers, lepers, and tax collectors. He challenges us to do the same."

"The whole 'preach the gospel without words' thing, right?"

"Exactly that. Teach by example. Live in love."

"Says the woman packing a Glock," Colt noted.

She shrugged. "Nothing wrong with being prepared, and not everyone plays by the rules."

She stood and stretched. "I'm going to bed. Morning's coming early. I'm glad the term is ending and we can adjust the schedule accordingly. And then I'll be happy to have school start again at the end of summer and get back to a routine."

Nick and Colt stood too. "You won't hate it if I move in here for a while?" Nick asked because he and Colt might be brothers, but they hadn't exactly been best buddies.

Colt faced him, serious for once. "This is home, Nick. And it's time for you and me and Trey to realize it. Besides, it will be good for you to be around all the time once they start building the new house. And with Dad and Hobbs unavailable, you being here makes the most sense." He studied the ranch image through the big plate-glass window. "You've worked hard to build this. Nothing wrong with being on hand to protect the investment."

"You're being nice." Nick wasn't sure what to make of this new and improved version of his know-it-all older brother. "It's a welcome change."

Colt pretended to scowl. "Don't mess with my persona. I'm the mean one, remember?"

"You sure looked all mean and gruff when you were reading Noah his bedtime story tonight." Angelina kissed him good night and started down the hall to the north wing of the broad house.

"I make occasional exceptions to the rule."

She sent him an over-the-shoulder smile, and when Nick looked back at Colt, the look of sheer love on his older brother's face gut-twisted him. Had he ever gazed at Whitney like that?

He didn't think so. Maybe he'd never really loved her in his youthful stupidity. Maybe what he'd loved was the idea and image of a perfect family, to show his father that it could be done with a beautiful woman at his side

Epic fail.

Colt's advice niggled him as he drove back to West Chelan Pass for the night. By giving Whitney a chance, he was living his faith, not just spewing it. He didn't need the money from the sale of the house in town to start the new house rolling, which meant it was available if he and the girls moved to his father's house.

Did he want Whitney to stay in Gray's Glen?

No, he admitted honestly to himself.

But if she could clean herself up, then it would be in the girls' best interests if she stayed. At least he hoped that was the case, but the thought of Johnny Baxter living drunk and disorderly all those years weighed on him. What if Whitney chose that instead? How would he deal with that? How would the girls deal with that?

He went to bed grim and woke up the same way. He didn't stop to check the time or his appearance. He simply got into the truck, swung by the café, and grabbed two coffees in town. He drove into the woods to see Elsa. He wasn't her patient, but he could use some insight, or maybe he just wanted to see her. Talk to her. In any case, he pulled into the woods long before the sun had a chance to dry the dew and rapped on her door.

EIGHT

*T*he knock startled Elsa, woke the bird, and set Achilles into a tail-spinning frenzy. He let loose with a series of woofs as he bounded in circles, determined to protect her. The crazy bird marched sideways on his roost, back and forth, scolding the world for waking him too fast and too early. "Let me in! Let me in! Let me in!"

"You are in, hush! Oh my gosh, what in the world is happening? You, stop." She signaled Achilles, but the mottled mixed breed only stepped up his game. She looked through the side window, spotted Nick, and sighed.

He looked good, even first thing in the morning, and she hadn't even run a brush through her hair. He spotted her in the window and held up the two coffee cups, and the lost-puppy look on his face was a deal clincher. She moved to the door, swung it open, and let Achilles out and Nick in.

"Sorry." He looked truly apologetic as he handed her a coffee. "I should have called."

"You think? Gimme." She reached for the tall sleeved cup with two hands. "I might have at least combed my hair and washed my face if you had."

"You look beautiful, Elsa."

His words trip-hammered her heart. She hadn't been called beautiful in a long time, and she certainly hadn't had any early morning male visitors. The combination delighted her emotionally. Mentally, she wanted a ten-minute warning so at least she could be out of her

Snoopy and the Red Baron pajama pants. "Buttering me up won't work, not until I've inhaled this coffee at least. Come in, sit down, and tell me what's going on. But this is not a professional visit."

"I don't swing by the Coffee Shack for most doctors," he admitted. He sat on the chair as she curled into a corner of the small sofa. "I never looked at the clock. Sorry."

"Which means the girls weren't with you."

"They stayed at Dad's." He splayed his hands, set his coffee on the small table, and almost didn't jump when the bird scolded.

"He's a jerk! He's a jerk! He's a jerk!"

"Oh good grief." She stood, crossed to Hoyl's cage, and unlatched it. Then she opened the door and let the bird go free. "Come back, you hear?"

The bird fluttered to the floor, hopped to the door, then took flight.

"What happens the day he doesn't come back?" Nick wondered, and Elsa raised her shoulders as she went back to the couch.

"I'll miss him like crazy, but I'll know he had a good life. A mix of two worlds. Risk costs."

"Exactly why I'm here."

She sat back, sipped the coffee, decided the hometown barista needed a raise because this was the best mocha she'd ever had, and waited.

"I'm thinking of moving into my father's house for a few months," he began. "Letting Whitney have a short-term contract for the house in town, and telling her she needs to go to AA if she wants the girls to visit."

Mental red flags made Elsa put her coffee down. "What's your reasoning on all this, Nick?" She wasn't sure she wanted to hear his reasoning because this was a big turnaround.

Did Whitney's return offer Nick hope of reconciliation? And why did her head jump straight to that as if it was the worst idea ever? Because her heart was involved, that's why. *Remember, he's not here as a patient. He's here as a friend.*

"Colt's idea, actually."

She almost spewed her coffee because that was the last answer she expected to hear.

"I know." He paused while she coughed and waited until she'd stopped before tossing her a napkin from his front pocket. "He surprised me too, but it makes sense."

"How, exactly?"

"You told me to put the girls first." He leaned forward and clasped his hands. "Having your mother walk out bites, and it bites for a long time."

Statistics and her experience agreed, so she nodded.

"If I make an effort to help her and she takes off again on her own, then at least Cheyenne has a chance to see the reality of both sides."

"True."

"If I roadblock her, then it looks like I'm the bad guy."

"Sometimes parents have to be the bad guy to keep kids safe."

"And that's why I'm here." He huffed, glanced down, and cringed. "What do you think, Elsa? Is she safe to be around the girls? Even with supervision?"

Whoa.

She did not want to be asked this. Not now. Not ever.

Tell him. Tell him why you won't offer an opinion on this. Isn't it better to know his reaction than presume it?

She couldn't. Not yet. Not when she was feeling like a strong, healthy person for the first time since losing those children. For now— at least for a little while more—she wanted to be considered normal. The fact that being around Nick and the girls made her feel more than normal, even special, wasn't anything she intended to minimize. "I can't offer advice on that, Nick. I don't know her well enough, I don't know you well enough, and it's out of my league. I've worked with kids, mostly."

"And families." He looked right at her, and for a moment she thought he must have run an Internet search, but then he added, "Your sister told me that when she suggested you."

She sighed inwardly, partially relieved, but maybe it would be better if he stumbled on her past through an impersonal online search engine.

Chicken.

Yes.

She didn't want Nick feeling sorry for her, and she sure didn't want to lose his trust, because she loved working with the girls. But next to the relief came the realization that she couldn't let him accidentally discover her past. It was up to her to tell him, and she needed to do that soon. But not today. "That wouldn't work in this case, for obvious reasons." She stared point-blank at him, and when he smiled, she knew she'd made her point.

"A conflict of interest goes both ways," he told her.

"But here's what I think." She faced him directly and waded in. "I believe in being nice. I believe in sharing blessings. But there are givers and takers in this world. Most of us are a fairly normal combination, but when a taker goes to extremes, their effect on those around them can be dreadful."

"A narcissist."

"Along those lines of behavior, yes. The lack of satisfaction, no matter how much they're given." She wrinkled her brow, not wanting to discourage him but wanting to hike his awareness. "True narcissism is a rare disorder, but selfishness and self-absorbed natures are running rampant in modern society. So you've got to be careful while being kind."

"Is this the therapist or the woman talking?"

She frowned and shrugged. "It's hard to draw a hard line because I'm both."

"How's your coffee?"

The change of subject made her smile. "Perfect. How's my hair?"

He laughed, and she should have been insulted. She wasn't because she felt at ease around him, as if messy hair wasn't a huge deal, although she was glad she'd taken time to brush her teeth when she got up. A girl could only stand so much embarrassment. "I think it's a good thing to do, Nick. If you're strong enough to set parameters and mean them."

"She likes to push the envelope."

Elsa conceded that with a grimace. "Typical for selfish types, bending rules because they don't think they really apply to them."

"That's Whitney."

"You need to write things down, like a contract. Give her a copy."

"You mean have her sign it?" Nick scoffed. "That'll never happen."

"No signature needed. Her promises probably don't mean a lot right now anyway. But if you put things in black and white, concrete rules of engagement, then she can't plead that she misunderstood or something wasn't clear. Because it is clear."

"That's actually a great idea."

She shrugged pretend modesty. "Every now and again I have one."

"I'll set it up." He stood, glanced at his watch, then made a face. "I had no idea it was this early. I'm sorry, Elsa."

She raised the coffee cup, then stood. "It got me coffee I wouldn't have had otherwise, so we're good."

"Are we, Elsa?" He looked down. Met her gaze. Held it. His attention shifted from her eyes to her mouth, as if wondering. And when his arm circled her shoulders, drawing her in, his next words sealed the deal. "Let's find out."

He kissed her. He kissed her long and slow as if they had all the time in the world, as if kissing her meant something wondrous.

Her toes went tight while her heart sped up, and when he deepened the kiss, rational thought dissolved into sweet emotional bliss.

"Elsa." He held her close, sighed, and pressed his cheek against her messy hair. "I didn't come here to do this, but maybe I did. Maybe I wanted to see for myself if kissing you would be as wonderful as I kept imagining it would be, and that's a stretch because I really don't have much of an imagination."

"Was it?"

He laughed softly. "It was on my end. On a good-better-best rating scale, I'd give it an outstanding."

"Off the charts."

"Absolutely."

She smiled against his chest, then sighed.

"Hold the lecture, Doc, I know what you're going to say."

"Add mind reader to list of interesting qualities," she muttered as if making a list.

"We need to hold back, go slow, make sure the girls are first and foremost."

"Yes." She handed him his hat and pointed to the door. "You've got work to do."

"And a better frame of mind with which to do it," he teased, smiling. "I'll call you later."

Such simple words to put bright expectation on her heart. "I'll look forward to answering."

He left, but when he turned and tipped the brim of his hat in her direction, she realized anew what a good, solid man Nick Stafford was.

He deserved to know the truth. Would he be able to see beyond the obvious, that she'd stumbled emotionally?

Or would a man who'd already been failed by the two most

important women in his life run for the hills when he realized her frailties?

Either way, she had to come clean. Honesty in a relationship wasn't an option; it was a basic need.

She hadn't always been overly careful. She'd accepted life joyously and worked her way forward. That all stopped on a warm, damp June day three years before.

In her self-prognosis, she wanted that part of herself back again. The spontaneous woman who listened well and embraced life. She'd shrugged off any kind of embrace since losing those children. Meeting Nick and the girls had highlighted just how much she missed it.

Nick came in from cutting hay midday, knowing the house would be a whole lot busier once school was out. Then there would be at least three kids running up and down the stairs, and all the noise and mess that came along with parenthood. As long as he could get through this week's first grade graduation, the upcoming dance recital, and maintain the increasing clutch of daily work on short help . . . and the alcoholic ex-wife . . . he'd be fine. He strode through the kitchen door, saw Colt holding Angelina, and stopped. "What's happened? What's wrong? Who's hurt?"

Colt drew a deep breath before he turned, and that was Nick's warning. "It's Dad."

Nick darted a look down the hall to the first-floor bedroom Sam had been using for months. "What's wrong? Is he worse? Is he—?" He couldn't say the words out loud because, for all their tempest, he wasn't ready to lose his father. Not until they'd settled a few more scores, and that might take decades because settling scores seemed to take record time in Stafford-land.

"He needs a transplant." Angelina said the words through a

tear-streaked face, and when Angelina gave way to tears, you knew things were in a serious way. "They've put him on the list, but they need to find a good match and then have him healthy enough to undergo the surgery."

"Oh, man." Nick thought his days had been full a few minutes ago, but the thought of actually losing his father brought up emotions he didn't want to deal with. He tipped his head back, gazed at the ceiling, then faced them. "What kind of a timeline are we talking?"

"Tight."

He sat in the nearest chair, and Colt and Angelina joined him. "What are the options?"

"We just told you," Colt began, but Nick shook his head.

"No, sorry, I mean how do we find out the options on procuring a liver? Is it a critical need list or best match? And is there a possibility that we can buy one?"

"Nick!" Angelina stared at him, appalled, but Colt nodded.

"I wondered the same thing. I don't mean on an illegal market," he explained when Angelina looked like she might pop both of them in the jaw. "There are ways to do this legally, I believe."

"I don't even want to know how you might know this." She leveled him a hard stare and sat up straighter. "It's a rating system. A mix of critical need, then the best match for the most critically ill. There is the possibility of a living donor transplant according to the surgeons. But it has to be a good match. And there's risk involved."

"Okay, that's ghoulish." Nick narrowed his gaze at her. "You can't live without a liver, so how can a living person donate theirs? And you thought the idea of buying one was out there. As if."

"The liver is one of few organs that regenerates itself." Colt faced Nick. "Remember that big scandal back east, where the doctor was doing too many of these surgeries to make money for the hospital and pad their stats?"

Like Nick had time to sit around and catch up on East Coast scandal sheets. "No. One of us was too busy impregnating cows, cutting hay, and dodging bulls to sit around reading newspapers. What's that got to do with Dad?"

"We've got to make sure that whoever works on Dad has no one to impress," Colt declared. "We're not after the hospital that does the most of these; we want the one with the best possible outcome percentage."

"And how do we find out if we're a match?" Nick asked. "Where do we go to get tested?"

"The doctors can set that up," Angelina told them. "We've got good hospitals all along the West Coast, but if we can't find a match, they said the waiting time is shorter in the Heartland."

Colt threw up his hands. "That makes no sense."

"Sure it does," Nick told him. "It comes down to numbers. Highly populated areas probably mean higher need, more patients."

Angelina nodded. "That's what they said."

The phone rang just then. She got up, looked at the read-out, and held it up for Nick. "Whitney."

He waved her off to buy time. "I'll call her back later. Right now—" He stood, hauled in a deep breath, and headed for the door. "I'll be back."

She let the call go to voice mail, and when Colt followed him out the door, Nick paced about thirty feet away and then turned. "How do we do this?"

Colt didn't look any too sure, but he pretended to be sure, and that just aggravated Nick further. "Day by day, same as always, I expect."

"We're down on help, we've got a ridiculous amount of work to do each day, we're committed to helping the town get back on its feet, and if one of us is a match, that means another man down. And I've got the whole Whitney situation to deal with now." He waved in the general direction of the town. "She'll be underfoot, wanting this, wanting that. What if I'm the match?" He turned toward Colt. "How do I keep an eye on Whitney and the girls if I'm off in some hospital undergoing life-threatening surgery?"

"You won't be in any such place, so don't worry about it."

Sam's voice, coming from over Nick's left shoulder. Could this possibly get any worse? He turned to apologize, but his father's glare stopped him.

Sam moved forward. He didn't falter as he walked, which meant Nick's tirade got his adrenaline pumping.

Great.

Sam stopped in front of his two sons, and the stern look on his face was contradicted by stark fear in his eyes. But Sam Stafford never let fear stop him, and today wasn't any different. "I don't need anything from anyone. Not now, not ever."

"Dad, I'm sorry, that's not what I meant to say."

Sam shook off his hand and his apology. "And I sure as shootin' don't need a half-baked apology. You spoke your mind, made your feelings clear, and that's that."

Nick started to speak. Colt warned him off with a shake of his head, so he waited until Sam let the screen door slap shut behind him before speaking. "I thought he was asleep."

"I realize that now." Colt winced. "Sorry, man. I never thought to mention he took a walk to the barn. Give him time to digest all that's happened today, and then apologize. Or give him part of your liver," he added cheerfully.

"That's not funny."

"It is in a way," Colt argued. "I'll call and get an appointment set up for the testing. No sense in us going separately."

"And I'll call Trey."

"To tell him, sure." Colt took a deep breath and faced the broad expanse of fields. "We'll be able to put him to work here, that's for certain."

"Well, that, and to have him get tested."

"You think Trey could be a match?" Colt asked, surprised. "Really?"

Nick shrugged. "When we arrange genetic cattle crosses, there are certain dominant traits that breed true. They say siblings are usually the best match, but if Dad's sister passed those traits down to Trey, he could be a match."

"I suppose." Colt saw Murt moving their way and he slapped his hat back on his head. "Me and Murt are drawing blood from the heifers today. I'll be back later. Unless you want to do Dracula detail and I'll cut hay?"

"I'm better up top, alone, where I can think about shutting my big mouth." Nick pulled his Mariners baseball cap down onto his head. "I'll be back at dark."

"I'll tell Ange and Isabo."

He took the four-wheeler east to the thick, lush hay field, and when he climbed into the cab of the monster-sized tractor, a heart-stopping view lay before him, sprawled in elegant beauty. And just as much moved north behind him, a stunning testament to Sam Stafford's hard work.

And here he was, stuck in the middle.

He loved this land, this ranch, the entire entity that was the Double S, and he'd been mad at his father for so long that anger seemed part and parcel of the family holdings. Sitting up top of that mammoth machine, he realized that in spite of his own childhood bitterness, Sam Stafford had built a larger-than-life legacy in Gray's Glen, a legacy that would pass to his sons.

But he wasn't ready for his father to die. He didn't want to say good-bye with old wrongs wedged between them. He should be proud of his father's newfound faith. He should be happy for him, but was he?

No.

He was resentful, thinking of those workers that came late in the day and got paid as much as the laborers who worked all day. Where was the equity in that?

There was no equity. There was just another story about a lamb, one of those parables that made you feel good until you realized that ninety-nine lambs were risked because one chose to go astray.

Colt had flown off to build himself a life in the east. Trey had stood his ground against Sam's tirades and gone south to Nashville, where he made a big name for himself. And Nick had stayed here, the good son, striving to build the ranch alongside his father while showing his father what a successful marriage looked like, right up until his wife proved him wrong and made him look foolish.

He'd paralleled Sam's life while trying to do the exact opposite, so who was the stupid son?

He scowled as the tractor jerked forward along the first edgy row of the sage-green field.

Colt had come back. And now Trey would return. Was he jealous that his effort meant little?

Or was he selfish, wanting credit for a job well done while the wandering lambs built their own way in the world?

Would Christ's analogy really work on a ranch? Percentages were a big part of the annual report because no farm was perfect, but God didn't rest on percentages. He wanted his lambs—his people—accounted for.

Nick eyed the remaining acreage and realized he'd have plenty of time to mull because this hay field stretched long and hard to the south and east, and maybe hours on his own would sweeten his attitude.

Your attitude was all right when you were kissing Elsa this morning.

Elsa, laughing at him. Talking to him. Letting him say what was on his mind without regret.

He aimed straight ahead and figured it wasn't a bad idea to say some prayers. There was a lot of ground to cover, a parable in its own right, and while he took care of the hay, he'd ask God about seeing to everything else. Given their current family dynamics, Nick figured the good Lord had his work cut out for him.

Elsa had discovered a new scientific theory yesterday. The power of one very well done kiss could provide environmentally friendly energy for the world, if harnessed correctly.

It sounded preposterous, but how else could Elsa explain the urge to scrape one side of the house to prepare it for painting, spackle dents and holes to discourage bugs, and bake double batches of brownies and cookies for the volunteer construction crews working on the church? She dashed in and out of the house, humming—*yes, humming!*—while she rotated pans in the oven and scraped the beige clapboard. Once the desserts were cool, she packed them into plastic containers and headed toward the construction site.

Her tire pressure light came on as she drove toward the main road, so she stopped by the convenience store on the way into town. She unscrewed the valve covers, then fed coins into the machine. When the air hose burst to life, she filled the low tire, then decided to check the others. As she rounded the back of the car to get to tire number three, she noticed two people coming out of the small, patched-together bar on the other side of the intersection.

Whitney Stafford and Johnny Baxter.

She watched, dismayed. Neither one looked sober. She didn't realize she was staring until the air pump ran out of time and the motor
shut off, leaving a silent gap.

The change drew their attention. Elsa felt Whitney's gaze as if taking measure. She set the hose down, moved around the car, and fed
more coins into the machine. It sprang back to life, but when she
turned to finish the last two tires, Whitney was approaching her.

She'd felt prepared to deal with Whitney on Sunday, surrounded
by Nick's family.

But here? At the corner of Rustic and Deserted?

Elsa's heart went into overdrive. Her palms broke into a cold sweat.
Her throat choked, and she had to mentally disengage herself from the
pure physiological reactions as Whitney drew near. "You're Nick's little
friend, aren't you?"

She could argue, admit it, or smack Whitney with the air hose and
run away. Option two won. "Elsa. Yes."

Whitney's eyes narrowed, and when she raked Elsa's T-shirt and
capris with a deliberately disparaging look, Elsa was pretty sure she'd
just stepped back into eighth grade. "Why were you watching us?"

She was trying to put Elsa on the defensive. That would happen
only if Elsa allowed it, and she wasn't about to give Whitney the satisfaction. She moved to the opposite side of the car and went back to
filling tires. It was impossible to hear over the roar of the air compressor,
so why try? And the wait might give Whitney time to settle down.

"You think you're pretty smart, don't you?"

The air compressor shut off just then, which meant she couldn't
help but hear Whitney. The choice of whether or not to answer was
another story.

"But who are you, Elsa?" The scent of liquor grew stronger as
Whitney moved closer. "Who does Nick have watching my girls,

because Johnny tells me no one knows all that much about you. But there are ways of finding things out, and if I want to know more about you, I can find it out like that!" She snapped her fingers for effect, but the snap missed and the dull scrape of skin to skin missed its mark.

Elsa faced the taller woman and spoke simply. "Your girls are beautiful. They're wonderful. And they miss having a mother, but if you're really interested in stepping back into the job, Whitney"—she sent a direct look toward the bar across the street before shifting her attention back to Nick's ex-wife—"you might want to consider some changes."

Whitney's face flushed, but Elsa didn't wait for a reply. She climbed into her car, started the motor, and pulled away.

She refused to let Whitney intimidate her. So what that her heart was pumping a mile a minute and she had to swipe damp palms against her khaki capris? She'd gone face to face with an angry parent and stood her ground, and if she was still in personal therapy, her therapist would have called that a victory.

Their little tête-à-tête had all the earmarks of a milestone. But the realization that Whitney was holing up with someone else who hated the Staffords might be cause for concern. Were they just a couple of foolish drunks feeding their habit in the local watering hole? Or were they getting together purposely to figure out how to even up old scores?

Don't apply rational thought to irrational people.

She drove into town determined to move forward. She'd baked for the construction crews, and she wasn't about to let a rude confrontation ruin her day. It took all her gumption to drive past the road leading into her woods, because it would have been so much easier to turn the wheel and head for home.

She didn't, and that was another solid success.

She parked, then carried her plastic totes of brownies and cookies toward the construction zone. One of the local families had opened their three-bay garage as a soup kitchen, offering free food and drinks to the men and women rebuilding the damaged buildings.

"Look what we have here!" A smiling heavyset woman with pinned-up gray hair hurried her way. "You're Rachel's sister, aren't you?" She angled a happy look of appreciation to the stack of plastic containers. "You've just made yourself a lot of new friends here in town. Come on back here and meet the folks on hand today. I'm Wandy Schirtz, and that gruff old-timer across the way is my husband, Ben."

She grabbed Elsa's hand and led her up the driveway and into the wide garage.

Extra lights had been rigged to brighten the shaded area, and tables had been arranged to make the best use of the space. Not too many folks were sitting right now, and the methodical movements of another older couple made quick work of table cleanup. "This is wonderful." Elsa turned back toward Wandy. "I'm Elsa. Just in case that bit of information hasn't gotten this far yet."

"Nice to meet you finally, Elsa. Ben there"—she nodded her husband's way—"is on the school board, so I know your sister well. Such a nice woman."

"She is."

Wandy glanced toward the construction area, then tapped a watch. "The next lunch will be here in five minutes. I don't suppose you have a few minutes to help, do you, dearie?" She gazed expectantly at Elsa, and how could she say no? It wasn't as if she lived a crammed full, hour-to-hour schedule anymore.

"I can help."

"Perfect!" She beamed Elsa's way. "Mary Kay's daughter decided to go into labor a few weeks early, so she's off to the hospital, naturally, and Jemma Myering came down with a spring cold and can't stop sneezin', so there's no way we want her around food, is there?"

Elsa couldn't argue the logic in that, so she shook her head. "No, ma'am."

"If I could have you serve up Rowen's chicken and dumpling stew, folks can help themselves to the biscuits alongside, and we've got just enough time to set out dessert trays before folks head over."

"You've got scheduled eating times?" Elsa moved down to the dessert table and began filling trays from the stack of boxes and plastic containers on a shelf behind the food tables. "This is the pinnacle of organization."

"Well, at first we just had folks come whenever, but then we'd have too few one minute and too many the next," Wandy admitted. "We'd run out of seats, folks had to wait in the rain, it was a mess. Course, there weren't as many daily workers then, because it was all groundwork goin' on. Diggin' and layin' block and stone and tearin' down burnt buildings with big equipment. Once they got to the above-ground stuff, we got hoppin' over here, and schedulin' just seemed to make sense. Oh, that looks so nice, Elsa!" Wandy was looking at the dessert trays she'd set up for the workers. The older woman's approving smile bolstered Elsa's self-confidence after her little run-in with Whitney. "And here come the troops. Get ready, folks!"

Wandy wasn't kidding.

A crowd of hungry people headed their way, and as Elsa served up bowl after bowl of chicken and dumpling stew from the cavernous pot, the steady stream of thank-yous and smiles made her feel like she was part of this small town. She filled the next bowl and started to hand it out when a strong hand covered hers.

She peeked up, knowing without looking, but needing to see.

"Mighty nice of you to help out, Elsa."

She felt the blush rise from somewhere around her feet. "I do what I can, cowboy."

His smile. The sweet look of affection in his eyes. The touch of his hand, firm and strong. The combination called to her, but behind all the normal lurked abnormal, and Elsa couldn't take that lightly.

"If you're done makin' moon eyes at the help, there's a few more of us waitin' on food, Nick."

He laughed, unoffended, gave her one last smile, and moved down the line, but the memory of that smile and his gaze kept her glancing his way while he and a bunch of others wolfed their food.

And he glanced back.

Each time he did, she blushed, which was ridiculous for a thirty-two-year-old woman. By the time the line trickled to a stop, the first arrivals were done eating. Most of them grabbed coffee from the front table or a soda from the cooler just outside the door beneath the wide overhang.

Nick came around her way. "You're still okay seeing the girls tonight?"

"Yes, I am."

"Good." He hesitated, then waved toward the street. "I need to fill you in on something before you see them, but I need to do it quietly."

Elsa was pretty sure nothing private should be said in the broad, busy garage. "I've got to go to Hammerstein's. Why don't I walk you back to the church and we can talk?"

"Perfect."

"Folks'll talk."

"Better yet."

She smiled, ducked out from behind the table, and waved to Wandy and Ben.

"You come back whenever you can, Elsa, and thank you for today! You got us out of a jam."

She was pretty sure the crew could have handled things just fine, but she loved being included. Did that make her needy or normal?

Maybe it just makes you part of the town. Part of something bigger than yourself. That's pretty good right there, isn't it?

It was, she decided. They walked a block east to the small park, and she took a seat on the bench. Nick did likewise, and he didn't waste any time explaining. "My father's worse."

The tenor of his voice spelled danger.

"He needs a liver transplant or he's not going to make it. They did some kind of scoring thing, and it put him fairly high on the list, and the higher you are on the list, the worse your chances are."

"Nick, I'm so sorry." She took his hand in both of hers. "What can I do to help?"

When he hesitated, she gave his hand a light squeeze.

"Don't shrug me off, because I mean it sincerely. Tell me the game plan and then plug me in as needed. I can do basic ranch stuff, I can handle kids and houses, and I heard there were puppies due any day."

"That's just it." He frowned and did the little clicking thing with his tongue. "There is no game plan and it's driving me crazy. All I see is everything that needs to be done, and we're already down on help. I've got summer hands, but that's not the same as someone who knows the Double S inside and out like my father, Murt and Hobbs, or me and my brothers. School's coming to an end, and Ange and Isabo are great with the girls and the house, but with Cheyenne's problems and Whitney's return, I'd be stupid not to be worried about being gone morning till night with Whitney around."

"You don't trust her."

"Not at all," he admitted. "And the shame of it is"—he turned to face her more directly—"she wasn't a terrible person, Elsa. Yes, she was pretty stuck on herself. I see that now, and I know we were both somewhat stupid and shallow when we got married, but nothing to this extreme. I can't look back and pinpoint when things went bad, but I'd say it was once the girls were born. With two little kids, she couldn't just run free the way she liked, and she started to edge away. There's a different look in her eyes now, as if she's on the hunt. And that's reason enough to be nervous."

It was on the tip of her tongue to tell him about her run-in with Whitney, but one of the guys called Nick's name just then. He stood and pulled her up with him. "I've got to get back. They need all of us on hand to raise this wall."

"We'll talk tonight," she promised. He squeezed her hand, then brought it up to his mouth for a kiss. Eyes locked with hers, he kissed her fingers, then dropped her hand gently back to her side.

"Thanks for listening."

"No thanks needed."

He strode one way, she went the other, and when she stopped by Hammerstein's to pick up a few things, she eyed the cowboy hat again.

"It looked mighty nice the last time you eyeballed that hat." Deenie Miller smiled from behind the dry-goods counter. "And at my age, I've learned to grab life by the horns and live it to the full."

"Which is all well and good," Elsa told her, "when you've got the money in your pocket, but eighty-dollar hats aren't part of the current budget."

"Twenty percent off for the next two weeks," Deenie told her as she folded two lengths of lace and wrapped them in brown paper. "I'd be glad to tuck it away for you."

Temptation nipped at her.

She loved the hat; she loved the thought of getting back in the saddle like she did as a girl. Who would have thought she'd miss the smell of horses, dogs, puppies, and dirt, or the noise of a tractor turning fresh hay toward the sun?

But she could work with Nick's girls and be at the ranch without a cowgirl hat. Trying to justify the expense meant it had no justification. "No need. But maybe I'll tuck away some of my summer money and grab one in September."

"And if that one's gone, there'll be other pretties to take its place," Deenie promised as she handed Elsa her change and her packages. "Thanks for stoppin' in again. Always a pleasure."

"Thanks, Deenie." Then she paused, realizing she'd never given this woman her name. "I'm Elsa Andreas." She reached out a hand, and when Deenie gave her a thoroughly tough western handshake, she smiled. "Nice to meet you."

"You know my boy, Jay. He delivered groceries your way now and again."

"Nice kid, great smile, tan jacket. He looks like you," Elsa noted.

"He said it was fun braving the woods in our farm truck, making sure not to get stuck or lost that first time. And that you were right nice to him, Elsa."

Jay had been the only person she'd seen for months, besides Rachel's family. It seemed silly now, to have hidden herself away, even understanding the reasons why.

She'd stepped forward, finally, and when she left the hardware store a few minutes later, she had a can of exterior paint, a three-inch brush, some sandpaper, and a sanding block. By the time Nick came by with the girls at five thirty, she'd painted eight clapboards from the top for them to see. "What do you think? Too crazy? Too bright?"

"It's gorgeous!" Dakota streaked across the lawn, twirled, and threw her hands into the air, leaving absolutely no doubt how she felt. "It's the best blue ever!"

Elsa turned toward Cheyenne. "Go ahead, kid. Hit me with a more mature reaction."

"I love it." Cheyenne looked at the color, stepped back, and eyed the tall mix of trees. "It's almost as if you brought the sky into the forest. It's really pretty, Elsa."

"I'm going to call it Elsa-blue!" announced Dakota, as if naming rights was her domain. "Queen Elsa wore a blue gown, just like this. So it's the perfect name."

She loved the girls' reactions, but Nick's expression made her hesitate. "You hate it."

"I don't. I think this is your stepping-out color, and at least the house won't blend into the hill quite so much. Anyone passing within a hundred yards will see it now."

"I'm not sure if that's good or bad, but it's more cheerful, don't you think?"

"Elsa, anything is more cheerful than earthworm brown." He made a face at the dull dirt-toned tan. "You had nowhere to go but up."

He laughed when she poked his arm, and then he did the sweetest thing. He shrugged an arm around her shoulders, tugged her close, and moved forward with the girls right there, watching. "I think it's beautiful. It's bright and nice. Congratulations, Doc."

"I agree," she said simply. She smiled up at him, wishing she could reach up for a repeat of their morning kiss, but she couldn't. She tweaked his hat instead and stepped out of the curve of his arm. "You head off. The girls and I have some work to do."

"Do you have to go?" Cheyenne asked. "You could stay here, Dad. Help us. And then we could all work together."

Work together?

Nick turned, surprised. So did Elsa. She gave the girl an approving smile while assessing her motives. "That's a really nice thought, Cheyenne."

Cheyenne didn't look complimented. She looked guilty, which meant she had a reason to keep Nick here.

"I'll stay another time."

Nick kissed Dakota, then Cheyenne. She clung to his arm, holding him back. "Can't we just chill?" Cheyenne wondered. "We can help Elsa paint."

"You are going to do exactly that, but this is a project for us, not your dad. Not this time," she added, hoping to relieve Cheyenne's concern. She indicated two lengths of white picket fencing. "We need to doll up this fence. There are smocks right there." She pointed to the metal-and-wood garden bench. "Grab those and check out the pattern ideas I've laid out."

The girls scrambled over, and Nick took the opportunity to raise his brows in question.

She shrugged, just as mystified.

"Give us ninety minutes this time please. We're expecting showers tonight, so the more we get done, the better off we are."

"A ninety-minute session it is." He climbed into the truck, backed around, and pulled away, but she heard the truck idle a few moments later, and when her phone signaled a text, she pulled it up and smiled. "Girls @ ranch tonight. Meeting w/W now. Meet me later?"

She texted back "Yes."

Could Cheyenne know Nick was meeting her mother? Was that why she wanted him to stay?

Possibly, but when she looked at the girls, Cheyenne was slipping into the smock Elsa had indicated.

She wouldn't delve and interrupt a moment of peace.

She stuck the phone away and focused her attention on the two beautiful children in her yard. Her morning encounter with their mother said their lives might be changed again, through no fault of their own. Being the target of small-town gossip and conjecture is never in a kid's best interest, and when their mother's behavior earns a top

spot in the gossip column, kids take the fallout, but Elsa had formu-
lated a plan.

If she could strengthen their self-esteem and awareness before everything around them went more ballistic, they'd have a better shot at
coming through unscathed, and that was her current goal. If she could
work with these two the next few months, maybe they could weather
whatever grown-up crazy came their way.

NINE

*Y*ou promised you'd be sober." Nick stared at Whitney, dismayed. To be wasted at this hour meant she started drinking hours before. He stepped back from the steps leading up to the inn and held his hands up, palms out. "I'm out." He turned on his heel and strode toward the pickup, not wanting a Center Street scene, but Whitney chased after him, yelling.

"Nick, wait!"

So much for discretion. He turned back between the sidewalk and the truck and folded his arms. "We had a meeting scheduled. You promised to be sober. You're not. End of meeting."

"You can't just dismiss me like this. I'm the mother of your children."

He bit back what he wanted to say, and it wasn't easy, because he'd had a lot of time to build up anger, but Elsa's wisdom kept him in check. *"Put them first. Always."* "Whitney, Dakota doesn't remember you. Cheyenne remembers the way you were years ago. This"—he waved a hand toward her—"doesn't enter into the equation. You say you've got problems." He shrugged. "So do I. But they don't get fixed with drugs and alcohol. If you love the girls at all, if you want to see them, you've got to get clean. It's that simple."

"Simple?" She didn't shriek the word; she hissed, and that drew the attention of two older women passing by, walking their dogs on a beautiful night. "Nothing about being with you high-and-mighty Staffords is simple. Nothing is easy, and barely anything is acceptable."

He couldn't do this. He wouldn't do it. He turned to get back into the truck, and she came up behind him and grabbed his arm. "Don't walk away from me! They're my girls too, and Cheyenne wants to be with me. You can see it in her eyes when she looks at me! Don't think because you're rich that you can do to me what your father did to your mother. Buy her out and send her off so he didn't have to deal with her influence in your life."

Buy her off . . .

Anger didn't snake Nick's spine; it catapulted.

He'd heard the rumors all his life, that the high-and-mighty Sam Stafford paid off his mother to leave because she didn't hold a candle to his first wife, Colt's mother. Johnny Baxter was fond of spreading it around on the worst of his bad nights.

Nick had never asked because he didn't want to know. What was worse? His father paying off a wife so she'd leave peacefully or a mother who took money in exchange for a child?

He hated both scenarios equally, so why search for truth when either truth might strangle the thin relationship he and Sam already had?

He controlled his face with effort and faced Whitney, a caricature of the woman she'd been. Buy her off?

If only that would work, and if only his conscience would allow such a luxury, but it wouldn't, so he decided to take another page from Elsa's book and kill her with kindness. He started to speak.

She took a step back as if in fear, and he sighed, pinched the bridge of his nose, counted to ten, then opened his eyes. "I don't want you gone."

"What?"

She looked dumbfounded, so that made two of them.

"I don't want you to leave or go anywhere. That would be the worst possible choice, Whitney."

She stared hard at him, then scowled. "You're lying."

"I never lie. You know that."

She gulped because she did know that.

"We've got two beautiful daughters. They deserve a chance to know and love their mother. I came here to tell you that, but I wanted you to be sober enough to understand."

"I'm sober enough." She folded her arms, mimicking his stance. "Mostly."

"I've got an offer for you," he went on, deciding to take a chance while wondering if he was downright stupid to do it. "A contract."

"Gotta get it in writing, of course. You've always gotta dot your i's and cross your t's when you're a Stafford." She slurred her words slightly, and he shrugged.

"It's how things get done. Here's the deal: The girls and I will move to the ranch for the summer. As long as you stay sober, you can have the house in town. I won't try to sell it until later. You come visit the girls on the ranch, and if you can stay clean and sober, we'll talk again next fall. But for now, I'd like to offer you a roof over your head and a clean bed to sleep in."

"How much?"

He frowned, confused.

"How much rent do you want? I'm pretty tapped out right now."

"No rent."

She stared as if trying to read his angle.

"I don't need the money, and you don't have the money. Why make the situation worse?"

"I get to stay there, rent free?"

"That's the gist of it. But no booze, no drugs, no partying that gets me hot-under-the-collar phone calls from the neighbors. And you need to agree to some kind of program."

"Not happening." She dug her heels in and glared. "A small town like this, you go to AA, everyone knows you've got a problem."

"Small town like this, everyone already knows you've got a problem," Nick reminded her. "At least if you're in a program, people know you're trying your best to get back on your feet. Folks around here like that."

"What do you know about folks around here?" Disbelief colored her tone. "You haven't spent time with the townies. You're too busy playing lord of the manor with Daddy to know what goes on with simple folks."

"That was true once. Not anymore."

"That's not what I hear."

He drew a mental line in the sand before she pulled him off topic. She could wade into deeper waters only if he allowed it, so he wouldn't. "I'm having my lawyer draw up the contract, just like I stated. We'll do a three-month trial basis to see how things work. Your only stipulation is to keep the terms. You visit the girls at the ranch, and no drinking or drugs."

She stared at him, then flicked a look around the town. "I don't need your charity, Nick."

"You do," he surmised softly, "but I wouldn't call it charity. I'd call it help, Whit. When things go bad or life kicks us in the head, it's nice to have a little help." He threw that out there, then waited, wondering.

Would she accept the offer?

Did she have the willingness to walk away from whatever sordid habits she'd adopted?

He didn't know, but if he never offered her the chance to come clean, he couldn't live with himself. His father might call him foolish. Colt might think he was weak or touched in the head, but they didn't have much skin in the game. It was his, and he did a lot better with an olive branch of peace than brute force. "Dakota's moving-up ceremony is tomorrow at eleven. Coming to it clean and sober might be a great first step, Whitney. She's already got three years of pictures without a mother present. It would be a nice way to change that up, don't you think?"

She stared at him as if disbelieving, then stepped back and rubbed her arms. "I don't expect I have the right things to wear."

"If Angelina takes you shopping in the morning, we could change that."

She stared into the distance, then shifted her gaze back to his. "She'd do that?"

"She said so."

"What time?"

"It's got to be on the early side. The mall's over forty minutes away."

"Walmart's closer. If I'm ready at ten, that would work."

He nodded. "Walmart works for me, Whit."

She hesitated as if tempted, then dropped her arms. "I don't have money. No money, no credit, no job, Nick." She held his gaze, and for the first time since she rolled into town, he felt like she was being honest. "I can't pay for the clothes."

"You had money enough to drink today."

"Johnny Baxter bought me a round or two. He saw I was down on my luck."

His ex-wife drinking with Johnny Baxter. That meant Johnny probably wanted to dig up dirt on the Staffords, or he wanted to wave a relationship with Whitney in Nick's face. It also explained the tough piece of information she flung at him. "I'll cover the clothes. Once you're working, you can pay me back or we'll put it toward something for the girls. We can figure that part out then. Right now, all we should be looking at is one day at a time."

Her eyes went wide, which meant she recognized the familiar phrase from Alcoholics Anonymous. "Tell your friend I'll be ready at ten."

"I will." He climbed into the truck and drove away, half of him glad it went all right, the other half stewing over what he really wanted to say.

He knew it wouldn't be easy, but he hadn't realized it would be this hard either. He'd had words to hurl, and in the end he had to swallow his pride and the words. He drove out of town, wishing he could stop by the church to spend a little time in thought and solitude, but the church was closed for the night and the pastor was gone. He punched a few keys on the radio, but nothing appealed to him.

The local baseball team was practicing on the town field, west of the village. He pulled off the side of the road, climbed out, and watched. He loved playing basketball as a kid. He loved being part of a team, which was why helping to rebuild the church felt so good. Straddling walls, walking scaffold, talking with others. He hadn't been part of a team effort in a long time, not away from the ranch, that is.

He liked the synchrony of it.

His phone warned him that it was almost time to pick up the girls. Once they were in bed, he'd talk with Elsa. That thought encouraged him. He'd handled these opening volleys with Whitney without making a fool of himself because he'd put Elsa's advice to work. She'd come into their lives when he needed her. When they needed her.

That had to be a God thing, because while it seemed that the timing couldn't be worse, he realized it couldn't be better. *"My grace is sufficient for you, for my power is made perfect in weakness."* Paul's words to the Corinthians—God's reassurance in times of trouble.

He pulled into Elsa's yard, put the truck in park, and climbed out.

"Daddy! Do you love it so much?" Excited, Dakota jumped up and down to point out the bright, merry, imperfect blossoms decorating the whitewashed picket fence sections. "Elsa's going to put it in her garden!" She swung her paintbrush in a wide arc, spraying droplets of water left and right. "And she let us paint the flowers all by ourselves."

"Gorgeous." He winked at Elsa over Dakota's head, scooped her up, and moved closer. "You guys got a lot done."

"Elsa bought some pretty paints. Finally." Cheyenne drew out the last word out, as if pained. "Not those dull colors she's got inside."

"There is a time for every purpose under the heaven, kid," Elsa reminded her. "Some things call for dull, and some moments call for bright. But it's never okay to fault someone else's feelings or choices, because you're not walking in their shoes. Got it?"

Cheyenne frowned but nodded. "Yeah, I guess. Did you go see Mom while we were here? And did you tell her to get out of town? She told me that's what you'd try to do, so I wondered all night if that's what you were doing."

At least she'd asked him outright instead of sitting around stewing. "I did go see her, but she was wrong, Cheyenne." When Cheyenne looked skeptical, he shrugged. "I told her I don't want her to leave, that you girls need your mother around, and that she could stay in our house for the summer and we'll move onto the ranch."

"For real?" Cheyenne stared up at him, and the look of hope in her gaze went deeper than words. "What did she say? Did she say yes?"

"She's thinking about it."

"I don't mind if she leaves." Dakota clung to Nick's neck and muttered the words softly. "I think it's okay to be just us, isn't it, Daddy?" She pulled back and gazed into his eyes. Distrust flattened her features. "But I'll love living on the ranch with Noah and Ange and all the animals."

"Why can't we all stay in our house, together?" Cheyenne set down her brush and faced off with him. "Like we used to? There's plenty of room, and you know it."

"We're not married anymore," Nick reminded her. "But that doesn't mean we can't be a family. It's only a fifteen-minute drive into town, Cheyenne. If your mom stays for the summer, she'll come out to the ranch and visit you."

"Which is a nice compromise on all sides, just like we discussed." Elsa's words suggested they'd discussed the merits of concession while he was gone. "Give a little, take a little."

Chin down, Cheyenne moved toward the truck.

"Cheyenne, use your manners. Say good-bye to Elsa and thank her for letting you decorate the fence."

She didn't turn and barely spoke. "Good-bye. Thank you." She climbed into the truck, plopped into the backseat, and turned away.

"Bye, Elsa!" Dakota reached down to hug Elsa's neck and almost flipped herself out of Nick's arms doing it. "I love the pretty fences so much! Can we do some for our house, Daddy? Elsa knows how to make things look special and pretty."

"She does." He locked eyes with Elsa. A growing appreciation for a kid-centric mind-set wrapped in a delightful feminine package swept him. "Let's get you guys home. Big day tomorrow with the graduation. You're moving up, kid."

"I know!" She clapped her hands together, then put them over her mouth as if the thought of graduating to second grade was simply too amazing to contemplate. "I'm so excited!"

"Me too." Nick tucked her into the back of the truck. She chattered all the way to the ranch.

Cheyenne sat in sullen silence, punishing him for decisions he had to make. Well, that's why he was the parent and she was the child, but his younger illusions about being the best dad ever flew right out the window on a central Washington breeze. And when he got back to the ranch and got the girls settled in, a call from the birthing barn stymied his plans to meet Elsa. He picked up the phone and dialed her number.

"What's up?"

The inviting quality of her voice sounded light and easy. "I can't make it, sorry. We've got a cow in a bad way."

"Why are you on the phone? Go save her."

"I'm heading that way," he promised as he hurried toward the barn. "Meet me at the graduation tomorrow. It's at eleven o'clock. Dakota would love it if you were there."

"Dakota's father would like it," she corrected him as he crossed to the barn. "But this is a delicate time in family relations, and I'm okay with taking a backseat as needed. I hope you invited Whitney, and I hope she comes. I'm going to keep painting my hobbit house and keep Achilles company. Now focus on the cow, and I'll talk to you soon."

She hung up as he entered the barn.

Murt met him halfway in. "I canceled the veterinary." His grim expression said the rest.

"We lost them both?"

"Yes."

Sam came through behind him. He caught sight of Nick and frowned. "You had her up here. You must have suspected something was wrong, but you took off and didn't bother leaving instructions."

He hadn't, Nick realized. He'd meant to alert Murt or Brock, but he was running late and forgot.

This was all on him.

The loss of the cow and the calf was his fault, and all because he didn't alert anyone that he'd brought her down low for a reason.

"I meant to check over here. I saw you out back earlier, and then I got hung up and by the time it occurred to me again, it was too late." Murt sounded angry at himself. "I should have come this way first thing."

"You're not generally sloppy, Nick." Sam didn't look like a warm, forgiving father right now. He looked steamed. "And we didn't build this place to where it's at on careless practices."

If he mentioned they were down two experienced hands and that cleaning up Hobbs's accident the other day had cost valuable hours, he'd sound like a whiner, and Nick Stafford never whined. "No, sir. I'll take care of it."

"See that you do."

He wanted to shout as his father pushed by. He wanted to profess that he was one person spinning a whole lot of plates right now, but what would his father know about that?

Nothing. Because he'd spun one ever-growing plate for decades, with one thing dead center. The Double S.

"He's hurting, Nick."

Nick said nothing.

"I mean in the gut, death-is-approaching kind of pain, but he won't take pain meds because then he can't function on the ranch. You might want to cut him some slack."

"Like he's done for me so many times?"

Murt winced and rubbed his jaw.

Sam Stafford cut no one slack. He worked hard, he excelled, and he expected the same from everyone around him, even the sons he ignored.

He'd left child raising to the handful of housekeepers and school teachers while he built his empire. He ate as needed and drank when he liked, and Nick could count on the fingers of one hand the number of school functions his father had bothered with.

Michael McMurty had come to more of Nick's basketball games than Sam Stafford ever had. The idea of putting the girls first wouldn't occur to the old Sam, and maybe not the new one either, from the looks of things. "I'll get the backhoe."

"I can do that, Nick." Murt reached out a hand. "It's a ranch. These things happen."

Nick knew that, but they usually happened when it couldn't be helped.

This could have been helped. He'd messed up, and at the end of the day, there was no one else to blame. He moved deeper into the barn. An aching sadness grabbed hold and refused to shake loose. "You go on, Murt. I've got this."

He didn't turn around, and after several seconds, Murt's footsteps moved off.

He propped the doors open, crossed the shadowed barnyard, and climbed onto the loader. As he steered the rig into the barn, movement caught his eye. He paused the rig.

Colt moved in from the side, not laughing, not joking. He didn't say a word. He just motioned for him to lower the big shovel.

Nick did. As he inched the shovel closer, Colt eased the pregnant heifer aboard with a gentleness that made Nick's throat go tight. And once she was safely tucked in the crook, Colt gave him a sign.

He brought the shovel up. Colt climbed aboard the opposite side, still quiet, and he stayed quiet as they drove the sad load out to the designated burial spot just shy of the first hill. And when they'd taken care of the heifer with a thick layer of soil, Colt climbed back in. "Isabo has soup."

Just that. Nothing more, nothing profound, but after a long day and long night, soup sounded good.

They parked the rig back in the yard and started for the house, but when Nick paused, so did Colt. Nick looked toward the barn, then his older brother, the man who'd gone off to build his fortune in Lower Manhattan and never looked back until this year. "Thank you."

Colt shrugged it off and started for the house again.

Nick reached out and stopped him. "I mean it, Colt."

Colt stopped. He sighed, staring off, then looked back at Nick. "I know you do, but from now on, when we help each other, it's okay to use words, but it's not necessary." He drew up straight and gazed into Nick's eyes. "We're partners, but more than that, we're brothers. And that means no matter what happens, I've got your back. Twenty-four seven. Got it?"

Nick's stomach calmed. His heart went soft. The weight that had been hanging on his chest dissipated. "Got it."

"And not for nothing . . ." Colt strode across the porch and drew open the screen door. "I'm hungry. Let's eat."

Rachel called Elsa first thing the next morning. "I need your opinion on something."

"My advice? On what?" Elsa asked. "And no, do not stop dying your hair. You're better blond. Leave it."

"Not the hair, this time. This is work. Career oriented. I've got the end-of-year things going on today, but if you can stop down before ten thirty, I could go over this quickly."

"I don't want a career. I believe I've made that plain."

Rachel sighed purposely. "That was then. This is now. You've stepped out of your self-imposed cocoon and eased Mom's worry."

"Mom isn't worried about me anymore." Saying the words, Elsa knew they weren't true. Her mother was probably concerned and pretending, a skill they'd all perfected the last couple of years. But she was tired of pretense and was truly enjoying the steps she'd taken toward mainstream existence. She woke each morning not just happier but invigorated.

It felt great.

"Of course she is, and you know that, but I don't want to do a phone chat dissecting the matter. Stop by the school before the day gets crazy on my end."

Months ago she'd have avoided the school at all costs. When had that changed?

Since meeting Nick and the girls. Since stepping back into life. And Rachel was right to push now, before school was out for the summer. "I'll get dressed and come right over."

"Excellent. See you in a few."

She didn't waste time with delaying tactics or she might call Rachel back and cancel. She drove to the school, parked in the visitors' lot, and walked to the main door as if she belonged there.

She didn't, of course.

She'd lived in Gray's Glen for two years and had never come to her sister's workplace. The doors, the walls, the sounds transported her back to Brant Park Elementary.

She paused, unnerved, but then looked around. As she did, she breathed a little easier. Was it because this was a different school? Or was she finally moving on?

The initial noise took her by surprise. Little voices mixed with teachers offering direction, the rustle and bustle of the last day. Kids on the playground and kids playing ball while sacks of well-used supplies sat atop many of the desks. At twelve fifteen, the bell would ring for the last time this year. The students would scatter far and wide across the valley, and the buses would stand parked in the transportation lot behind the middle school building.

She moved down the hall leading to the main office. When she opened the door, the woman manning the front desk waved her in. "You must be Rachel's sister. Come on in. Door's open, right through there. I'm Casey Szady, the office assistant."

Elsa put out her hand. "Elsa Andreas."

"Nice to meet you." Casey clasped her hand in a quick, self-assured grip.

"Elsa." Rachel popped her head through the open door to her office. "Come back here. I've only got about ten minutes but I wanted to run this by you. Thanks, Casey."

Casey moved toward the office door. "I'm going to make sure the teachers are all on schedule for the K through one festivities, but I'm going to do it personally so we don't have a repeat of last year's snags."

"Perfect." Rachel stepped aside as Elsa approached her office. "I'll be in the auditorium by ten fifty."

"Mr. Harvey texted me that he's conducting a sound test right now."

"Good."

Elsa crossed into the principal's domain and gave it a quick once-over. "I like it, Rach."

"Me too, but I spend too much time in it these days. You'd think the age of technology would sidestep red tape and bureaucracy, but it doesn't, even in a fairly small district like ours. Here." She handed Elsa a sheet of paper. "I wanted you to see this before they do the public posting."

Elsa read the job description for the grades five through eight school psychologist, then lifted her brows. "This isn't subtle. In fact, I'd call this the *opposite* of subtle."

Subtlety had never been Rachel's forte. She admitted that as she closed the door. "I only practice sensitivity with my K through three crew, and honestly, the third graders barely make the cut."

"Eight-year-olds are in a whole new league these days, aren't they?"

"Unfortunately so," Rachel agreed. She eased one hip onto the edge of her fairly plain desk. "This is tailor made for you, Elsa, and I didn't want time to get away from us. They're doing interviews the week following Independence Day, so there's plenty of time between now and then to refresh your resume and send it in if you decide to throw your hat in the ring. I'd love to have you on board in this district. You like junior high, and you've got the credentials."

"I didn't come here to stay." She'd come to Gray's Glen to get her feet back under her. Or she came here to hide, a skill she polished until pushed to work with the Stafford girls.

Rachel faced her directly. "Not then, no. But I think you like the valley. The hills, the peace and quiet when you need it, and maybe now a little activity to balance that out."

She did like it here. She liked the sun-soaked valley and the shadowed gloaming. Acres of rich, fertile farmland lay in every direction once she came down the hill, and more stretched beyond.

She glanced around.

"It's just an application process, and if they call you for an interview, you don't have to go." Rachel shrugged. "But it's a step, Elsa."

It was.

A month ago she'd have said no instantly, but a month ago Rachel wouldn't have mentioned the opening. Had she come that far?

Cars began streaming into the west-end parking lot of the elementary school. She folded the posting and slipped it into her bag. "I'll think about it."

Rachel stood.

Elsa wanted to say more. She wanted to tell Rachel how much her unobtrusive support had meant, that the phone calls, the drop-by visits, the invitations—even the ones she ignored—had kept her in the loop of normalcy when life seemed cruelly abnormal. She faced Rachel, and her sister waved her off. "You've got that sentimental look on your face, and I can't be a bucket of tears in here and then walk out on stage and be Miss Congeniality for the moving-up festivities. I love you, Elsa."

"Me too." She hugged her quickly. "No mushy stuff. Got it." She opened Rachel's office door, then crossed to the second door before she turned back. "Thanks, Rachel."

"You're welcome."

Elsa opened the door.

Parents and grandparents clogged both ends of the hall leading to the auditorium. People chatted as they moved, a kaleidoscope of bright clothing and happy faces.

This is the normal, her conscience scolded softly. *What you see right here, right now. This is what God intended, for his people to pass through life sure footed, to care for their young with love and compassion. Don't blame God for what man has put asunder.*

"Elsa?"

She turned toward Nick's surprised voice. "Hey."

He spotted Rachel behind her and nodded. "Mrs. Willingham, I know you're busy, but I'd like to thank you for recommending your sister to work with my girls." He settled his gaze on Elsa just long enough to make her wish it were longer. "She's making a difference already."

"I'm glad." Rachel tapped her watch. "I've got to run. Mr. Stafford, there are seats saved down front so you don't all have to walk so far."

Sam was coming up behind Nick, flanked by Colt and Isabo. Angelina followed with Noah. Sam looked aggrieved at first, then nodded. "I'd appreciate not walking too far, actually."

"I've always been a front-row-seat kind of guy." Colt tipped an imaginary hat Rachel's way. "You've got my thanks, ma'am."

Rachel grinned and moved off as they followed her to the first access door.

Nick turned back to Elsa. "Stay."

She almost did. It was on the tip of her tongue to say yes when Whitney strolled through the door.

She spotted Elsa standing near Nick. Her countenance changed.

Her affect darkened and her gaze narrowed as if looking for confrontation. Elsa wasn't about to give her the satisfaction. "I've got to get things done today, but I needed to meet with Rachel first thing. I'll be ready to start with the girls tomorrow, all right?"

He began to say something, then paused and let it go. "Cheyenne's teacher sent home three study guides. Math, language, and reading with spelling lists too. They're pretty big books."

"We've got all summer, and we'll take it day by day." She moved another step back as Whitney drew close. "Enjoy the moving-up ceremony."

"We will."

It wasn't Nick who answered. It was Whitney, smiling up at him as if he mattered. Touching his arm as if they were a couple. Standing close enough to send a proprietary message.

Her body language hinted one thing. Her eyes said another.

Nick eased away from her proximity. He kept his arms firmly at his side and didn't make eye contact with her. Elsa started to turn, then remembered their last conversation. "Nick, I forgot to ask about the cow. How is she? How's the calf?"

He shook his head.

"Oh, Nick. I'm so sorry." She was too. Her parents had taken animal losses seriously on their smaller ranch. Maybe it didn't mean quite so much on a big holding, but Nick's expression indicated otherwise.

"Rough night." He splayed his hands slightly. "Today's another day."

She grimaced because she knew he meant more than the ranch loss.

Whitney looked bored. Maybe worse than bored. Disgusted was a better term, as if the thought of the ranch and the animals and the everyday dance of life and death annoyed her.

"Well, if you need an experienced hand on deck when those puppies come due, I'm happy to jump in."

"Thanks, Elsa."

"See you tomorrow."

Whitney said nothing. She didn't acknowledge Elsa's existence
with anything more than a cold hard look. She turned toward the auditorium and tugged Nick's arm as Elsa moved toward the door.

Explosive.

The word filled Elsa's mind as she went outside.

Whitney was a powder keg, waiting to explode, but why? Because
of Elsa?

That made no sense. She'd left of her own accord and had been
gone for years. So what was driving her return and the negative attitude? Lack of money? Regret? A combination of the two?

She started her car, and as she appropriately circled the parking lot
to the exit, late arrivals pulled in, ignoring the exit arrows, using the exit
for quick access to the school. As she waited, then threaded her way
through, she was a salmon, swimming the right direction, but the
wrong way, it seemed.

In Rachel's office it had seemed momentarily right and tempting to
take that next step forward. Did she dare?

Her bag had flopped open on the passenger seat. The folded sheet
of copier paper lay tucked just inside, inviting her to take a chance.

*You have nothing to lose and everything to gain. Why not? Are you
willing to let one person's horrid choice steal your life too?*

No.

She made up her mind as she took a left into town. She'd always
have regrets about Will Belvedere's precious children. But it was his
choice, not hers, that stole two sweet lives that warm spring day.

She stopped by Hammerstein's Mercantile and bought cream for her coffee and coarser sandpaper for the neglected shutters. And then she went back to the woods, determined to use this time to help shape up the odd little house, because if she did get a job . . .

She breathed deep and it felt good.

When she started working, she wanted something cheerful and friendly to come home to. She parked the car, made a cup of coffee, and got to work.

———⟶⟨⟩

Ladies first. Nick allowed Whitney to precede him through the auditorium door and regretted the action as they descended the long, sloped ramp. Their entrance through the emergency exit door turned heads, and Whitney made the most of the moment. She paused, not quite striking a pose, but with a "notice me" stature, and Nick was pretty sure at least eighty percent of the crowd noticed her, all right.

He moved right by, refusing to be part of her charade. Colt had kept a seat at the far right, while Isabo had saved one at the near left.

He slipped into the tufted seat next to his brother and whispered, "Thank you."

"Yup."

Eyes forward, Colt ignored Whitney's approach from the left, and when she made a show of smoothing the bottom of her dress over her hips before she settled into her seat, Nick bit back a sigh.

God, grant me the serenity to accept the things I cannot change, courage to change the things I can, and the wisdom to know the difference.

He'd used that prayer long ago, and it helped. Then he spent some years not praying at all. Once he'd married Whitney and had Cheyenne, he prayed for show, he and his perfect family lined up in church.

He wasn't sure when he'd started praying sincerely again. Sometime between Whitney's departure and that second Christmas alone, when he realized it was time to be something better than a fake example to his daughters.

The program started, and as the kindergarten and first grade classes marched in wearing miniature caps and gowns, adult drama faded.

"'Kota!" Colt pseudo-whispered her name as she walked by. She giggled, hands up to her mouth, and sent her dad and her uncle a look of delight. The line had to pause as they mounted the steps on the right-hand side. Row by row they marched up, each child taking a seat on the graduated risers. Dakota peeked back over her shoulder. She waved to Angelina, then to Sam and Isabo.

And then she turned back toward the teacher, dismissing her mother completely.

Nick refused to glance Whitney's way.

Kids had their own ways of getting a message across, and Dakota had made hers clear. She didn't remember Whitney, she didn't think she needed her mother, and she wasn't about to acknowledge her. Did that hurt Whitney? He didn't know, and if it took years for her to regain ground with their youngest child, so be it. He didn't walk out. She did. Simple science said reactions generally met actions headfirst. If that held true, Whitney would be working her way back into Dakota's good graces for a while.

Elsa's sister moved to the podium. The teachers instructed the first row to stand and come forward. One by one their names were called to accept their scrolled diploma from the principal. And when it was Dakota's turn, she clutched Rachel's hand with a squeal of delight. "Mrs. Willingham! Your sister is coming to my house this summer. To help us! Isn't that so special?"

The crowd tittered.

The Staffords exchanged looks, unsurprised because Dakota wasn't one to hold back her enthusiasm.

Whitney froze.

"It is." The principal smiled down, squeezed the little one's hand, then turned for the next student.

Dakota hurried down the left-hand steps, curls bouncing, and when she passed in front of their seats again, she waved to her family, a picture of innocence. She made eye contact with everyone in the row, starting with Isabo and working her way down. And once again she ignored Whitney's existence.

As the program drew to a close, teachers released the students to their parents, ready to begin summer vacation.

"Daddy!" Dakota launched herself into Nick's arms, then held on tight. "I'm so glad you came!"

"Wouldn't miss it for the world, sweet thing. We're going to gather up your sister from her class and take everyone out to lunch. Sound good?"

"Even her?" She whispered the words, but when she pointed to Whitney, her expression made it clear that she didn't consider her mother to be part of the family.

"All of us." Angelina didn't wait for Nick to answer. "Because we're all quite proud of you, little one."

"And I was so good!" Surprise hiked Noah's voice and made people smile around them. "Can I have chocolate chip pancakes for lunch, just like Uncle Nick's?"

"Well, little man"—Nick aimed his gaze down—"there isn't a restaurant around that makes chocolate chip pancakes better than the Christine Stafford original recipe. Your grandma started the tradition a long time ago. I'm just happy to keep it going."

"Huh?" Noah looked up, befuddled.

"The restaurants won't have the right ones," Nick explained in easier terms. "But I'll make your favorite ones soon, if you're good."

"I'll be good," Noah promised.

"Me too!" Dakota squeezed Nick's neck in a big hug. "So maybe I'll just get chicken nuggets to celebrate today, okay?"

"Me too!" Noah fist-pumped the air. "And then we can play, 'Kota!"

"Some of us can." Cheyenne came toward them. Stubborn reluctance dragged her steps. Nick had given her the choice of staying in class or being excused for Dakota's special moment. She'd stayed in her classroom. Now she totally ignored the joy of her little sister's moving-up ceremony as she shifted her gaze from her mother to Nick and back again. "I bet if I lived with Mom, I wouldn't have to do stupid summer school every single day and miss out on all the fun stuff kids are supposed to do in summer."

Angelina started moving toward the door, but she shot a quick look over her shoulder. "You should have considered that last fall, darlin'. You set the stage by your choices then. And now you have to fix those choices."

"Like you and Elsa know so much," the girl muttered. She folded her arms and glared at Nick. "Why do so many people get to boss me around? All I need is one mother and one father and not so many bosses. Why can't we just be normal?"

She'd raised her voice as she spoke, until she ended on a note loud enough for half the thinning auditorium to hear.

"We're as normal as anyone else these days, kid." He reached out to ruffle her hair.

She edged away.

"Why is she doing summer school?" Whitney faced him much like

Cheyenne had done, and the resemblance wasn't lost on Nick. "Kids are supposed to be able to relax and enjoy summer. Not be tied down to a desk. That comes soon enough, doesn't it?"

This from the woman who'd worked for less than four years of her thirty-one years on the planet. "She needs to make up work she missed this year."

"Why did she miss it?" Whitney's eyes went sharp. "Was she sick and you didn't tell me, Nick?"

He refused to play her game and let Cheyenne and Dakota think this was his fault. "You were unreachable, as you know. And she wasn't sick. She simply didn't complete assignments. Now she needs to make them up. It's that simple."

"Were they too hard, baby?" Whitney bent low and gazed into Cheyenne's eyes. "Did you ask for help and no one helped you?"

"All right, before this enchanting little display of enabling behavior gets out of hand, Cheyenne and I have this all worked out, and none of it is open for discussion. Everything's arranged, and if she doesn't like it?" Nick shrugged and started for the door. "Maybe she'll work harder next year. Let's go, girls, the family's waiting."

"Isn't Mom coming?" Cheyenne hung back and put a death grip on Whitney's arm. "I'm not going if Mom's not invited."

Should he count to ten? Or discipline Cheyenne for her very public display of bad manners? He almost stayed calm, then didn't. "Go to the car. Now."

Cheyenne froze, staring up at him.

"Nick."

"Go." He ignored Whitney and leveled a hard look at his daughter. "I'm the parent, I make the rules, and no kid of mine is going to issue challenges to me. Got it?"

She scowled and scuffed her feet all the way out of the auditorium and probably to the car. He turned back to Whitney. "Listen, you're more than welcome to join us for lunch. Cheyenne would love it and that's reason enough for me, but you've been gone, Whitney. You walked away and gave up custody of them three years ago, so don't think you can stroll into town and start making waves. You can't. You need to abide by my rules for them or leave them alone. We've spent three long years without a mother's help, so don't think you can instantly reassume the role. You made your choice, just like Cheyenne did in school, and in the real world, those choices have consequences."

Dakota buried her head in his shoulder.

He sighed.

He shouldn't be doing this here, in front of his little girl. He took a deep breath and began again. "You're welcome to come along. We're going to Mustang Bob's off I-90. But there can't be any more talk of Cheyenne getting out of schoolwork. It's not an option."

She glared up at him, then lifted one shoulder in an insolent shrug. "You go have lunch with your family, Nick. I've lost my appetite."

She stalked off, and when they both reached the parking lot, she made a show of stomping to her worn car, enough of a performance for any remaining people to notice.

Whitney had always loved a public fuss, but they used to be more positive in nature. Her love for attention came flooding back into his memories as he crossed the asphalt and settled Dakota into the backseat.

Colt pulled up alongside, his window down. "We'll get a table. See you up the road. And congratulations, kid." He smiled down at Dakota from his higher vantage point. "Nice job."

"Thank you!"

Her smile returned and she wriggled in delight.

Nick climbed into the driver's seat, torn.

He didn't want to fight with Whitney. Yes, things were easier with her gone, but he understood that having your mother shrug you off was one of those things you never forgot. To this day he still wondered why his had never bothered looking back. Or returned just to check up on him.

Had Sam paid her to leave?

He'd never asked. What if his father confirmed the rumor? What kind of woman could be paid to abandon her child?

He didn't like to think about it, so he didn't, but if he purposely pushed Whitney away, he'd be guilty of the same thing, laying the groundwork for his girls to ask the exact same questions.

He didn't want that gaping hole for the girls, but he didn't want a drunken caricature of a mother either. At the moment those appeared to be the only two choices he had.

Elsa finished painting the trim, put a first coat on the clapboards lining the south side, and lightly sanded all six shutters.

Then she cleaned up her hands and studied the school district application she'd just printed.

The ideal job. Perfect for her credentials. And the weaker pay scale of a smaller district didn't pose a problem for her here. Her costs were low, and she kept her needs minimal.

A job. With kids. Surrounded by coworkers. Tackling the things she'd loved.

You loved it then. Are you strong enough to take this on?

She studied the multipage document while she pondered that question.

She'd stepped out of the shadows, ready to embrace the light, but applying for this job would bring everything out into the open by necessity. Professionals would handle her past based on facts and discernment. They'd assess if she'd overreacted, and they'd decide if she'd done anything wrong.

But it wasn't their rejection that made her fingers grip tighter. What if Nick couldn't handle it? Would his reaction send her back into doubt and despair? Was she ready to take a chance on the truth?

"Trust in the LORD *with all your heart and lean not on your own understanding."*

She'd tried that. She'd been a staunch believer, a front-pew cheerleader, but grievous actions had doled out a mind-numbing dose of reality. Professing love for God and others did little if the mind clung to the poisons of hate.

She sat on the bench and let afternoon sounds churn around her. Achilles came around from out back. He moved quietly through the yard, then sat at her feet, staring out, mimicking her stance.

The finches had chorused all morning. Now they sat silent, enjoying an afternoon nap. Birds flitted above, darting for food here and there, but other than the pass of their wings, the forest was quiet. Waiting. Wondering. Just like her.

Our Father, who art in heaven . . .

Her phone interrupted the old prayer. She saw Rachel's name and lifted the receiver. "Hey, Rach. What's up? How did your little-people celebration go today?"

"It was marvelous and cute and reminded me of all the reasons you and I focused in on working with kids. They're an absolute pleasure, most of the time, which is why I printed off the job posting for you. But that's not the reason I called."

"Then what?"

"I'm having second thoughts about you working with Nick's girls."

This was about the last thing Elsa expected to hear. "A little late now."

"It's not too late. It's never too late, Elsa. I shouldn't have pushed it. There's no reason a well-off guy like Nick Stafford can't take his kids into the city for treatment. I really think it would be better if you didn't see them anymore."

"Why?"

"A number of reasons. He likes you. You like him. Let's just cite conflict of interest and be done with it."

"How about we don't cite that at all," Elsa replied. "Nick and I are working well together, and that's been a positive for his kids. I've made a promise to Cheyenne to tutor her, and I'm not going to break that promise. Especially now, with her mother's unexpected return. For Cheyenne's sake, I think continuity is in her best interests and outweighs other factors."

A moment of silence yawned between them, and in its wake Elsa sensed the truth. "Whitney makes you nervous."

"I don't want to get into this, Elsa. I just want—"

"You're afraid she'll tip me over the edge. Or worse, that she's a danger to those girls and I'll feel responsible."

"There are plenty of therapists around. He can get someone else to counsel them. And someone else to teach Cheyenne. Honestly, Elsa, it's for the best."

"A few weeks ago you thought this was a great idea."

"I was wrong. Not the first time, won't be the last," Rachel admitted.

"But if not now, when? If not me, then who?" Elsa asked, and when Rachel started to answer, she interrupted. "I'm being rhetorical, Rach. I hear what you're saying. I understand your concerns. But if I don't step out and take hold now, I'm afraid I might never do it. And besides, who better to be observing than someone with my experience? Maybe I'm here for just that reason. Have you considered that?"

"And if she messes things up? If she does something rash? I knew her years ago," Rachel pressed. "And this Whitney is like a shadow of the former one. A dark shadow. Looking at her today I got weird, menacing vibes, and I don't want anything to happen to you, Elsa."

"Me either," Elsa assured her. "But I don't want to slip backward again. No more living in the shadows. I intend to stick with the plan to help Nick's girls, and I'm filling out the middle school application as we speak."

"The application is fine. Testing Whitney Stafford's claws is probably not the best idea. Please remember that when I suggested all this, she was nowhere in sight. That's a game changer."

Rachel's concern had the opposite effect. Instead of worrying Elsa, it empowered her. "I've made a commitment, Rach, and I intend to keep it. What can go wrong in a house full of Staffords? As discordant as that family can be on the outside, they've got a solid internal bond. Real family. Like ours."

"You're sure, Elsa?"

"Positive. Now stop mother-henning me. I've got papers to fill out."

"I'll hound you daily."

"If you do, I won't answer," Elsa replied. "Treat me normally please. At least that way I feel like I've regained ground. Okay?"

Her reply didn't sit well with Rachel, and she didn't like that her sister picked up bad sensations from Whitney. But Elsa understood what Angelina and Rachel couldn't see: those early days of coming off addictive habits drove the self inward. If Whitney got through the first few weeks of sobriety and still sent off stress-inducing vibes, then Elsa would take the warnings more seriously. For the moment, the woman needed a chance.

Wasn't that why Christiana and Braden's mother brought civil charges against you? For giving Will Belvedere too much of a chance?

It was.

But she'd done nothing wrong in her recommendations or her treatment. She'd come to understand that. What Will did *wasn't* her fault. But how she wished she'd followed her instincts that day.

She hung up the phone and moved into the wide patch of late-afternoon sun.

She could help Cheyenne and Dakota. She loved being around Nick, and he seemed to reciprocate the feeling. But could she differentiate the rest of the family dynamics enough to assess Whitney?

She didn't know, but it came down to this: she believed the kids were safer with her around, and that made the decision to stay involved a no-brainer.

TEN

Nick faced Whitney across the porch the following week and stared in disbelief, certain he'd heard wrong. "You want what?"

"I want the girls to come live with me. That way I can come and go with them as I please. If they want to go shopping, we go shopping. If I want to take them to a movie, we go to a movie. That's the way it should be, Nick. I'm their mother."

Nick had to bite back the host of reasons that wasn't about to happen, and it wasn't easy. "Have you talked to your sponsor about this?" When she hesitated, he sighed. "Between the church halls and the community centers here and in Cle Elum and Roslyn, there are AA meetings every single day. I know because I checked. Morning, afternoon, or evening. You said you'd go."

"I'm not like the people in those meetings. Have you been there, Nick?"

He shook his head and replied, "I think they're people trying to get back on their feet, day by day. Maybe not so different, Whitney."

"It's not the place for me."

Arguing over it would get them nowhere. She'd agreed to go, but she was staying sober, and Nick was pretty sure it had been a rough eight days. "You've been sober for just over a week, Whitney. I've given you a house to live in, food, and clothes. But that's just the beginning of getting healthy. The next steps are up to you, and they don't include the girls living with you. And besides, how were you expecting to pay for all these little excursions?"

Her blank stare indicated she expected him to foot the bill.

He started to turn away, then didn't. If she needed a reminder, he'd give her one. "You signed over sole custody to me over two years ago, as part of your quickie divorce, remember? And you stayed out of their lives for three long years. Your youngest daughter doesn't even remember you, so no. They're not coming to live with you. End of discussion."

"It's not the end of anything," she shot back. She moved in front of him to block his path. "You let Cheyenne get on a horse and get hurt. I heard all about it, Nick. And I saw her working her routines at dance class this week. She's not practicing hard enough, she's not nailing her numbers, and that's because you've let her slack off."

"Or it's because she doesn't like dancing and she'd rather ride herd with her dad," Nick countered. "She's already made the decision to stop taking dancing and gymnastics lessons. Dakota too. Once the recital's done, they're done. We're going to spend the next year learning about horse care and riding. The girls want to explore their heritage on the ranch, and I think it's an excellent idea."

"That's Colt talking. Not you. You wanted them safe and sound, just like I did."

"And then you disappeared," he reminded her.

"We're talking about the here and now." She shot a dark look at the house. "There was nothing for me there, Nick. I was always the outsider, and that's a wretched place to be when you're up against Team Stafford. Your father might be sick, but he's still formidable. He doesn't like that I'm here, and that makes my time with the girls uncomfortable. It would be better for all three of us for me to have time with the girls at my house. We'd all settle in more quickly."

Surprise pushed Nick's brows higher. "*Your* house?"

She flushed as if hoping he wouldn't catch the slip. Oh, he caught it all right, and Whitney needed to realize that she wasn't claim-jumping the house in town. "You do remember I bought you out of that house for the cool sum of a hundred-and-ten grand two years ago, right? I don't want to know what you did with the money, Whitney." He held up both hands to stop any explanation she might want to throw his way. "That's your business. But don't forget you're in that house temporarily. The excavators are scheduled to break ground for our ranch house here next month. If you want to buy the house on West Chelan, I'll be happy to sell it to you. But first you need a job. If you're staying in town, you've got to be able to make your own way."

"It's always easy for the rich to pass edicts on the poor." She gave him a cold hard stare. "When you're born to a life of ease, I guess it's hard to see the struggles of the little people you Staffords crush beneath your feet on a regular basis."

"Nobody crushed you, Whitney." If anything, he'd given sway too often until nothing he or the girls did satisfied her. "Nobody wants to crush you. But you've made choices, and you can't just pick up where you left off. We've had a lot of hurt and heartache to deal with here. So get that notion out of your head. The girls are living here, you're wel-come to visit them here, and I've got cows to tend."

She swore under her breath, but Nick kept walking.

She needed cooling-off time.

So did he.

Her audacity galled him. Stripey dashed past as he strode to the barn, which meant Dakota was probably chasing the kitten. He paused, and when his youngest daughter raced around the corner of the house, she ran right into her cowboy father. "Are you supposed to be playing over here?"

She gulped. "No. But Stripey—"

"But Stripey nothing. Cars come in and out of this area. Big tractors come down from the fields. I do not want my little girl hurt because she won't follow directions. Now go play on the other side with the rest of the kids or I'll have Angelina put you under house arrest."

She made a tortured face. "Not that!"

"If clipping your wings is the only way to keep you safe, I'll do it, 'Kota. And you know it."

"I'll be good. I promise!" She hugged his legs and dashed back toward the wide, grassy front slope, totally ignoring her mother on the side porch.

Whitney stared after her, but he didn't see a sad mother, anguished by the lack of relationship with a beloved child. He saw a chasm, as if any bond they'd once shared as mother and infant had dissolved. Could that happen? Could a rift of nothing form from what had been something? He understood Dakota's end; she was a preschooler when Whitney left. But Whitney's lack of emotion formed the puzzle piece. Isaiah's words flooded him as he moved toward the barn, God's promise to remember his children, even if their mothers forget them.

He didn't get it.

He'd lived his life wishing for a mother. Praying for a mother. Angry at Sam Stafford for his mother's abandonment. But Whitney's facial expression was a wake-up call.

Maybe not everyone was meant to be a mother. Putting kids' needs first wasn't an easy deal. He didn't mind it because it felt right to him, but what if you hated making the daily sacrifices, and resentment grew?

He moved into the barn realizing that maybe his father wasn't always the bad guy, and that was a revelation nearly thirty years in the making.

Elsa had assigned Cheyenne earbuds and a skill-building math website with graduated tracking. Once Cheyenne mastered mental addition and subtraction in the allotted time-per-problem ratio mandated by the program, she'd move on. In the meantime, Elsa was glad the girl hadn't heard the heated discussion just beyond on the side porch.

Angelina heard it though. She came into the house through the front door and indicated the open back door with a nod. "I wasn't about to walk into the middle of that," she said softly as she brewed a fresh cup of coffee. "And I can't believe she had the nerve to push to have the girls come into town her second week here. In Nick's house." She looked at Elsa, then frowned. "Sorry, I don't mean to put you in an awkward spot. You're easy to talk to, which is probably a plus in your profession, but it loosens my tongue."

"We'll classify anything you say as confidential," Elsa told her as Whitney slammed the door of her car without poking her head in to say good-bye. Of course, she treated Angelina and Elsa like hired help, so why should she bother with pleasantries? "Nick said there's a buyer coming in from Montana today and one from Wyoming tomorrow."

"This is the time of year when deals are struck," Angelina explained. "They buy and sell in advance of pregnancy. This year's calves are all sold."

"Ranchers preorder calves?"

"They sure do." Angelina raised her coffee cup. "Coffee? Tea? Iced tea?"

"I brought some, actually." When Elsa withdrew the tall bottle of premade tea from her bag, Angelina groaned.

"That's not real. That's . . . something else entirely. I have a whole pitcher of fresh lemon tea in the fridge. With no weird things in it. Put that away."

"Nick is right; you are bossy. But I can see why the whole family loves you. And obeys you instantly." Elsa plunked her tea onto the counter, opened it, and drank. "I like this stuff, chemical aftertaste and all. Perhaps it's an acquired taste."

Angelina squealed, then dashed around Elsa and threw open the back door. "Another prodigal comes forth! Hail the missing son!"

A cowboy stepped in, grabbed Angelina in a hug, and spun her around. "Thank you for your constant updates and for sacrificing your life by marrying my stupid brother. If being married improves Colt's disposition, we will be forever in your debt, Angelina."

"Oh, you like him and you know it." She smacked his arm, then hugged him again. "I've been praying you'd get things wrapped up, because we need you here. Colt and Nick won't admit it, but with Sam and Hobbs both down and trouble on the home front"—she tipped a look Cheyenne's way—"and rebuilding a church, we're swamped."

"How is Dad?" The cowboy met Angelina's worried look and sighed. "Okay. That says enough."

"Did you get tested as a possible donor match?" Angelina asked softly. "Or do you prefer not to?"

The cowboy looked surprised. "Of course. They said they'd send the results to the medical team here."

"You're a good man, Trey."

He shrugged that off, then noticed Elsa. "I'm sorry, I didn't mean to be rude. I'm Trey Stafford. The youngest son."

Elsa put out a hand in welcome. "Nice to meet you. I'm Elsa. I'm working with that one." She pointed toward the table. Trey poked his head around the corner and grinned. Cheyenne caught a glimpse of him, tossed her earbuds aside, and jumped up from the chair. "Uncle Trey!"

"Shh. Grandpa's sleeping," Elsa cautioned her, but it was good to see normal, happy emotion in Cheyenne's instant reaction.

Trey hugged Cheyenne tight, but when he shot Elsa a look over the girl's head, she read question in his eyes. "So who is this nice lady, Cheyenne? She's mighty pretty."

"This is Elsa." Cheyenne turned toward Elsa while clinging to her uncle. "She's helping me do schoolwork this summer."

Trey looked right into Cheyenne's eyes and didn't scold her for needing help or tease her about blowing off the year. He just gently bumped his forehead to hers and smiled. "I'm glad, honey."

Nick had told her Trey was the easygoing brother. His gentle interaction with Cheyenne proved it.

"Me too." Cheyenne whispered the words and hugged him again as if his acceptance meant something. "Are you staying this time? And are you staying here?"

He stood, accepted the mug of coffee from Angelina, and answered both questions. "I am staying to help with things, and no, this house is a little crowded right now. I'm going to stay in the cabin that Isabo and Noah used before they moved in here. I need things a little quieter when I'm writing songs."

Elsa looked closer. Her mouth dropped open. She shut it, but not before Angelina caught the look and laughed. "You didn't realize that Trey Stafford and Trey Walker were one and the same."

"Not a clue," Elsa confessed. "But this family is full of surprises. Why not one more?"

"Not everyone's a country music fan." Trey's smile said he understood.

"But I am," Elsa told him. "Huge. I have every one of your CDs, and my iPod loves you."

"And you live in Gray's Glen." Trey made a face of total disbelief. "So much for the hometown lovin' on one of their own. We'll change that up while I'm here."

Elsa was pretty sure everyone else in town knew who Trey Walker Stafford was. Two years of reclusive living kept her out of the local gossip stream. "I'm probably the only person in central Washington who didn't know, so don't go too crazy. Besides, once your brothers see you, the only thing you'll be seeing is a saddle, I expect. Or the front seat of a Mule. Welcome home, Trey."

"Trey!" Hobbs's excited voice broke in as he came by the open window and spotted Trey in the broad kitchen. He pivoted back toward the barn, cupped his hands around his mouth, and yelled, "Nick, Trey's here! We'll be okay now!" Then the weathered cowboy crossed the porch, threw open the screen door, and rushed inside as Trey moved toward him.

"That's a tall order for a guy who's been doin' more singin' than ridin' these past few years," Trey told the older man as he grabbed him in a hug. "But I expect I remember most everything you taught me, except how to get along with two know-it-all big brothers."

"Same as always," Hobbs proclaimed. "Ignore 'em and do it right, like I showed you when you were a pup. Them others got nothin' you don't got. Never did. Never will."

"Stop babying him, Hobbs. He's richer than any man has a right to be, and if we give him a little baptism of fire, it'll toughen him up. Hey." Nick's words sounded gruff, but when he clapped his brother on the back, then pulled him in for a hug, Elsa read the affection in his eyes. "Welcome home. You have no idea just how badly we need you right now and how happy I am that you made it back this week. Have you seen Dad?"

Trey shook his head. "Just walked in, although if he's sleeping through all this racket, more power to him. Maybe I should take my things over to the cabin, get settled in there, and then come back. I've got an early July charity gig I have to leave for, but other than that, I'm here as needed. I figured I'd drive back from that and cart more stuff in the SUV."

"Coulda done that now, couldn't you?" Hobbs asked, and Trey made a face.

"I didn't want to waste days when we're down on help here, so I flew into SeaTac and grabbed a rental car."

"You're staying in the cabin?" Nick looked surprised, then shrugged. "I suppose it makes sense."

"It does if he wants to keep his sanity," Angelina noted sensibly. "And write songs. The big house isn't conducive to quiet thought at the moment. Would you like some help taking your things over?"

"That would be great, actually." Trey moved toward the porch door. "I'll change into ranch clothes and Nick can put me to work."

"But we'll feed you here," Angelina told him as she pulled out a bank of steaks from the double-door refrigerator. "Starting with fatted calf on the big grill for dinner."

"Elsa, you'll stay, won't you?" Nick must have seen her edge toward her bag. "Have supper with us. Achilles seems happy on the front stoop."

Achilles loved coming to the ranch. He'd spent the first day sniffing anything and everyone, then found a shady corner of the front porch and claimed it. Within hours he'd adapted to sun and shade, a wonderful combination. And she'd left Hoyl inside at home today, just in case she was gone longer than expected.

"I'd love the help in the kitchen." Angelina pulled the makings of a monster salad out of the other side of the fridge. "If Mom's watching the kids, it'll be just the two of us in here. Which means you men are on grill duty. No complaints."

"Cheyenne, how would you like to ride over to the cabin with me?" Trey asked. "Help me unload my stuff?"

"I'd love to! Can we listen to your music in the car?"

"We sure can."

"This is so cool." She gripped his hand and tugged him toward the door. "See you guys in a little while, okay?"

"Hold it, Chey. Did you get all your work done today?" Nick

asked before they got to the door. "And I expect the answer to be 'Yes, Dad.'"

She smiled because she was holding Trey's hand, not because she'd been happily working while Whitney visited earlier. She'd pouted and fussed, but when Elsa didn't cave, she'd gotten down to work. "Yes, Dad."

"Then you can go."

Trey exchanged a look with Nick before he and Cheyenne went through the door, and when he did, Elsa noted the emotional resemblance between the brothers. They didn't look alike in any obvious way, and she was pretty sure they grew up fighting like a litter of ill-mannered pups, but there was a bond between them.

She'd seen it with Nick and Colt despite their different natures. And now she saw it with Nick and Trey, as if something deeper than blood or relationship bound them.

Bound by loss.

Three motherless boys and a clueless father who spent too much time building his financial legacy and too little time being a dad.

"I'm glad you're staying." Nick's voice brought her gaze to his, and she smiled because when she looked at Nick Stafford, the urge to smile overwhelmed her. It felt good to smile again.

"Me too. And hey, I heard the back-and-forth on the porch earlier. With Whitney."

"Before she stormed off in her car?" Nick scrubbed a hand through his hair and grimaced. "I figured you did, and I hoped Cheyenne didn't. If you've got advice, Doc, I'm ready to hear it because I'm caught in a meat grinder and I'm not sure how to turn it off."

"Keep doing what you're doing." She moved forward and gripped his hands.

"God will lead; you will follow. God shows the way." Angelina pulled out a bottle of steak rub and liberally dusted the meat, first one side, then the other. "When we forget that, we make wrong turns."

Elsa hadn't found faith that simple in recent years, but maybe she had long ago. Back before she lived a purposely jam-packed life and tragedy hit full swing.

"I've got computer work waiting." Nick faced Elsa. "You're okay if I go do it?"

"And why wouldn't I be?" She looked from him to Angelina and raised one brow. "Isn't that the primary rule we're trying to instill in Cheyenne? To get work done when it's supposed to get done?"

"It is." Nick's smile said she'd done something really right. "I'll be back in an hour."

She saved Cheyenne's work into an electronic folder on the laptop, then filed the girl's hard-copy work into her bag before she took her place at the counter. "I'm walking a fine line here, Angelina."

Eyes down, Angelina kept working on food. "Tell me something I don't know."

"I can't be Cheyenne's counselor and Nick's girlfriend."

"My immediate response is, too late. My more measured response is, why not let life take us along the path and then choose as we go? Is it better to see the path ahead or to worry about unseen bends in the road?"

"I used to plan everything. Down to the minute, daily."

"But you haven't done that for a while, I expect."

She hadn't. Elsa shook her head as she chopped lettuce.

"I'm going right back to letting God lead the way," Angelina told her. "When we forget that, we take ourselves too seriously. We take on too much. We're the humans. He's God. The times I've gotten myself into trouble are when I've forgotten that simple truth."

It seemed awfully complicated to be called a simple truth, but maybe Angelina was right. Maybe she was mentally confounding things instead of believing in God's plan. But did he have a plan? Or did things just happen because people chose right or wrong?

"... *thy kingdom come. Thy will be done* ..."

God's will or man's choice?

"I saw a lot in Seattle."

Angelina's words put a halt on introspection, but Elsa kept chopping cucumbers, then celery.

"There was a part of me that spurned God and faith for a while. Maybe because I was too into myself, maybe because I was surrounded by greed and evil."

"Maintaining a distance isn't easy."

Angelina's expression didn't agree. "I thought that too, but then I realized my choices put me in that situation. I was too busy with life to bother with faith. Too busy ladder climbing at work to remove myself from the presence of evil often enough. And after a while you get jaded, as if you expect evil. And that wasn't good."

"But you jumped off the roller coaster before you got burned," Elsa noted. "And before anyone else got hurt. That says you were in charge and made strong choices."

"While that *sounds* real good, the truth is I came here to hide after my father was gunned down in cold blood as retribution for something I did. I was part of a unit that brought down a major drug and human trafficking ring."

Elsa stopped chopping and stared at her.

"I put my mother and my son into seclusion to avoid further retribution. I changed my name and became a cook and a house-keeper. For two years my son didn't see other people or have friends or visitors because I was too afraid to bring him out of the shadows and into the light." Elsa must have looked as surprised as she felt, because Angelina nodded. "It's all true. Sam Stafford took me in, gave me a job, and hid my family. In return, God has given me the man I love, a father for Noah, an amazing friend and father in Sam, and he's brought my family out of hiding. But only once I turned over the reins."

"I had no idea."

Angelina smiled as she pulled a potato casserole out of the refrigerator and tucked it into the preheated oven. "Life dares us to live it, Elsa. God longs for us to live it fully, in his name."

Her kind words fell like a blessing on Elsa's ears. It made sense, put that way, as if God's hopes and dreams for her, and for every person, were that of a kind parent for their child. The longing of joy that comes in the morning. She reached over and gave Angelina a spontaneous hug. "Thank you."

"It's my mother you should thank. She had a stubborn daughter who took a long time to listen, but once I did?" She smiled and shrugged. "I listened well."

Isabo came through the back door, toting a laundry basket of line-dried sheets. "It is the perfect day for drying! Sun, breeze, laughter!"

"Did Lucy already come by to pick up Belle? Lucy is the next farm over," she explained to Elsa. "Single mom, three cute kids."

"She did, yes!" Isabo set the laundry basket down by the back stairs. "She was in a hurry to get back home and get things done. Those boys are getting big, but I wonder if they're truly a help at the Fresh Market or too busy being pesky boys."

"Most likely the latter. It's a long day for them," Angelina remarked. She pointed east as she set the meat aside so the rub would season. "Lucy owns the Christmas tree farm east of here. Isabelle spent the day with us while her mom took flowers and plants to the fresh air market near the highway."

"The little one with all the curls and a face like a Precious Moments figurine?"

"And a nature to match," said Isabo. "A gentle heart, easily broken. Her mother's child."

"Lucy's toughened up," Angelina said. "She's got a heart of gold, but she's gotten stronger."

"I'm taking Noah and Dakota to visit Kita." Isabo moved toward the back door as she spoke. "Her puppies are due and I saw her making a nest."

"I can't wait to see the puppies," Elsa told them. "We bred dogs on my parents' ranch up north, and I helped with a lot of birthings before I went to college. My sister wanted absolutely nothing to do with it, and my brother preferred big animal work, but I loved working with the dogs. The miracle of birth, those sweet babies, weighing each one, keeping logs. And then watching them grow. It was marvelous."

"Be careful." Angelina slid her gaze to the screen door and the sound of male voices beyond and then leaned close, as if sharing a secret. "The minute they realize you *can* do something, they expect you to do it. It isn't a bad idea to keep our abilities understated around here. If you get my drift."

Elsa laughed as Colt and Murt clopped along the side porch. They kicked their boots off outside. Two summer hands followed, which meant the kitchen was about to get noisy, and at that moment, the sound of Sam's walker softly thumped in the back hall. "I'll stay here and see to Sam and these guys," added Angelina. "Why don't you walk with Mom and the kids to check the dogs? We're expecting Kita to deliver any day. BeeBee will follow with her first litter in a week or so. The girls would love to show you, I'm sure."

"You're okay here?"

"Fine, now that the salad's done and my future husband has set a fire in the big grill."

Colt grimaced, turned, and went right back out the door with Elsa. He shoved his feet back into his boots and went toward the party-sized cooking area.

Elsa headed toward the barn and followed the contagious sounds of children's laughter.

———❧———

Nick had given Whitney an inch and she wanted a mile, which meant not much changed in her time away.

Did she honestly think he'd let her take the girls? Yes, she'd stopped drinking to the best of his knowledge, but she was shrugging off self-help programs and didn't seem to realize how her abandonment affected her children.

A shriek of joyous laughter eased his encroaching stress.

Dakota was happier here on the ranch, pure country. Cheyenne wasn't really happy anywhere yet again, but her confidence was growing, and that was a major step. He stood, stretched, and clicked Save on the files for the coming calves. He'd sent acceptance e-mails to a half-dozen buyers. Ninety percent of their designer calves were sold before they hit the ground, and that was a good-faith gesture. His father had studied genetics before genome sequence had been cataloged, and now that it had, they'd fine-tuned production to reflect science, not chance. The result was an amazing ranch filled with high quality cattle possessing an enviable feed-to-pounds ratio. Farmers across America were buying Stafford stock.

He closed the office door and headed toward the voices at the far end of the newest barn. "What've we got?"

Dakota's face puckered. "Nothing. Isabo says that Kita is making a nest, but she's not having any babies."

"Having babies takes time." Nick squatted low and stroked the

Aussie's head. "And remember that animals tend to like dark, cozy places to have their young."

"But, Dad, the cows have babies in the field all the time. In the wide open." Dakota offered him a skeptical look. "I don't think that's the problem."

"It could be the problem because dogs are different from cows." Elsa sank down onto the straw stacked along the inside of the stall and kneaded the dog's neck. "When we were breeding police dogs at my parents' place, we always let the mother seek out her spot. But then we moved her indoors with the puppies as soon as she started giving birth so we could give them round-the-clock care."

"Did that help reduce the loss rate?" Nick asked and Elsa nodded.

"Well, sure. Big dogs tend to have big litters, and my father had developed a line of dogs that served on a lot of police forces across the country, so they were valuable puppies. My mom and I took turns sleeping by them and caring for them. But my mom always respected that nesting process before birth."

"That's brilliant."

She tipped a smile his way. "Sometimes simple is best."

"I concur. So . . ." He pointed beyond the dog and hooked a thumb. "Now that I have you out here, would you like the grand tour?"

"You have time?"

"I'll make time." His words brought color to her cheeks. She gave the dog one last stroke, then stood. Nick reached out a hand, hopeful.

She slipped her fingers into his and sighed when he gripped them gently.

It felt right, holding Elsa's hand. Talking to her about school and dogs and crazy birds. "Where's Achilles?"

She smiled as the sunlight touched her face. "Still napping. He dashed around in the sun like a puppy while the kids were playing earlier, then found the deepest shade he could and collapsed in a heap under the porch swing. He's barely twitched a muscle since."

"Racing around with kids takes a little getting used to, for certain." He headed out the near end of the barn, then pointed back. "Office, laboratory, treatment areas."

"Treatment for . . . ?" She arched a brow in question.

"Anything necessary. That area has a private pasture on the west side so we can keep animals close as needed."

"Was this your father's vision years ago? Or did it all just kind of grow, being in the right place at the right time and using science to augment nature?"

"Both." He mulled the question as they moved on. "I think the vision for what could be sprang from his partnership with Murt and Hobbs—seeing this, trying that, back in the day. They both had a great eye for crossbreeding animals. The science aspect came later, but it fit, and Dad saw an opportunity to blend the two concepts."

"So he engineered nature?"

"To a degree."

"And that doesn't seem weird to you?"

He laughed. "No. But then I was raised around it, and the whole thing made sense. Did your parents run a lot of cattle?"

"Nothing like this. It was a small, hands-on operation, and I was so glad to leave it. To move on to school, and then the city. And then I ended up missing it once they'd moved to an island in the Sound. Maybe that's why I enjoy being here so much." She gazed around as they emerged from the barn into the light. "It's like a second chance to appreciate what I had."

"That's the only reason?" He bumped shoulders with her. When she smiled, he knew he'd made his point.

"There are multiple reasons to enjoy being here, and having a hot country music star on hand isn't exactly a bad thing." He pretended to scowl and she laughed. "I had no idea that Trey Walker was your brother until today."

"The disadvantages of reclusive living."

"So it seems. I was still on the coast when he lost his wife."

Nick had been caught up in his own drama then. Looking back, he knew he hadn't been as supportive as he should have been. Colt gone, and the younger two brothers facing life-altering crises, not one of them smart enough to ask for help. "It was rough. He stuck by Kathy through all the craziness, the rehab, thought he was finally on solid ground, and then repeated the whole thing."

"Except she didn't make it through that last downward spiral," Elsa said softly. "It was like watching a fairy-tale romance go up in smoke."

"Mostly illusion," Nick told her bluntly. "But they were already married before he realized the truth. Trey lost both parents to drug addictions. My father adopted him when he was just a little guy and raised him as carefully as he did any of us." She squeezed his fingers and made a face of sympathy. "Then Trey married someone who followed his parents' pattern, and I married a woman who walked out, just like my mother did. So maybe we're destined to repeat the mistakes of those who went before us."

"That's not one bit true."

"It feels kinda true." He paused at the split-rail fence and leaned forward, elbows propped. "You'd think we'd have learned from our parents' mistakes, but we didn't come close."

"Which is why you brought the girls to see me," she told him softly. "Children can't be expected to understand loss and motivation on their own. A few might, but the majority try to fill voids with what feels right. And sometimes what feels right is the same old wrong we knew twenty years before."

He saw that now. Funny how he'd missed the sensibility of that dynamic a dozen years before. He was younger then. Angrier too. And he'd always felt like he had a lot to prove. To Colt, for appearing so perfect with seemingly little effort. To his father, to show him he was the *good* son, the one who stayed to help the Double S establish the success it enjoyed today. And to show his father what a good marriage was all about, to pick a perfect bride, have the perfect family, and rub his father's nose in it.

He'd tried to re-create what he'd lost as a child when Rita Stafford walked out the door with a simple good-bye. And he'd done it, all right. Right down to marrying the wrong woman. Or maybe being the wrong man. Either way, there was nothing to rub Sam Stafford's nose in, and that might be a wake-up call of its own.

Maybe Sam *wasn't* a horrible husband. Nick had no clue; he'd been a little boy.

Perhaps his mother simply hadn't liked being a mother. "We've had cows reject calves."

Elsa nodded, quiet.

"I've never understood it." He folded his hands, elbows set on the rail as he watched a field of dark red Angus browse in quiet contentment. "I'd reintroduce the calf, and sometimes it would work. Most times, actually." He paused, still watching the cow and calf pairs gently plod through the thick grass field. "But when it wouldn't take, when the mother kept rejecting the baby, I would tell that baby he did nothing to deserve it. It wasn't his or her fault. It had done nothing wrong."

"Because when a parent leaves us and doesn't look back, in our hearts we feel we're to blame. Even when common sense and timing and age tell us otherwise, the child heart within us wonders what we did wrong."

He turned to face her. "But we did nothing wrong."

She nodded in quiet agreement.

"So if Whitney runs off or if I follow the temptation to encourage her to leave, the girls face life wondering what they could have done better?"

"For Cheyenne, probably. She was older and has spent this time re-creating reality with her mother in it. She's invested herself, her time, and her hopes and prayers. Dakota was younger, and she's got a more 'show me' nature. She's able to keep a distance because she doesn't really remember a bond, and her nature doesn't try to cling to the bond."

"Where Cheyenne's does, for all her tough-girl ways."

"Yup."

"A part of me wishes Whitney gone," he admitted. "I don't have the slightest desire to expend the energy to deal with her, to contend with her problems, or to listen to her rationalize irrational behavior."

"I know."

"But I understand the downside of having a mother who doesn't care, and I'm not sure which is worse for the girls." He paused again. "A mother who came back, carrying a host of problems they have to deal with on a regular basis, or the quiet, aching loss, wondering why she left and never returned."

"What if it's not your choice?"

It wasn't. He knew that. But he also knew money could change things around, and he'd be lying if he pretended the idea of paying Whitney to leave hadn't occurred to him.

"We tend to mess things up more by trying to fix what we should simply leave alone," she went on. "Why make it convoluted or make yourself the villain? Why not take each day as it comes and deal with it?"

"Because I like control."

"There's a Stafford trait that bred true." She smiled and nudged his shoulder with hers, and when she did, he looped his arm around her shoulders and drew her close to his side.

It felt right, having her there. Just right. Her quiet presence, the plodding cows and dancing calves, and a soft June breeze.

He turned his head.

She turned hers. And then he was kissing her, loving the feel of Elsa in his arms, snugged against his heart. She brought quiet joy into a frenzied dynamic. Being around her both soothed and aroused, as if her presence made his more whole.

He didn't want the kiss to end.

He held her close, her head to his chest, breathing in the soft scents of farm and fruity shampoo. "I've been waiting to do that again."

"I can't deny the thought has crossed my mind as well."

"Well." He smiled and kissed her again, taking his own sweet time about it, and when he finally released her, he dropped his forehead to hers. "That was perfect."

"Mmm hmm."

"Glad you agree." He hugged her, then led her over to the back paddock and pointed up. "These cows are carrying the future of America's beef."

"I don't want to burst your bubble, but cows have been doing that all along, I believe."

"Not exactly like these, but . . ." He shrugged and nodded. "Yes."

He took her hand again and led her into the nearby barn. "Birthing center, used as needed but only if problems occur. Generally, nature's pretty good at taking its course."

She looked around the barn setup and made a face. "So tell me the truth, Nick."

"Uh-oh."

She smiled, like he hoped she'd do. "Does the science and numbers of it all remove the wonder of birth? The miracle of life? Does the volume make it less personal and more of an income-based outcome?"

It was a natural assumption. Most folks would expect that, especially on a ranch this size, but in truth— "No. As unbelievable as that sounds, we take any loss personally."

"Like you did the night you lost that cow and her calf."

He couldn't deny it. "Yes. It's not about percentages. At that moment, it's all about life and death."

She stared off, past the cows, then motioned up the hill. "Are those horses segregated because they're sick?"

He looked where she was pointing and grabbed her hand. "Come on." He tugged her back to the Mule, hopped in, and turned the key. He drove the four-by-four around the barn and up the lane and pulled up short, just shy of the small field where two horses grazed nonchalantly. "Nate and Bess, meet Elsa. Elsa, this is Nate." He waved to the aging black horse. "And his sister, Bess."

"They're old."

"Fairly ancient by horse standards, yes."

"But—" She looked down at the paddock full of perfectly produced cattle about to produce more of the same. "This doesn't add up."

"Nate and Bess were the first horses on the ranch. Dad rode Nate. Colt's mother rode Bess."

"That means they're thirty years old."

"Midthirties, actually."

She stared at the pair, and when she blinked hard, Nick heard her sniffle. He scrubbed a hand along the back of his neck. "Don't do that."

"What?"

"That," he insisted. He wrapped his arms around her from behind. "No crying allowed."

"I'm not crying. I'm . . . thinking about crying."

"That either."

"Well, then there's no place for me here, Nick Stafford, because I've been known to openly weep at a Hallmark commercial."

"The one where the woman goes back to thank the teacher for believing in her?"

"Stop. You're only making this worse." She hauled in a deep breath and smiled as Bess plodded close, looking for a treat. "I've got nothing for her."

"I do." Nick pulled an apple out of a compartment in the Mule and whacked off a piece with his pocketknife. "You feed her. Unless you're afraid she'll slobber on you."

"As if I care." Elsa chirruped to the horse, arm extended. Bess took the apple with no small amount of drool. Nate plodded over, ready to make friends as long as food was on the line, and when she gave the old gelding the other half, he slobbered too. Nick was just about to offer his sleeve when Elsa swiped both hands across the thighs of her jeans.

And they were mighty nice-looking jeans.

He fell in love with her right then. She hadn't faulted their ranch or their systems, she didn't chastise him with dog shelter numbers for having two breeding dogs, and she handled feeding the old horses like she was born to the farmyard. "Want a wipe for your hands?"

She shook her head as she ran a gentle hand down Nate's nose. "No need. I'll wash up before supper. Which, by the way, I can smell cooking, so we better get back. Angelina might need help."

He didn't want to leave the idyllic moment. Peace had been fleeting these last years, but she was right. They climbed back into the four-by-four and headed toward the house. From his seat on the Mule, he could see the open plot of land slated for his new cabin. They'd staked out the utility areas that morning, so a field of blue and orange flags marked the spot where his new home would sit.

He could picture her there, on his front porch, Achilles curled up on the floor or in the green grass beyond, and the bird . . .

Maybe she'd let him build a birdcage in the barn.

He grinned, knowing she'd never do that, and not caring. Not

caring in the least because the thought of Elsa reading a story or painting a picture in their shared home made him want to build faster.

He should have gone to see her last fall, like her sister advised. He'd
have known her an extra eight months that way. His bad.

But he knew her now. He breathed the scent of her, even when she
wasn't around. She looked right at him when he talked, as if what he
said mattered. She could talk dog, cow, and horse and didn't shrink
away from the convoluted crazy of his ex-wife showing up.

Tranquility.

She brought him a new sense of serenity, he realized as he drove the
Mule into the barnyard. Realization struck as he put the four-by-four
into park.

She needed peace too. Comfort to wipe away the stain of sadness in
her gaze, the shadows in her eyes. He longed to make her happy, so
happy that she never had to reach for somber paints again. Maybe he
didn't have that power, but he would spend a lifetime trying because a
woman like Elsa should never have to hide herself away.

"Elsa!" The kids raced over as she stepped out of the Mule. Dakota held a tiny toad. Noah just shrieked in laughter each time the
tiny critter tried to bound away. "Look what we found! There's a mil-
lion of them over by the pond! They've come out of the water! I love
when that happens!" Elsa laughed and let them pull her across the
yard, racing toward the pond. "This is unbelievable, guys, look at
them. So many!"

"Come away, O human child! To the waters and the wild with a
faery, hand in hand. For the world's more full of weeping than you can
understand."

Nick turned as Angelina moved beside him. "Huh?"

"Yeats. It fits." She directed her gaze toward Elsa and the children.

He considered the words, watching. "It does. When'd you get so
poetical, Ange?"

"Trying to rationalize my life surrounded by a bunch of cowboy yahoos," she replied. "A little whimsy becomes essential."

Whimsy.

He bet Elsa would like whimsy. The word fit, so that's what he'd do. He'd chase the shadows from her eyes with the lighter side of life.

Like you're some expert on that? his conscience scoffed. *Dude, you'd best get a book because whimsy isn't exactly your thing. And what made those shadows in the first place? A smart man would want to know, wouldn't he?*

He shushed the internal warning, washed up, grabbed a drink, and went to help Colt grill the steaks and a rack filled with seasoned, sliced summer squash.

Whoops of laughter drew his attention toward the pond. Then Trey came up the drive in his rental car with Cheyenne riding shotgun. "Things are a little different around here, aren't they?" Colt made the observation as the meat sent up a sizzling invitation.

Nick couldn't deny it. "Night and day."

"Who'd have thought so many discordant chords could come together?" Colt's gaze took in Elsa at the pond. Trey laughing as he picked up Chey and tossed her over his shoulder before he raced across the yard to see what was going on at the water's edge. Isabo setting out food on the porch tables, humming softly, while Angelina brought out more platters.

"And make beautiful music?" Nick added.

Colt snorted. "Aw, ain't that nice? The cowboy poet." He made a gagging sound that almost got him punched, but he was holding a long, thick fork so Nick thought twice.

"Well, you've been doing your share of sweet-talking these days," Nick noted as he raised his drink in a toast to Angelina, chatting with her mother as they finished getting things ready. "I expect you're no stranger to a rhyme or two yourself."

Colt grunted, then shrugged. "A man's got to do what a man's got to do."

Nick laughed. It felt good to laugh with Colt. "That's the truth of it." He wanted this to last. The joy, the laughter, the ambiance.

It wouldn't, of course, not round the clock, but if they could reclaim some joy in being family at long last, Nick Stafford would be okay with that.

ELEVEN

*C*hey, come on. I've got to get you ladies to the school hall for your dress rehearsal in ten minutes. Let's move." Nick jerked a thumb toward the clock as he grabbed one last cinnamon roll from the elevated breakfast bar on Friday morning.

"I need my other costume!"

"I need my ballet shoes!"

"I need—"

"Here, here, and here." Angelina thrust various necessities into the girls' hands and pointed toward the door. "Go. Do not be late. Your instructors have many numbers to go through, not just yours."

The girls dashed out. They didn't look thrilled, but they weren't grumbling either, so that was a plus. "I've got my phone," Nick told her. "Call if there's a problem, okay?"

"I've got Colt, Trey, Murt, and all the others. Your father and Hobbs will be comfortably grumbling on the porch, citing their inactivity as a major source of annoyance. You go, and don't worry about us. I think you're going to have plenty on your hands in that school because Whitney will most likely show up in 'dance mom' mode. Good luck with that, by the way."

He dreaded the thought, so he scowled, pocketed his phone, and headed out.

"Dad, hurry! Mom said she'd meet us there and she's the *only one* who knows how to do my hair!"

"I'm coming." He slipped into the seat, and ten minutes later they pulled into the high school parking lot with a hundred other parents.

Cheyenne pulled her rolling bag full of costume parts. He brought Dakota's bag and the six ironed, hanging costumes. He found the dressing room and started in, but shrieks of dismay stopped him at the door.

Heat burned his cheeks, and Nick had stopped blushing decades before, but he'd almost walked in on a room full of girls getting dressed.

No Whitney.

He stared around the corridor, spotted one of the teachers, and explained his problem.

She gave him a blank look, then made a face. "The other rooms are locked. I can call Bill from maintenance to open one up for us. And I'm so sorry I never thought about needing a room for dance dads to help their girls," she added. Sincere dismay darkened her gaze.

Nick hadn't either because Angelina had helped them the past two years, and Whitney had promised to be here today.

"Dad, I need Mom!"

"We need to get dressed!" Dakota added. "I saw Stella and Clara, and they're both dressed already, Dad!"

What were his options? Angelina was swamped at the ranch. Did he dare ask Elsa to help get the girls into costume?

Absolutely. He dialed her number, started to explain his problem, and didn't get through the first sentence before she cut in. "I'll be right there."

Eight minutes later she walked in the door sporting blue jeans, a pullover shirt, sneakers, and a ponytail. Utterly simple and absolutely beautiful. "You're a lifesaver. Whitney was supposed to meet us here, but she must be running late."

She didn't make a fuss or roll her eyes as if she expected Whitney to mess up. She smiled and shrugged one shoulder. "Happens to all of us. Come on, ladies." She grabbed the girls by the hand and ushered them both into the classrooms doubling as changing rooms.

He paced the hall, and when Dakota pranced his way ten minutes later, he finally breathed again. "You look great."

"Well"—she sashayed the little cowgirl outfit with just the right amount of sass—"I like wearing real ranch stuff, but I can be a dancing cowgirl today. And tomorrow. But I'd rather be home, seeing if Kita's having puppies."

"Angelina's on puppy watch, with Isabo. They'll let us know. I promise. You head back to your class, okay? I think Miss Debbie's about to line you guys up for rehearsal."

"'Kay. And, Daddy?"

"Yes?"

"Thank you for bringing us to the ranch."

Emotion swelled. He knew exactly what she meant. Not that he hadn't taken them to the ranch consistently over the last years. They'd been there often, in Angelina's care while he worked. Now he'd made a commitment to them and the ranch, to become a unit. A true family enterprise. And that's what Dakota meant. He'd brought them home, at last. "You're welcome, darlin'."

Cheyenne and her troupe raced out of the dressing room, more like a stampede of young bulls than a dance class. She didn't look his way, didn't thank him for calling Elsa in. He hoped she had the grace to thank Elsa. If not, he would.

Elsa appeared right then. She gave Chey a thumbs-up, waved to Dakota, and moved his way. "Done for the moment. Let's go watch the rehearsal, then I'll get them ready for their next numbers, if Whitney doesn't make it. There's a long lull before they need to be in costume again, so why don't you go do big ol' cowboy stuff and I'll stay here."

"I can't ask you to do that," he protested, but already he was thinking of ten things he'd rather do than sit for hours of dress rehearsals with other people's kids.

She patted her purse. "I've got a book, and I'm not afraid to duck out to the café for coffee as needed."

"How about I bring one back to you? A mocha with whipped cream?"

She one-upped his offer. "Add in a trip to Cle Elum for maple bars, and I'm all in."

He grinned and bumped knuckles with her. "Deal."

"I'll bring the girls back to the ranch when we're done. With this many kids it will probably run long. You'll be here for three hours tomorrow for the actual performance. I think it's okay to spell you today."

He hugged her, not caring who saw, and several people did. "I appreciate it, Elsa."

"You should," she muttered and gave him a teasing elbow jab to the side as costumed girls dashed in and out of changing rooms. "Let's go watch these first numbers and then you can be on your way."

"Perfect."

It should have been perfect. It should have been a chance for the girls to dress up, practice, and perform the well-rehearsed numbers with their friends. And it was, until Whitney walked in the door midafternoon, clearly hung over and wanting to help.

"Mom's here, at last! Mom!" Cheyenne spotted Whitney as they were heading to the changing room one last time. "Where've you been?"

"I must have overslept," she cooed to Cheyenne, but when she raised her eyes to Elsa's, the confused mix of emotions sent up mental red flags. "But I'm here now, darlings."

Dakota shrunk into Elsa's side. "I want Elsa to help me," she whispered, more into Elsa's jeans than into the air.

"Elsa's not your mommy," Whitney reminded her. Steel knifed her tone. "And I promised you I'd be here."

"But you weren't," Dakota pointed out matter-of-factly, as if that settled everything. She reached for Elsa's hand. "How about you help Cheyenne and Elsa helps me?"

"That's a great solution," Elsa told her. She started to move into the dressing room with Dakota, but Whitney's voice cut deep.

"I'm here to help my *daughters* get ready for their dance recital. Plural. So give me my kid and get out of the way."

Put the girls first. Always.

Elsa weighed the options. She could insist on helping Dakota and make Whitney mad, or she could turn a reluctant Dakota over to her belligerent mother and disappoint the child. Dakota's fear and reluctance were as real as Cheyenne's overexuberance.

"Or we could do it together," she suggested easily, keeping her voice soft. "I'd be okay with that, Whitney."

"Well, I wouldn't." Whitney had folded her arms across her chest, spoiling for a fight Elsa wasn't about to give her. "Give me my kid."

Dakota's dance instructor swooped in from out of nowhere, an answer to unspoken prayer. "I'm going to get Dakota ready with the rest of her group in the next room. I grabbed her costume, and we're good to go! Come on, 'Kota."

"Okay!" Dakota dashed off willingly with the vibrant, young teacher.

Elsa stepped aside. "I'll be in the auditorium, watching, Chey. And then I'll take you gals home after rehearsal."

"I'll take them."

Oh, man.

There was no way she could allow Whitney to drive the girls anywhere, but arguing the point now would upset Cheyenne, and that was the last thing she wanted to do. She moved down the hall, around the corner, and texted Nick. "Whitney here, insisting on driving girls. Help needed."

"On my way," he texted back, and she took a seat in the back of the auditorium, half-fuming, half-praying.

The girls didn't need a scene. Neither did she. Usually she could spot a way to diffuse situations, but as she waited for Nick to arrive, she realized she'd gotten too close to the girls—and their father—to see this clearly.

And that was a problem.

He must have been out on the ranch because he smelled of horse, hay, and lumber, but he got there in time to thwart the face-off, and that's all that mattered to Elsa. Nick had custody of the girls, so there was no arguing with his choice to drive his daughters home. Once both girls had gone through their final numbers to their teachers' satisfaction, he moved into the hallway leading to the only unlocked door, becoming an effective blockade.

Dakota got changed quickly, spotted her dad, and raced down the hall. Elsa slipped into the extra room, gathered Dakota's costume from the last number, then watched as Whitney crammed the pretty, delicate costumes into the bag, ignoring the hangers suspended on the rolling rack nearby.

Cheyenne went pale, watching. "Shouldn't we hang them up, like Angelina did?" Nervousness pinched the girl's voice. That might mean a raise in her awareness of her mother's behavior, or simple fear that Angelina would promptly murder her for being careless with the pricey outfits.

"That's the housekeeper's job," scoffed Whitney. She glanced around and spotted Elsa, but the questioning look said she didn't see Dakota. "Let's go find your sister and I'll take you guys home."

"You mean back to the ranch, right?"

Elsa's ears perked up. Cheyenne was questioning her mother, a healthy sign.

"I said *home.*" Whitney stared down at the girl, and Cheyenne backed down instantly.

"Okay."

Peace at any cost. Elsa wondered how much of Cheyenne's little-girl life had been governed by that mandate. Whitney straightened, grabbed the rolling duffel, plowed it into two folding chairs, swore, and powered her way out of the room.

The remaining kids stared at her, then Cheyenne, then back.

Cheyenne's cheeks went red. Head down, she didn't look left or right as she aimed for the only escape, the far door leading to the hallway. Elsa sized up the situation and forgot she was supposed to be disconnected. She intercepted Cheyenne midway, looped an arm around her shoulders, and kissed her forehead. "Great job today. Ready to head home?"

"Yes."

"Me too, honey."

Cheyenne pressed into her side slightly, just enough to show she appreciated the gesture, and when they moved into the hallway, they had one choice. Duck back into the room or move down the hall where Nick and Whitney were facing off. *Let this be peaceful, Lord. Let common sense and love for these children prevail.*

"What are you really doing here, Nick? Because I'm perfectly capable of taking the girls home."

Holding Dakota snug under one arm, Nick stared at her a few seconds too long.

Whitney didn't squirm. She reacted. "You don't like what you see, cowboy? Well you did, back in the day."

"Mom." Cheyenne's urgent whisper should have softened Whitney's stance.

It didn't. If anything, it gave her a power punch of self-defense. "Your father didn't want much to do with the old man back then, did you, Nick? But now that Sam's at death's door, you want to suck up because of the will, no doubt, because that's the Stafford way. Do whatever it takes for the almighty dollar, and if you trample a few lowlies on the way, that's their problem. Not yours. That about sum it up?"

"Grandpa's dying?" Fear spiked Cheyenne's voice as she zeroed in on Whitney's words. "Dad, is he? For real?"

"I love my grandpa so much!" Dakota took Nick's face in her two little hands. "Is he gonna die, Daddy? Like my first Stripey cat?"

Nick bent low to meet Cheyenne's worried gaze. "He's sick. We know that. But he was breathing just fine when I left him, girls, and we've got great doctors helping him. The rest is up to God, like always." He shot Whitney a dark look, took the roller bag handle, and moved to the big double doors leading outside. "Elsa." He held the door wide, letting Elsa and Cheyenne through before he bumped his way through with the duffel.

"Daddy, my costumes are all wrinkled now." Overwhelmed, Cheyenne looked up at him. Her chin quivered. She blinked hard, twice, pointing toward the rolling bag.

He frowned, not understanding.

"They're supposed to be on hangers." Silent tears streamed down Cheyenne's cheeks. "Angelina worked hard to iron them and now they're all messed up."

Elsa reached for the bag's handle to give him a moment with his daughter. So much sadness, so much drama, so much crazy adult confusion. Why couldn't kids just be kids anymore? Because that's how it should be, as much as possible. Loved, sheltered, protected, and enjoyed.

If she ever had the chance to be a mother, she'd jump in joyfully,

both feet, because there was little on the earth more amazing and wonderful than the gift of a child.

Her costumes . . .

Now Nick was starting to get it. Cheyenne was talking about costumes, but what she meant was life. For the first time since Whitney's
return, Cheyenne was recognizing her mother's frailties. "Costumes
can be fixed, Cheyenne. An iron. A needle and thread. Angelina always
knows what to do."

"Because we hire her to."

Nick bent low, confused and concerned. "Because she loves you,
Chey. She loves all of us. We're family."

Whitney stormed out of the school door just then. She didn't look
their way. She stomped down the stairs and to the adjacent parking lot
as if they didn't exist.

She didn't wave to the girls or wish them luck for the performances
tomorrow. She left in a flurry of turns and tires, heading out of town,
maybe to another bar. The thought of choosing alcohol over their two
beautiful daughters made him want to punch something. But he
couldn't. Instead he wrapped his arm around Cheyenne's shoulders,
wishing he could protect her from everything, which was part of what
got them into this mess in the first place.

Cheyenne's face shadowed. She stared after her mother as Whitney
tore out of the parking lot like some spoiled kid, and then she sighed.

*You wanted Cheyenne to see her mother's true colors, didn't you?
There you go.*

He'd wanted Cheyenne to take a more realistic view of the situation, but he hadn't realized it would be at the cost of Cheyenne's
heart . . . and that broke his.

"I'm starving, Daddy!" Dakota hollered as she worked the buckles
of her shoulder belt. "Can we get chicken fingers for supper? Please?"

"Yes, sure, honey. We'll swing by on the way home."

Elsa's car was parked two rows away. He opened the door for Cheyenne, made sure she got in, then held up two fingers. "Give me two minutes to walk Elsa to her car, okay? And then we'll order chicken fingers."

"Thanks, Dad!" Dakota gave him an enthusiastic thumbs-up with both hands.

Cheyenne stared at the school as if wishing she'd never have to go there again, and she hadn't been any too pleased with school in a long time.

Great.

"She's had a dose of harsh reality. Her dream bubbles were just burst in front of all her dancing peers because Whitney made a scene in the dressing room, so use kid gloves tonight, okay?" Elsa's grimace said whatever happened inside wasn't pretty.

"Come up to the ranch. Please," he added because the last thing he wanted was to end this day on a sour note. "It would be wrong for us to let Whitney's behavior mess up the rest of the day. Come have supper with us. You and Cheyenne can check the dogs together, anything that makes her feel like part of her life is still going right. It was hard to give her the positives she needs without Whitney here. Now it looks like it might become a daily struggle. But maybe if Chey compares the positive influence of you and Ange and Isabo in her life, she'll start to understand that people make their own choices. Good and bad."

"She's eight," Elsa reminded him, but when he started to speak, she held up a hand. "But I agree, totally. She was struggling to succeed in her dream world before. At least this is reality, and if Cheyenne's going to mature and be self-sufficient, she's got to deal with reality."

"I hate that," Nick growled. But then he sighed. "But I hear you, and I should have stopped soft-pedaling things for the girls a couple of years ago. I messed up some too." He stared back toward the truck for a moment. "I need to fix up some old regrets, and I seem to do that better with you around. How about it? Supper with me and my little cowgirls? And maybe later we can figure out if there's something we can do to help Whitney."

"You've got some nice horses on that ranch, Nick."

He nodded, puzzled.

"And when they need water, you can lead them to it—"

"But I can't make them drink." He passed a thoughtful hand over the back of his sunburned neck and frowned, first because if he had half a brain, he'd have slathered some sunscreen on his neck, and second because she was right. He was already trying to solve Whitney's problems for her, and his ex-wife knew exactly what she needed to do. Stop drinking. "Gotcha. Isabo's got shepherd's pie at home, and I'm getting the girls chicken tenders at the diner. Which would you prefer?"

"Both." She smiled up at him and he wanted to hug her. Hold her. Tell her how much her gentle manner meant to him, what it had brought to him, but he had two girls who needed him right now, so he bumped knuckles with her instead.

She grinned as she waggled her fingers in the air afterward. "Bah la la la la."

The film reference made him smile because it was one of the girls' favorites. *"Big Hero 6."*

"One of my faves," she admitted. "Baymax wasn't afraid to sacrifice for love, and that's how every one of us should be. Always."

He'd been mad for a long time because his father had never sacrificed for love, but when he turned up the Double S driveway twenty minutes later, he realized how wide off the mark his thinking had been. Sprawling before him was a work of great sacrifice, a legacy, a glory to behold, which could mean he was mistaken here too.

Was his father right to sacrifice so much of his time with his kids to build it?

No. He knew that as the girls trundled their dance bags toward the house.

But looking out over the wide, rolling fields of Stafford land, a new reality dawned. He'd been struggling for three years to raise two little girls and work on the ranch with a full-time house manager and a solid ranch staff.

His father had raised three boys, two of his own and the third one adopted, and built an empire because he saw the future of modified beef production before most people knew it would be humanly possible, and he implemented it. Was it perfect?

No.

Was it awful?

He stared across the patchwork-quilt crop fields and knew it wasn't. So why did he feel like he'd gotten the short end of the stick all his life?

Because your mother walked out and never came back.

Did it all come down to that root cause? A motherless child always searching to fill a void?

"You're thinkin' hard, son."

He was. Maybe questions that had no answers. Or maybe answers he didn't want to hear.

He turned as his father walked his way. "And you're looking stronger today."

"Up and down." Sam shrugged, leaned his arms against the fence rail, and surveyed the broad-reaching ranch. "Can't deny I'm hopin' this transplant business will do the trick, if it's available. But if not?" He aimed a look at Nick. "I'm leaving my boys a piece of me that will live on forever because land never dies."

Nick's chest went tight. So did his throat. Was it because of Sam's words or Whitney's caustic proclamation? Maybe both. "I'd be okay with you staying around awhile more, Dad. If you could arrange it."

An almost smile softened Sam's face. "I've been in conference with the Big Man Upstairs. He says I'd best leave it to him at this point, since I wasn't good at doing that before. So I am."

"Then I'll let him know I'm not ready to say good-bye," Nick noted softly. "No sense building all this and leaving us shorthanded. I'm pretty sure God will understand that."

"From your lips to his ears," Sam agreed, but he kept his voice gentle too, a rarity with the Stafford men.

The dinner gong sounded from the front porch. Both men turned. Sam met Nick's gaze as Elsa's car came up the driveway, squawking a protest as it rolled to a stop. "That woman's a rare find. Not that I'm telling you what to do, but I'm just saying. A mighty rare find." He waved to Elsa as he crossed to the front porch where Hobbs was setting up a game of checkers on the rustic table. "Get that game outta my sight, Hobbs. We aren't old yet, nor dead. You and me are going to find some way to be helpful around here because I've got no intention of being put to pasture before God and I say . . . But first, food."

Hobbs gave him a crooked grin and followed him inside as Nick crossed the stone yard to meet Elsa. He held out a box of maple bars and watched her eyes brighten in appreciation, and when they did, he leaned down and swept a gentle kiss to her mouth, so sweet and light.

He'd messed up before. He'd married Whitney more to show his father another way, that Nick could and would do his own thing and be successful, much like his father had done after losing Colt's mom.

Two men, pretty much alike and both fairly stupid.

But kissing Elsa felt smart, and right, and good, and perfect.

He'd prayed on a lot of things these past few years, not the least of which was his daughter's life earlier that spring. And God had shown him so much.

Cupping Elsa's chin gently, he gave her one last breath-stealing kiss, then paused. "I could get used to this, Elsa." He let his gaze linger with hers, then stroked one finger along the curve of her pretty cheek. So soft. "I could get real used to this, and that's all I'm sayin'."

She sighed.

The sigh about did him in because the veiled sadness behind the sigh made him want to make everything better in Elsa's world. But what had she just told him about Whitney? That you can lead a horse to water but you can't make it take that life-sustaining drink.

He wanted Elsa's trust and, yes, her love. He could admit that now, absolutely. But he *needed* her trust because love without trust was, well, not love. And he wanted both with this woman.

She could get used to this too, Elsa decided when Nick finally broke the kiss.

She could get used to the heartfelt attentions of a strong, good man, the scents of ranch and farm pulling up sweet memories of a younger Elsa, the sounds of children running and laughing, arguing and singing.

It wouldn't take much, and maybe it was too late already, because something about the Double S made her feel right, and Elsa hadn't felt right in a long time.

Cheyenne, Noah, and Dakota raced to the front porch. "Gotta get washed up for supper," Noah yelled, as if they were silly to delay Isabo's good dinner by something as inconsequential as kissing.

"Should we check Kita first?" Elsa hesitated before they went in. "I think we should. I can always warm stuff up later."

"Then, yes. Chey?" Nick called through the screen door. "Let's check the barn, okay?"

Cheyenne came quickly. "Before supper?"

"Babies can't read clocks. They come when they're ready, and it's better to have a feel for what's going on," Elsa told her.

She followed them quickly. "I think it's a great idea, Elsa. We can eat anytime, right?"

"Exactly." Elsa smiled down at her, and when Cheyenne took hold of her right hand, she also took hold of Elsa's heart. A whimper from the back of the foremost barn said something was happening. They found the mother dog pacing the far corner of a clean stall. She gave another worried whimper, then moved forward and pushed her snout into Cheyenne's outstretched hand.

"Is she okay?"

"She's in labor," Elsa told her. "That means someone either brings supper out here or we eat later, because we need to be on hand for this."

"You don't mind?" Nick asked, as if she might be a few cards short of a full deck, but Elsa was too busy making him a list.

"Sharp, short scissors and alcohol preps. Or just a bottle of alcohol will do. Some kind of bowl or basin, a nesting box with a clean old sheet or towel in it, extra towels and old sheets, a scale, a notepad for listing weights as the puppies grow so we can track the growth of any laggards, a warming light, a coffee for me, and a latte for obstetrical assistant, Cheyenne. Oh, and aprons or old T-shirts for us to put on so we don't ruin our clothes."

Nick looked surprised and pleased, but mostly surprised, and when he and Angelina came back with a tote full of supplies a few minutes later, Elsa smiled her thanks and pulled on one of his old Gray's Glen high school basketball shirts. Then she draped a table she'd found in a far corner with an old sheet and had Cheyenne set up a nursing station right there.

"I forgot a pencil for recording weights," Elsa said as the red-and-white dog started to circle, pawing up straw into a rounded pile. "Or a pen."

Nick brought back a pen from the barn office as puppy number one entered the world.

"She's having them, Dad!" Cheyenne's eyes went round at the sight. "I can't believe this! I'm watching puppies be born! Isn't this the coolest thing ever?"

"It is," Elsa agreed happily, keeping her voice soft. "Now we'll just wait while she tends the first one or two. The trick is not to bother her until we need to. Kita is the best judge of how things are going. She's had a litter before?"

"Two years ago, a little earlier than we intended."

"Life has a way of doing that, doesn't it?" Elsa quipped as she took a seat on the ground. Cheyenne followed suit, and when Elsa crooned words of love and encouragement to the beautiful and industrious dog, Cheyenne did likewise. Nick found an office chair, set it down, straddled it backward, and leaned his arms against the chair back. "Now what?"

"We wait," Elsa answered softly. "Our goal is not to interfere, but if it's a big litter, we need to be able to give the newest babies first dibs on Mom while we tuck the firstborns aside."

"Will she miss them?" Cheyenne asked. "Won't that worry her?"

"Giving birth keeps them pretty busy, so it works," Elsa assured her. "And each new pup deserves some time with its mommy, time to be cleaned up, cuddled, rolled around."

"That's just weird," Chey whispered back. "Rolling a brand-new baby around?"

"It stimulates them to breathe and stretch," Nick explained. "It gets the baby dried off, gets the blood flowing and the baby taking nice big, deep breaths. That way any moisture in the puppy's lungs gets pushed out, and then the lungs are nice and clear."

"Like a cow."

"Yes. Only they usually only have one baby to worry about. From the looks of Kita, I'm thinking seven or eight puppies."

"Really?" Cheyenne clapped her hands together silently, and her thrilled expression said the angst of the afternoon had been forgotten in the beauty of this new moment.

God's perfect timing.

Elsa hadn't thought of that in a long time. Circumstances had made the possibility of his timing surreal, but now she realized those circumstances were all about man's selfishness. The glow on Chey's face said this opportunity charted the beginning of a new course. Cheyenne Stafford, ranch hand and general cowgirl. When Kita began the process of delivering puppy number two, Elsa picked up the first puppy and dictated stats to Cheyenne. "Twelve ounces, boy, liver and white, both ears liver colored." She deftly set the tiny boy pup back down alongside his mother while Kita tended the newest member of the family. "Nick, can you check on BeeBee? Even though she's not due for days, it's not unusual for them to go early."

"Good idea." He left and returned fairly quickly. "All is quiet on that front. But she's been pawing straw into the corner, so it won't be long, right?"

"Sometimes they do that for days," Elsa answered. "And sometimes they do it when they're in labor." Elsa exchanged looks with Cheyenne. "Eventually you need to rest tonight because you've got a big day tomorrow, Miss Cheyenne."

"I can sleep during the day," Cheyenne supposed, and the excitement in her voice said dance recitals were the last thing on her mind. "This is so much more important."

"Nick, how much do you generally ask for one of these pups?" Elsa wondered, and when he named a price similar to what her father had drawn for their puppies, she swallowed hard. "That ups the stakes a bit, doesn't it?"

"Nah." Nick reached out and laid a hand against her cheek. "It's never about the cost, remember? It's always about life."

She fell head over heels right then because Elsa was pretty sure that

most people—well, most businessmen—would see each pup as a miniature bank account. But not Nick. And he'd told her the same thing
about his father when he pointed out the pair of equine pensioners loll-
ing in sweet green grass up the hill. Life first.

Angelina and Colt showed up just then. "We wanted to see if you
guys need anything. We can bring supper out here."

"That would be great." Cheyenne got up and hugged Colt, then
Angelina. "I can't believe I get to help Kita and the puppies. And Bee-
Bee will be having hers soon too. It's like a miracle, isn't it, Uncle Colt?"

Nick's rough and tough older brother peeked into the stall. And
then he locked eyes with his fiancée, and the look they exchanged re-
flected the world that lay before them, filled with joy, babies, and second chances. Oh, Elsa wanted that. All of it. Seeing their happiness
sharpened the ache she'd carried for three long years.

God wants his children joyful. The voice of her conscience chided
her gently. *Throw off the mantle of sadness and wear joy. It's time, Elsa.*

"I think number three is on the way," Nick said softly. Elsa picked
up the second puppy while Kita was busy delivering its brother or sister,
weighed her, and reported the statistics to Cheyenne.

Colt nudged her shoulder once she'd replaced the puppy into the
stall. "Nice system. That way you can keep track of their gain and keep
them straight from the beginning."

"It's what we did at my parents' place. It's basic but effective."

Colt faced Nick. He kept his voice soft but loud enough for Elsa
to hear. "If you let this one get away, I will never let you forget it.
Understand?"

Nick scowled at him but then winked at Elsa. "I've got this."

"You do?" Elsa arched a brow and looked from brother to brother,
but then she smiled. "Well. Maybe you do, at that. Did you guys leave
Trey in there with the other kids? Because that's kind of mean, isn't it?"

"Trey loves kids, but you're right. If we hang out here too long,

Dakota and Noah will be clamoring for a visit, and I told them they have to wait until morning so that Kita and the pups have time to relax a little."

"That's perfect, Colt," Elsa agreed. "Too many people make mothers nervous. Nervous mothers make mistakes."

"I like having an expert on hand." Colt draped his arm around Angelina's shoulders. "Let's go get supper for these guys. Then we can make a fire so the kids can roast marshmallows tonight. We'll listen to frogs and gaze at the stars."

"I'd love that."

Elsa stared after them.

Kids and campfires and frogs and stars. Keeping it real.

A puppy whined. She turned and caught Nick's appraising gaze, and when he smiled, heat climbed her cheeks.

He edged closer as Cheyenne retook her nursing station position on the floor. "My brother is rarely right, and when he is, he has a tendency to never let me forget it, but in this case"—he shoulder-nudged her gently—"I'm totally willing to take his advice. Not letting you get away has become a new, *and very nice,* goal. Just so you know."

She faced him full on so he'd understand the import of her words. "And just so you know? I've got no intention of going anywhere. I'm enjoying being right where I am."

His smile widened to a grin. "Well, then."

"I think we've got another one coming." Cheyenne's excited whisper turned them back to the stall.

"Cheyenne, I'm going to have you pick up puppies one and two and put them in the box so Kita can concentrate her efforts on the newest puppies. And, Nick, do you guys have a caged warming lamp someplace?"

"What's a caged warming lamp?" Cheyenne asked as she gently cradled the first puppy into the box nearby.

"A hot light with a protective shield around it so it's less of a fire hazard."

"Oh."

"It's almost summer." Nick pointed outside. "Warmth comes with the territory."

"I know, but optimum temperature for puppies is ninety degrees the first week, then down by five each succeeding week."

He stood. "I'm on it. They're in the back barn, so it'll take me a few minutes."

By nine fifteen, nine perfectly healthy puppies lay in a row along Kita's side, four boys and five girls.

"I can't believe it." Cheyenne reached out and gave Elsa a spontaneous hug, an embrace that felt good and right. "Elsa, thank you for letting me help."

Nick cleared his throat.

"Oh, and you too, Daddy!" She peeked up at him from the circle of Elsa's arm and grinned. "But I'm so excited that Elsa let me be a nurse, weigh the puppies, keep an eye on things. That's like the best night of my life ever."

"Mine too," Elsa whispered, and she hugged the girl one more time. "But you need to go shower and get to bed."

"Are you going home?" Cheyenne wondered. "Who's going to watch over the pups tonight?"

"That would be me." Hobbs ambled into the barn with a tall mug of coffee. "I'm fairly useless for a few weeks yet, but I know how to keep an eye on all kinds of things, pups included. And might I add, little missies, you done a right fine job of tendin' this mama. The important thing is keepin' mama calm and pups straight, and Miss Elsa here's got the lowdown on that. Mighty fine work, both of you."

"Thanks, Hobbs." Cheyenne hugged him gently, mindful of his bad arm.

"You're welcome, sweetheart. Sleep well."

"Oh, she will," Nick whispered as he watched her race off. "And she'll be up and out here early to check on things, no doubt. Why did it take me so long to see that she's an animal lover with a rancher's heart? Was I just stupid or too protective?"

"The resident psychologist pleads the fifth," Elsa said with a laugh.

"Which means both," he supposed with a wry smile. "Hobbs, thanks. A little shuteye would feel good right about now. Elsa, you want to stay here for tonight? We've got a daybed in the office. I can take that, and you can have my room."

"And that way you're here if BeeBee starts having puppies." Hobbs set his coffee mug down on the long, low table they'd used for weigh-ins.

She could wake up with the crazy of ranch life burbling around her. Tend puppies and children and see Nick. But it wasn't her place to do that. Could it be, someday?

Perhaps. But not when secrets lay between them. Secrets that had gone on long enough. "I'd love to, but I have to tend that crazy bird and take Achilles home. I'll come back in the morning, though, unless Bee-Bee starts into labor tonight. She looks comfortable right now, so I'm guessing we've got some time. But I could be wrong."

"I'll call you if she starts," Hobbs promised. "You're most likely right, but first-timers can be a dickens to manage."

"Thanks, Hobbs."

"My pleasure, Doc."

On the way to her car, Nick dashed into the house, got his keys, then came back outside. "I'll meet you at your place."

She glanced from his truck to her car and back. "Why?"

"I'm seeing you home."

Warmth escalated again because what kind of man did that? Thought of that?

The best kind.

"Nick, there's no need. I'm a big girl; I can find my way home—"

His kiss stopped the argument, and she had to admit, kissing was more fun than talking. "Stop fussing. It's how it's done, Elsa. The right way."

"Okay." She drove home, happy. Calm. Excited. The blend of emotions took her every which way, and when Nick walked her to her door a few minutes later, she realized that happy had become the norm again.

And it felt marvelous.

"Thank you for seeing me home."

He grinned a lazy grin in the slanted lamplight. "My pleasure." And when he leaned in for a kiss, then paused, making her wait, her heart about paused too.

She could live a life with this man, a full and contented life with this man, whose grace and goodness shone in all he did, and when he finally touched his lips to hers, she wanted it to be forever.

He sighed, bumped his forehead to hers, and sighed again. "I'm falling for you, Elsa. I know we haven't known each other long, but that's the truth of it. I needed to tell you."

A mental warning knell made her pull back. It wasn't his speed that caused the internal nerves.

He thought he knew her, or was getting to know her. But he didn't know the dark side, the oppressive anxiety that had weighed her down. If he did, would he trust her with his heart? With his children? "Do we have to rush?" She leaned back against his arms and faced him. "Can we take some time and let things develop? There's a lot we don't know about each other, and so little time to talk. Private time, I mean."

"We're here now." He held her loosely, waiting.

They were, and that might be fine if she could predict his reaction. She couldn't, and she wasn't going to throw the already heightened drama of the dance recital into a bigger tailspin than what had happened today. She shook her head. "Tomorrow's going to be stressful enough for the girls, and I don't want long, drawn-out conversations to mess up the day. But maybe tomorrow evening? Once the girls are settled and the recital's over?"

"Sure. But Elsa . . ." He waited until she met his gaze. "I don't think there's anything you can tell me that will change the way I feel."

Oh, Nick . . .

He had no clue what he was saying. She knew that. And when he kissed her good night, she prayed he was right, but she understood the raw truth. Two unstable women had played havoc with his heart already. She was pretty sure Nick Stafford wouldn't want to take a chance on a third.

TWELVE

*P*uppies? Healthy and nursing. The ranch? Being overseen by Murt with a steady barrage of advice from Hobbs.

Trey was bringing Sam to the recital; Colt was bringing Angelina, Isabo, and Noah. Nick had picked up Elsa two hours before, leaving enough time to check the puppies and BeeBee and think about what life could be like in the future.

He climbed into the driver's seat, started the engine, then paused because the rightness of it all seemed unbelievable. Elsa beside him; the girls in the backseat, not fighting. Peace in the kingdom—a welcome rarity. Bliss, he decided as he turned the SUV around and drove down the long, sloping drive. Right now he had all the elements of the life he'd wished for so long ago. Family. Faith. Friends. A woman he could trust. And his ranch, brimming with strong, healthy animals, a tribute to good stock-raising standards. It wouldn't last. Life had a way of throwing unhittable curve balls.

Whitney could start some kind of firestorm and mess up the day. The girls could stumble through their performances and come undone. Or a crucial piece of hair ribbon could be misplaced, inciting tears of frustration.

They'd handle it like Elsa suggested. One problem at a time, day by day.

He was blessed; he knew that completely, and as he paused at the roadside, he motioned to Cheyenne. "Hey, Chey, can you send that box this way please? To Elsa?"

"Sure can." The girls giggled as Cheyenne passed a wrapped package up to the front seat.

"What's this?" Elsa looked at them, then Nick. "Is this a present?"

"Yes!" Dakota fist-pumped the air as if Elsa's conclusion deserved amazement. "That's exactly what it is!"

"I'm not opposed to presents as a general rule, but why am I getting one?" Elsa wondered as she slipped the ribbon from the big floral-wrapped box. "It's not my birthday."

"I don't even know when your birthday is," Nick confessed. "Which means we do need to talk."

"October fifth, and it's perfect because I love fall," she told him. She maneuvered the ribbon, then slipped off the box cover to reveal the hat she'd admired at Hammerstein's. "Nicholas Stafford. How did you know?"

He grinned because he couldn't help it. "You like it? Really? Deenie said you would."

"Not like, love. I've looked at this hat every time I've gone into Hammerstein's. I've tried it on twice, but I knew it would blow my budget out of the water. Nick, you shouldn't have. Really."

"Says the woman who just helped deliver nine pricey puppies. I figured I owed you something, darlin'."

"You called Elsa darlin'!" Dakota half-screeched. "You love her!"

"When you're really good friends, sometimes you use sweet nicknames like that," Elsa explained logically.

"Do you like it so much, Elsa? A lot?" Cheyenne leaned up, which meant her seat belt wasn't snugged as tight as it should have been. "It looks amazing on you."

"Tighten your seat belt," she scolded, then turned so Cheyenne could see the hat better. "You think?"

Cheyenne snugged the belt and nodded quickly. "Oh, yeah, the turquoise and silver go with your eyes. It's so pretty!"

"Chey's right. It looks great on you."

"But I can't wear it into the dance recital," Elsa noted as Nick pulled up into the student drop-off loop. "I'll leave it here, and then I'll wear it all around the ranch."

"Today and tomorrow? And every day?" The innocence of Dakota's question hung in the air.

"Well, I'm not promising every day," Elsa said. "But I do love hanging out with you guys."

"Church tomorrow?" Nick asked as he met Elsa around the back of the car. "Because I'd like that. A lot."

"I'd be honored. As long as BeeBee's not in the middle of whelping."

The sincerity of her words stirred his heart.

She'd be honored to be with him. *With them.*

A future he'd once discounted spread out before him. A future with Elsa and the girls. He'd been down for so long that feeling happy and expectant almost felt wrong, but it wasn't wrong. He knew that. He knew it was time to let God take the lead and believe in the goodness again.

He leaned down, swept a quick kiss to Elsa's mouth, then kissed each of the girls. "I'll see you inside. I'm going to grab seats on the left side after I park the car."

"I'll find you."

She would, too, because honest women like Elsa meant what they said, and Nick hadn't had that, well . . . ever. The change went beyond refreshing to just plain, old-fashioned nice. And he was okay with that.

The high school auditorium filled quickly. Parents and grandparents, siblings, aunts and uncles, friends, and neighbors all congregated at the high school on dance recital day. Refreshments were sold in the spacious cafeteria, and area vendors manned displays of goods and services aimed at dance moms and the community in general. Merchants understood that dads were more likely to hand over money or plastic for their princess performers on recital day, and the thickening crowd buzzed with anticipation, conversation, and gossip.

"Elsa, I can't find my—"

"Bright pink ribbon? The one pinned to your outfit?"

Cheyenne made a face. "Sorry!"

"Uh-huh. Come here, let me tie this around the bun." Elsa looked at one of Cheyenne's fellow students, studied the bow, then frowned. "I'm not sure how she rigged that." She tried twice, failed, then waved another mother their way. "Can you show me how to make that knot? Mine comes out looking more like a pretzel than a bow."

"Sure." The mother had Cheyenne sit, wove the ribbon around, down, up, and through, then back. "There we are."

"I am forever in your debt," Elsa told her. A distant door creaked open, and the sounds of Maroon 5 came through softly. "That's the older girls. Dakota's crew will be next, you're up in three numbers, then you've got a break. I'll meet you back here, okay?"

"Yes. Thank you, Elsa!"

"You're welcome, honey." Cheyenne's group moved out to line up backstage.

Elsa hauled in a deep breath.

She'd stayed out of schools purposely for years. Working in classrooms, picking up kids for counseling, and meeting with team professionals to discuss a child's issues had been a regular part of her day as a push-in consult in Brant Park.

Facing school halls, classrooms, and lunchrooms had dredged up a past she'd tried to bury, but the old anxiety didn't rise up strong today. She felt good being here for Cheyenne and Dakota. As if she belonged. And tonight she'd tell Nick and let the pieces fall into place. No matter how he reacted, she would take each step forward, knowing she was on more solid ground.

For the moment she pushed it all aside. This was a day for pleasure and normalcy. A day to celebrate. She hurried, eager to join Nick and the family. Dakota should be lined up, Cheyenne was with her troupe, and Elsa should have about a half hour to sit with Nick and whatever Staffords had made it into town. And then back to a costume change for Cheyenne.

Dancers flitted in and out of classroom dressing rooms. Fairies, ballerinas, and street punks joined preschool zebra-looking creatures. So cute, fresh, and innocent.

She moved through the propped-open access door, tiptoed down the carpeted aisle, and spotted Nick. They'd saved a seat for her on the outside of the row, an easy spot to access when costume changes ruled the day. She sat down and sent the Stafford group a smile and a wave, enjoying the grace of a perfect afternoon. By the time the performances were over and awards presented, the kids and the audience were tired. Angelina intervened as Elsa moved toward the door. "Let me stow their stuff away. You've been in and out of the changing rooms a dozen times between the two of them. Take a minute to relax."

A nice offer like that should never be shrugged off. "Thanks, Angelina." She turned as Isabo and Sam moved toward the nearby ramp. Noah had hit his dancing tolerance over an hour before. Colt had taken him to the town playground, a friendlier environment for a little guy who got tired of sitting. Nick was following Isabo and Sam up the ramp. She stepped through and held the hallway door open for them.

Background confusion filled the air. Relatives and kids milled back and forth, a crowd of people in a confined space. Voices rose and fell from multiple directions, for varying reasons. Congratulations, instructions, reassurances, questions.

Lots of people in a limited space with a crush of voices.

Elsa stepped against the wall, as far from the action as she could get with limited options. The push of bodies and the loud, jumbled voices hit too many simultaneous triggers.

Reporters. Cameramen. Throngs of people outside her office and then her apartment when the Internet yielded her address. Shouting questions, pushing microphones in her direction. Wanting to know if she suspected anything. Had she seen anything to indicate Will Belvedere's state of mind. Why had the judge ruled in the mother's favor for custody? And did she regret her recommendation to the judge?

Who would ask those kinds of questions? And yet . . .

Could she have prevented that awful event with a simple phone call?

She moved closer to Sam, trying to focus on him, not the crowd.

"They did well for themselves." Pride and exhaustion thickened the sick man's words. "But I can't say I'm sorry they're turning in their dancing shoes for riding boots." Sweat soaked Sam's face, and he mopped his forehead with a white hanky as Nick took hold of his arm in a kind, caring gesture. "But it was good to be here to see them, Nick. Real good."

Sam's face swam before her, out of focus. She closed her eyes, willing herself to be strong in the moment, the joy of *this* day, *this* time.

"It was." Nick's steady tone fought through the haze. "I'm glad you could be here, Dad."

She centered on Nick's voice as she pushed the unwanted surge of adrenaline down. *Focus on Nick. Focus on now. You're fine. Everything's okay.*

"And their mother never showed," Sam added, and there was no missing the disgust in his voice. "Though I was guilty of that too many times myself, so I won't mention it around the girls."

Elsa heard Sam's words, but her thoughts clung to one word only. *Guilty.*

Sam was guilty.

Elsa was guilty.

Emotions crawled to a spiral around her, slow at first, then faster, an approaching storm.

"Cling to God, Elsa! When those moments come, when they start to take hold, hold on to him who made us, who made the heaven and the earth." Her mother's words during the worst times. She grabbed hold of the wisdom now. Isaiah's sweet verse of comfort, a favorite . . .

"So do not fear, for I am with you; do not be dismayed, for I am your God. I will strengthen you and help you; I will uphold you with my righteous right hand."

"I expect the girls noticed Whitney's absence anyway." Nick's voice, answering Sam.

Of course they would notice. Elsa knew that. Kids always did. They discerned more than grownups gave them credit for.

"I'm so scared, Elsa."

Christiana, sharing her fear with a person of trust. Longing for help. Seeking safety from those around her.

"Absolutely not!"

A loud voice rang out above the hallway melee. Loud, yet harsh and controlled, a strange combination. A combination she remembered too well.

Elsa turned quickly. Others turned too.

"It's my weekend, Aubrey, which means Kaitlyn's going with me, and that's that. But nice try." The man's powerful voice matched his appearance. Broad. Strong. And angry.

"I made a promise to my daughter, and I intend to keep it." Bitterness deepened the young mother's tone. She fisted her hands.

"That's your problem." The father stood tall and grim, football player size. Massive shoulders filled out a nondescript golf shirt. He crossed thick, muscular arms over his chest, and his voice, deep and low, resonated throughout the hall. He wasn't shouting. She was. But it was *his* voice that commanded attention. A voice that sounded very much like Will Belvedere's from three long years ago. "Your problem," he repeated. "Not mine. My weekend started at five last evening and ends at five tomorrow night. That's what the court said. That's how we roll. There are no other options, Aubrey."

"I had no other options . . ." From Will Belvedere's rambling note, as if excusing himself of his heinous crime.

Angry tears rolled down Aubrey's cheeks. She hissed at him with such venom that he should have stepped back.

He didn't. He did nothing to defuse the moment, and any minute their little girl would come out of the dressing room into the middle of bitter chaos.

"I refuse to live like this, Peter."

The mother's angry words put Elsa's heart into a barrel roll. *No other options . . . Refusing to live . . . I'm so scared, Elsa . . .*

Voices merged into a high-pitched tone, pulsing in her brain. She raised her hands to block the sound, but it was no longer the current sounds that were forcing the issues.

It was the voices from the past, silenced by the grave, voices she should have listened to more carefully or more closely.

Voices that were now gone forever.

Eyes closed, hands up, she slipped to the floor and put her head between her knees, once again wishing it would all go away.

"Nick!"

The fear in Angelina's voice pulled Nick's attention away from the arguing couple. She pointed behind him as she pushed her way through the crowd.

"Dulce María, madre de Dios, ruega por nosotros." Isabo muttered the old prayer as she released Sam's other arm and bent low.

He spotted Elsa, head tucked on the floor, and his heart jumped rhythm. He squatted too. "Hey, hey, what's wrong? Elsa, are you sick? Are you—"

Angelina copied his stance on the opposite side. "Let's get her out of here."

"But what if she's hurt?" Nick laid a hand of caution on Angelina's arm. "We don't know what's going on, Ange, maybe—"

"Panic attack. Help me get her out of the crowd, okay?"

Panic attack?

Nick didn't have time to process the words. They brought Elsa upright while Isabo cleared a path to the exit. As they moved through the doors, Isabo touched his arm. "I will go see to Sam and the girls with Trey."

He didn't remember nodding, but he was grateful to have Isabo and Trey on hand.

"Elsa. Sit."

He started to chastise Angelina for being too abrupt, but she surprised him by pulling out a tiny packet, snapping it open, and putting it beneath Elsa's nose. "Smelling salts, Elsa. Breathe."

She did. Her head came up, eyes wide as the ammoniated scent hit the air. She inhaled again, raised her eyes, and spotted him. Her sad expression cut him to the quick.

He bent low. "Hey." He put a hand to her cheek and kept his voice soft and tender. "It's okay, Elsa. It's okay. It was stifling in there." He jutted his chin toward the school. "I expect you weren't the only one feeling faint."

She stared at him. Her throat convulsed. Tears filled her eyes, then ran over. When he reached out to comfort her, she drew back as far as the seat would allow. She began to speak just as the school door flung open.

The fighting couple barged out. The man strode forward in long, hard strides. He held a little girl's hand on one side and a rolling bag on the other, and the child had to run to keep up with his pace. The mother hurried after him, carrying the argument all the way to the car, letting everyone—including a sweet, brown-haired little girl from Dakota's class—hear her litany of complaints.

Elsa stared after them, eyes wide. Her jaw quivered, and Angelina slipped onto the stone wall beside her. "Elsa."

Elsa cued into her voice and turned her way.

"You're safe. You're fine. There's nothing here to hurt you. Or her." She indicated the little girl with a look that way.

"How can we be sure?" It was Elsa's voice, but tiny, as if not daring to say the words out loud. "How can we ever be sure, Angelina?"

"We can't." Angelina held her attention with a firm hand on her arm. "So we do our best and let God take charge. The Alpha and the Omega, the One who sees all, who welcomes the innocent into his kingdom with loving embrace."

"I want to believe that." Elsa gripped Angelina's arms with both hands. She held so tight her knuckles strained white, and her expression cinched a knot around Nick's heart. "I want to believe that so badly. And I was doing so much better. Wasn't I?"

Better? Better than what?

"Take it one day at a time, just like you've been doing, and don't you dare let one misstep push you backward. You've come so far."

Angelina's tone both scolded and comforted. "God sees. He loves. He knows."

"He knows what, exactly?" Nick looked from one woman to the other. They might be privy to this conversation, but he didn't have a clue what they were talking about, and that didn't sit well with him. He had tried to be open and honest from his first meeting with Elsa. He took his hand away from Elsa's shoulder and rocked back on his heels. "Would someone care to tell me what's going on? Because if there's something wrong, I should know. Don't you think?"

Elsa looked at him. She began to answer as his phone vibrated. He ignored the phone, but when it went off again, almost instantly, he grabbed it.

Rye Bennett was calling from the sheriff's office. For Rye to call twice and not just leave a message meant something was wrong. "Rye, what's up?"

"It's Whitney."

Elsa was falling apart in front of him, and the sheriff was calling about Whitney? "What about her? What's happened?"

"She's had an accident up on Route 970. She's all right. The car's a mess. My guess is that she totaled it."

"Is she sober?"

"Yes."

At least there was that to be thankful for. He'd started the day happily, looking forward with hope and confidence.

That changed a few minutes ago.

He'd trusted Elsa. Sure, he knew she had issues. Who didn't? And with all their talk of trust and harmony, putting others first, he figured if there was anything seriously amiss, she'd tell him, because she preached honesty and integrity.

It seemed clear right now that she didn't practice what she preached, and he'd already been down that road a couple of times, once with his mother and once with his former wife.

He didn't just *want* honesty. He longed for it. He needed to be able to trust his relationships going forward.

Trey came through the school door right then. He held it ajar for Isabo, Sam, and the girls, and as the kids rushed his way, he couldn't look at the sadness in Elsa's eyes.

Put the girls first.

She preached that loud and long, so that's exactly what he'd do. Whitney could stew at the local jail, waiting for a ride, and Elsa could . . .

He had no idea what Elsa could or would do, and right now . . . he didn't care.

Elsa watched Nick stride away and didn't blame him. She'd do the same thing if the situations were reversed, except she couldn't imagine big, strong Nick Stafford falling apart. Getting mad, yes.

Collapsing into a blubbering heap?

Not likely.

She pulled a deep breath and stood.

"Better?" Angelina kept her tone level.

"Yes. And embarrassed."

"Pff." Isabo had walked back up the steps from the parking lot. "We all have moments when things from the past creep up on us. After a cowardly cur of a man shot my beloved husband, I had many such moments. Time and faith have eased them. And love." Isabo grazed Angelina's face with one hand. "Let's get back to the ranch and enjoy food and peace and quiet."

"I don't know how much peace and quiet there will be when the men react to Whitney's accident. But I sure could use a cup of coffee, Mami." The women began to walk toward the parked vehicles. The crowd had thinned. Colt had gone back to the house with the rest of the family.

"I, as well," Isabo confirmed. "And it is wise to give Nick some time, I believe."

"The trick with Staffords is, how much time?" Angelina unlocked the SUV and the three women climbed in, with Isabo taking the seat behind her daughter. Elsa slumped against the cool leather.

Angelina glanced right, then left as she pulled out onto the road. "Too much and they're stuck-in-the-mud stubborn, and that's gotten them into plenty of trouble before. Let's go home and get things done, and we'll let things unwind around us. Eventually they will," she added. "Sam and his boys don't generally take the easy or quickest path. But they get there after a while."

Elsa leaned forward slightly. "Can you drop me at home please?"

Angelina met her gaze in the rearview mirror. "Because?"

She hesitated, wishing she could have been different. A different woman with a different past, but she wasn't. "It's better that way."

Isabo groaned.

The noise made Angelina grimace. "My mother needs no words to voice her opinion, as you can see."

"Your mother's a tough woman," Elsa said softly. "Tough and wise. Her strength becomes her." She sat back, wishing she lived close enough to walk. A walk would give her time to decompress.

"You sure you want me to do this?" Angelina asked at the intersection. "I think you should come to the ranch with us. Cheyenne and Dakota will want to see you. And it will give you and Nick time to talk."

"I think I've caused Nick enough worry for one day, don't you?"

"Elsa." Angelina turned and faced her once they pulled into her gravel driveway. "Your reaction surprised him, yes. So now you need to see him. Explain."

She knew that, but right now her nerves were stretched thin. She needed the gift of time, something she'd learned to give herself.

She climbed out of the car. She didn't dare meet Angelina's eyes. She knew what she'd see. Concern. Disappointment. Worry.

She'd seen it all before.

She walked into the house as the big SUV pulled away. Then she sank down along the wall onto the floor.

She dropped her head into her hands and let the tears fall. They fell for Christiana and Braden, for Cheyenne and Dakota, for that little brown-haired girl, caught in a maelstrom. She wept for all the little children whose parents disappointed or hurt them.

Achilles budged his way under her right arm.

She ran tear-soaked fingers through his fur, and when her fingers touched the cool, flat metal of his nametag, she didn't have to read the tag to remember the inscription. "There is a little good in all evil." Wilson Rawls, *Where the Red Fern Grows,* a book that helped inspire her life, her career path.

She'd hung that tag on Achilles purposely. The old dog had been left to die, wandering a train track. She and the old mutt had a lot in common back then. They still did, a pair of loners, shirking others, avoiding the sunlight.

But as she fingered the tag, she remembered the beautiful story of Big Dan and Little Ann and a boy, growing up before his time. Or maybe it was right at his time. Maybe people didn't get to choose what experiences molded and melded them into contributing members of society, but they did get to choose how to handle those experiences.

She'd loved dogs all her life. And horses. And she didn't mind cows at all, so maybe part of her was never supposed to be encapsulated in an office in a big city or suburban professional building all her days.

Maybe . . .

Just maybe . . .

She was supposed to be here and now, with Nick and those girls. If that was true, she needed to face Nick and explain her past. Maybe her past could bring understanding to the present.

She sat straighter against the wall, then pushed herself up, grabbed her keys, and went out the door.

Angelina was right. It was foolish to hide, foolish to wait in the dark when she could be her own catalyst once again.

She hopped into the driver's seat, turned the small car around, and headed for the Double S. She was done with waiting. Nick would form his own opinions, as it should have been all along, but to wait anymore would show cowardice, and Elsa never wanted to be cowardly again. If there was a time to every season, she needed to claim her season now. In Gray's Glen.

THIRTEEN

Nick punched a fist into the passenger door of his brother's SUV as they drove to the sheriff's office. They had left the girls, tuckered but content, at the ranch with Trey and Sam. "If you can't drive faster than this, pull over and I'll take the wheel."

Colt stayed calm and didn't mock him, a possible notation for the brotherly record books. "We're almost there. Let's keep it cool. And what the heck was Whitney doing up on 970 when she was supposed to be watching the girls dance?"

That was the question of the hour, wasn't it?

Right now his emotions were on high and his brain was jumbled. "No clue. I realized again today that I know absolutely nothing about women, but that's not exactly a big surprise, is it?"

"Not a pity party." Colt groaned on purpose. "Spare me that. And what is it you think you need to know?" Colt asked, and he sounded so sensible that Nick had to work not to wail on him, which would be dumb since Colt was driving. "Because whatever it is, you'll be wrong, so why bother? You picked wrong the first time. The world didn't end. This time you've actually found a good match, and not just a good match for you."

Nick snorted.

"But a match for the girls," Colt continued, when what he really should do was just be quiet.

"And the ranch."

Obviously quiet wasn't top priority for his older brother.

"You found a smart, beautiful, funny woman who isn't afraid to get dirty and likes animals. Clearly a mistake, of course." He turned into the sheriff's lot and parked. "So if you need a little time to get to know her better and understand why she came unglued today, take the time. It's not like you're going anywhere. Breathe. And give the girl a chance to explain."

"She could have explained any time in the past several weeks," Nick retorted. "I don't do lies and half truths. You know that—you're the same way."

"Like you didn't know she'd been hurt before?" Colt shot him an incredulous look that matched his tone. "Hey, newsflash, Captain Obvious. People don't walk away from their lives and hole up in the woods over a broken fingernail. The words *delicate psyche* were written on her face the first time I met her. You didn't notice?"

Heat climbed Nick's neck. "I knew there was something. I figured she'd tell me in time."

"Except that you've only known each other a little while."

True. But. "It seems longer. It seems . . ."

"Like it was meant to be. Like God put her in front of you and said, 'Hey, Einstein. This is the one, right here. Your match. Your destiny.'"

"Without the sarcasm, but yes."

"Why do I have the feeling you're going to totally muck this up because a rough few minutes tweaked the emotions of an amazing woman?"

Put that way, it did sound kind of dumb.

"Listen, it's not my business—"

"Like that's ever stopped a Stafford."

Colt shrugged off the truth in that. "When I realized I was falling in love with Angelina and Noah, I had two choices. Stay or go. Which meant I had one choice because there was no way I was about to leave the best thing that ever happened to me. Once we've got things settled, you stop and think about that. And yeah, pray about it. Because I've never seen you as happy as you've been the last few weeks. Having Elsa around made a difference in you and those girls. For the first time since I came back last winter, you all started to look happy. No matter how many fancy cows you raise or how many cattle you sell, you can't buy that look, Nick. And my guess is it's mighty hard to replace."

He knew his brother meant well. He knew he was right in many ways, but the one thing Nick had always wanted, had always prayed about, was honesty. It was how he treated others, and it wasn't too much to expect to be treated the same way in return. *Love without trust isn't love.*

He'd found that out the hard way when his mother left. And then he'd repeated the mistake with Whitney.

Yeah, maybe he'd chosen wrong. He could own that in retrospect.

But two little girls made the stakes much higher now. Could he— no, wait, scratch that—*should* he risk their stability and happiness?

No.

His gut soured.

He was doing what Elsa taught him to do, following her advice to the letter. Putting the girls first, exactly as he should. They'd finally gotten to a leveled playing field, only to trip up the present with the past. His past. Her past.

Which meant it might be better to live separate paths.

He climbed out of the car and moved toward the sheriff's office. Rye met him just outside the door. "She got tired of waiting and called for a ride."

"She what?"

Rye shrugged. "We weren't charging her, she didn't do anything wrong, and when you didn't drive right over here, she used our phone and called Johnny Baxter. She said she had something to celebrate and she'd already lost a lot of time."

Something to celebrate?

Not her daughters. Clearly they weren't important enough to set aside a night of partying. "Did she say where?"

Rye shook his head. "She didn't, but I overheard Johnny call a friend for a ride later, which is at least a smart thing to do. He told him to meet them at the Little Luck around eleven. Said he'd be out of money by then."

The Little Luck Tavern was a hole-in-the-wall bar north of town, which explained why she was out on Route 970.

"You might want to have your say tomorrow, Nick. Considering they've been gone nearly an hour already."

Rye was right. Nick didn't want to face Whitney when she'd been drinking, but they'd made an agreement for her to stay in the house rent free, and she was north of town breaking that agreement right now. "It'll hold till tomorrow. Did they tow her car into Sal's?"

Sal's Auto was one of the businesses hurt by the spring fire, but Sal was working in temporary quarters while his shop was being rebuilt.

"Yeah, Sal radioed me that he had it. And that there were liquor bottles in it, but they were unopened. Two broke. The rest were fine. He set them aside."

Nick turned toward Colt. Colt shrugged. "No clue."

He turned back toward Rye. "She's got no money, unless she lied about that, but I don't think she did. Where did she get the funds to buy liquor?"

Rye splayed his hands. "A question for the lady, my friend."

Colt set a hand on his shoulder. "Isabo made a killer lasagna. Let's go home and eat, maybe find out what Angelina knows. We can do all this tomorrow."

"Like I have a choice?"

Colt shook his head. "And since you don't, why let it make you crazy?"

He was right. He thanked Rye and climbed back into the car. They drove home, and the first thing he noticed as they pulled into the wide drive was Elsa's car, parked to the left.

His heart stepped into quicker rhythm. He stopped, tightened his shoulders, and blew out a breath. Angelina approached him from the side. She looked from him to the car, then the barn.

So . . . He started walking that way but paused when Angelina called his name. He turned and waited, figuring it was one more person about to have their say, but then she surprised him. She faced him, waited, then took a step back. "I'm staying out of it."

She should stay out of it. Everyone should stay out of it. Out of his business, out of his hair, stop telling him what to do, what not to do.

He walked into the barn, and the first thing he heard was the sound of Elsa, humming in the distance.

He didn't think his heart could beat faster.

It did.

He didn't think he could possibly move slower, because what could he say? Do? How could this ever be right?

Elsa hadn't gotten a little shaken up at the school. She'd gone into full-blown meltdown. Nick was right that Angelina seemed to know something. And why was she privy to the information?

Give her a chance to explain. It's the decent thing to do.

He didn't feel all that decent right now. Right now he felt like every woman he'd ever cared about had gone rogue on him. Why should he want to step into that quagmire all over again? If once burned was twice careful, then three times burned was just plain stupid, and Nick was done with being stupid.

She didn't turn as he approached.

Embarrassed?

Maybe. Or stubborn. That thought brought to mind their initial meeting, where she shut the door in his face.

His vote went straight to stubborn. "I looked in on Kita. She and the pups look fine."

She didn't look up, just stayed in her corner of the whelping stall, watching BeeBee. "Here too, and I think we've got a little time yet. Instinctive mothers have the best outcome."

He'd noted that with cows over the years, and lived the lack of it, so Nick understood.

He sat down in the opposite corner of the stall.

"Those are your good clothes and you're sitting on a barn floor."

"I know."

She accepted his admission without looking up. Was she waiting for him to open the conversation? He picked a piece of clean straw from the nearby bale and worked it between his fingers. "I expect we've got things to talk about."

That brought her head around, and when she aimed that sea-green gaze at him, it was all he could do not to cross that floor, gather her into his arms, and promise her everything was going to be all right. Except it wasn't.

"Not if Cheyenne's coming out here. She doesn't need to hear all this stuff. Not at her age."

"But it's probably stuff *I* should have heard, Elsa." He didn't try to hide the disapproval edging his tone.

"I agree. And every time I went to tell you I chickened out."

"I'm here now, and the kids are playing. There's time enough."

She flinched, then sat straight, her back flat against the wall. "I was part of a big, busy practice in Brant Park. I had a jam-packed schedule, a great reputation, a nice office I shared with two other counselors, and I'd been named a school consultant for the Brant Park school district. I did a good job. I know this because many of my early patients have gone on to high school and college. They're thriving. I've gotten up-dates and thank-you notes from all over the country, and there were times when those notes were the only thing that kept me going, Nick."

He stayed quiet and still, wishing he didn't care, wishing they didn't have to have this conversation. But there was no choice.

"I was brought in on a case of a girl about a year older than Cheyenne. Her name was Christiana. No one was allowed to nickname her; she wasn't allowed to be called Chris or Chrissy or Christy. It had to be Christiana, always. She had a six-year-old brother, a sweet little boy named Braden. He was cute, funny, and didn't like to sit still, but a good kid. Their mother initially hired me to see the kids. She was going through a tough divorce, a divorce that made all kinds of headlines. Her husband—ex-husband," she corrected herself, "was a big-name pro-football player. She said he'd been displaying odd behaviors, mood swings, anger issues. But these weren't documented by anyone else; there was a lot of money involved and weekly headlines. Neither one was opposed to slandering the other in public, which made the whole thing a chronic mess for the kids, while feeding a tabloid frenzy of he said–she said. The judge had asked that my report be part of the custody hearing. Their father objected to it, saying I was biased toward the mother."

"Were you?"

Elsa's face went grave. "I didn't like either of them. They were two selfish, self-absorbed people who didn't have a clue how blessed they were in multiple respects. I wrote my report, turned it into the judge, and then saw the kids for one last time for an exit interview, recommended by the court. That day we talked about change. About dealing with change, getting used to things, looking at the bright side. I wanted to give them every possible skill I could think of because no matter what that judge decided, and based on their parents' self-absorbed behaviors, their lives would most likely be filled with turmoil. And then, as we said good-bye, Christiana reached out and hugged me."

Her face changed, remembering. She flexed her hands, then swiped them against her casual jeans. "She'd never done that before. She was a private, distant child—beautiful but definitely a loner. Until that one time, that moment, and when she let me go she looked right up at me and whispered, 'I'm so scared, Elsa.'"

Chills ran up Nick's spine.

"So scared." Elsa whispered the words, staring at the young dog in a nest of clean straw. "I said, 'Of what?' and she said, 'My daddy.'"

"I stared down at her, wanting to take her back into the room. Find out what she meant, but I couldn't. At least I felt like I couldn't.

"Technically, our time was up. The door was open. Her mother was there, waiting to take her home, always in a hurry. Braden had already waved good-bye and dashed out to her, and as she motioned for Christiana to come along, Christiana took my hand and squeezed it hard, as if begging for help. And then her mother called her name and she went." She locked her hands around her knees, eyes down. She stared at her hands for long seconds, then sighed. "I didn't know what to do. My report was in, the exit interview was just that, until that last moment. I tried calling her mother later but got no answer. And then the next morning, when I should have called the school to relay what she said, I had second thoughts. What if I ruined someone's life by repeating the words of a child? It wasn't as if she'd given me any basis for concern at this point. But I knew, Nick."

She sat straighter, her hands gripping her knees, her gaze directed across the stall, but he was pretty sure it wasn't the liver-and-white dog she was seeing. It was a little girl, asking for help. "He picked them up from school that day. Sometime during the day, the judge's ruling had come down, giving custody to the mother with shortened visitation to their father."

"He didn't like the judge's ruling."

Her jaw went lax. Her forehead furrowed, and then her chin

quivered, but still she stared at that wall, just over BeeBee's head. "He killed the children and himself that day, and when the authorities finally found them, they realized he'd been planning this for days, maybe weeks. If he didn't like the judge's ruling, he intended to take matters into his own hands."

Sympathy flooded Nick.

This wasn't what he'd expected. He didn't know what he had expected, but murder/suicide involving two small kids hadn't been in contention.

"The mother blamed me. She said she heard Christiana tell me she was scared and that as a trained professional, I should have done something."

Now anger vied with sympathy. "That's not fair. It's not like we can be responsible for other people's actions, their choices, their decisions."

"Well." She huffed out a breath and stood. "No one ever said life was fair, Nick." She turned and started out of the stall.

"Where are you going?" He stood too.

"To the woods."

"Elsa, I—"

"Don't." She shook her head, and now, finally, she looked up at him. "I didn't come here to erase the fact that I should have told you from the beginning. I was working with your kids. You had a right to know."

She was right. She should have told him. What if she'd gone into some kind of crisis like today with the girls around?

"I couldn't deal with the lawsuit on top of the loss. I couldn't practice with so much hanging over me. How do you help others when you can't get yourself up and dressed in the morning? I pretended I was all right to my family and friends, right up until I considered taking my own life."

Her words tore at him.

Her face, the pain, the sadness, so stark, so worn. "But you're better now." The minute he said it, he realized the truth of his statement. She wasn't just better; she was amazing. Marvelous. Caring. And yet she'd lied by omission.

She looked at him, then the dog, and then made a little face of regret, a face that said how nice this all had been. "I am. And part of that is because I met you and your wonderful girls at just the right time. But you told me once that love without trust isn't love, and you were right. I should have trusted you. I should have been honest from the start, but I wasn't and there's no going back. I want you to know that I am better. I'm good now, and you and the girls were a big part of making that happen. So, thank you."

She started walking away, away from the dog, from the barn, from him, from the girls. "Elsa."

She didn't turn. She didn't say any more. She lifted one hand in a quick flit of a wave and went out the door, crossed to her car, and got in.

Kita crooned to her puppies behind him, puppies Elsa helped whelp. It had all seemed so right and so good last night. And now it wasn't anything of the kind. He moved to the graveled drive and wanted to stop her. Beg her to stay.

He didn't.

She backed the car around and eased down the driveway. Brake lights marked the first curve. Then the old car with the faded paint job disappeared from view, leaving nothing but thinning summer light in its wake.

ow can I help, son?" Sam had come up alongside quietly, but when he put his hand on Nick's arm, it didn't feed old fuels of resentment, and that was surprising enough. Nick thrust his chin toward the town beyond the raised hedge and the route Elsa had just taken. "Tell me how to fix the unfixable."

Sam stayed quiet.

Nick turned his way because if the old man wasn't going to try to help, what was he doing here? One look at Sam's hurting face made him bite back words of frustration. "I've got this, Dad."

"I see that." Sam paused and leaned against the broad barn door. "Didn't doubt it. But I'd still like to help if I can."

What could an aging, ailing cowboy do? Nick tapped his tongue to the roof of his mouth, then faced his father. "I wanted to show you up in the worst way."

Sam didn't look all that surprised.

"I wanted you to see that I was the best son for the ranch, for the business, for production. And then I wanted to show you how a good marriage was handled, that if you paid attention to your wife and worked *with* her instead of against her, everything would work out all right and we'd all live happily ever after. I wanted my success to show how you messed up so completely with my mother."

Sam grimaced. "I passed a lot of good qualities down to you, Nick. But that one, the one that's always got to have a hand in everything, besting everyone, that's one I wish you'd missed. Because in the end, what does it matter?" He shrugged. "Folks talk all the time about how if they could go back, they wouldn't change a thing. Well, they're stupid."

Nick watched him. "What would you change?"

"I'd have taken Colt to school that day like I was supposed to with his mother. We had it all planned out, to drop the little guy at preschool and grab lunch, then pick him up later. But something came up, I didn't go, and I lost the most precious thing I'd ever known. I didn't know what to do, how to handle any of it, and when Rita showed up and offered to help, it seemed like the smart thing to do. We'd dated in high school, and then there she was, quietly helping out, taking care of Colt. Marrying her seemed brilliant at the time."

"Did you love her?" Nick wasn't sure why that mattered, but it did.

Sam didn't lie. "I was grateful to her. She'd stepped in and was willing to take what I could give then, but in the end it wasn't enough."

"I wasn't enough."

Sam stared at him and straightened. "It wasn't about you, Nick. It was about her, and what she wanted. And that wasn't us, or the ranch, or Gray's Glen. She wanted a husband who loved her first, and that could never happen because Christine's shadow was everywhere around us. In Colt's smile. In his eyes. In the pictures on the wall, even after I had them taken down."

He didn't want to ask, but he had to know. He faced Sam and held his gaze. "Did you pay her off? Pay her to leave?"

Sam studied him. "You think that? That I would pay your mother to abandon you?"

"People have said as much."

"The dumb ones. I asked her to stay. I begged her to stay, and I'm not the begging sort. But she said I'd left no room in my heart for another woman and she wasn't playing second best, ever again."

"She didn't take me."

"Well, now, that wouldn't have been allowed." Sam faced him. His gaze went tight. "I'd have shared, Nick, because she was your mother, but she was bent on going to Texas, to family that had moved there, and there was no way I was letting her take my son so far away. If she'd stayed local, it would have been different, I expect. But she wouldn't hear of it. I sent her pictures of you every year. You remember that picture you made of you and her when you were in first grade? With her curly brown hair and big brown eyes?"

He remembered. In retrospect it was probably more of a caricature, but he'd looked at that picture and saw Rita Stafford, his mother, looking back. "I remember."

"I sent that to her and asked her to come visit. I even said we'd come visit there."

Sam had offered to go to her? To bring him to visit her? "We never went to Texas, Dad."

"She said no. She'd moved on with her life, she was remarried and expecting a baby, and she didn't want to face old regrets."

He was a regret.

Emotion swelled his throat so tight it ached.

"And right about then Sandy and EJ overdosed, and I had to make a run to California to find Trey, and then it was the four of us, with Murt and Hobbs. I wish it had been different." Sam sighed. "I wish I'd been different. But your mother didn't leave because of you, Nick. She left because of me and her, and she couldn't see her way beyond that. Maybe I was wrong, saying you couldn't go, but how does a father let something so special just slip out of his hands? I couldn't do it, and I hope you don't hate me for it."

Sam, professing his feelings for Nick. The big, rugged, faded-jeans cowboy saying how important Nick was to him.

He hadn't bought Nick's mother off. He'd asked her to stay.

It made a difference, somehow. The thought that Sam had been willing to sacrifice to keep things together way back then made a difference now. *"And there we have the difference between the adult point of view and childlike perception."*

The common sense of Elsa's observation rang true. Those early wounds had festered into gaping holes he'd tried so hard to fill, but in the wrong way.

He couldn't solve Whitney's problems by making her path smoother. If anything, that would probably enable her. But he could forgive her and move on, because he was sick to death of grudge holding.

He would go see her tomorrow, after church. If Rye's information was correct, she'd broken their agreement, and she'd skipped the girls' recital to do it.

He'd help Cheyenne work through it. And he'd respect his younger daughter's trepidation, unless Whitney did a full three-sixty, because if he couldn't understand his former wife's choices, how could he expect a six-year-old to rationalize them? He couldn't and shouldn't.

Putting the girls first was bound to make Whitney unhappy, but that was her problem now because one of them had to be the responsible parent, and in this case it was him.

~~⁓∈☙~~

Nick walked the girls into church the next morning. It had rained gently overnight, a five-hour soaker, just enough to give thirsty plants and ponds a needed drink. Damp morning air met glorious sunlight, while evaporating moisture scudded thin clouds along the ground, rising into the trees as the sun moved higher.

Sam had stayed home, tired from yesterday's outing. Hobbs had remained at the ranch with him, but everyone else flocked to church. Everyone but Elsa, of course.

Nick reminded himself *not* to look around the church for her, so when they walked through the double oak doors, that was the first thing he did.

She wasn't there.

His gut tightened.

Was she skipping the service because he was there? Most likely.

He rubbed his jaw, troubled. Messing up a person's faith quest hadn't been on his list of things to do that day, and yet . . .

Elsa wasn't there. Was she all right?

She seemed pretty calm and cool when she walked away from you last night.

She had, at that. As if despite her troubles, she was in charge, the same thing he'd sensed about her at their first meeting.

"Dad!" Dakota grabbed his pant leg, leaned back, and peered up. "Elsa said she was coming to church with us! I don't see her! Can we go get her?"

"She promised." Cheyenne didn't look up as she muttered the words. "And Mom promised to come to our dance recital. Big deal."

Her disillusioned tone seemed to expect grownups to break promises. Elsa wasn't like that, but he didn't know how to excuse her absence.

"Dad." Dakota wasn't about to let up, a true Stafford quality. "She might be sick. Or maybe Hoyl flew away and didn't come back and she needs our help." She tugged his arm. "Come on, Dad, we have to hurry! What if she's in trouble?"

Angelina leaned their way as she waited behind them. "I'll text her. If she needs help, we'll run right over there, okay?"

"Yes! Thanks, Angelina!" Dakota whispered her gratitude as they moved to a pew.

Nick shook himself mentally.

He could have put Dakota off that way too, but his brain wouldn't function once he realized Elsa hadn't come to church. She wasn't there because of him. She'd suffered a panic attack in public and was probably embarrassed, and he'd done nothing to assuage that embarrassment.

He'd been so angry about the lie of omission that he'd forgotten to be caring and tender. He'd thought about her horrible experience half the night, and when he couldn't sleep, he'd opened his laptop and searched her name.

And there it was, linked to the Belvedere tragedy.

He'd lost that cow and calf earlier that month, and he felt the loss grievously. His negligence had been a factor. If he'd told someone that he'd brought her into the barn, she and her calf might be alive today.

He didn't.

For Elsa, a moment's indecision had cost three lives.

As he settled into the pew, single notes sounded from the keyboard. Familiar notes, warm and true. And when their small choir began singing "Amazing Grace," the words didn't just speak to him. They flowed over him, reminding him of lost times and finding his way back to faith, to God. And here he was, ready to walk away from the most wonderful thing that had ever happened to him because she was flawed.

Who wasn't?

She kept a mighty big truth from you. That's something to think over, isn't it?

It was.

Staffords might be tough negotiators. They might be savvy, always looking for a good deal, but they were honest, and Nick was proud of that. Maybe more because of how his mother left and his wife bailed out of their marriage. As Dakota kept leaning up, peering toward the entrance, another thought rang true.

The girls trusted Elsa. She kept them focused, the way a ranch kid should be focused. Work first, play later. Follow directions. Don't shirk.

Reverend Stillman crossed the simple sanctuary. He raised his hands and smiled, letting his gaze roam the filled church. "May the peace and joy of the risen Christ be with each and every one of you this day."

Peace and joy.

Nick centered himself on those two words. Perhaps if he focused on them more, they'd be granted to him. That was something worth praying about, right there.

Elsa saw Rachel's name and accepted the call. "Hey, Rach. Good morning."

"Good morning!" Rachel sounded happy to have her back on track. Would she rethink recommending Elsa for the job once she heard about yesterday?

"Am I seeing you in church this morning?" Rachel asked.

"You aren't."

Her sister cued into her voice instantly. "How come?"

Elsa didn't mince words. She'd had enough of that. "I had a panic attack at the dance recital. The good thing is that Angelina was there with smelling salts and snapped me out of it. But the whole thing gave Nick a wake-up call he wasn't expecting. Let's just say he was less than thrilled with my reticence."

"Elsa."

She appreciated the note of sympathy in Rachel's voice. "On the plus side, a fighting couple kept the crowd quite engaged, so no one even noticed me."

"Oh, honey. I'm sorry."

"I am too. But in a way, it's good," Elsa admitted. "I got deluged with reminders, but once it was over, it was over. I didn't revert to hiding, I didn't want to revert to hiding. I mostly wanted to smack both of the fighting parents, then shove it behind me and get on with my life, and that's huge. Huge to me, anyway."

"It is. Do you want me to come over?"

"Nope. You go to church with your family. I heard that the reverend is doing a fresh air service in the hills this afternoon. I might pull out for that. I like praying outdoors."

"You're sure you're okay?"

For the first time in a long time, she *was* sure. Sure of herself, because falling apart yesterday wasn't a crushing blow. It was more like a rough ride on a bad trail, and for a ranch girl, those things happened. "Yes. Talk to you later, okay?"

"Okay."

She set down the phone, then picked it back up as a text buzzed in. Angelina's number came up in the display. "Are you okay? Coming to church? Dakota's asking."

Dakota. Not Nick.

She texted back quickly. "Yes and no . . . In that order. Give girls kisses and hugs for me."

"On it."

So the girls were wondering where she was.

Did Nick wonder? Or was he relieved that she stayed home to avoid an awkward situation?

She pulled out her scrapers and began working on the front of the house. As she completed her doll-up of each side, the house seemed happier. More inviting.

She turned on a modern country station, and when Trey Walker's "Find Your Way Home" came on, she sang along softly.

Hoyl flapped, as if approving the song. Or maybe he was just happy that she stayed home. He flew off as Achilles plodded to her side. The shaggy dog sat, eyed the car and then her, and whined.

"We've got work," she told him.

He pawed her leg gently, then looked toward the car again.

His meaning was clear. She'd given him a taste of life outside their hermitage and he liked it. Now that she'd opened the floodgates, he wasn't content being stuck in the woods.

Neither was she, but for the moment it would have to do. "We're staying put right now. Stop begging."

The dog thumped to the ground, drew his front paws over his snout, and sighed as if she'd let him down.

He liked going to the ranch.

So did she.

But that wasn't an option any longer. If she had to get used to it, so did he. Once the front was painted, she'd take her canine friend for a ride. It wouldn't be the same as hanging out at the Double S, but it would be all right. Elsa was sure of it.

Trey climbed into the passenger's seat of Nick's SUV once the service had concluded and sat back. "Let's do this."

Nick lifted a brow in question. "Do what?"

"Go see Whitney. You. Me." Trey waved a hand between them. "You can't bring Colt because nothing will get accomplished once they start sparring, and I'm the next best thing."

"I figured I'd see her alone. But thanks."

"Guess again," Trey told him. "Just in case you need a witness or a pal when this is all said and done, I'm coming."

"Listen." Nick faced him. "I appreciate all this brotherly love stuff, but I've got this."

"Never doubted it. I'm still coming." Trey settled back against the seat and tapped his wrist. "Colt's got the girls; I've got all day. Take your time."

Nick started the engine. It was probably smart to have someone along because there was no predicting what might happen. He drove west and turned into the subdivision. He pulled up to the curb outside the house, got out, and walked to the door, while Trey waited by the car.

Nick rang the bell. Would she answer? Was she even here?

The door opened quickly, surprising him, but then she looked just as surprised to see him standing there. Was she expecting someone else?

He motioned her outside. "We need to talk."

She didn't look great, but she didn't look terrible either, and Nick was grateful for that. She nodded. "I know." She stepped through the door and spotted Trey. "Hey, Music Man. How are things?"

He lifted one shoulder, cowboy easy. "Can't complain."

She laughed as if he'd said something funny. "Well, that's a quality that didn't come down from the Stafford side, did it?"

Trey didn't engage the comment. He hung out, next to the car, looking as if he didn't have a care in the world.

"Listen, Whitney."

She turned back toward Nick. "You're upset because I missed the girls' recital."

That was all she had to say? She'd been in a wreck, her car was totaled, and she'd broken promises to him and her kids. "The girls expected you. They looked for you. Cheyenne has worked for years doing something she doesn't even like, just so you'd be proud of her when you came back home. And then you didn't even bother to show. How can I explain things like this to them?"

She had the decency to look guilty when he mentioned Cheyenne's hard work. He continued, "Then you had Rye call me, and when I came to pick you up at the sheriff's office, you'd gone off with someone else."

"I don't wait on Staffords anymore, Nick. Not now. Not ever again."

He frowned. "You can have all the issues you want with me, but the girls need to know where they stand with you. They're kids. Your kids," he added with meaning.

"It matters to Cheyenne, maybe. Not Dakota." She studied his face as if looking for something, then sighed. "She's your little girl, Nick, through and through. She doesn't need me. And she sure doesn't want me around."

His brain went right back to the cow story he shared with Elsa, how the occasional one showed no interest in her calf despite an udder full of milk. "She doesn't know you," he offered reasonably. "She's a little girl. You're her mother. Don't you think it would be good for her to have a relationship with you?"

"Good for her?" She held his gaze deliberately. "Why would that be good for them? I'm not exactly mother-of-the-year material, now am I?"

What could he say to that? Nothing, so he let it be. "Kids want to know their mother loves them, because the opposite of that leaves you on the outside, looking in, for an awfully long time. I want more than that for them, Whitney."

She shook her head. "I've got money, now, Nick. Not a lot, but some. I can get by."

He heard the words and frowned, confused. "What's that got to do with anything?" But even as he asked the question, he knew. He'd known it from the minute she'd rolled into town, pretending they mattered.

"Nothing if you're rich, but when you're down on your luck, a little bit of good fortune is a solid surprise. Aunt Rose's trust fund just came down to me. It's not Stafford huge, but it's more money than I've seen in a while. Enough to fund my way out of this one-horse town."

Another out-of-the-blue surprise. "You're leaving?"

"I can't stay here. You know that. I don't want to be under your thumb, or on someone else's schedule, or at someone's beck and call. I like calling the shots. You should know that about me, Nick."

Oh, he knew it all right. "By someone's, you mean your daughters?" Her words prickled. Or maybe it was the disdain in her voice because being a mother would tie her down.

She squared her shoulders as if spoiling for a fight, but he didn't want to fight. He wanted that peace and joy the reverend talked about earlier. "When are you leaving?"

"I'm going over to Sal's to check out the used cars he's got on the lot. Once I have wheels, I'm heading back to the coast. Real cities. Real people. Places where folks won't look at me like I'm the odd one."

"I need you to do one thing before you go." When she huffed, he put a hand on her shoulder. "Let me bring the girls over to say good-bye. They're at the playground; it will only take a few minutes. It would be real rough on them if you just disappear again."

She hesitated, glanced around, then shrugged. "Sure. I'll be right here."

She wouldn't; Nick was pretty sure of that. He looked at Trey.

Trey moved over to the driver's side and climbed in. "I'll be right back." He pulled out, leaving Nick and Whitney standing there, and just like Nick had predicted, Johnny Baxter rolled into the driveway while Trey was gone. He looked at Whitney, then Nick, waiting.

Whitney moved his way.

"Give me ten minutes, okay? I've got to say good-bye to my girls."

"Is there coffee inside?"

"Help yourself."

"Don't mind if I do." He smirked as he walked by Nick, as if coffee mattered.

In the whole scheme of things, Johnny Baxter grabbing a cup of coffee was no big deal. Nick saw Trey making the turn back onto West Chelan. He drew a breath.

He wasn't sure how the girls would handle this, but no matter what happened, they had him and the whole Stafford family to offer love and support. They'd be just fine. He'd make sure of it.

FIFTEEN

ow are them pups doin', Miss Cheyenne?"

Nick strained his ears to hear Cheyenne's reply on Thursday morning, but Trey rolled through with equipment just then. He heard nothing, so he walked that way. "They grow fast, don't they?"

Cheyenne hung the clipboard on the nail he'd put in the stall post. "About an ounce a day, Dad. I think that's good, right?"

"I expect it is," said Hobbs. "Steady like, not too fast, not too slow."

"Except this little one." Cheyenne pointed out a distinctly smaller puppy. "She's only gained three ounces in six days, and if I put her on the graph Elsa made, she's not on the right line. Do you think there could be something wrong with her?"

Nick started to answer when Cheyenne grabbed his hand and his heart with her next words. "Elsa would know. Can you call her and see when she's coming over? She'll know what to do, Dad."

What could he say? He dodged the question and felt like a first-class jerk for doing it. "We can get puppy supplement for that one, Chey. She'll catch up."

"I expect they've got some at the feed store in Cle Elum. I'll check it out," Hobbs assured her. "I was runnin' that way in any case because I can still drive and run errands with a bum arm."

"Can't we just ask Elsa first?" Cheyenne wasn't letting him off the hook easily, and the intensity of her gaze underscored that. "And isn't she supposed to be here to work with me this week?"

Hobbs moved away, muttering something under his breath, unwilling to be part of whatever tale Nick was about to spin. He started to scrub his jaw when a pitiful moan came from farther back in the barn.

"BeeBee." Cheyenne dropped his hand and dashed around the corner and down the center of the barn. "Oh, BeeBee, what's going on?" The young Aussie had found her way into a back corner. She'd scratched loose straw into a nest and paced worriedly, poking her nose into the broken strands, pausing to pant now and again. "Hey, girl." Nick leaned down and stroked the dog's head. "How about we get you into your stall, okay?"

"Remember what Elsa said, Dad?" Cheyenne turned, concerned. "That we should let her pick her spot and move her after the first puppy is born because then she won't care."

Elsa had said exactly that, so Nick squatted low. "Then we'll let her get on with it here for the moment."

Cheyenne worried her lower lip and gazed out the door. "We need Elsa, Dad."

He knew that. He hadn't been able to stop thinking of how he needed Elsa since waking up Sunday morning to the reality that he'd let her walk away. He'd handled taking the girls to church and then to see Whitney. He'd juggled her good-byes and Cheyenne's look of loss, but she didn't fall apart when they watched Whitney drive away.

Her eyes had grown wet and a few tears found their way down her pale, soft cheeks, but when they got back to the ranch, she didn't stomp off like she used to. Was that because Elsa's wisdom had spurred strength in the young girl or because the reality of having Whitney in Gray's Glen didn't resemble Cheyenne's happily-ever-after fantasy? Perhaps a combination of both.

Instead of having a hissy fit, she'd changed her clothes, gathered some things, and moved into the barn to keep an eye on the dogs and the pups. She hadn't left the barn for more than a few minutes since, camping out with a sleeping bag and pillow alongside Kita's whelping stall for four nights. He'd wanted to object, but he'd done the same thing himself when calves and foals were due, so how could he fault her for great animal empathy and instincts?

Call Elsa.

He couldn't. If BeeBee seemed to be in trouble, he could run her to the veterinarian and get an expert opinion.

"Dad. Elsa would want to be here and she told me to call. Remember?"

He remembered, all right.

"Give me your phone. I'll call her."

She wasn't going to let it go, another good characteristic of solid animal husbandry.

Nick took one look at the hard-working dog's face, pulled out his phone, and hit Elsa's code in his speed dial. When she answered, he waded right in. "Elsa, BeeBee's in labor, and Cheyenne was hoping you could come."

"I'm on my way."

Click.

Just that, nothing more. She sounded crisp and businesslike, as if she got called to midwife dogs on a regular basis. When she hurried into the barn ten minutes later, his heart swelled, then ground to a stop.

Beautiful.

She strode into the barn, wearing a fitted dress with open-toed heels, looking fashion magazine lovely, but if she'd shown up in a classic tee and barn-friendly blue jeans, he'd have thought the same thing.

"You came!" Cheyenne flew to her. "I knew you'd come," she told her as she hugged her tight around the middle. "I told Dad to call because you'd promised."

"That's right." Elsa smiled right into his daughter's eyes. "And I try to keep every promise I make. What's going on?" She started to move toward the whimpering dog, but Nick stopped her.

"You've got good clothes on." He hurried into the nearby office, pulled one of his long-sleeve T-shirts off the hooks, and came back just as quickly. "You don't want to mess up that dress."

"I don't." She slid into the tee as she followed Cheyenne. "I was at a job interview when you called."

"A job interview?" That was about the last thing he'd expected her to say. "Doing what?"

"Exactly what I'm trained to do," she replied, not looking back. She crouched down next to BeeBee, and Cheyenne did the same along the dog's other side. "How long has she been laboring like this?"

"About twenty minutes since we found her."

"And has she been straining like that?" Elsa indicated the dog's futile efforts to deliver the first puppy.

"Yes. And she doesn't look happy, Elsa."

"You've got a good eye." Elsa smiled at Cheyenne, then gently rolled BeeBee to her back. "Hey, there." She crooned the words to the anxious dog and with gentle hands pushed one way, then the other.

"What could be wrong?"

"Well, she's got a good-sized litter in there, and my guess is that puppy number one is either really big or badly positioned and lying across the opening to the birth canal. If he's crosswise, it's hard for him to slide out."

"I've watched Daddy move calves around." The proud look she shot him made Nick feel distinctly taller. "He knows how to reach in and change things up. But cows are a lot bigger than dogs."

"Do we need a C-section?" Nick kept his voice soft, but if the dog needed help delivering, he'd pay the price gladly. "I can call Doc Wendel and take her right in."

"Have we got everything set up for delivery here?"

Cheyenne pointed to the stall they'd selected the week before. "Everything's there. I got it ready on Sunday, just in case."

"Good girl." Elsa's approval lifted Cheyenne's chin and put a distinct sparkle in her eyes. "Then let's try one of my mother's old tricks before we take her to the vet, okay? Can I have a collar and a leash?"

"Sure."

Cheyenne put her trust in Elsa instantly. When Elsa looked his way, he could do no less. He hurried to the first barn door and took a fairly dusty collar and leash from the pegs mounted just inside.

Elsa rolled BeeBee back over and coaxed her to stand. Then she slipped the collar over her neck and attached a leash.

"Aussies aren't leash dogs, generally." Nick rubbed the back of his neck. "She's run free all her life. We keep those handy for trips to the vet."

"Which is fine, but she's probably a little indignant that I want her to walk right now, so the leash will act as a persuasion." She started walking backward, coaxing the dog to follow. Cheyenne did the same thing, mimicking Elsa's movements. BeeBee moved forward, slow at first, and when the dog aimed a sorry look at the straw bed, Nick almost caved.

He didn't, though, because Cheyenne was placing her trust in Elsa, and that was too important for an impatient, interfering father to interrupt.

Elsa quickened her pace to a slow jog, and when she reached the barn entrance, she pivoted and increased her speed.

So did Cheyenne and so did BeeBee.

Elsa circled the wide drive, encouraging the dog, and when they'd gotten halfway around, BeeBee lurched free.

The leash slipped from Elsa's hands, and the dog whirled about, hurried straight back to her nest, and delivered a big, wet puppy onto the floor.

Elsa and Cheyenne followed her in and gave each other enthusiastic but quiet high-fives.

"You did it!" Cheyenne looped her arms around Elsa again. "How did you know?"

"Well, we had this happen a time or two on our place. Our ranch wasn't big, we didn't have a ton of money, and it would have cost my parents over fifteen hundred dollars to have a litter of pups delivered by C-section. When a dog runs, it stretches its body from front to back, and that can help the first puppy slide into place. And once that happens, well"—she put an arm around Cheyenne and they smiled together—"you see the results."

Nick moved closer to her side. "That's a pretty neat trick."

She didn't look up.

He wanted her to, but she didn't. And when puppy number one was cleaned up and nursing, they moved BeeBee and her newborn over to the prepared stall, midbarn. "You sure this won't bother her?"

"It shouldn't. She's occupied now, and she's about to deliver the next pup, so she won't even know we moved her as long as her babies are nearby."

"You know so much, Elsa." Admiration filled Cheyenne's eyes. "I can't believe how good you are at all this."

"Years of practice."

The second pup presented right then. Nick brought them hay bales to sit on, and when puppy number three was born, Elsa let Cheyenne take over completely with the weighing, checking the umbilicus, then charting the numbers and identifying marks. "Well done, farm girl."

Cheyenne folded her arms over her chest as she watched BeeBee happily greet the newest member of the Double S Ranch. "I love this." She whispered the words with a happy sigh as if her mother's departure hadn't knocked her world completely out of whack a few days before. "It's like what I was meant to do, Elsa."

"I know."

What she was meant to do . . .

Nick received another mental kick in the head. He'd fought his daughter's urges, trying to reshape destiny. It was a foolish mistake, one he didn't intend to make again.

"Elsa." Angelina strode into the barn, hugged Elsa and then Cheyenne. "Ooh . . ." She bent and crooned to the new lives before her. "So very precious. And I expect you'll be on midwife duty for a bit, so how about if I send lunch out here to you? Or you can wait until the pups are all delivered, but that might be a few hours."

"We might get a lull midway," Elsa told her. "She's been laboring for a while, so if she dozes off, we could break for lunch then. But a coffee now sure sounds good, Angelina."

"How about you, Chey?"

"A coffee, like Elsa?" She perked up at Angelina and shot her father a quick look of question.

"I'll go light on the coffee and heavy on the milk," Ange promised. "They're beautiful puppies, guys."

"I know." Cheyenne grinned with pure delight, a reaction Nick hadn't seen in a long time. "I can't believe it."

He should get to work. There was plenty to do, but Trey was baling hay with Brock in the upper field. Colt, Murt, and a couple of other hands were shifting pastures for the heifers carrying seed calves, and the lure of new life held him here. Or maybe it was the joy on his daughter's face as she followed Elsa's quiet directions. Or perhaps it was Elsa herself.

Just before one, he texted Angelina that BeeBee had fallen asleep. Isabo brought lunch to the office, and when Cheyenne rushed off to the house, it left him alone with Elsa. Only a fool would waste those moments. He had things he needed to say and the chance to say them. He moved closer and sat down by her side.

"I want to thank you for coming."

She stayed intent on Isabo's yellow rice. "Of course I came; I promised her. Thanks for calling."

"How did the interview go?"

She shook her head.

"It didn't go well?"

"It didn't go at all. I left when you called."

He sat straighter as her words registered. "You mean you were actually *in* the interview when I called?" Guilt mushroomed inside him when she nodded. "And you left?"

She frowned as if confused. "I told Cheyenne I'd be here when she needed me. The interview wasn't supposed to happen until after the Fourth of July, but the hiring committee was on hand to talk to a few prospective teachers, so they asked if I could come in today. So I did."

"This was with the school district?"

"For a position as a counselor for grades five through eight, yes."

"And you're okay to do the job?" It came out wrong, as if he doubted her. She'd demonstrated her strength and skill set from their first meeting, going toe-to-toe with him, and he hadn't questioned her ability once. In fact, he'd learned from her. Things about kids, about himself, about dealing with loss.

"I'm more than okay." She faced him with a cool look. "I've come full circle, and I think I'm even better equipped to handle kids and crises because of what I've gone through. I've seen the inside of the monster and fought my way out, so if I can do it, anyone can."

"Elsa."

"Delicious rice." She turned her attention to the *achiote* flavored dish. "I wonder if Isabo will share the recipe."

He ignored her effort to change the subject. "Listen, I—"

"Nick." She raised one hand, and he paused to let her talk. "It's all right," she told him, as if comforting him, but she was wrong.

It wasn't all right; nothing was all right.

"I should have been up front with you from the beginning and I wasn't," she continued, "but that brief chance to be part of the girls' lives, to be part of all this"—she swept the barn a quick glance—"has meant a lot to me. It helped me see that I *can* do anything, the same premise I've taught kids for years. So thank you."

"Don't do that."

She knit her brow. "Do what?"

"Act like there's nothing between us. As if there wasn't something amazing and wonderful happening before Saturday."

She let the plate rest quietly in her lap. "But things changed."

He leaned back against the wall and watched her. "Someone once asked me which of the Staffords were the calm, patient ones."

A tiny smile indicated she remembered asking the question.

He moved closer. "I'd like a second chance."

"Nick—"

She didn't look at him. She looked beyond him, trying to figure out how to let him down nicely, no doubt.

Nick Stafford had no intention of being let down easy. He'd go down swinging for the fences, just like he did when he played hardball as a kid, because this was way more important than any ball game. This was his life. His heart. His home.

He reached down, lifted her plate, and set it on the desk, then drew her up. "First of all, you're a big fan of second chances. I know this for a fact." He settled his arms around her and waited for her response.

"I've been known to say exactly that," she admitted. "But I've also advised time and caution. Patience too. Because no matter what you see on TV, life doesn't get fixed in sixty-minute increments. It builds over time."

"I've got time, Elsa." He held her gaze steady. "No matter how long it takes. When I realized that you had issues you didn't share, and

Whitney was messing with the girls' heads, everything piled up. It was a dumb reaction and I'm sorry. Will you forgive me? Please?"

"Nick, I—"

"I said please." He raised his brows and stroked a thumb along the soft curve of her cheek, sweet and gentle.

"You did."

"A trick I learned from Dakota. It generally works for her."

She sighed softly and his heart did a little leap for joy.

"Elsa . . ." He murmured her name, raised one brow, and then shifted his gaze to her lips. "I do possess other powers of persuasion."

"You do?" She lifted her gaze from his mouth to his eyes, then back. She frowned slightly. "I don't quite recall . . ."

He grinned, moved forward, then paused with his mouth just above hers. Close. So close . . . "Allow me to refresh your memory."

He settled his lips on hers and lost himself in the kiss, the feel of Elsa in his arms.

She fit. She fit the way he remembered so well, as if made to be there, with him.

"This is how it's supposed to be, Elsa." He whispered the words against her cheek, her hair, loving the scent of her hair and her skin. "I can tell because everything feels right, and when you're not here, it feels all wrong. Which means I deserve a second chance, don't I, honey?" He snugged her close and brushed the gentle question to her ear, her cheek, hoping for the right answer, but if she needed more convincing, Nick Stafford wasn't afraid to do it.

He called her honey.

He wanted a second chance, a chance to begin anew. To see where this might lead.

So did she.

Her heart was doing a happy dance, pounding against her ribs.

BeeBee made a noise across the way.

She leaned back against his strong arms and indicated the whelping stall with a glance. "We've got work to do."

He brushed the back of his big, rugged hand to her cheek and smiled. "We do."

"And Cheyenne still needs tutoring."

"She does."

"And after examining my summer calendar, it appears that I'm available as promised."

"I can't deny I was hoping that was the case, Doc. Because I've heard summertime is the best time for courting a pretty gal in the PNW."

His quaint cowboy talk made her smile. "Do tell."

"Campfires. Walks in the woods. Along with possible volunteer efforts on that new church building."

"Well, Wandy Schirtz did invite me back to help, and my brownies were a big hit with the volunteers."

"There you go."

He smiled. Then he settled his hand along the back of her neck and drew her in for a kiss as puppy number seven took its first breath.

He pulled back when Cheyenne's footsteps dashed their way. "Number seven!" She grinned up at them when she spotted the newest baby dog. "Oh, isn't this the most amazing day ever?"

When Nick slung an arm around Elsa's shoulders and grinned, she looked right at his delightfully headstrong daughter and nodded because Cheyenne was absolutely right. "It truly is."

$\mathcal{S}$am Stafford watched as his growing family raced around the yard for their first annual Fourth of July celebration.

He'd never bothered hosting anything like this at the Double S before. He'd been too busy amassing his fortune to worry about parties and holidays, so whatever the cooks had done to create a day, they did, and he was no part of it.

But now he watched as Colt took the kids on wagon rides through the lower fields. Angelina and Noah were tucked up on the old wagon seat beside Colt, while Nick's girls, Elsa, and Nick rode along in the back with Rye Bennett's kid sister Jenna.

Murt had fashioned a nice campfire, and Hobbs, Rye, and Trey were keeping an eye on the spit as it made slow circles above the rotisserie Murt put together nearly twenty years back.

Nick shouted something to Colt from his seat on the wagon bed, and Colt laughed out loud, just loud enough for Sam to hear. Two boys, at each other's throats from the time Nick was old enough to walk . . .

Now brothers, bound in love and respect, at long last.

One to go.

Trey, his beloved third son, the child he'd plucked from a den of squalor when the boy's foolish parents overdosed. His nephew by blood, his son by law, and Sam had no intention of dying before he saw Trey happy too. If God entertained the idea of answering prayer and granting wishes, all he wanted or needed was to face his Maker knowing he'd left all three sons happy, and anyone with half a brain could look at

Trey and see that sorrow wound tighter than a calf roper's knot around his gentle heart.

Isabo came through the door, carrying two large glasses of iced tea. He was actually starting to like tea, but he wasn't about to admit that to anyone. "Thank you, Izzie."

She settled into the rocking chair next to his. "It's a fine view from here, Sam."

She wasn't talking about the verdant valley or the rolling rise of the Cascades surrounding them. She meant family. His. Hers. And friends. "It is."

"You're making a difference, Sam." She reached out and covered his hand with hers.

"Enough?" He turned her way and she shrugged.

"For God to say, not us. We do what we can, as we can."

He snorted. "Easy enough to say when you've lived a good life being nice to others."

"God sees the heart, not the accomplishments."

Did he, Sam wondered? Did he know how sorry Sam was for all those years of being a jerk?

Trey moved their way and climbed the steps as if everything was fine. He faced his dad with the sincere expression country music fans knew and loved.

Sam knew better.

"I'm flying out on Thursday to be back in Nashville for a charity event," Trey reminded him, and Sam didn't miss the flash of reluctance in his youngest son's eyes. "Then I'm going to load up the SUV with as much stuff as it can hold and head north again."

"You don't mind coming back?" Sam took Trey's hand, much like he'd done over twenty-five years ago when a neglected three-year-old with wet pants won his heart.

"No, sir. Glad to. And I'm looking forward to an easy cross-country trip. It's been a while since I was able to just get in a car, point north, and drive."

Sam gripped his hand. He wanted to say more. So much more.

Wait.

He felt the caution like a breath of Cascade wind and stayed quiet. And when Trey squeezed his hand lightly, leaned down, and kissed Sam's forehead, the older man had to choke back words of remorse.

Colt had found his way.

Nick was the happiest he'd ever been.

And if Sam was truly ready to put the reins firmly in God's hands, he needed to turn this big-hearted youngest son over too. But this might be the hardest of all, because in the world's eyes, Trey seemed like the most balanced of them all, but they hadn't seen how that little boy lived the first wretched, impressionable years of his life.

Sam did. And it broke his heart to this day.

"I love you, Dad."

"I know." Sam had to choke the words past the lump in his throat. "You always have, Trey. I love you too."

Trey winked, breaking the serious connection, and Sam allowed it because his third son would need to find peace in his own way, in his own time. Sam just prayed he'd be around long enough to see it and celebrate it.

God's timing. Sam was real hopeful that he and the good Lord were still on the same page.

"Trey, can you grab the basting sauce?" Hobbs called across the spread of deep green grass.

"Will do." Trey ambled inside, and when his footsteps sounded against the kitchen floor two rooms back, Isabo reached out a hand once more.

"For this one," she whispered, "we pray together, my friend. For his joy, his peace, and his faith."

She took his hand in both of hers, and in her face he saw the confidence of a true believer, the very thing he longed to achieve. Looking into Isabo's heartwarming gaze, Sam Stafford finally believed it might really be possible.

FROM THE KITCHEN
OF THE DOUBLE S RANCH

ISABO'S YELLOW RICE

1/4 cup olive oil

2 packets Sazón seasoning

3 cups water

1 teaspoon salt

1 tablespoon chicken base

1 1/2 cups rice (Isabo likes to use basmati or jasmine. Me too!)

A couple of stalks of chopped celery

A couple of carrots, peeled and chopped (Isabo would laugh
   if I pretended she measures. So let's humor her!)

1 can whole kernel corn, drained

Pour olive oil into a four-quart saucepan. Sprinkle with Sazón. Heat gently. When oil is hot, add water, salt, and chicken base. Mixture will bubble up. Stir to combine. Add rice. Bring back to a boil, cover, and reduce heat to low/simmer. After ten minutes add chopped celery and carrots. Cover and cook about six minutes more. Add drained corn. Simmer about four or five more minutes.

This is great right away, it's good cold, and it's wonderful reheated. This recipe is family size but can be doubled or tripled for bigger gatherings, something Isabo is quite accustomed to out on the Double S!

Elsa's Cheesy Biscuits

2 cups Bisquick

2/3 cup milk

2/3 cup sharp cheddar shredded cheese

1 stick butter, melted

1 teaspoon garlic powder (more or less to taste)

2 teaspoons parsley

1/4 cup grated Parmesan cheese

Mix Bisquick, milk, and shredded cheese. Spray baking pan or cookie sheet with cooking spray. Drop biscuits by generous spoonfuls onto baking pan. Bake at 400 degrees for 12–15 minutes or until just golden. Remove from oven. Cool for five minutes (if you can wait that long!).

Mix garlic, parsley, and cheese with melted butter in bowl.

Dredge each biscuit in the buttery, cheesy mixture. Serve warm. Amazing!

ACKNOWLEDGMENTS

Huge thanks to so many people on this book . . . First to my beloved literary agent, Natasha Kern, a woman who sets the standards high for those who work with her, but whose confidence and faith are always a loving inspiration! Thank you, Natasha!

To Shannon Marchese, who gave me this chance to formulate new westerns with their own flare. Your advice is a wonderful addition, even when it takes me a few days to remember to be grateful. ☺

Thanks also to my husband, Dave, and my son, Seth, who are always willing to put their hand to the plow with new ideas. Their willingness to work long hard hours in all kinds of weather amazes me.

Thank you to Yvonne Joslin Bagley for her advice about flowers and flora native to the area so that I could paint realistic pictures of a land not my own, and to the Washington Cattlemen's Association website for lots of pertinent information. And I can never write a cattle book without giving author and friend Mary Connealy and her husband, Ivan, a shout-out for all of their willing advice, which ranges from funny to cryptic to sensible.

To all of the teachers, day-care workers and nannies, and counselors out there who work the front lines with kids every day, in particular Amanda, Lisa, Karen, Seth, Lacey, and Beth. You guys bring warmth and balance to young lives in the rise and fall of life. Thank you for that. You never know when some small thing you do makes a great difference to a child.

Additional thanks to Beth for helping me keep things going last year. I couldn't have done it without you!

To McKenna Tydings who inspired my version of Cheyenne

Stafford. McKenna, you are part of my heart, and your strongly held emotions helped shape this delightful (and stubborn!) character. You'll always be "part Ruthy" no matter how much your parents try to fix it! I love you to the moon and back, and your heartfelt letters have made me smile . . . and cry. You're an amazing girl.

And to MacKenzie and Anna Blodgett, two little darlings who made writing Dakota's character a piece of cake. They are truly sugar with a whole lot of spice, and they've made wrapping their daddies around their fingers an art form. I love you, girls!

A Selection From

PEACE
in the
VALLEY

Book 3 in the Double S Ranch Series

Coming March 2017

F or once in his life, Trey Walker Stafford had aced his two
older brothers. The fact that he had to risk his life and offer
up a chunk of his liver to claim the title made it a dubious honor.

The irony wasn't lost on him as Trey drove his packed SUV west
on I-90 through central Washington. The thought that of three sons, it
was the orphaned, adopted nephew whose DNA provided the best possible outcome for his adoptive father fit today's reality TV scenarios too
well.

But then their lives up to this point had seemed like a reality television show, so why change now?

The fingers of his left hand thrummed a senseless beat on the leather steering wheel. He drove the roads he'd known for so long, intent on getting back to the ranch. He meant to do whatever he could to help his father. But surgery, painful recovery, and possible death weren't on his agenda. His agent made that clear, multiple times this past week, and by every possible available media.

Trey could imagine the speech now. "You'd risk everything you've earned, everything you have, your home, your ranch, your music, your life, to help the man who threw you out of the house because you loved music? You're a better man than I am, Trey. That's for sure."

He wasn't better. He knew that. He was guilt-ridden, and fairly vacant inside, like one of those black holes yawning wide in an endless universe. So solid. So dense. Yet empty. And it had felt that way for a long, long time.

"Poor little boy."

The voice. *Her* voice, the voice of his mother, Sandy Lee Stafford. Beloved on her early country music recordings, that voice turned utterly scathing when it came to her little boy.

She'd stood over him, smelling unwashed and looking hateful, and that's all Trey envisioned anytime someone mentioned his mother. They said a three-year-old doesn't have the capacity to remember actual events, that they might have snatches of recall, here and there. Whoever they were, they were plumb stupid, because Trey remembered enough. Too much.

"There ain't no one in this world 'bout to feel sorry for you, Trey-Trey. Least of all, me."

He must have been crying. He couldn't remember the tears, but he remembered the wetness on his face.

And then she was gone, and his father was gone, and the next thing he knew, Sam Stafford strode into that police station, larger than life, scooped him up, and took him home.

And now Trey would donate part of his liver to keep his father alive. A good Christian man would go forward boldly, embracing the opportunity. Trey marked that up as another out-and-out failure because he tried to live out his Christian faith in every way.

But not this.

His internal guilt spiked like an overwound E string on his guitar, but Trey spent so much of his life feeling guilty that today shouldn't be any different. But this change—*this summer*—would be life and death. And that made a difference, right there.

He exited the highway and took the right-hand turn leading away from Gray's Glen, the town he grew up in. Broad fields stretched on either side, filled with lush grass and the gray-green sagebrush growing thicker as the hills climbed. Dark red cattle dotted the upper pastures like a generous sprinkling of cayenne pepper on steamed broccoli.

He was hungry.

Tired.

Nervous? Yes, that too.

The Ellensburg deejay segued into Trey's newest single in a way that made him cringe. "Ya wanna talk a Cinderella cowboy story? We've got it right here, as central Washington's own Trey Walker tugs the heartstrings while he rockets up the charts again with 'You Only Live Once'."

Trey shut the radio off.

He had no desire to hear himself croon sage words of advice to trusting fans. They thought he understood their plight.

He didn't.

They sensed he had a heart of gold.

Wrong, again.

They believed in him, in his music, his calling, his faith.

How he wished he could believe in himself. He—

The aged, dark blue van came out of nowhere. Trey hit the brakes, too late.

The van shot into the intersection.

Trey cut the wheel and prayed. The SUV squealed in protest.

The van spun about in a desperate move to avoid the crash. The maneuver worked, but then the van raced up the embankment and tipped up and over before landing on its side in the small creek running into the glen.

Trey shoved the SUV into park and jumped out. He raced across the two-lane country road, jumped the hill, and hit 911 on his phone at the same time. He leaped into the water and yanked himself up onto the side of the tipped van. Wet fingers made the grip difficult, but once he gained a leg up, he was able to pull himself the rest of the way. He reached down to jerk open the van door.

It wouldn't budge.

The driver, a woman, was facing away from him.

She didn't move. Didn't wiggle. Didn't—

His heart stopped. He pounded on the door, not knowing what else to do, then realized he might be able to get in through the back hatch. He jumped down and ran through the knee-deep water, bent and grabbed the latch on the back hatch.

It opened.

His relief was short-lived. The entire back of the van was filled with floral debris. Upended plants, baskets, planters, and trays of seedlings blocked his way. Utter destruction filled the banged-up van from top to bottom.

"No."

He looked up.

If despair had a face, it was the one he saw right now as the driver spotted the complete wreckage. "Unlock your door," he ordered, then slogged back through the water. He climbed up again and braced himself. The van's angle made pulling the door tough. Its weight worked against him, but instinct dictated he needed to get her out of the van. And what if there was a passenger? He hadn't seen anyone, but the visibility was poor.

He pushed down on his heels and tugged the door upright. It blocked his view, and he didn't have the best footing, but he hung on for dear life. "Can you climb out? I'm afraid to let go of the door to help you. It might fall and hit you."

"I can climb."

Trey prayed.

He doubted the effectiveness, because while *he* believed in God, he was pretty sure God took a detour somewhere north of his Virginia home a long time ago. But then, why wouldn't he?

He and God knew the truth. He was here, seeking absolution. Seeking . . . something.

Trey wasn't stupid. The prospects of finding peace in the broad, lush green valley of central Washington were slim to none. He wasn't being pessimistic. It's just how things rolled these days.

A hand appeared, then another, then a mass of long, gold-and-brown hair tumbled over the side, accompanied by a face.

An absolutely beautiful, very angry face.

Great.

AVAILABLE IN 2017

DOUBLE S RANCH BOOK 3

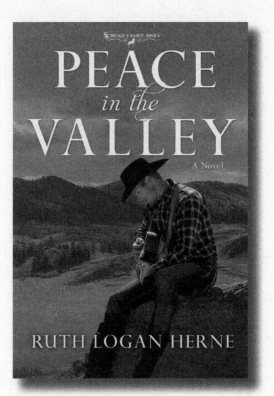

WATERBROOK

DOUBLE S RANCH BOOK 1

A PRODIGAL COWBOY
COMES HOME

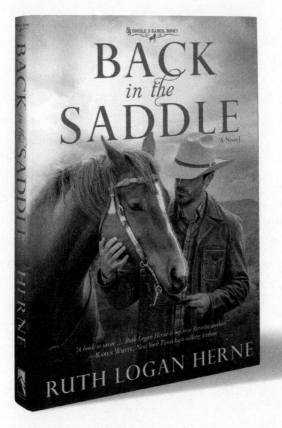

Read an excerpt at WaterBrookMultnomah.com!